I Bloom

At Last
I Bloom

Cas Sigers

URBAN BOOKS
www.urbanbooks.net

This is a work of fiction. Any references or similarities to actual events, real people, living or dead, or to real locales are intended to give the novel a sense of reality. Any similarity in other names, characters, places, and incidents is entirely coincidental.

URBAN SOUL is published by

Urban Books
1199 Straight Path
West Babylon, NY 11704

ISBN-13: 978-1-59983-092-6
ISBN-10: 1-59983-092-2

First Printing: February 2010
10 9 8 7 6 5 4 3 2 1

Printed in the United States of America

1

Necessary Sabbaticals

There is nothing like a sabbatical with friends. After last year's ups, downs, and turnarounds, white sand and blue water were not only a refresher but also a necessity. I chose St. Lucia for the getaway and initially, I had one partner in crime, Tam. She and I were supposed to have a girlfriend retreat. However, Evelyn convinced me that she also deserved to get away and that she wouldn't have anyone to go away with if she couldn't go with us. Her argument, though pitiful, worked and we sat there enjoying our drinks on the balcony of the hotel over-looking the Atlantic.

"I wish Stan was here," said Tam.

"Can't you enjoy yourself with us, without talking about your husband?" I said to Tam with a frown.

Sarcastically Evelyn chimed in, "Are we not good enough for you?"

Tam rose from the table and moved toward the railing, without answering. Evelyn and I looked at each other and laughed. Although we snickered, we understood her statement. If only we had a "Stan" in our lives to enjoy this moment with. Not that a vacation with friends is not fulfilling, because it is. There is nothing like camaraderie between girlfriends, yet it can't compare to a trip with that special someone. It's apples and oranges and one is no substitute for the other.

"I'm going to take a dip in the water before dinner, you guys coming?" offered Evelyn.

I quickly declined as Tam finished her drink.

"I think I'll stay here," said Tam.

Evelyn rose, removed her sarong from the back of the chair, and wrapped it around her waist.

"Hey, Evelyn, the nude beach is only a mile down the road. I hear it calling your name," I said, laughing, recalling our beach episode last year when Evelyn gladly stripped down to her skimpy bottoms in front of all of us, boyfriends included.

"Ha, ha. You know that's not my style anymore, but I may just walk down there to enjoy the sights," she said with a smile before walking away.

It was amazing how things could change in twelve months. Last year at this time, Evelyn was on the beach naked, pursuing my man and offering me a deal to switch with hers. Now she is a more mature, church-going woman, trying to get into heaven. She still has her ways, but it's good to see progress, and although I don't completely buy her transformation, it is a welcome start. She was still finding herself; hell, we all were for that matter. Nevertheless, some people find the discipline of religion a basis for starting over and I realize that some people need that in order to ground themselves. Plus, our spiritual side must be fed in order to be completely healthy. I only hope she doesn't get so caught up in regiments of church that she misses the purpose entirely.

"I'm glad that Evelyn came with us and I am more pleased with your tolerance of her. You know she doesn't have many friends, this means a lot to her," Tam said as she sat at the table.

With an intentional, careless expression, I moved my chair beside hers to face the ocean. Leaning back in our chairs and extending our legs onto the wooden railing of the balcony, we sat in silence staring into the massive body of water. After minutes of silence, Tam softly placed her head on my shoulder and spoke.

"She was a little girl."

Without her prefacing this statement, right away I knew she was talking about her miscarriage last year. This was the first mention of it. She never wanted to discuss what had happened, how she felt about it, or the sex of the child. I vividly remember seeing her lying on the floor of the baby's room wrapped in a yellow blanket as Evelyn and I walked in to comfort her. All she said was "I love you guys." That was it. I guess it had taken her six months to heal. Not sure what to say, I placed my hand on top of hers and gently squeezed it as a sign of comfort.

"I think about her every day, I just don't say anything. Stan wants to try again, but I don't think I can go through the pain of losing another child."

With my legs stretched across the chair, I sat silently and listened to her purge.

"I want another child, but I don't know. I'm a good

person. Do you think God would make me deal with this over again? Maybe it wasn't meant for me to have a child. We even talked about adopting, but I know that would be the last option for Stan."

Her thoughts, though random, made perfect sense.

"If I couldn't have kids, I don't know how he would feel about me. I know he would still love me, but I think it would be a little less. I know that if I don't at least try, he will look at me differently," she said with a sigh.

Finally, I decided to but in. "Stan is a good man, he is going to love you regardless. With your strength, I know you can deal with whatever God gives you. We all go through adversity. How you deal with the difficulty is the key."

Tam lifted her head from my shoulder and kissed me on my temple. Suddenly she shifted the topic of conversation from her adversity to mine. "So, I know you still think about Dick. When was the last time you spoke with him?"

I laughed and asked, "Why must it always come back to Dick?"

"You tell me," she said.

"You started it," I said.

"You wanted me to," she bantered in return.

I looked away into the body of water and gave a heavy sigh, yet Tam continued.

"I promise this will be the last time I say this, but you know you love him, why don't you just admit it?"

"You sure have a lot to say," I mumbled.

Tam shrugged and stared until I commented on her statement.

"I told Dick that I loved him. What more can I do? He has a fiancée."

"Girl, come on. You know Dick wants you. He's settling for Celeste, because you gave him such a hard time. Celeste came along and she was easy, so he gave in. I want to see you two together."

Becoming a little angry at Tam's remarks, I stood and moved away as my pitch rose.

"What do you want me to do, conveniently make Celeste disappear? Dick is gone. He has moved on and I have moved on! That is it. I haven't spoken to him in months. Let it go!"

"If you didn't love him so much, you wouldn't get so angry," she said, just as calm.

I placed my drink on the table and walked away from the balcony. Tam called out as I entered the room, "It's not over, mark my words."

I closed the door on the echo of her voice to block out her insanity.

"It is over," I said to myself, leaning against the sliding glass door. Yet, as I said these words, I longed for him, just as Tam desired Stan. Nevertheless, wishful thinking keeps us grounded to the land of fantasy. I must rise to reality and begin to plan my life without Dick. Last time I saw him, we were together in the park. He was telling me how he thought I never really wanted to be with him, but that I was only after him because he was now with another woman. He was so wrong, but after that conversation, I realized he didn't know me at all, and so I too moved on.

I changed my clothing and joined Evelyn on the beach. I saw her wading close to the shore, so I called out for her attention. Seconds later, she came out of the water and with little persuasion. Several men watched her glide across the sand. With her petite frame and golden skin, they couldn't help themselves. Evelyn was definitely cute; she sort of looked like a pixie doll and she used this to her advantage. I convinced her to walk down to the nude section of the five-mile beach, and there we placed our towels on the sand and shared a huge blue and white umbrella. We crossed our legs and enjoyed the beautiful highlights of St. Lucia. Instantly, idealistic thoughts of my Dick were replaced with the reality of many dicks swaying in the light breeze. Evelyn and I giggled like little girls as we talked about the sizes and shapes of each island man's anatomical structure.

"It's such an odd-looking thing, don't you agree?" said Evelyn.

"Why do we like it so much? It's actually quite ugly," I concurred.

"And yet amazing," Evelyn said in awe of this sculpted caramel, nude figure passing by.

We both stare at his defined pecs and his rippling right biceps adorned with a colorful tattoo of an angel inscribed with a name. Gleefully, we watched him walk away, which was as delightful as his approach. His broad shoulders and strong back narrowed down close to a thirty-two-inch waist. He reminded me of Dick. Factually, most everything did and I absolutely hated it. I snapped my fingers in front of Evelyn's eyes in order to get her attention, for she was still gawking at Mr. Caramel.

Just then Evelyn turned around and spoke. "He reminds me of Dick."

"Don't start. I already had to listen to Tam," I retorted.

"That's all I was going to say," she responded, leaning back onto the towel.

I put my shades on and continued enjoying the sun.

"Watch out!" called someone from the beach.

Hurriedly, we whipped around in the direction of the voice, and I saw Mr. Caramel rapidly moving toward our towel. With his back facing us, he leapt to grab the football being tossed in our direction. Evelyn sat up as he landed on the edge of her towel and fell back onto our laps. Our mouths flew open as his naked body stretched across our legs.

"Sorry, ladies," he said, looking into our faces.

"No apology necessary," flirted Evelyn.

He slowly turned around as his manhood brushed against Evelyn's leg. She looked at me as her eyes opened wide. Facedown and still on top of our legs, he introduced himself with a smile.

"My name is Pierce," he said with a Caribbean accent, and then lifted himself off the towel.

"My name is Lily and this is Evelyn."

Reaching over, Pierce kissed both our hands.

"Would you like to play?" he offered, holding up the football.

I quickly turned to Evelyn and put her on the spot. "Evelyn, weren't you just saying you wanted to play? Here's your chance."

She briskly began to shake her head no.

"Come on. It will be fun," said Pierce while lightly lifting her from the towel.

Evelyn eventually joined Pierce in his game.

"Yeah, Evelyn!" I cheered from the sandy sideline as I watched this very interesting game of football.

How intriguing the game becomes when there are more balls involved.

"I could get used to this," I uttered.

The day passed rapidly as most vacation hours do. We only had one more day here and I dreaded going back to the States. Island life was stress free. I am sure the natives stress over the same things as we do in America, but they seemed to handle pressure in better ways. Our country is definitely uptight in comparison. I vote for nude beaches everywhere; I think they are a start in the right direction.

Around 8:00 p.m., the girls and I arrived at the Line Restaurant for dinner. As soon as we took our seats, Pierce and two gorgeous acquaintances walked through the door.

"Oh my!" gawked Tam.

Astonished at their beauty, we all agreed that these island men had been blessed with a wonderful gift— the gift of being fine. We soon learned that Pierce was one of six boys. Three of his brothers were married and he and two other brothers were single. That night we had the pleasure of being wined and dined by the single three. We ate, danced, and laughed as we watched the sun go down into the ocean water. Leaning into my date, I whispered, "I love eating outside overlooking the ocean. Everything is so picturesque, it's easy to forget that you have an ordinary life back at home awaiting your arrival."

He gave me a charming smile and stroked my arm. I assumed he thought I was flirting with him. I was, a little, but only for fun. I didn't want to give him the wrong impression, and so I quickly grinned back and averted my attention elsewhere. Before we noticed it, it was 1:00 a.m., and it was evident that none of us wanted the evening to end. Even Tam, though happily married, seemed to be lost in the stories of the gorgeous island brothers. She didn't mention Stan once during the evening. Upon realizing that we were the only six people left in the restaurant, we thanked the guys for dinner and parted ways. However, somewhere between the eatery and the hotel we lost Evelyn. She was walking with us down the street one minute, and then Tam and I noticed her slowing down to talk with Pierce. Next thing we knew, she disappeared with him.

"Where did Evelyn go?" asked Tam.

"I think the church lady has gone to get her some island lovin'," I said with laughter.

"Whatever. She's a grown girl and we're not waiting around for her, I am tired," Tam griped while pulling my arm.

We retired to the room and believe it or not, little Miss Evelyn did not make an appearance until nine thirty the next morning when she strolled out onto the patio to join Tam and me for breakfast.

"Good morning, ladies," Evelyn said with an interesting look on her face.

"Oh, you're finally up?" I asked.

"Up? I just got in," Evelyn answered with a peculiar smile.

Tam and I slowly turned around, nonchalantly acknowledged her presence, and then continued our conversation. Evelyn hated to be ignored, and we knew the best way for her to spill the beans about last night was for us to act like we didn't care. Immediately, Evelyn pulled up a chair and sat in between the two of us; however, we did not halt our conversation. After a few seconds of our talking around Evelyn, she couldn't contain herself any longer.

"Pierce and I had the most wonderful evening, don't you want to know what happened?" she asked.

"Not really, can you pass me the pitcher of water?" I asked.

Evelyn quickly turned her attention to Tam. "Tam, we went back to the beach and walked along the shore for hours."

"Did I ask you what you did?" Tam responded with a frown.

"Come on, guys, why won't you listen to me?" Evelyn whined.

Tam and I looked around at each other and began to laugh. That was all Evelyn needed to start the ball rolling.

"He held my hand and we walked on the beach. We talked about dreams and goals. He wants to move to the States and train to be a firefighter. Two of his brothers live in New York and he visits them every other year. We sat on the beach and talked about how vast the ocean is compared to humans and how silly we are to think that we are the greatest things on this earth. We are so connected," she continued.

Interrupting her girlish babble, I commented, "That was around one, it is now nine thirty. Did you talk about nature all night long?"

"Of course not, we talked about a lot of things, God, science, healthy eating—"

"Did you sleep with him?" interrupted Tam.

Evelyn gasped. "How is that your business?"

"What! You're the one interrupting our breakfast with Pierce this and Pierce that. If you want to keep us interested in your little story, you best come up with something better than walks and talks," I said.

Evelyn turned toward Tam in hopes for a better response, but Tam nodded in agreement.

"Well, I'll tell you everything if you promise not to judge me."

"Girl, we didn't judge when you were a whore, we surely aren't going to judge you now," I said.

"Tam!" Evelyn shouted.

"Lily, be nice. Go ahead, Evelyn," she said, just as eager to hear the details.

"Okay. We go back to his place and he put on a few records. He has an amazing collection of old jazz records. Records are so much more romantic than CDs," she rambled on. "Anyway, we danced and talked, and then he slowly undressed me and we made love on his beanbag chair," Evelyn said with excitement.

"His beanbag chair!" questioned Tam.

"Yeah! Anyone can do it in the bed. The chair is a different experience."

"We aren't questioning your love experience on the beanbag, we are questioning why he even has a beanbag chair," I replied in bewilderment.

"Will you let me finish?" exclaimed Evelyn. "Then we walked to the roof of the building where they have a Jacuzzi, and kissed and cuddled until the morning." She giggled.

Tam and I sat boggled by this so-called wonderful experience. Neither of us knew what to say, and so Evelyn continued to speak.

"We were going horseback riding today, but he had class this morning."

"Oh, is he a teacher?" asked Tam.

"No, he's a junior at the university."

"How old is this man?" Tam continued to interrogate.

"Twenty-two."

Tam and I both burst into laughter. Evelyn frowned as if she were appalled by our behavior.

"He's a baby," I said.

"He's not. He's an adult," she argued.

"You are thirty-one years old," Tam said while knocking on Evelyn's head.

"I knew I shouldn't have said anything. You two are just jealous," she said while walking into the other room.

"What about God and commitment and waiting until the right one comes along?" Tam called out.

"That's right. The only one you are supposed to be having relations with is God. He is going to be pretty upset that you cheated on Him," I chimed out right behind Tam.

Tam and I were still laughing. We couldn't believe that Evelyn had come to St. Lucia and lain up with some boy she didn't know, when just a week ago she was judging a friend of ours for doing the exact same thing.

"Can you believe her?" asked Tam.

"Oh yeah! That's the real Evelyn. She can pretend all she wants, but deep down, your friend is a freak and I am going to enjoy reminding her of it over and over again."

Recalling her expression about the beanbag made Tam and me laugh all over again. We retired from the balcony and continued our fun in the sun. We didn't see Evelyn the entire day, and that evening we packed up our things and prepared for our flight back home the next morning. Around midnight, we heard Pierce and Evelyn outside the door saying their good nights. It was so sweet and so juvenile.

"It reminds me of a summer camp romance," Tam whispered from across the room. "Lily, do you hear them?"

"Of course I do. Are they for real?"

"Shh! Hear she comes, here she comes," Tam said hurriedly.

We closed our eyes and pretended to be asleep as

Evelyn walked in. She went over to the sofa and lay across the cushion with her feet dangling over the edge. She stretched out her arms and spoke.

"I know you heifers aren't asleep, so you can stop pretending."

Tam and I continued to keep quiet.

"Just so you know, I am not going back with you two tomorrow."

"What!" Tam and I simultaneously yelled as we sat up in our beds.

"I'm not going back. I have decided to stay a couple more weeks."

"Did you leave your virtue and your brain on that beanbag? You can't stay here. What about everything at home? What about your job?" questioned Tam.

"I have no one at home and I'll call my father and tell him that I will be staying awhile longer and that he can fax me any paperwork he needs me to look over. I'll just say that mentally I couldn't return and I need a few weeks longer to recoup."

I sometimes forgot that Evelyn's family had money and that she worked in land development for her father. I guessed she could stay here as long as she liked. Yet I was still amazed.

"But—" Tam tried to speak, but Evelyn interrupted.

"But nothing. He asked if I could stay, so I'm staying. I'll be back in a few weeks. It's no big deal."

"You don't know him. What if he's crazy?"

"So what, I'm crazy. We'll be two crazy people enjoying each other's company."

"Well, you got the first part right, your ass is crazy, and I'm not going to debate with you about this. Have fun. Let me know what happens when you meet his mama, Stella," I said.

Evelyn picked up the sofa pillow and tossed it in my direction but missed. "That's not funny," she said.

Tam stayed up and tried to convince Evelyn to come back with us, but I went to sleep. I wasn't ready to return, but my daddy didn't write my paychecks and so with or without Evelyn, I had to get my behind back to reality by tomorrow.

2

Back to Life

I walked into my house, flipped on the lights, and like mold I could feel the loneliness sponge over my body. Suddenly I realized that Evelyn's idea of staying a few weeks longer wasn't so bad after all. I would love to hear my boss's remark if I told her that I was mentally exhausted and needed an additional two weeks attached to my vacation. Some of us have it made and the rest of us work in Corporate America, where two weeks' vacation per 365 days is the only recouping one gets.

I had been gone from my office for one week and my desk was piled with at least ten folders. It was as if everyone dumped his or her unwanted projects on my desk. I'd come in early to get a grasp on everything, but it was going to take me a few weeks to catch up on this mess. A few hours after I was there sifting through the folders, Sarah appeared from nowhere handing me a small bouquet of wildflowers.

"Welcome back! Did you have fun?" she asked.

I stood and gave my favorite coworker a hug. Her light freckles and naturally bright red hair always put a smile on my face. I enjoyed my job as a writer, but truthfully, talking with Sarah was often the highlight of my day. The writers here didn't normally mingle with the receptionists, but I didn't care. Sarah's youthful energy was always uplifting.

"I wish you could have come with us," I responded.

"Please. You know I cannot leave the country with a five-month-old attached to my nipple. But next year, I am definitely going."

Sarah moved the pile of papers over to one side, sat on the corner of my desk, and sipped her morning tea.

"So, did you meet anyone?" she asked.

"Aren't you nosy?"

"I have to live through your exciting life because mine is the same ole boring business day after day."

"I didn't meet anyone, but Evelyn met a young man and decided to stay down there with him for a few more weeks."

Sarah's eyes grew wide as she leaned in for more details. "Isn't Evelyn the rich girl you don't like? Where did she meet him? Is she coming back?"

This was right down Sarah's alley. She loved good gossip, and though she never spread information around the office, she thrived on others' excitement. Like she said, she lived vicariously through it. Deep down, Sarah wanted to live on the edge and be daring, but she was a country girl from Kentucky who still desired to be accepted by her peers, and so she kept it simple.

"I don't dislike Evelyn, I simply don't like all of her ways, but she's growing on me. She met her friend

Pierce on the nude beach playing football. I'm sure she'll be back in a couple of weeks. Then again, who knows with Evelyn?"

"Pierce? He sounds fine."

"Oh, he is. He is also twenty-two."

Sarah slammed her cup on the desk and yelled, "Get out! Isn't she thirty-something?"

I nodded as Sarah began to laugh.

"Well, at least she has someone. You need to follow her and get you someone. You haven't been on a date since Carmen was born," Sarah mentioned.

Sarah and I went through this once a week, and she knew that I was purposely not dating. Last year I had done nothing but run from one relationship to another. I left Romance, my boyfriend-turned-fiancé of two years, for Will Dickson, aka Dick. He was a tall, dark-skinned singer with big, bushy, curly hair. Dick was the epitome of fineness. We ended up having a fling that turned out to be much more, but not enough to call a commitment. Then I moved from Atlanta to Kansas City not only for this great job with America's favorite greeting card company, but also to clear my mind of the male chaos I had created back home. However, I came here and became involved with Mr. Wealth Fulmore, whose affluent background allowed him to shower me with elaborate gifts and expensive trips. So caught up in that nonsense, I didn't realize he was cheating the entire time. After these fiascos, I decided it was time for a break. I need to be with one person and one person only—myself.

"Sarah, I don't want to date. I am enjoying my life. I have more time to write, and I started volunteering at the youth shelter. You know how much I've been enjoying that."

"Writing and volunteering are fine, but you know you miss dating. There's nothing wrong with one date, once a week. Let me fix you up with an old friend of mine. He moved here from back home. He is really sweet and cute. He's short, but his personality is tall. Please go out with him," she said while squeezing my arm.

"Hell no. No offense, but your taste in men sucks."

Sarah lightly punched me in the arm. However, she knew I was right. Omar, her man and the father of her child, was slowly getting his act together, but in the beginning he was a mentally and physically abusive asshole, whom she should never have gone out with. She met him through Wealth and though I sometimes felt responsible for bringing him into her life, Sarah was an adult. Thank God for Omar's mom, Claire. She was there to pick up the pieces of her crazy son. Sarah and her daughter, Carmen, lived with Claire, who was an absolute angel.

I slowly lifted my eyes from my paperwork and saw Sarah was still pleading with me to go out with her friend.

Finally, I responded, "One date. That's it. I do not care how sweet and cute he is. I do not want a boyfriend. I want to be alone, and I don't like short men."

Sarah's eyes lit up as she leaned over and grabbed my phone. I immediately placed my hand on top of hers to keep her from lifting the receiver.

"Have you already told him about me?" I asked, already knowing her answer was yes.

"Kind of," she said with a funny face.

"Only give him my work number."

Sarah tried to pick up the phone again, but I slammed it back down. "And go to your own desk and call. I have to start work."

Sarah jumped up from my desk with the fervor of a twelve-year-old as I continued giving her instructions.

"Do not put him through, tell him to call me this afternoon."

Sarah eagerly nodded and spoke. "His name is Donnie, but we call him Patch."

"Patch?" I questioned curiously.

"His family was poor and his mom used to patch up his pants with old tablecloth fabric. At first it was a joke, but then it never went away."

"And what does Patch do for a living?" I asked.

Sarah turned back and winked before walking down the hall.

"You'll see," she said before disappearing.

I leaned back in my chair and thought. If I remembered correctly, Sarah had convinced me to go out with Wealth the same way. I must stop letting her do this. I knew she meant well, but her record was not in good standing. I was extremely leery about my future date with this guy named Patch.

Immediately after lunch, I returned to my desk, and as soon as I sat down, Patch called. Our conversation was very brief because of my two o'clock meeting with Nehri, my new presentation partner who replaced Dale, my old partner. Yet he and I agreed to meet for dinner the next night. I had never been on a blind date, and I had a strange feeling it was going to be my first one and my last.

I got home around seven that evening and instantly plopped down on the futon. Exhausted, I leaned my head onto the back, closed my eyes, and as soon as I began to doze, my phone rang.

"Yes," I answered.

"Hello, Miss Lady."

"Who is this?" I asked quite irritably.

"It's the Fulmore brother you should have dated."

"Winston!" I said with excitement. "Where have you been?"

I had called Winston a month ago and he never returned my call. I assumed since I was no longer dating his twin, Wealth, that he didn't want to communicate.

"I've been out of the country on research. How have you been?"

"Wonderful, and you?"

"About the same. I just got back from Africa last week. I've been there working with infants infected with HIV and AIDS. I enjoyed my trip, but I am so glad to be home," he said.

It was so good to hear his voice. Winston and I were close, probably a little too close. We had an odd but special situation, and I so badly wanted to see him.

"So, when am I going to see you?" he asked without delay.

Thank God, he read my mind.

"Whenever you have the time," I quickly responded.

He paused for a second before continuing. I heard talk in the background and it sounded like Wealth.

"Is that Wealth?" I asked.

"Yeah, he stopped by to pick up something. Hold on."

The good thing was that Wealth and I were still acquaintances. We no longer hung out at social gatherings, but were respectful and friendly when we saw each other. However, I still thought he would have a problem with me hanging out with his brother.

"I'm back. Wealth says hello," Winston commented.

"You told him I was on the phone?" I whispered.

"Of course, he knows we still talk. I told him I was going to take you to dinner."

"What did he say?"

"He said she loves Italian."

"And what did you say?" I hastily interjected.

"I said I know."

This was such a sticky predicament, and I felt so uncomfortable when he spoke about Wealth. It was as if I were being passed between brothers. I couldn't help but think they were going to compare notes.

"Well, I have to go, but I'm going to call you next week once my schedule settles. We'll discuss dinner then," said Winston.

"Okay. Talk with you soon. Bye."

I hung up the phone with a big smile, went upstairs, and prepared for bed. Although it was only eight, I was done in. I took a long bath to relax, slipped into my long cotton tank, and slid into bed. I popped in a CD of Dick's band, SoulTyme, and I giggled remembering how Dick used to call and convince me to have phone sex. I had never done such a thing before meeting him. In truth, I never did several things before meeting him. He would tell me what to do and it would make me so uncomfortable at first, but then eventually it seemed normal. Thanks to him, I was much more comfortable with my body. He brought out a sexual side of me that eventually boosted my confidence. He made me feel pretty and deep down we all want to feel like a pretty girl. I pulled out my journal and wrote about that before turning in.

PRETTY GIRL

There is gold beneath my surface
Though many never see
I come and go as I please
I blend amongst the common
I rarely dress my looks with colors and sparkles
Funny, those who do think there is something wrong
Ironically, they are the ones with the problem
They don't realize how valuable I am
They don't see the treasure within
I laugh to myself when they judge me
For they are the fools sitting on oil land
Refusing to dig below the surface
They want a pretty girl
But they can't see
That the prettiest of all girls
Is me

Giggling, I laid my pretty self down and slowly drifted off to sleep.

Good night.

3

Blind Date
or Blind Man

Around noon the next day, I remembered that I was supposed to have dinner with Sarah's friend Patch. I wanted to reschedule, but I figured I might as well get it over with. Thankfully, the workday wasn't hectic and I left work on time in order to go home and change.

I arrived at the restaurant fifteen minutes early. I wasn't sure what Patch looked like, but we had agreed to meet each other at the bar. He said he would be wearing a white shirt and black slacks, and once I arrived, I realized Patch's ensemble was going to identically match the waiter's wardrobe, which was pretty funny. I ordered a glass of lemonade and waited at the bar. While I was waiting, a handsome gentleman walked up to me and initiated conversation. He was definitely not Patch, although I wished he were. He was a high school math teacher named Bruce. This teacher was an interesting change of pace from the men I normally dated. Maybe that was where I had been going wrong. I wondered, *Could math teachers be exciting?* Better yet, excitement was what caused problems. Math teachers were stable and practical, which could be good for me. Then suddenly the word *boring* popped into my head.

Why was it that girls loved artists, bad boys, or brave guys? A firefighter was going to win a date over an accountant any day of the week. The girl may eventually marry the accountant, but not until she's burned a few flames with the firefighter. However, this teacher was quite interesting. He leaned over and handed me his card and just as I was taking it out of his hand, I felt a tap on my arm. I turned away from Bruce and looked over my left shoulder to see a brother in an oversized white shirt and black pants greet me. He was wearing a Kangol hat, but the most obvious feature was the black patch over his right eye. Immediately, I knew that I was going to kick Sarah's ass.

"Patch?" I questioned, praying that it was only a coincidence.

"The one and only," he said with confidence.

I turned back around, excused myself from Bruce, and slowly moved a few seats down to have conversation with Patch.

"Sarah told me you were smart, but damn, she neglected to say that you were beautiful," he said, kissing my hand.

"Well, well, she told me absolutely nothing about you."

The hostess came over and told us our table was ready. I walked a few steps behind Patch. Not that I was embarrassed to be with a man with a patch over his eye, but he looked like the rapper Slick Rick minus the gold chains. I should have known that tablecloth story was a hoax. He pulled my chair out and we sat down for dinner.

"So, Patch. You're moving here to Kansas City?"

"Thinking about it. Right now I'm here working on my sophomore album."

"Oh, you're in music. What do you do?"

"I rhyme. You know what I'm saying?"

Ugh! He spoke that horrible phrase that I hate. Why start a conversation with "you know what I'm saying" before anything is really said? It's just dumb.

I plastered on a fake smile and replied, "That's nice."

Our server came over to take our order, yet she was so overwhelmed by my date that she couldn't concentrate. Finally, she took a breath and asked for his autograph. He obliged, and then she left without taking the order.

"People know who you are?" I asked, quite astonished.

"Yeah, yeah, you know what I'm saying. I can go some places without people recognizing me. That's why I wear the hat. It doesn't always work, though. I don't mind the autographs. When they stop asking for them is when I'll worry."

At the end of his sentence he excused himself, reached down into his pants, pulled out his iPhone, and proceeded to type in a message. As soon as he finished, he had to pull it out again and type another message. He finally put it away as two more young female servers came out with a plate of appetizers.

"Excuse me, we haven't ordered," I said to them.

"I know. We put together a special plate, a sampler of each of the appetizers. I hope you guys like it," she said, beaming at Patch.

He smiled and asked me if I was ready to order.

"I'll have the chicken fettuccini with a house salad and vinaigrette dressing," I responded.

"I'll have the T-bone steak with french fries. No salad for me."

The young girls giggled, took our menus, and walked back to the kitchen. As soon as they left, I felt Patch's leg rubbing against mine under the table. At first I thought it was an accident, but as he continued I realized he was trying to woo me. It was not working.

"So, Sarah tells me you're a writer. We have a lot in common . . . Excuse me."

Once more, he began typing on his phone. We had only been here fifteen minutes and he had spent ten of them talking to someone else. Though this would never work, I was still going to attempt to make conversation.

"So, what was the name of your first album?" I asked curiously.

He smiled and looked up from his phone while answering. "*Bloody Murder Coming at Ya*," he boasted.

I sat quietly pondering his answer before responding. "Hmmm. Interesting."

I wasn't even going to ask him the name of his second album. Just then my cell phone rang. Normally, I would not answer it during a dinner date, but this was not a normal date.

"Hello," I answered quietly.

"Hey, girl. Are you surprised?" Sarah asked.

I tapped Patch on the arm and excused myself from the table. I didn't dare let him hear what I was about to say to his friend Sarah.

"Should I be surprised, Sarah? Should I?" It was clear that I was not pleased.

"It's Patch. You know, the rapper Patch," she said with excitement.

"I don't know Patch from snatch! Why did you lie to me about some little poor boy who wore patches on his knee?"

"That wasn't a lie. He did wear tablecloth patches. The name stuck, so he decided to wear a patch over his eye to go with the name."

"So you're saying he doesn't need a patch, but that he wears it as part of some costume?" I said with disgust.

"Yeah. As far as I know, he can see fine."

"Bye, Sarah, we'll talk tomorrow."

I hung up the phone and walked back to the table.

"I'm sorry about all of the interruptions. I cut my phone off so we could enjoy dinner," Patch said.

I nodded and smiled and within minutes dinner arrived and we ate with very minimal conversation. He paid for the meal, left the server a twenty-dollar tip, and walked me to my car. We leaned against the door and said our good-byes.

"I had a nice time. Thanks for dinner," I said to Patch.

"I'll be here for a few months, maybe we can do it again. Know what I'm saying?"

He handed me a piece of paper with his four phone numbers. I thought to myself, *Why do you need four numbers?*

However, I didn't ask, I simply replied, "We'll see."

Patch leaned over and kissed my cheek before opening my door. I sat in my SUV and watched him walk away to his brand-new black Range Rover. I had to admit, he was a gentleman, but I would not like that lifestyle. Between the phone calls, the groupies, and the touring schedule, there would never be time to nurture a relationship.

The more I thought, the more questions arose. Why in the world would he wear a hat to hide his identity and still wear that damn patch over his eye? It seemed he would have removed the patch as well unless he really wanted recognition on some level.

People can pretend all they want. Yet their true character will eventually be revealed.

This would be a good title for my next journal entry. Either way, Patch was too much drama for me. I thought, however, I would call Bruce, the math teacher. I saw it like this: all men have a wild side to unleash and if the math teacher had a normal gig, one can just imagine where he might release his wild side. *Know what I'm saying?*

4

Next Level Blues

The last two days of the week crept by. I had had the intention of working that weekend. Conversely by Friday, my plans had altered. I didn't want to think about work again until Monday morning. As I was getting my things together to leave work, my phone rang. I was so tempted not to answer, for fear it would be my boss, but since I had fifteen more minutes before five o'clock, I did.

"Hallmark, This is Lily."

"Hello, lady. What are you doing?"

It was Winston. I was so glad I answered.

"About to leave work. I thought I wouldn't hear from you until next week," I said.

"Well, my day has been light and I'm done here, so I thought we could do something this evening."

"I have plans. I'm going bowling with the youth home. I would love to see you, though. Why don't you come?"

"I don't know. I haven't bowled in years," he said with hesitance.

"So what, I can't bowl at all."

"Where is it?" he asked.

"At the lanes on Tenth Street at seven thirty p.m."

"I might come."

"Call me on my cell either way," I stated before ending our conversation.

I hung up with Winston, grabbed my purse, and headed home. I rushed upstairs and changed clothes. After a few phone calls, I made my way to the bowling alley. The youth home had special events once a month and bowling was always a favorite. I have always enjoyed working with kids and I was finally taking the time to do some of the things I had always wanted to do, which was volunteer teaching a creative writing class.

I had a special little sister at the home. Her name was Samantha, known as Sam, and she was twelve going on thirty. Sam's mom died when she was six. Her father, a drug user, would use Sam as a punching bag when he could not get a quick fix and she was taken from him at the age of eight. She had no other relatives to take her in, so the courts placed her in the home. She was a sweet, smart girl. However, for obvious reasons, she was riddled with low self-esteem. I gravitated toward her and I tried to take her to special events whenever I could. What she needed more than anything was for someone to show her how precious she was. Becoming a teenager was difficult enough. Becoming a teen without parental guidance had to be hell. I really wanted to make a difference in her life.

As soon as I walked into the alley, I heard the kids near the last four lanes. While I was exchanging my sneakers for the multicolored bowling lace-ups, I felt a pair of arms squeeze around my chest. I didn't have to turn around, because I could tell it was Sam from the various colors of fingernail polish. That girl never wore the same colors on any of her fingers.

"It's about time you got here," Sam said.

I turned around, and pretended to choke her while answering, "It's only seven forty. You haven't been here long."

Grabbing my arm, Sam smiled and dragged me down the walkway to the rest of the gang. I sat and watched the kids bowl a few rounds before attempting to bowl myself. Finally, I decided to bowl a game with Sam. She knew I was a terrible bowler, so before each roll she stood beside me and showed me everything that was wrong with my form. She actually improved my game, but unfortunately we still lost. Her next game, she traded me in for another partner. She was sweet about it, though.

"I think I should bowl with Greg now. He doesn't have a lot of friends, and you told me I should extend my friendship to those in need."

"Just say you don't want to lose another game with me. I understand."

Sam softly patted me on the arm and spoke. "I don't want to lose another game with you."

We both laughed and I moved over to the video games and quickly one of the boys challenged me in *Madden NFL.* I had no idea what I was doing; nevertheless, I was going to give it a try. I got on the right joystick as he began to explain the rules. I didn't have time to ask questions, for he pressed the start button as soon as he finished. The game started and I vigorously moved the joystick back and forth while continuously pressing the red and blue buttons. I didn't know if I was defense or offense, I only knew that my team was wearing black. When I started the second quarter, Winston surprisingly walked up behind me and caused a distraction. I was about to score, so I couldn't turn and look. Yet when he pressed his body against mine and whispered in my ear, I quickly snapped around.

"I have a few moves I can show you," he said.

"Oh, really?" I responded.

"Oh, really!" he replied with a simper.

I moved aside and let him finish my game. Unfortunately, he was no better. He didn't even score. After his pitiful display, I walked him over and introduced him to the kids. Of course, everyone loved him. Together, we sat and watched the kids throughout the evening.

"Sam has had an unstable life since she was six," I said.

"Yeah, it's sad."

"Most of these kids have been in homes their entire life. They've seen things in the first decade of their life that most adults never see in a lifetime."

"When I was in Africa I sat in that hospital and wondered why the Creator picks and chooses what obstacles we will have. Why are some born with a silver spoon and some born with no spoon at all?"

"You don't have to go all the way to Africa to ask those questions," I replied.

We continued to watch the kids and talk until eleven, when the kids started to board the bus. As we were walking out, I saw Sam hugged up with one of the older boys. She caught a glimpse of my eye, immediately removed his arm from around her neck, and ran over to give me a hug.

"What was that about?" I asked her.

She tried to play innocent. "It was nothing, we're just friends."

"You know a guy's interpretation of *friends* is a little different than a girl's."

"It was nothing," she reiterated.

Sam hugged my neck and rushed back to the bus. Although she looked sixteen, she was only twelve and that is too young to date.

"I think I'm going to have to talk to her about boys," I told Winston.

"What do you know about boys?" He smirked.

I looked him straight in the eye and responded, "They are nothing but trouble, especially the fine ones that grow up to be doctors."

He chuckled and we waved good-bye to the kids as the bus pulled off.

"So, where are you going?" Winston said.

"Any suggestions?" I responded.

He leaned against the hood of the car and pulled me closer.

"You want to come to my house and watch a movie?" he asked.

I didn't know what to say. I really didn't want to go down that road with Winston.

"What are you doing?" I asked.

"I am asking you to come over."

"That's not what I mean. Your tone changed. One minute we were friends and now it's different. When did this happen?"

"It's been happening all the while. Where were you?" he stated.

I thought silently for a moment, then turned around and looked into his eyes. It was amazing how much he looked like Wealth. Yet his energy was completely different. "I'm not sure about this."

"I'm not going to do anything you feel uncomfortable with."

"It's not that. I just like things the way they are, at least for now."

Winston kissed me on the forehead and then on the lips. I knew this was trouble. I'd only seen him a couple of times since Wealth and I ended things; however, we'd had a few late-night conversations that were intimate and revealing. It was amazing how close people can grow through simple dialogue. We both knew that there was something there, but we both had been avidly avoiding it. I presumed this had been happening the entire time and I guessed Winston was ready to make his move.

"Look, you have to follow me halfway home to get to your house. If you decide to come over, just keep following."

With that comment he moved away and walked to his car. While driving, I contemplated his invitation. I had been by myself for close to six months. This was a record for me; I normally jumped from one relationship to another, and if I were not in a relationship, I was definitely dating someone. This time, my goal was to be single for at least a year. I wasn't sure why I decided on that time frame, but twelve months sounded like enough time for me to get my head together. My desire was to master being alone without having the feeling of loneliness. I wanted to feel complete without the company of a man and I didn't think that I was there yet. I needed to go home, so when we got close to my exit, I called Winston on his cell phone.

"I'm going home. It has nothing to do with you and everything to do with timing," I said in a solemn tone.

"You're a special lady," he responded.

"I'll call you later," I said as I quickly hung up before I changed my mind. I wanted to work out my issues and everything, but it was a full moon and a week before my period. In other words, my hormones were raging.

Once home, I got undressed and took a long hot bath. I sank my head back onto my bath pillow and closed my eyes. Almost immediately sexual images of Winston appeared. Ironically, I never had sexual images of Wealth when we were going out and I was so glad that we never had intercourse. This way if I ever did sleep with Winston, they wouldn't have any sex notes to compare.

I think that no matter how old men get, they always compare notes. It's not until one of the men actually starts to love a woman that he stops comparing. It's the same for women. We gossip about everything from penis size to bedroom skills. Yet we always keep quiet about the man we think might be around for a while. We don't want our girlfriends knowing about him; it's distasteful. Furthermore, we don't want to pique their interest in our man. Dating is a funny, funny thing. It's a desired pain in the ass.

Just before turning in, I talked to Evelyn and was surprised to hear that she and Pierce were still going strong. She'd convinced him to start going to church and everything. While we were talking, Sarah beeped in, but I opted to call her back the next day after church. Better yet, I decided to call her in the morning to see if she wanted to attend church. She was always telling me to send up some prayers for her and Omar. It was about time she start praying for that mess herself.

5

Going to the Chapel?

I woke up early the next morning around nine o'clock and fixed breakfast before I headed out to church. I walked down to the kitchen and before I could start cooking my phone rang. I slid over to pick up the phone after seeing Tam's name on the caller ID.

"What's up, lady?" I answered.

"Not much. I just woke up," she responded.

"I talked to Evelyn last night."

"Her crazy tail will be back next week. She really likes that little boy. She says she's going back to visit him in a few months."

"He must be doing something right."

Tam laughed and paused for a moment. I could tell something was on her mind.

"Listen. I ran into Celeste and Dick last night. They were leaving Houston's as we were about to go in—"

"Yeah, and . . ." I interrupted.

"Well, Celeste invited Stan and me to the engagement party. I just thought you should know," she said.

"Why are you telling me this, Tam? Why?" I moaned.

Tam was silent. Nonetheless, I knew what she was telling me. She wanted me to call Dick and convince him that he was making a mistake. What she didn't realize was that it no longer mattered. I was not making a disaster out of someone else's life.

"You know he is only marrying her because you rejected him," she said. "I saw the look in his eyes last night. It's like he wanted me to call and tell you," Tam added.

"Tam, I have to go. I'll call you later," I said, hanging up the phone before she could get another word in. "Damn it!" I screamed.

I slammed the pan down on the stove and leaned over the counter. My appetite was ruined. I knew he and Celeste were living together, but he told me the ring was just a commitment promise and that no dates had been set. Then again, that was six months ago.

"Oh God, I feel sick," I griped, hunched over the counter.

Why did he still do this to me? I was supposed to be over him. I didn't want to do anything now. I didn't want to eat, I didn't want to shower, and I definitely didn't want to go to church. I slowly walked into the living room to become one with my confidant, the futon. As I held my arms close to my stomach and closed my eyes, the phone rang again. I rolled over, grabbed the phone, and prepared myself to tell Tam a bald-faced lie.

"Look, Tam, I don't care if he is marrying that ballet girl. Please don't talk to me about Dick anymore."

"Don't be mad at me. I just thought that if you knew—"

"Okay, well, now I know and I said that I would call you back. Good-bye."

I knew that I was being harsh, but why did she call me on a glorious Sunday morning to tell me some bullshit about Dick and Celeste? Once again, my phone rang.

"I am going to hurt this girl," I said aloud before answering.

"If you tell me one more thing about Dick and Celeste, I am going to come through this phone and ring your neck. I told you, I don't care!" I yelled with my teeth clenched together.

"Well, you sound like you care to me," said the man on the line.

"What? Who is this? Winston?" I asked anxiously.

There was a silence on the phone.

"Who is this?" I yelled.

"It's been too long if you have forgotten the sound of my voice."

"Dick?" I questioned while holding my breath.

"Hi, beautiful," he said.

There was another silence on the phone as I nearly choked.

"Are you okay?" he asked calmly.

Dick could always read me like a book, and he knew that I was not okay. He also knew that Tam had called me with the news of the engagement. He was probably trying to beat her to the punch.

"I'm fine, Dick, how are you?"

"I'm so-so," he replied.

"Well, you should be doing splendid, seeing that

you are getting married and all," I joked with a very southern accent.

"I'm sorry I didn't call to tell you. I was . . . um. Shit, I have to be honest, I was scared."

"Scared of what?"

"Scared that you would stop caring about me."

I paused momentarily for sentimental purposes, but then the rage hit me.

"You are so full of shit! You decided to keep seeing Celeste and gave her the ring. You didn't have the nerve to tell me about her, until I met her at the club. Then when I told you that I loved you, you read me my own poem stating that I had taken you for granted. You told me you were happy with her, so why in the hell are you concerned about my feelings for you?" I bellowed.

"Because we are friends and I don't want to lose that."

"Well, you know what, Dick? This friendship is not working for me. I don't think we should continue it."

He was silent. I couldn't even hear him breathing on the phone.

"Do you hear me?" I asked with anguish.

"Oh, I hear you and let me tell you something. I'm not the only one full of shit. Since you want to recall old memories, here are a few more. You're the one who pushed me aside because you thought you wanted your ex back. You're the one who moved away to start a new life, without even considering that you could have had a new life with me. You're the one who welcomed me to Kansas City, fucked me, said thank you, and then sent me on my merry way. When I asked you to move back, you said you couldn't. The only time you showed true emotion with me is when I told you I had another woman. It sounded more like jealousy than love. Several times I had to be your friend and sit and listen to stories about you and Romance or you and Wealth. I didn't want to hear that shit, but as your friend, I listened. But now that I'm calling you with something you don't want to hear, you no longer want to be my friend. Well, Lily, if that is what you want, you got it, baby."

"Forget you, Dick!" I shouted.

"Right back at ya!"

I slammed down the phone, placed my hands over my face. "I hate him. I hate him. I hate him."

I continued this phrase over and over again until the yells turned to wails and the hates turned to loves. The thin line between the two words had disappeared and I realized that love and hate just might be the same exact emotion. A feeling we choose to call different names at varying times to suit our mood.

At that moment, my mood was askew; the only thing I could do was write. I went back upstairs, pulled my journal from my nightstand, and crawled back into bed. With my teddy bear and my tissues by my side, I wrote:

Emotions run deep, I can't control them
What is this hold on my heart
I'm not bold enough to part

Yet I was told from the start
That what this is . . . is what this is
No more, no less, no more
And still I pour, and I still pour
My feelings overflowing to the floor
I continue to trip, I continue to slip
Please help me up, please take a cup
And scoop up my remains
Though they'll never be the same
I may need them again someday

I have no more words to tell
My courage resides in hell
Still you overwhelm
Me!

I couldn't believe how a day that started so great could end up so awful. This was too much energy over a stupid phone call. I refused to spend the day in bed. I was going to get up and take my goddaughter, Carmen, to the park. No matter how bad a mood, children could always find a soft spot to ease the pain. I rose from bed and called Sarah. She was excited about having a few hours alone to take care of personal business. She asked that I give her some time to pump some milk and then Carmen and I could walk in the park until the sun went down. I knew she was only kidding, because any time I had Carmen, she called every thirty minutes to make sure all was well. She would be sick if I kept her child out all day.

Two hours later, I was driving to the park with Carmen cooing in the backseat. It took nearly thirty minutes to find a place to park, for Sunday afternoons at Mill Creek Park were quite popular. I placed Carmen in her stroller and we headed down the walkway. It was a beautiful spring day. In the large field at the south end of the park, I heard music so I strolled to that section in order to see what was happening. There were four guys playing percussions while two ladies seemed to be practicing African/Latin dance moves. I wasn't sure if they were a group, but they had attracted a small crowd. I removed the blanket from the bottom of the stroller and Carmen and I took a seat. She loved music, and was already trying to move her head to the rhythm. As soon as I sat her up on my lap, I started getting eyes from neighboring blankets. This happened whenever I took Carmen anywhere. Her mother was Caucasian and her father was African-American, and Carmen's skin was very fair. Her hair was deep red with huge curls and her large eyes were dark brown. I found that people stared at Carmen first, looked at me, and then back at Carmen. They would try to figure out the combination. Today, I heard a neighboring couple gossiping about it.

"She must have a white daddy," one of them said.

It was so silly how people spent time wondering about others who had nothing to do with them. This child could have two black daddies. They didn't know and they shouldn't care. A great factor about people of color is that we can produce any shade of color from ecru to jet-black. The unfortunate thing is that whenever people meet Carmen, the first thing they are going to wonder about is her ethnic background. All her life she is going to hear that dreadful question.

"What are you?"

As if she were an alien. I have several friends with multiracial backgrounds and they all abhor that statement. It's a shame that we are more obsessed about what people are instead of how they are.

Carmen and I sat there for about thirty minutes until she became fussy. I placed her back in the stroller and headed back to the car. As soon as the car started rolling, Carmen quieted down and went to sleep. I had only been gone for an hour, so I decided to take Carmen to my home in order to give Sarah a little more time to herself. When I pulled up to my home, I saw a note on my door. I got the baby inside, went to the front door, retrieved the note, and read:

I was in the neighborhood, cell phone is dead, so I stopped by to take you to brunch. Call me later. Winston.

Winston was sweet and he liked me. Was I a fool to keep avoiding his advances? Was I going to miss out on another good man? How many chances was I going to get? I walked down the foyer and placed Carmen on her baby blanket. I called Winston and left him a message on his home phone.

Over the next hour and a half while Carmen was asleep, I started cooking dinner. Like clockwork, Sarah called every thirty minutes to make sure Carmen was okay. I was proud of Sarah; she was doing an amazing job with Carmen. If she could get Omar to put his two cents in, they might make a good family.

Around five, I headed back to Sarah's house. On the way, Carmen started screaming. I had fed her right before we left the house, so she wasn't hungry. But she was not happy and she was letting me know it. I was trying everything. Talking, singing, and making funny faces were not working. To top it off, my cell phone started ringing. I pulled over at a convenience store to answer the phone and try to calm Carmen.

"Hello!" I yelled over the screaming baby.

"What are you doing?" asked Winston.

"Trying to get Carmen quiet."

"Is she hungry?" he asked.

"No, I fed her not too long ago."

He listened to her crying in the background and then gave specific instructions.

"Lift her up so that her chest is just over your shoulder. Tap her lightly on the upper part of her back until she burps. She has gas. Call me back," he stated.

I did exactly what he said and seconds later she burped and soon stopped crying. Knowing a doctor has its advantages. I placed her in the car seat, got in, and returned Winston's call.

"Thanks so much. She is much better now. How did you know she had gas?"

"I could tell by her crying. Have you forgotten I deliver babies every day? Listen, what are you doing for dinner?" he asked.

"I cooked. Would you like to come over?" I said without thinking.

"I need to stay close to the house. I have a patient who may deliver tonight. I too am cooking. If you want, you can come right over and pack your dinner up for lunch next week," he offered.

Without hesitation, I accepted his invite.

"Give me directions. I'll be there shortly."

I wasn't sure what had changed between his last invite and this one, but I had decided to spend time with him. He gave me directions and after I left Sarah's house, I headed toward Winston's neighborhood. My stomach was beginning to flutter. Although nothing had been said, I knew I was about to go do something wrong. I sat at the end of his driveway hesitating and anticipating at the same time. Winston lived south of the city in an area where the homes start at five hundred thousand dollars, and I quickly became lost in the admiration of all the beautiful homes in his community.

Finally, I got out of the car and immediately he came to the porch wearing nothing but a pair of old jeans and his glasses. As I walked up to the front door,

I couldn't help but feel as though I were in a Levi's commercial. I had never seen this side of him, because I always saw him either with his family or after or before work. He was always in slacks or khakis with a button-up shirt. However, this look, with the jeans, the low haircut, and the five o'clock shadow, was working for him and surely working for me. He'd been compared to Boris Kodjoe and on that day I really saw it.

Winston greeted me with a kiss, pulled me into the house, and closed the cherry-wood doors behind us. He spun me around like a child greeting her father and sat me down on the lounge chair. His home was very spacious and open. He had very little furniture, yet his light tan walls were bedecked with huge, wonderfully framed oil paintings. Each of his rooms had looks from different countries and the paintings were indicative of these countries as well. His living room and dining area was Africa, and his study was Asia.

"Something smells mouthwatering," I said to Winston as we walked into the kitchen, which was decorated without a theme.

"Dinner should be ready in a moment. Make yourself at home."

I slipped off my shoes, placed them by the door, and walked into his study. I wanted to see what kind of books he had to read. You can tell a lot about a man by the books he reads. The first two shelves consisted of medical journals. However, the third shelf was filled with books on entrepreneurship and small business marketing. More interesting, the fourth shelf consisting of hardback books of old Hollywood celebrities. Rare photos of Marilyn Monroe, Frank Sinatra, Sophia Loren, Dorothy Dandridge, and others completed his collection. I took a seat and opened the book on

Sophia Loren. As soon as I opened the cover, a *Hustler* magazine fell onto the floor. I knew he had layers, but this guy was like an onion. Flipping through the pages, I wondered what else I might find in here. As I was placing the magazine back into the book, Winston walked into the room.

"It's okay if I look at these, isn't it?" I said, startled.

"Why look at nude pictures when I can show you the real thing?" he said with laughter.

Slightly embarrassed, I looked away and demurely stated, "Who are you?"

Winston continued to laugh.

"I'm not talking about the *Hustler* magazine. I meant the books," I continued.

"Does that mean I can't show you the real thing?" he replied.

I looked up from the book with a smirk, yet I gave him no answer. He grabbed a few of the books and asked me to follow him into the living room.

We sat on the floor looking through the photos while dinner was cooking.

"I love this period," Winston commented. "The women were so gracious and regal. The men were strong," he said, pointing to a picture of Harry Belafonte and Dorothy Dandridge on the set of *Carmen*.

"Are women today not as gracious and regal? Are the men not as strong?" I asked.

"Men are fighting to be strong, but they don't want to come off too strong, for it may offend the women. And women are so busy trying to be strong to survive on their own, they sometimes forget how to be gracious. I don't place blame on either sex. Society has done a number on gender roles."

His speech and ideals were turning me on. There is

nothing sexier than an intelligent man. Why was he
not taken?

"Why are you still single?" I asked.

"Well, you know about my ex. After she left me, I
had a difficult time trusting women. Therefore, I put
all of my energy into my practice. With my schedule,
I don't always have time to foster a relationship and
there are so many women who want to date me just
because I'm a doctor. I'm single because the right
woman hasn't come along, and you?"

"Oh, we had enough talks last year for you to know
why I'm single," I responded with a bit of laughter.

"Timing is so important," he said, looking into
my eyes.

"It is," I said, staring back.

Winston leaned in and brushed my hair aside. He
kissed me on my forehead, then my nose, and lastly
my lips. Just as he was parting his mouth and I started
to feel his tongue on my bottom lip, the oven timer
went off. He pulled away and started laughing. Simultaneously, we both commented on his previous timing
statement. I leaned my head back onto the chair and
quietly sighed. I couldn't believe how excited I was.
We had always had great conversation, but every exchange had underlying meanings. My appreciation
for Winston had increased threefold.

"Do you need any help?" I called out.

"I got it, just relax."

As he opened the oven and the aroma of the food
hit the living room, I could only think of one thing. *I
am going to have great sex tonight.* It had been six months
and I did not want to wait any longer. I was so glad that
I was a woman, because the decision of sex usually falls
in the hands of the female. All men can do is wait

around for our actions in order to react. They really have no control. A woman usually decides to take the man's number or give him her number. A woman dictates if a good night kiss is appropriate. A man may coerce, but a woman decides when will be the first time the couple has sex and a woman indisputably decides when will be the last time a couple has sex. I wouldn't trade being a woman for anything.

Through my peripherals I saw Winston placing the food on the table. "You don't have to set the table, we can get it off the stove."

He looked up and raised his oven mitten in the air. "Will you let me do this?"

"Yes, sir, I will," I said meekly.

I closed my eyes in order to gather my thoughts and calm the butterflies breeding in my stomach. I didn't understand why I was so nervous. I was not normally uneasy in the company of men. However, Winston was different. I almost felt inferior to him. I knew I could hold my own when it came to conversation and I knew I was an attractive woman with a great personality. But I felt I should be more of a woman when I was around him. I was even questioning his interest in me. He was so dynamic; he deserved a dynamic woman. Could I be that dynamic woman?

"You may come to dinner."

He pulled out my chair and handed me a napkin.

"I would have fixed your plate, but I didn't want to give you too much," he stated.

"Everything is lovely," I responded.

We sat and ate baked chicken with steamed vegetables and rice. The chicken was a little dry, but who cared? His effort truly outweighed moist chicken.

"You know I have never been jealous of my brother

and he makes more money and gets more women. Yet the first time I saw you at his house, I have to admit I was a little envious."

I held my head down and smirked. He was really laying it on thick. Winston was in Super-Mac-Daddy mode.

"What are you thinking?" he asked curiously.

"You really want to know?"

He nodded with hesitance.

"I'm thinking that you can stop with the compliments now. I have already decided to give you some."

Winston gave a hearty laugh. "Well, maybe you need to start complimenting me so that I can decide to participate as well."

I leaned my head to the side, raised my voice an octave higher, and gave him my best southern belle accent.

"Winston, your eyes are so captivating. I get lost in them when listening to you speak such eloquent words of wisdom. To put it plainly, you turn me on."

I rubbed the ball of my foot against his slightly erect penis.

"Is that right?" he replied with a one-sided grin.

"Oh yeah. I can hardly contain myself, how about you?" I continued in character.

Winston shyly lowered his head and chuckled. "Lily, finish your dinner."

I grinned as we finished our meal with silent stares across the table. I helped him load the dishes in the washer and we retired to the living room. With light jazz playing in the background, Winston began playing in my hair. I sat between his legs as we stretched across the sofa.

"Why do you have so many small business books? Is there something else you want to do?"

"Yes, I want to open up a youth center for inner-city kids. I want to have professionals come in, teach classes of interest, and set up work-study programs. Then I want to have a scholarship program through the center that allows the kids to attend their choice of school."

Was he for real? He was a gorgeous doctor, and he had a good heart. I didn't want to start looking for any faults, but damn, he was too good to be true. Winston moved his hands from around my waist up to my breasts. He began to caress them as he kissed on my neck. I was anticipating this as if it were my first time. His penis swelled and pushed against my lower back. I slowly turned around, lay on his chest, and kissed him on his chin. As I rubbed my nose against his five o'clock shadow, he pulled my lower body closer to his. After minutes of kissing, Winston leaned up and my legs automatically wrapped around his hips. He picked me up and carried me into his bedroom. Laying me down on the bed, Winston lifted my shirt, pulled my bra to the side, and circled my nipples with his tongue. Finally, he pulled my shirt and my bra completely off and thrust his weight against my hips. With his left hand gently holding my wrists together above my head, his right hand lifted my skirt and removed my panties. His kisses moved down my body to my waist and as he subtly sucked on my thighs, Winston took off his pants, and leaned over to remove a condom from his nightstand drawer. Handing me the condom, he whispered in my ear.

"Put it on."

Nervous, I couldn't get it on fast enough. I got so confused that I fumbled and began to put it on inside out. Finally, I got it right and as soon as I rolled it down over his shaft, he entered me. With my skirt still around my waist, Winston grooved his pelvis with mine. I placed my hands under his arms and grabbed his shoulders for more support as I interlocked my ankles around his back. Our bodies began to dance just as Winston froze. I had started to ask the problem when I realized that he was reaching his orgasm.

"What da hell?" I said under my breath.

Sure, it was a very exciting, passionate 4.3 minutes, but I didn't want a commercial. He could have at least given me a thirty-minute drama. Without even searching, I had found his fault. Dr. Winston Fulmore was a minute man. I tried not to make eye contact with him, for I was never one to hide disappointments. Winston gently slid himself from within my womb and went to the restroom, without saying a word. I lay there in utter disbelief. Those four minutes were great. I could only imagine how wonderful they would have been multiplied by ten, or at least five. What should I do? He knew he was a minute man; I wondered how that made him feel. Another great advantage of being a woman is we never have to deal with such embarrassment.

As he approached the bed, I closed my eyes and pretended to be resting. He got back in the bed and lay beside me while placing his leg over mine. Within seconds, he started kissing my neck. I couldn't understand why he was teasing me. I wished he would just stop and go to sleep, so that I could leave. Just then he pulled me on top of his body. Frustrated, I folded my arms and looked him in the eye.

"What are you doing?" I said with apparent disappointment.

He reached up and gave me a quick response. "Did you think that was it?"

And with that comment, Winston Fulmore's penis became more erect than the first time. With a poor attempt of my southern belle accent, he asked me to tell him my desires. However, his attempt to get into character was destroying the mood, so I quieted his mouth with my breasts. Amazingly he climaxed two more times before the evening was over. He beat me by one, and that was a first. Within hours, he went from little minute man to super multiple man. I kept looking behind the door for his blue leotard and red cape. One thing was for sure, during his years as an ob/gyn, Winston had learned his way around the vagina. Ironically, I have never liked doctors, but on that day I gained a new appreciation for their talents.

After our incredible evening, I still had to go home and prepare for work the next day. Funny, I was just as nervous now as I was before we started. I wondered how this was going to change our relationship. I valued his opinion of me. Moments ago we had been talking about women being gracious and regal, and at that moment I was hoping that I was still a respectful lady in his eyes. That was the issue with impulsive sex.

Rubbing his hand through my hair, he whispered, "Thank you for a beautiful evening."

Halfway grinning, I didn't know how to respond. I disliked when men were thankful for sex, as if it were a favor. I was sure he meant no disrespect, yet it was tacky. His phrasing had such prostitute tendencies. Then again, it could be my conscience.

Sexual thought patterns of men and women are so different. Men consider sex a favor, because the woman could very well have said no. However, when women hear thank you, it sounds like sex is a service and men are thanking us for providing great service. Women have so many hang-ups when it comes to sex. Don't do it too soon or you're a whore. Don't wait too long or you're frigid; don't be too wild, don't be too tame. All of these rules really mess with the female psyche.

"You okay?" Winston asked.

"I have to go," I whispered.

He pushed me off his body and spoke. "Good. I was hoping you didn't want to stay the night."

Shocked, I was silent. Yet, within seconds, Winston relieved my trauma with laughter. I smothered his face with the pillow, got up, and got dressed. The entire ride home, I thought about Winston and the possibilities. These were exactly the feelings I didn't want to feel for another six months. I wasn't going to be able to date him. I would never be able to hang out with him and his family. His mother would look at me like a flip-flopping floozy. I wasn't sure what Wealth would think, but I would feel uncomfortable around them all.

I got home, took a shower, and grabbed my journal. My first thoughts were—I want to talk with Dick. As incredible as my evening had been, it didn't make up for my argument with Dick. I had spent the day trying to forget about him, but it hadn't worked. No matter what I did, I couldn't shake this man.

6

Displacement in This Place

I had a restless night, which made my morning very groggy. Thankfully, the next morning at work was slow. I could finally see the wood on my desk and the paperwork was dwindling into one stack. Around noon, I called Sarah's desk to see what the plans for lunch were; however, she was not answering. Oddly, I hadn't seen her at all today, and so I grabbed my purse and walked around to her desk, only to see that she was not there. Her things were untouched, so I assumed she was not at work today. I used her phone to call her house and Margaret, the housekeeper, answered.

"Ms. Sarah had an appointment this morning. She should be at work this afternoon," she said.

"Thanks, Margaret."

I hung up and called Nehri to see if she wanted to

go to lunch. She obliged and we went down the street for Mexican. Nehri was extremely talented, but she was too serious. We were writers. Our job required goofing off from time to time, but it was like she was afraid to let loose, and so conversation with her was normally restricted. Other than that, we worked well together. We always finished our assignments ahead of schedule and rarely were there creative differences.

After returning from lunch, I got so wrapped up in working that I forgot to check on Sarah until the end of the day. I called her desk a few minutes before five and she was still not there. Sarah never took a day off without telling me, so this was strange. As soon as I cranked up my SUV, I called her cell phone, yet there was no answer and she was still not home.

I walked in the door, threw my keys on the counter, and went upstairs to undress. This was going to be a peaceful week. I wasn't doing anything with the youth center, Winston had to work every evening, and I was not babysitting. I planned to clean up the house and reorganize my closets in an attempt to make room for spring shopping. After I took a shower, I turned up my music, opened both my closet doors, and stared into the mess for at least thirty minutes. It was so difficult to get rid of old clothes. I had things in my closet I hadn't worn in years and yet I continued to justify their significance. I think women are so attached to our clothing because they are an extension of who we are and more importantly who we were. For example, I had a section of nothing but baggy, holey, loose-fitting jeans. I never wore these jeans, but they remind of the time when I was carefree and rebellious. Not that I was currently a conformist, yet at that time in my life I rebelled against the entire beauty statement of fitted clothing and lacy dresses. I held on to those jeans because they meant something. I held on to my dashikis because they too had their significance. They would never go out of style, although I never wore them anymore. We change scenes, friends, and jobs so frequently that our closets need to have some form of familiarity. So I continued to buy new things to suit my ever-changing moods, yet never threw anything away. Hence, the necessity for more closet space grew more and more each year.

Eventually realizing that this process was not going to start tonight, I closed all closet doors and walked downstairs. As I was rounding the corner to enter the living room, I heard a key in my door. Startled, I rushed toward the door yelling for the culprit to answer.

"It's me, Sarah."

I pulled the door open as she walked in. Her eyes were swollen and her face was as red as her hair.

"What in the hell has Omar done now?" I shouted.

She placed her head on my shoulder and began crying. I held her and slowly we walked to the futon.

"Where's Carmen? Is she okay?"

"She's with Margaret," she whimpered.

Sarah sat down and attempted to tell me about her troubles. However, because of her incessant crying it came out as gibberish.

"Sarah, slow down. What are you talking about?"

She rose and walked to the bathroom for tissue. When she returned, she was more composed to speak.

"At first I thought my chest was lumpy due to breast-feeding, so I ignored it. I went to the doctor a few weeks ago and I mentioned a lump in my right breast, so he checked it out."

Her tears began to flow with more consistency

as she continued. "I went to the doctor this morning and he . . ."

Sarah never finished her sentence, she simply wailed and buried her head in my lap. I sat back on the futon, pulled her legs up in the chair, and gently stroked her temples until she cried herself to sleep. Last year, all of Sarah's episodes had dealt with Omar. I would never have thought her issues after that would be breast cancer. Sarah was only twenty-nine.

After she fell asleep, I retrieved a blanket from the closet to cover her legs. I went upstairs, got in the bed, and stared at the ceiling.

"What is the key to passing all of life's tests? If our expiration date as humans is already predetermined, why must we go through false alarms? I thought it was to make us stronger, but sometimes it just breaks us down. Life is a constant reminder that we as people are so . . ."

FRAGILE

What could last a lifetime
Could vanish in a second
We can guess our purpose
We can assume our timeline
But since we never know
We should value quiet moments
We should treasure life
We are strong
We are Fragile

I prayed I would be able to make some impact on my friend's life before she broke.

* * *

Sarah took a couple of personal days to get herself together. By Thursday she returned to work and began to mentally prepare for treatment. She was concerned about taking time off from her job considering she just returned from maternity leave. But I assured her that Susan, our boss, was going to understand and an hour later, Sarah came to my desk with a huge smile. Her meeting with Susan was uplifting. If Sarah had to leave work because of her treatment, Susan said she would hold her position until it was complete. Her chemotherapy was going to last for eight weeks. Luckily, the cancer was not in her lymph nodes; therefore, she got to forgo radiation. She had planned to work during the weeks of chemotherapy, but it was a relief to know that her job was not in jeopardy.

While I was at her desk speaking with her about the meeting, I noticed her attention shift from our conversation to the front door.

"I thought you were done with Wealth?" she commented.

"What? I am," I confessed.

"Then why is he here?" she said, pointing to the guy walking down the corridor.

I turned my attention in the direction of her finger and I saw Winston. Without saying a word, I swiftly made my way down the hall to greet him. Grabbing his arm, I walked him back to Sarah's desk. As soon as we walked up to her desk, she extended her arms.

"Wealth, it's so good to see you again. It's been a while. Does this mean what I think it means?" Sarah said with a smile.

Both Winston and I looked at Sarah with blank expressions.

"What?" she asked innocently.

Finally, I pulled her close and whispered, "This is Winston. Ask no questions."

Sarah looked up and smiled quietly after apologizing. Winston and I walked back to my desk. The awkwardness was already starting.

"What are you doing here?" I asked him.

"I had a few hours before I started tonight, so I thought I would surprise you. Have you eaten?" he asked.

"It's the end of the day, I am about to leave."

Leaning against the corner of my desk, Winston began to stroke my leg. "Well, why don't we go for some coffee or dessert?"

I began to organize my papers and called Nehri to let her know that I was leaving for the day. While I was on the phone, Susan walked up to my desk, introduced herself to Winston, and conversed with him until I got off the phone. As I hung up, I formally introduced the two and mentioned to Susan that I was leaving. She handed me a folder and asked me to review it by tomorrow afternoon. She finished her conversation with Winston as I organized my things and grabbed my purse.

Winston and I left the office and stopped by Starbucks for drinks. I had chai tea and he had an iced Frappuccino. We sat at our table making dauntless eye contact. As soon as we finished, Winston rose and without saying a word, firmly grabbed my arm and walked me to his car.

"Where are we going?" I asked.

He got in the car and drove to my house, which was a few blocks away. He parked his car in the driveway, got out, and opened my door. Winston hurried me to open the front door and quickly closed it behind us.

"We have fifteen minutes," he whispered.

With that statement, Winston quickly stripped off his shoes and pants. He lifted up my dress and pulled down my panties.

"Damn! I forgot the—"

"In the kitchen drawer by the oven," I quickly interrupted.

With his pants around the bottom of his left ankle, he rushed into the kitchen, rambled through the drawer, and returned with the condom already on.

"The kitchen?" he asked with a look of confusion.

"Shhh. We don't have time," I said, covering his lips with my index finger. Before I could finish my sentence, Winston Fulmore was screwing me against the wall. It was so raunchy and yet a sexy delight, as he worked our bodies down to the foyer floor. He cupped his hands underneath my bottom to prevent the hardwood floor from rubbing my skin, and went deeper inside as I closed my eyes just before I climaxed. However, when I opened my eyes I no longer saw Winston on top, but I saw Dick. I closed my eyes again, praying for the delusion to vanish, but no such luck. All I saw were images of Dick and this was making me sick. It's one thing to enter my dreamworld, but he was taking it too far by disrupting my orgasms. Just then, Winston's body tensed up and the veins in his neck engorged. Luckily for him, there was nothing stopping his moment of glory. With five minutes to spare, Winston jumped into the shower and dried himself off. I hit the hot spots, changed my underwear, and we headed back to Starbucks to pick up my car. Talk about whirlwind sex. The entire experience gave me a head rush. I said good-bye to Winston before jumping out of the car. I had no desire to kiss him, I just wanted to get in the car and go home.

"Are you all right?" he asked.

"I'm fine," I mumbled.

"You don't look fine. I wish we could talk about it, but I have to go. I'll call you tonight if I can," he said before kissing my cheek.

I got into my car and he drove off. I banged my head on the steering wheel, for I felt the entire thing starting over again: total displacement of emotion. Sleeping with one man while desiring another. This was exactly why I needed to be alone, but now I had opened the gate.

It is wise to take the time and prepare to receive love. Yet it is foolish to let great opportunities pass by because of lack of preparation.

Winston was indeed a good man, and I was going to get over this and make it work. I went home, immediately stripped, and took a shower. Late that evening, I called Tam to tell her about my day's events.

"There I was, thinking about one man with another man inside me. Is that sick or what?" I said to her.

"So what are you going to do?"

"Winston is a great guy. I could give you a long list of his wonderful attributes and I could give you a longer list as to why I should be with him."

"Is 'I love him' on that list?"

I was silent, for we both knew that "I love him" was not on that list.

"I care a lot about him. The love will come. He wants to be with me," I said.

"Lily, Lily, Lily," Tam said with despair in her voice.

"Don't say my name like that."

"If you want to settle, so be it. Winston is a great runner-up. He may be better for you than the actual prize. But the prize is what you want and anything else will always be the runner-up."

"I'm going to go now. I'll call you later this week," I responded sadly.

We hung up and I began pacing the bedroom floor.

"Get it together, Lily," I stated aloud. "Winston likes you. He wants to take a chance with you. Take a chance. Do not give up on him in search of something that is not going to happen. Do not be a fool."

I continued to preach to myself for the next hour and got in bed. However, I couldn't sleep. I stared at the phone.

"Dick is not going to call," I whispered. "You've got to get over him."

I grabbed my journal and began to write.

Okay, Lord. I have got to get over this. I need your help. I know I need to work on earthly lust and a few other sins, but if you help me get over Dick, I am going to straighten up and fly right. I'll commit to you and the man you give me. I'll commit altogether. Is that cool? Amen.

Good night.

7

But He's My
Man ... I Think

Over the next few weeks, I was consumed with work deadlines and overtime. Sarah started her chemotherapy treatments, which unfortunately made her sick, and I ended up keeping Carmen a few nights a week. Although Omar's mom promised Sarah she was going to help her with Carmen, she was away in Greece for a month. Omar came by from time to time to play with his daughter; still, he didn't help Sarah with the caretaking. He was trying to get his act together, and taking anger management classes, but he had a long way to go.

Winston and I were still hanging in there, but his schedule had picked up and we were down to seeing each other once a week. Either he came over here or I went over there. We ate, had sex, laughed a little, and went to sleep. He asked me several times to attend parties at Wealth's home, but of course I declined. There was no way I could go with Winston to Wealth's parties. Winston seemed to think that it was no big deal, and for him it wasn't. I, on the other hand, didn't want to look like a first-class gold digger. Furthermore, I couldn't bear his mother knowing, and I made Winston promise not to tell her. Sometimes, I thought the entire thing was so inapt that it would never work. Winston and I couldn't be secret lovers forever. This pimple would eventually pop; I only hoped it didn't scar.

That evening, I went by the youth center to teach my creative writing class. I had twelve brilliant students whom I enjoyed working with every Thursday. They inspired me to create and their candidness inspired me to become more forthright with my own demons. That evening, I was doing an interesting exercise with them. I asked them to get out a sheet of paper and write, in one word, something that they feared. I told them not to sign the paper, for this assignment was anonymous. Then they were to write about that word in a paragraph or poem. I always joined in on their exercises, so I got out my sheet of paper and without much thought I wrote:

Holding back hides my past
Holding back slows my future
Holding back keeps me sane
'Cause to let go may reveal too much of me
Never liked vulnerability
And what if . . . it's love

Afterward, I collected all of the papers and redistributed them for the class to read aloud. Samantha came up to me and asked why I didn't put my paper in the stack. She felt that if they had to share, I too should share.

"I'm the teacher, I do not have to share if I don't want to," I responded.

"Well, that's real mature, Ms. Lily," she said with the tone of an adult.

I rolled my eyes at her, recollected a few papers, added mine, and redistributed them. I had to admit, these kids had some interesting topics. Death, drugs, spiders, and boys were just a few of the subjects read. But the one that stuck out the most was read by one of my new students. It was entitled:

LONELINESS

It starts as just a thought
A simple thought
Will it always be this way
Will they one day understand me
Will I always be lonely
As I view the world around me
I am not a part of it
Though I exist within it
I am alone
And my lonely thoughts become my disposition
I no longer long to belong, I'd rather disappear
I don't fear
I embrace loneliness
Because it's the only thing
That ever embraced
Me

At times, I looked into the eyes of these kids and I knew that their souls had been around for a long time.

"Great class tonight. I'll see you guys next week."

I gathered the stack of papers and placed them in my folder. I wanted them to make a book of their work, so over the next several weeks, I wanted to work on grammar and punctuation. It was important that they expressed themselves, something most of these kids hadn't been able to do since birth. Correcting their spelling was nothing compared to convincing them that it was okay to release their emotions.

"Next week is my birthday," Samantha said as she sat down in my chair.

"Is that right?" I said, pretending not to care.

"Yes. I will be thirteen. What are you going to get me?"

"Who says I'm getting you anything?"

Samantha looked at me as she spun around in the chair. She tapped her fingers on the corner of the desk as if she were a big executive. She leaned in and whispered, "I want a party."

"I'm sure they will let you have one."

"I want a party at your house," she said with widened eyes.

I began to laugh, for I could tell by her expression that she had been plotting to ask me this for weeks. I continued gathering my things.

"Miss Lily, did you hear me? Can we have a party at your house?"

"I don't know. We'll see," I responded.

"Just ask, please. It will only be me, Shannon, Kate, David, and Keisha."

"You will not have boys at this party."

"Why can't I have a boy at the party? I live with a whole bunch of boys. Besides, David is gay."

A little stunned, I stopped shuffling papers. I don't

even think I knew what gay was when I was twelve. I surely never said it aloud. I simply cut my eyes at her and shook my head no.

"Fine. But ask about the party. Okay?" Sam continued to beg.

"We'll see," I said while walking out of the classroom.

Just before I gave her a hug, Sam continued with her list of party favors. "And I want cake, gifts, games, and strippers."

"Excuse me!" I said with a puzzled look.

"I went too far, didn't I?" she said with a crooked smile.

"Indeed."

I got in my car thinking about Sam and her birthday request. I would like to give her a party. It would probably have to be in the center, because I was sure they would not release the girls in my care for the evening, but I was going to give it a shot.

The next day I called Ms. Gaither and told her about Sam's appeal. Ms. Gaither thought it was a good idea. She said that she overheard Sam saying she had never had a birthday party and that they were planning to give her one at the center. I suggested to Ms. Gaither that we have a slumber party at my house and asked if she thought that could be approved. She said she would get back with me and that if she attended the slumber party it might not be a problem. I didn't want Ms. Gaither to be there, but if that was what it took, so be it. Ms. Gaither was a fifty-something widow who had dedicated her life to helping kids. She was a nice woman, but she was old-fashioned and boring.

As I was getting off the phone, I saw Sarah walking slowly down the hall. Once she got to my desk, I saw a single tear roll down her face.

"What's wrong with you?" I asked.

"Look," she said, pointing to her head.

Sarah turned around and moved her head closer to my face.

"What am I looking at?" I asked with a bit of confusion.

"My hair. Don't you see it? It's falling out," she whimpered.

Although I couldn't see what Sarah was talking about, I was silenced. I might not have seen it then, but it was certainly going to happen. Her hair was going to fall out. Although it was only hair, we as women place so much stock in it. How can we not? As little girls, that is all we hear. We are taught hair is a part of being beautiful

"Her hair is so pretty, her hair is so long."

Having hair is part of being a little girl. When infant girls have no hair, people automatically assume it's a little boy. Accuse a little girl of being a little boy, and parents go ballistic, as if someone mistook their baby girl for a baby goat. The longer and curlier the hair, the cuter the baby becomes. It is only natural for this to assimilate from childhood into adulthood.

"I don't see what you are talking about, Sarah, but you know the doctors said that you have to be prepared for this."

"What am I going to do with no hair? I will be ugly with no hair. I'm going to scare Carmen," she started to whine.

I got up and walked with her into the bathroom. "Look, let's go get your hair cut really short. Then it won't be such a drastic change."

Sarah looked in the mirror while slicking her hair back. She tried to imagine what she would look like.

"You're a pretty girl. Pretty girls can get away with having no hair. Demi Moore and Sinead O'Connor once did it," I said, attempting to make her laugh.

"But what if I look like Annie Lennox?"

"She's cute . . . in a European kind of way," I replied.

Sarah nodded while making a dreadful face in the mirror.

"At least you won't have to shave your legs for a while."

Sarah grinned.

"You're going to be here for me, right?" she whispered.

"Where else do I have to go?" I said with a smile.

I gave Sarah a hug and we returned to our desks.

Monday morning around nine, Ms. Gaither called with good news. Mr. Collins approved the party as long as she was in attendance the entire time. We decided to keep it a secret from Sam until the day before. This way she would have no more time to add to her list of requests. I was so thrilled that I called Winston right away with the good news. He called me back an hour later and when I told him about the party he was just as excited. He wanted us to go shopping on Wednesday to get Sam a gift. I hurried and got off the phone, because I had a meeting in an hour and I was not prepared.

After my meeting my boss asked to speak with me. We remained in the room after everyone left and I prepared myself to be bombarded with questions about Sarah. Surprisingly, Susan didn't mention Sarah at all. The only person she was interested in was Winston.

"I had no idea you knew the Fulmores. I heard rumors last year about you dating the real estate brother, but I didn't know you were so close to the family," she said.

I feared where the conversation was heading. This town was so small, and I couldn't stand mixing business with pleasure, but here there was no choice. Therefore, I sat politely and smiled.

"So you're dating the other brother, correct?"

"Last year, we dated for a while."

"And you and Winston are friends, correct?" she continued to interrogate.

"Yes, we are friends."

"Well, I know he is single, so I want you to fix us up," she stated with a sly smile.

This was so wrong. She wasn't supposed to be asking me to fix her up. She was my superior, not my girlfriend.

"How do you know he is single?" I asked.

"I did my research. I have a dinner party I must attend this Sunday and I would love for him to be my date. Make that happen."

"Well, you ask him. I'll give him your number," I responded.

"I have his card. He gave it to me the day he was here."

Why would Winston give her his card? I wondered. More importantly, why would I tell her to ask him out? I couldn't believe I was saying this. But if she asked him, he'd say no and that would be that. Then again, I could say he was gay. But the way rumors spread around here, it would get back to him, before I got back to my desk.

"I'll ask him, but you give him a little nudge. You look out for me and I'll look out for you," she hinted.

This was a mess. My boss wanted me to hook her up with the man I couldn't admit I was dating. She knew I had dated Wealth, so mentioning Winston was my man was a definite no-no, but I couldn't ask Winston to go out with her. Slowly, I walked back pondering how I was going to mention this to him. He was going to be upset that I didn't acknowledge our relationship. I felt the pimple coming closer to a head.

Wednesday afternoon, Winston met me at the mall to shop for Sam's birthday gift. We went to The Gap, J.Crew, and Kohl's, and after we finished shopping, Sam had enough outfits to last a month. We probably had overdone it. After shopping, Winston and I went to the food court to have a snack. I thought this would be a good time to tell him about Susan's offer.

"Do you remember talking with my boss?" I asked.

He paused as he took a bite of his sandwich. "Yeah. What's her name again?"

"Susan. You gave her your card, remember?"

"Oh yeah. She said she was looking for a doctor."

"Hmm, I forget you look at coochie for a living."

"Anyway, what about her? She seems nice," said Winston.

I wasn't going to beat around the bush any longer. "Well, she likes you. She wants you to be her date for this function on Sunday."

Immediately Winston began to laugh. "That's funny. What did she say when you told her we were dating?"

I continued eating and pretended that I didn't hear him, but Winston tapped my hand to get my attention.

"You did tell her, didn't you?" he said with concern.

"Are we dating? Is that what we are doing?" I asked.

"Lily, don't play with me," he said seriously.

"She knows that I dated Wealth. I couldn't say that I was dating you too. It's tacky."

"How long do you plan on keeping us a secret?"

"It's only been a month," I responded.

Winston said nothing as he continued to eat. After a couple of minutes of silence, he looked up and spoke.

"What? Am I supposed to go out with her?" he said with a frown.

"No, you can turn her down. She asked me to nudge you into saying yes. She wants to call and ask you herself. She did mention that if I persuade you to say yes, she'll look out for me."

"So you are going to sell my services for your own benefit."

"No, just don't go."

Winston pushed his chair away from the table, threw his trash away, and grabbed his shades.

"I have to go," he said without giving me a kiss good-bye.

I sat at the table and watched him leave the mall. I finished my food, grabbed the bags, and headed home. I got in the house, placed the shopping bags in the living room, and checked the phone messages.

After my shower, I pulled all of Sam's gifts from the bags and began wrapping them in tissue paper and placing them in colorful gift bags. While I was removing tags I decide to call Tam.

"Hi, Stan, is Tam available?"

"Yeah, hold on," he said.

"What's up, girl?"

"Nothing much, wrapping gifts for a birthday party this weekend. I saw you called. What's up?"

"Evelyn and I went to the engagement party this weekend."

"You went to the party? You are so Judas."

"Anyway, listen. I had an interesting conversation with Dick. He says you cursed him out and have no intention of speaking to him again. He seemed upset about it."

"Why were you two talking about me at his engagement party? It makes no sense," I remarked.

"He started it, not me. Why are you not speaking to him?"

"Why are you asking me about this?"

"You know why," said Tam. "This is senseless. The entire time, Evelyn and I were saying that you should have been here with him."

"He didn't ask me to marry him, he asked Celeste," I commented loudly.

"He asked you to move in with him and you said no, twice. I'm sure he would have asked you to marry him, if you had given him a chance."

"Look, Tam, I love you, but do not call me about this man anymore. It's starting to make me sick."

"You called me and I have one more thing to say. He mentioned that the tour would be in Kansas City next month. He wouldn't have told me if he didn't want you to know. I'll talk to you later. Love ya," she added.

"Bye."

I hung up the phone as my stomach began to churn. Tam meant well, but she was making this situation harder than it had to be. She acted as if people don't move on. Life is full of breakups. Dick and I were one of many.

I finished wrapping Sam's gifts and placed them in the closet. I called my mom and talked with her briefly about her visiting this summer; then I watched a little television. I spent more time flipping through the channels than actually watching, though. Programming is horrible. It's all about reality television. Shows that are still scripted and edited, and so we only see what the networks want us to see. TV programming is exactly that. Programming, meaning encoding, training, and brainwashing.

They feed us bullshit and we actually believe we can live like that. It's so easy to get wrapped up. This was why Tam was calling me about Dick. She believed in perfect romances with perfect endings. But life has no perfect endings; it is what we make it. A perfect ending for me may seem disastrous for another.

Realizing perfect *is just a word is the key to perfection.*

8

Girls Just Want
to Have Fun

Friday mornings at work were usually hectic. However, this morning everyone seemed to be at his and her desk doing work. I spent the first two hours whizzing through my work because I wanted to get home in time to prepare for the birthday party this evening. Sarah agreed to come help and Ms. Gaither was to have the girls at my home around seven. During lunch, Sarah and I went to the store to pick up food, snacks, and drinks. I didn't keep much junk food in the house, but since it was a party with teenagers, I figured I should stock up. When we returned from lunch, I rushed back to my desk to finish my day. However, once I sat, I noticed a blank envelope placed in my chair. I opened the envelope, took out the card, and began reading.

Thanks so much for nudging Winston. I spoke with him yesterday and he agreed to be my date for Sunday. I'll tell you how it goes. Susan.

"What in the hell is this?"

Why didn't he turn her down? I wondered. Was he doing this for me, or did he want to go out with her? This was some mess and once again, I was creating my own havoc. I attempted to do some work, but the thought of this date was tormenting me. *What were they going to do? Where were they going to go?* The unfortunate thing about having a creative job is that the creative process is hindered when the mind is occupied. I spent the final three hours at work accomplishing nothing.

I arrived home at five thirty and finished my last-minute cleaning. I started preparing dinner and at six fifteen Sarah arrived. She rushed in the door while dialing on the phone.

"I have to call Omar. He's keeping Carmen and I am so nervous," she whispered.

"He's kept her before, right?"

"Never overnight. I was going to bring her with me, but he begged to keep her. What if she starts crying? What if he leaves her unattended? What if—"

"Hello!" Omar answered.

"Hey, I just wanted to make sure everything is okay," Sarah said, trying to sound confident.

She quickly gave him a list of things to do if Carmen started crying.

"She should have plenty of milk, but give her water right before she falls asleep. Call me if you need anything."

She hung up the phone and brushed her sweaty palms against her jeans.

"This will be good for Omar. He'll be fine," I stated to soothe her nerves.

She nodded and agreed, yet her eyes said just the opposite. Sarah then walked into the kitchen to assist me with the spaghetti.

"Where's the cake?" she asked.

My eyes bulged as I turned to her. "Shoot! I forgot the cake."

Just then the phone rang and Sarah answered. I heard her talking as I looked through the pantry for cake mix. Within minutes she hung up.

"Winston will bring a cake when he comes," she said calmly.

"He's coming over?" I asked.

"Yeah, he said he had to bring something over and I asked him to stop by the grocery deli and pick up a birthday cake."

Sarah popped in one of the rented movies and ten minutes later, the doorbell rang. We both ran to the front door with as much enthusiasm as the teens on the outside. We opened the door and the four bright-eyed girls rushed into the house. They threw down their blankets and pillows and flopped on the floor to watch television. Ms. Gaither slowly followed. Samantha gave me a huge hug and thanked me for the party.

"Are you girls hungry? I made spaghetti," I yelled into the living room.

"Yes," they replied in unison.

Sarah got out the paper plates and cups, and the girls piled into the kitchen to fix their plates. We all retired to the living room to eat and watch the movie. Ms. Gaither sat back on the futon and immediately fell asleep. She had only been there for thirty minutes and she was knocked out. The girls giggled as they placed her legs up on the chair and covered her with a blanket. As a matter of fact, the girls giggled continuously. We continued watching *Legally Blonde II* until Sarah picked up the remote and muted the television.

"What's today?" she asked.

"March twelfth," Sam responded.

Sarah tapped my arm and asked, "Do you know what today is?"

Looking at Sarah, I shrugged. She smiled while walking toward the phone.

"Today is Will's birthday."

Puzzled, I continued to shrug.

"Will Dickson, Dick. Today is his birthday."

In all of the chaos, I forgot that this was his birthday, and I always forgot the irony that Sarah and Dick were friends from college.

"What are you doing?" I asked, pointing to the phone in her hand.

"Let's call him. What's the number?"

I got up and snatched the phone from her hand. "We will do no such thing. Besides, he's on tour."

"Who is on tour?" asked Sam.

Sarah turned and answered, "Dick."

"Who is Dick?" Sam continued to ask.

"Lily's love supreme," Sarah said, pointing at me.

"But I thought you loved Doc," she said to me, referring to Winston.

Before I could answer, Sarah gave her the scoop. "Winston is her friend, but she *really* likes Dick."

"Enough talking about me," I shouted.

Suddenly Sam's friend Shannon jumped.

"How do you know Dick?" she asked Sarah.

"Because I dated him in college."

"Ooooh! Where we come from you would have gotten your butt kicked, Ms. Lily," said Sam.

Finally I stood and ended the talk about Dick. "Enough of this. We are not going to discuss my personal life at this party."

"Well, I don't know Dick, but I like Doc. I think he should be your boyfriend," Sam continued.

Sarah leaned over and whispered in my ear, "I hear he's going out with Susan this weekend. Isn't that funny?"

"I can't contain my laughter," I commented with obvious sarcasm.

We finished watching the movie as the girls got seconds on their spaghetti. As the flick ended, Sam stood and wanted to play truth or dare.

"Ms. Lily, you and Ms. Sarah have to play," she said with her hands on her hips.

Sarah immediately agreed; however, I was very hesitant. In my mind, I knew where this game could go and I didn't think I wanted to hear some of the girls' comments. I pulled Sarah's arm, while shaking my head in disagreement.

"I don't think that is a good idea," I told Sam.

"Well, the girls and I have been thinking. We want to ask you guys some serious questions. We don't have anyone to talk with and there are some things we want to know," she said sincerely.

"You have Ms. Gaither."

Sam looked at me and sighed. "Look at her. She's old. She don't know nothing."

"I think it's cool. I wish I had someone like a big sister to talk to. I'll participate," Sarah commented.

After a few seconds of thought, I agreed to listen. At least they felt comfortable enough to talk with us, and if kids don't come to responsible adults with questions, they are bound to get wrong information from other teens.

"Fine. But keep your voices down," I said.

All of us moved into the foyer area and spread out on the blankets. I heard Kate, Sam's friend, whisper for Sam to go get the paper. Sam kept refusing, so finally I asked about the commotion.

"What is this paper?"

"Well, we wrote these questions down, but they're stupid so I was going to make up some new ones."

The other girls disagreed and coerced Sam to pull out the paper. I felt this was going to be an intense hour. I knew these questions were about sex and I was praying that I could make it through this conversation without a headache. Sam reached into her book bag and pulled out a sheet of notebook paper folded into a tiny square design. She flattened the paper on the floor and began reading.

"Why do boys like to give hickies?"

I immediately began laughing.

"I told you these questions were stupid," Sam yelled.

"No, no. They are not stupid. I just remembered wanting to know the same thing and it brought back memories."

Maybe this wouldn't be so stressful, I thought. These were innocent girls trying to deal with the awkward phase of growing up. However, I was so glad Sarah was here for backup. She answered that question.

"Boys are show-offs. They like to brag. A hickie is just one way that a boy can say, I kissed her neck so hard that I left my mark. But remember that they have big mouths. So don't do anything with a boy if you don't want his friends to know about it."

Sam and the girls listened intently, marking off the questions as if this were a quiz.

"Okay, this is a good one. How old were you when you first did it?" asked Kate.

Sarah and I looked at each other waiting for each other's response. I wanted to encourage the girls to wait until they were in a committed relationship and/or married. However, I had to be realistic. These girls were basically rearing themselves with the help of the system. They looked up to us. Yet I didn't want them to feel they should do just as we did.

"If I had to do it all over again, I would have waited longer, but I was twenty-one," I said as Kate wrote the number 21 by that question.

"Hold up, why did you write that?" I asked quickly.

"So we can remember," she said innocently.

"This does not mean you should do it at the same age. You should wait until you are in a relationship with a man you love and plan to marry. Better yet, you should be married."

They looked at me as if I were a PSA on public television.

"Okay. Well, how many men have you slept with?" said Sam.

My eyes grew wide as I looked at Sarah. Hastily, I turned and responded, "We're not going to answer that."

Sam frowned up and whispered to her friends, "It must be a whole lot."

Sarah giggled quietly.

"It's not a lot, I'm just not answering it. There are some things ladies don't discuss and that is one of them. Move on to the next question," I said forcefully with discontentment.

Sam passed the paper to Shannon, but she read the question silently, shook her head, and passed it on to Kate, who passed it to Keisha, who in turn passed it back to Sam. Finally, after grunting aloud, Sam quickly read the question.

"Why do boys like blow-jobs and how close do you have to be to blow on it?"

"Jesus wept!" I said.

Suddenly the doorbell rang. Thank God for great timing.

"We're done with truth or dare," I said, rising to get the door.

Winston and one of his friends walked in. The young girls perked up as if their dates had just arrived. They each stood up and hugged Winston. He handed me the cake and I placed it in the kitchen. Winston handed Sarah a medium-sized gift bag.

"Happy birthday, Sam," he said. "Did you like your things?"

"What things?" she said.

I went into the closet and pulled out the bags as Sam deliriously jumped up and down.

"I have gifts! I have gifts!" she yelled.

All of the girls rushed to open Sam's gifts.

"Listen, I know it's Sam's birthday, but I brought a gift for everyone," Winston mentioned while taking the bag from Sarah and handing it to Keisha.

The girls tore open the bags as if it were Christmas morning and Winston was Santa Claus. We stood back and watched the girls' excitement. Winston purchased each of the girls iPods and Best Buy gift certificates. I gave him a hug and thanked him for his generosity. I was so elated about the girls that I almost forgot about his date with Susan. However, Sarah's big mouth was a quick reminder.

"I hear you're going out with our boss on Sunday," she said, nudging his arm.

"Yeah, your girl hooked up the entire thing," Winston said with a caustic stare.

"Excuse us," I said, peering at Winston as I pulled him outside.

As soon as I closed the door behind us, I fired away with the questions. "Why didn't you turn her down?"

"Why didn't you tell her we were dating?" he rebutted.

"I told you why. I also said you should turn her down. I can't believe you are actually going on a date with her."

"Look. You started this little game. I am not going to be the bad guy, she's a nice lady."

"You could have said you have to work."

"So I'm supposed to lie, because you can't tell the truth. No, I'm not doing it. We are going to this function on Sunday. I have no plans to see her again after then, but you are going to have to come clean," he said before kissing my cheek.

"Don't kiss me," I said, wiping his moisture off my face.

Winston grinned and walked back into the house to be tussled by four very excited teens. Shannon pulled on his shirt and motioned for him to lean down as she whispered in his ear.

"Let's get the cake," said Sarah.

We went into the kitchen and sang "Happy Birthday." Ms. Gaither finally woke in time to join in on the singing. Sarah helped the girls cut the cake just before

Winston and his friend left. The girls got their good-bye hugs and I walked Winston to his car.

"Thanks again for everything," I said.

He stepped back, leaned his head forward, and peered from underneath his brow.

"What?" I asked, questioning his look.

"So Dick is your love supreme?" he asked with an awkward grin.

I covered my mouth as I laughed. "What did Shannon say to you?"

"She said that although Dick is your love supreme, she thinks that I should be your boyfriend."

I continued to laugh aloud.

"Yeah, keep on laughing. Is this the same Dick I met last year at the painting party?" he asked.

I couldn't believe he remembered. Eventually, all circles collide. Winston walked around and got in his car.

"Hey, call me Sunday when you get home," I said before he cranked up his engine.

"If I make it home Sunday, I'll call you," he said, winking.

With a crude finger expression, I indicated my dislike of his humor.

"Just jokes," he said, smiling.

"Whatever," I said.

Winston pulled off and I went into the house and enjoyed the rest of the birthday festivities. As Sam put on a fashion show, we ate cake and Sarah continued to make calls to Omar. The girls attempted to stay up all night, but after we watched two more movies, they soon faded off to sleep. However, just before Sam fell asleep I asked her to come to my room. After those questions from truth or dare, I wanted to speak to her in private.

Before I could start, she blurted out, "I know what you want to talk about."

"Oh yeah, what?" I asked.

"Sex."

"You are correct, and I'm not going to beat around the bush. You are too young, Sam. I hope you are not thinking about having sex."

"I'm not," she confessed.

"I'm not going to judge you but I am going to be honest. Sex is not just an act. It comes with a heap of mental responsibility."

"I just told you—"

"I know what you said, but I want to be clear. You can always confide in me, and I prefer you come talk with me before you do anything."

"Yes, ma'am, I will."

I looked at little innocent eyes and I knew she was telling the truth, but I also knew she was living in a world filled with pressure.

I extended my arms and she squeezed her lanky arms around my body.

"I just want to make sure nothing happens to you," I whispered.

"Why?" Sam asked.

"Because I love you, knucklehead," I said as we remained embraced.

"Okay," she mumbled.

We headed back downstairs, but Sam stopped just at the bottom of the steps and looked back at me.

"Do you love me for real?" she asked.

I walked closer and responded, "Yes, love is not a play-play word and I don't take it lightly."

Sam's face lit up and she quickly trotted back to the girls and snuggled into her sleeping bag.

* * *

Sarah left early the next morning while Sam and Shannon cooked breakfast with pancakes, eggs, and turkey sausage. At first they frowned at the fact that the sausage was made of turkey instead of pork. However, once they tasted the meat, they were sold. Keisha and Kate cleaned up the mess and the girls prepared to go back to the home. Ms. Gaither needed to have them there by noon and it was already eleven. Before they left, each teen informed me of her birth date and hinted that a party would be nice. However, Sam was sure to give them her opinion.

"Lily is *my* big sister. That was why she gave me a party. You have to get your own big sister to give you a party."

Sam laughed as she was telling the girls, but at the same time she was serious. I gave the girls hugs and told them that I would see them Thursday for class. Sam rushed back from the van and gave me another hug just before they left.

"Thank you again, Ms. Lily, and I love you too."

Her sentiment instantly melted my heart. I think it was at that moment I wanted to make a bigger difference in her life. I decided to speak to Ms. Gaither that week about spending more time with Sam outside of the home. I wanted to look into a foster program.

I walked into my house and collapsed on the futon. I had only had three hours of sleep that night and my body was not going to make it through the day without more sleep.

I cut off the television, grabbed a blanket, and cuddled up for a few hours. While I was asleep, I dreamed about a wedding. I was standing in a white dress talk-

ing with my friends. I walked down the aisle and
smiled at the groom, but I couldn't see his face. Just as
I was about to stand next to him, the phone rang and
awakened me. I leaned over, grabbed the phone off
the floor, and heard Omar's voice on the other line.

"Hello," I answered.

"Lily, Sarah is sick, what should I do?"

"What? Go to the hospital."

"She's throwing up and she's in pain. Carmen is
crying and shitting all over the place and she is out of
Pampers. I don't know what the fuck to do!" he yelled.

"Omar, put Carmen in the car seat and get Sarah in
the car. You live three minutes from the hospital.
Drive there. I will meet you."

He hung up the phone.

"Damn!"

I got up, put on my shoes, and headed out the door.
I stopped by the store, picked up some Pampers, and
pulled into the hospital lot ten minutes later. I rushed
inside to find Omar pacing back and forth while trying
to calm Carmen. She was having a difficult time because Sarah had to immediately wean her from breast
milk. I rushed up to Omar, who immediately handed
me Carmen and ran into the restroom. I walked over
to the nurses' station to get information on Sarah. I
didn't know what could have happened; she had been
fine last night. The nurses said that these were symp-
toms of patients going through chemotherapy, and
she mentioned that they would have to keep Sarah in
the hospital for a few days, because of dehydration.
Omar finally returned from the restroom and when I
told him about Sarah, he began to panic.

"What are we going to do about Carmen?" he said
while walking in circles around the baby and me.

"*We* aren't going to do anything. *You* are going to keep her for a few days until Sarah comes home," I said, attempting to hand him his daughter.

"Nah, nah. I can't do it. I have to work. Besides, I don't know a thing about keeping a baby."

"I have to work too. So Margaret can keep Carmen in the day and you can keep her at night. This will be your chance to show Sarah that you are responsible."

Omar paused while looking Carmen in the eye. He smiled; then she smiled. Suddenly her smile turned into a frown and she let out the highest-pitched scream I'd ever heard.

"That's it. I can't do it," Omar said as he threw his hands in the air.

"Look, hold your child while I go in and see Sarah," I said while handing him the baby.

I walked down the hall, looking for Sarah's room. Once I got to 316, I gently tapped on the door and walked in. Sarah was resting on the bed with an IV in her right arm. As I sat on the bed she awakened.

"Where's Carmen?" she asked as soon as she opened her eyes.

"In the hall with Omar. Don't worry about Carmen, you just concentrate on getting better. The nurse said they're going to keep you for a few days."

Sarah nodded slowly.

"You'll keep Carmen, won't you?" she asked.

"I think Omar should keep her."

Sarah's eyes widened as she tried to sit up.

"Are you crazy? He can't keep her. My child will be dead by the time I get out of here. You have to keep her. I don't have anyone else," Sarah pleaded.

I sighed, shaking my head as Sarah continued to

beg. Seconds later, Omar knocked on the door and walked in.

"Where's Carmen?" Sarah and I asked simultaneously.

"She's good, she's right there with the nurse."

"What nurse?" I said, rushing out of the door as Sarah raised her voice and began to yell.

"Do you know how many babies get stolen every year? Where is my baby?"

I went outside the door to retrieve Carmen from the nurse. After thinking about Omar's irresponsible actions, I reconsidered Sarah's request. I guessed it wouldn't kill me to keep Carmen for a few days, until Sarah came home. I'd just have to get up a little earlier to take her to Margaret, but other than that it shouldn't be a big adjustment. I asked the nurses if it was okay for me to bring Carmen in the room for Sarah to say good-bye. After they complied, we walked in, and Sarah's eyes lit up as if she were seeing Carmen for the first time.

"There's my baby," Sarah said as she extended her arms to rub Carmen's arms.

Omar sat by the bed and apologized for his actions. I could see in his eyes that he was sincere; however, he was going to have to step up to the plate. Sarah really needed him and this necessity was only going to grow as she went through these steps of her illness.

"My mom will be back from Greece in two weeks. I know you miss her. She'll be able to help out."

"Your mom is not Carmen's daddy," Sarah said, rolling her eyes at Omar.

I leaned Carmen over the bed for Sarah to get a kiss.

"We're going to go. I will stop by your house and get

some clothing and Pampers. What about her food?"
I asked.

"Call Margaret. She should have some milk, juice,
and baby food at the house. Her stroller should be
there as well. Do you need money?" Sarah asked.

"No. I'm good."

Omar stood and pulled out a hundred-dollar bill.

"Please take it," he said, pushing the bill into my
hand.

I looked at Sarah, who motioned for me to take the
money.

"If this will help your conscience," I said to him.
"We'll call you tonight. Omar, I need the car seat," I
said as I closed the door.

Carmen and I made our way down the corridor
while Omar straggled behind. We got to the deck and
Omar brought the car seat to my SUV and put it in the
backseat. He kissed Carmen on the forehead and shut
the door. As soon as the door shut, I grabbed his shirt-
sleeve, pulled him close, and whispered, "Get your shit
together. Sarah is really going to need you. You've
messed up enough. If you don't get it together, Sarah
is going to move on and find someone else. Then another man is going to be raising your daughter."

I got in the vehicle, pulled off, and left him standing speechless on the deck.

Two hours later, I entered into my garage, grabbed
Carmen with my right arm, and her bag with my left. I
walked into the house and I was ready to fall out, but I
couldn't because little Carmen's eyes were wide awake.
I had a feeling the next few days were not going to be
a piece of cake. I placed Carmen on the futon and
walked into the foyer closet to get a blanket. On my
way to the closet the phone rang. It was Sarah. She

wanted to make sure that we made it home all right. I assured her that all was well as I walked back into the living room.

"*Oh no!*" I shouted.

"What's wrong?" Sarah shrieked.

How was I supposed to tell her that her child just fell head-first on the floor? Thank God it was on top of one of my pillows.

"Uhhh . . . nothing. We'll call you later, don't worry," I said, eager to get her off the phone.

I threw down the phone and rushed over to Carmen, who was lying on the floor with a startled expression. As soon as I picked her up, she began to howl. I bounced her up and down in my arms.

"Come on, baby Carmen. Don't cry. Crying creates swollen eyes. No one likes puffy eyes," I said with humor, but she was too young to care, and continued to cry.

I placed her on the blanket and gently rubbed her back. Her crying ceased to a whimper, but she was nowhere near sleep. Going through her bags, I pulled out her stuffed toys and built a fort around her tiny body.

"Okay, baby Carmen, here are your toys. Play with them until you fall asleep."

Which I hoped would be soon, because I was not going to be able to stay up much longer. I walked into the kitchen and made a sandwich while I watched her move up to her knees and attempt to crawl. It was funny, as soon as she revved her body up and scooted her knee half an inch forward, she collapsed down onto her stomach.

I turned on the television and ate my sandwich. Television was my only vice for staying awake. However, it was Saturday evening and nothing was on. I finally ran across a station playing reruns of *The Jeffersons*, *Who's the Boss?*, and *Family Ties*. Talk about three different TV families. I remembered some of these episodes. What was amazing was that I remembered when these weren't reruns. I recalled the original episodes that we used to talk about at school the very next day. TV had seriously changed. These shows were innocent, no mention of sex and the only crude behavior was George Jefferson kicking people out of his apartment. TV families of the millennium sure are different. Parents are catching kids having sex and using drugs. Older brothers are giving younger sisters condoms. *Damn*, *hell*, and *bitch* are no longer censored but part of everyday vocabulary.

I glanced down at Carmen, who was finally dozing off to sleep, and wondered what sort of TV episodes she would discuss in school. I could only imagine.

"Did you see it when they did it on the floor and the guy forgot to use a condom and now she thinks she's pregnant? I hear her abortion will be the season finale."

Not that television should be a complete fantasy, but I wondered if it would ever go back to the days of innocence or would it continue to defile? I lay next to Carmen to make sure she was asleep. I was scared to move her upstairs, because if she woke up again, I was going to mix some Ambien in with her applesauce and I didn't think Sarah would like that. I slowly closed my eyes, thinking I would finally get some rest, but then the phone rang.

"Shoot! I forgot to mute the ringer," I whispered, jumping up to catch it before the next ring.

"Where is the damn phone?"

I glanced over at Carmen as she started to move her body. I dove to catch the phone before the last ring, but was too late. Her movement had become a stretch and then a scream. I picked up the phone steaming mad.

"What do you want?" I yelled.

No answer, they hung up. Now I was really mad. I cut the ringer off, tossed it on the futon, and rushed to quiet Carmen.

"Baby Carmen!" I called out. "Do you want to go visit your daddy?"

She began to quiet down. Apparently, babies understand more than they let on. Within minutes, she went back to sleep. It was now 8:00 p.m. and my entire day was gone. My last prayer of the evening was "If you love me, God, you will let this baby sleep through the night."

9

Babysitting
Birth Control

Carmen woke up at 5:40 a.m. and underneath my
breath I began to curse her little ass out. I was not a
gracious host when I was tired, and this little girl was
quickly wearing out her welcome. I put on cartoons
for her entertainment while I lay down at her side.
Yet I was afraid I would fall asleep, and so I forced
myself to get up and move around. I grabbed my cell
phone and saw I had twelve missed calls from Sarah.
As I was trying to call her back, she called again.

"Where are you, is everything okay?" said a panicky
Sarah on the other end.

"Yeah, why?" I questioned.

"Because you weren't answering your phone. I've
been calling since last night."

"My phone was on vibrate, and I cut the house

phone off ring once Carmen went to sleep, and why are you calling me this early? She could still be asleep."

"Please, she's been up for at least fifteen minutes," said Sarah.

"How do you know?"

"She wakes up every morning between five thirty and six."

"Something you could have mentioned before I volunteered for this babysitting mission."

Sarah began to laugh. "It's only been one night. You can't be tired."

"Look, girl. I had four teenagers in my house the night before last. I had a six-month-old in my house last night. My home is officially an advertisement for safe sex," I ranted.

Sarah laughed even harder. "Well, this is my life and you wonder why I look like I do some mornings."

"Everything is fine here. I'm going to cook some breakfast and we're going to get dressed for church."

"Good. I should be home by Tuesday. So you only have two more nights, Godmommy."

"Okay, girl, I love you. Bye."

I hung up with Sarah, picked up my phone, and turned on my ringer. I checked the caller ID to see who had hung up on me last night. The number looked familiar but I didn't recognize it. Picking up Carmen, I placed her in the bathroom while I took a quick shower. This was so crazy, what if I had to do number two? Was she supposed to sit in there and watch me? This baby thing was no joke. I suddenly thought, this would be a great lesson for Sam to learn. Just before cooking, I called Ms. Gaither and asked if I could pick up Sam for the day. Keeping an infant was the perfect birth control. Ms. Gaither approved it and said I could come through anytime. I decided to grab Sam on the way to church.

I threw on some clothing, cooked breakfast, and fed Carmen. An hour later, I got dressed for church, changed Carmen, and then dressed her. Next, I sat her on the floor and made an attempt to do her hair. I remembered how my mom used to sit me down in between her legs and do my hair before church. She would get out the brush, comb, and ribbons. She put her heart and soul into doing my hair and she would be so proud of my glorious hairdos. I never understood the big deal; it was just hair. Carmen was too young to sit in between my legs, but I made my best attempt. She had a lot of hair for such a young child. I tried to put her little barrettes in the front, but she kept pulling them out. I gave up.

Thankfully, the home was on the way to church and even better, Carmen went to sleep during church. However, as soon as we started heading home, she woke up screaming. It was already driving Sam crazy.

"Is she going to do that all day?"

"She's just getting started."

I pulled over, let Sam get in the back, and let her give Carmen the bottle as we drove home. Sam wanted to go to the mall, but I didn't bring enough milk so we had to stop by the house first. I showed Sam how to repack Carmen's bag and get her prepped, and then we left. We had to take a break while there to feed and change Carmen, and Sam was ready for that baby to go home. My plan was working.

"Can you imagine having to do this all the time?" Sam asked.

"Can you?" I retorted.

Sam just shook her head and continued to window-shop.

Later on, once we got to the house, Sam wanted to watch a movie, but I had to do some work. So I asked her to watch Carmen while I worked. Carmen was asleep when Sam first started the flick, but thirty minutes later, she woke and started to cry. Sam came rushing into my home office.

"She's up again," she said.

"Check to see if she's wet. I showed you how to change her. And she's probably hungry."

"Again? She just ate."

Carmen let out a huge scream, and I motioned for Sam to go attend to her. Sam grumbled and ran into the other room. Then I heard a shrill from Sam, so I rushed in to check it out.

"Look, look, it's everywhere," Sam said, obviously grossed out by Carmen's fully loaded Pamper. "And it stinks," Sam added.

"It's just poop, quit being so dramatic. Get the wipes."

"You want me to clean this up?" Sam said in disbelief.

I nodded and went back to the office. I heard Sam whining and complaining the entire time. I peeped around the corner into the living room after everything was quieted down to see what was happening. Sam was playing with Carmen, who was inside her playpen. Then I overheard her speak.

"You made me miss my movie, Carmen. I'm not happy about that."

Carmen laughed and cooed.

"That's not funny," Sam said, but Carmen continued to laugh at Sam's dramatic expressions. I went back to the office and worked for another hour. Carmen went to sleep and Sam came into the office to talk to me. She sat next to my computer and asked about my job.

"I want to write," she said.

"You do? What kind of stuff?"

"Poems, like you."

Sam went into the other room and retrieved her book bag. She pulled out several wrinkled pages of her work. "I have more, but they are in my folder at home."

I went to my bookshelf, pulled off one of my unused journals, and handed it to her. "Here, now you can keep all of your work in here."

Sam looked at the journal, and looked up at me. "Why are you always giving me stuff?"

"What?"

"You are always giving me stuff. Why? People don't just do nice stuff for no reason."

"I like you. That's my reason."

"I thought you loved me?" she stated.

"I like you and I love you."

"Hmmm," Sam said, and continued to flip through the empty pages of the journal. "I had a diary one time, I used to write some poems in there, but this girl stole it. We got into a big fight about it and I got in trouble for hitting her."

"You shouldn't have hit her," I said. "You should have told someone."

Sam looked up at me as though I had no clue. "It doesn't work like that. You have to fight for what's yours. If not, people will take advantage of you."

"But you have to fight smart, and sometimes that doesn't include using our fists. But trust me, I used to fight when I was a little girl, so I understand."

"Really?" Sam said, very intrigued.

"Yep, all the time. I got suspended from school, thrown off the bus, and in school detention."

Sam laughed, and spoke. "You're too scrawny to fight."

"I know, that's why I had to start fighting with my brain."

"Got tired of getting beat up, huh?"

I playfully mashed Sam in the head; just then Carmen started whimpering. I looked at Sam and then flicked my eyes toward the living room.

"I know. You want me to go see what's wrong with Carmen."

"Could you?"

Sam rose and griped as she walked out of the room, "I'm never having a baby."

My mission was accomplished. The rest of the evening was calm. I finished up my work and took Sam back to the home.

"I want to come stay with you again," she said before I left.

"Definitely."

"But next time, let's do it when you're not keeping Carmen."

I nodded and watched her walk down the hall to her room.

Carmen was quiet on the drive back home and really didn't fuss anymore the rest of the evening as long as I was in her sight. It was when I left the room that she cried. Yet when I rubbed her little stuffed blue dog in her face, she instantly burst into giggles and grins.

Poor Carmen, I'm sure she didn't know what to think. Over the last few days she had stayed with her irresponsible father and her crazy godmother. Babies may not be able to communicate it, but they know when there is something wrong. It must be frustrating to be unable to verbally communicate with those in your daily surroundings. I knew how she felt. I hate when I am screaming at the top of my lungs for help and everyone around me can't seem to understand what is happening. But the difference between infants and adults is that within seconds infants bounce back. They find joy in the simplest of things, and the turmoil never lasts long. Sure, they don't have the responsibility of adults, but stressing over responsibility keeps us from taking pleasures in the simplicities of life. Now, that is a great subject for my journal writing.

Adults should be more like we were as children, when we were truly happy for no reason at all, instead of now, when we pretend to be happy for millions of reasons.

If we could be more like children, in that respect, I bet the suicide, drug, and insanity rate would drop dramatically. As I started writing, my phone rang.

"Hello."

"Guess what?" said Tam on the other line.

"I don't know, what?" I said with little enthusiasm.

"Come on. Guess," she stated, forcing me to play her little game.

"Evelyn and Pierce are getting married."

"No."

I sat down to await the end of this guessing game. Finally, after no more guesses and a second of silence, Tam broke out with the good news.

"I'm pregnant!"

"Wow. Congratulations."

"What's wrong? You don't sound really excited."

"I'm very happy for you. It's not too soon, is it?" I asked with concern.

"No, the doctors say I'm fine. Don't worry. I'm going to be okay, the baby is going to be okay, and you're going to be a godmother."

"Tam, I'm so happy for you. Really. You deserve this more than anyone I know."

Carmen started whimpering.

"What's that?" Tam asked.

"Carmen, I'm keeping her while Sarah's in the hospital."

"Oh, that's right. Is she doing better?"

"She is, and thank God. This baby is wearing me out." Tam started laughing.

"Just you wait. When you find the right one, you will be more than ecstatic to have his little ones running around."

Minutes later, Carmen began preparing her voice for her nightly performance. I congratulated Tam again, and then hung up, changed Carmen's Pamper, and turned on the television. Before I realize, it was close to 10:00 p.m.

My day had been so hectic that I forgot the function with Susan and Winston was today. If only this thought had stayed in the caves of my memory, but it didn't. After I thought about it for thirty or so minutes, I decided to call Winston. But as I grabbed my phone, it rang.

"Hello!" I said with excitement, thinking it was Winston.

There was no answer.

"Hello!" I continued.

No answer again. Finally I hung up. "Who in the hell is calling me and hanging up?"

I grabbed the phone and dialed star 69, but it was restricted. Irritated, I hung up the phone once more, and I decided against calling Winston, and he never called me. I wasn't going to make a big deal of it, but I was certainly not pleased.

I checked on Carmen, who was asleep. It was amazing how peaceful she looked. How could something so calm raise so much hell?

I grabbed my journal again, but I didn't have the energy to write anything more than a poem. I glanced back at Carmen again and smiled.

Babies are so much like . . .

NATURE

She sleeps like still air
Calm
She awakens like a gust of wind
Sudden
She shrills like lightning
Sharp
She screams like a shout of thunder
Deafening
She cries like a hurricane
Downpour
She sleeps like still air

Good night.

10

Adolescence
Always Lingers

Although the alarm was set in time, Carmen's little body was equipped with her own alarm clock. She woke up three hours before the alarm rang, and so I also had to get up at 3:00 a.m. I fed her and made a poor attempt to get her back to sleep. Finally, she dozed off around five thirty, which was thirty minutes before the alarm was supposed to sound. I placed my head beside hers and closed my eyes for what I thought would be three seconds. However, the seconds turned into forty-five minutes and I arrived to work a half hour late. If I continued to keep Carmen, I would be late to work every day. Again, I didn't see how working mothers did it. Not to mention single, working mothers. I loved my goddaughter, but Sarah needed to come get her child as soon as possible.

I dragged my feet to my desk, pushed my chair out with my heels, and fell down into the seat. It took me five minutes to notice the bright pink Post-it stuck to the front of my desk. After focusing on the note, I realized that I was late for a morning meeting that had started fifteen minutes ago. I really didn't want to walk into the meeting late because everyone would stare as I opened the door and look around the room to find a seat. Then Susan would stop speaking until I got to my seat and I finally would have to explain why I was late to everyone in attendance sometime throughout the day. The entire ordeal made me continue sitting at my desk, and so I grabbed the Post-it, ripped it up, and tossed the shreds of hot-pink paper in the trash.

"I'll pretend I have no clue about the meeting," I mumbled to myself.

I grabbed my folder from my desk and started my day. Around forty minutes later, I heard the meeting break up. I grabbed several sheets of paper and colored pencils and scattered them haphazardly over my desk. With a pen in my left hand and paper in my right, I buried my head into my work. I wanted to appear extra diligent, especially if I was to convince Susan that I had no idea about the meeting. Through my peripherals, I saw her walking toward me. Thus, I kept working as if she were not there. She came around my desk and tapped me on the shoulder. I slowly lifted my head and sighed as if I had already put in a full day's work.

"We missed you at the meeting this morning," she said.

Seemingly confused, I looked at her with squinted eyes and spoke.

"The morning meeting?" I asked.

"Yeah, I told Nehri to leave you a note."

I scanned my desk pretending to search for the note I threw away moments ago.

"Well, never mind. Here are the notes. Make a copy and place the originals in my box. What are your plans for lunch?"

Why was she asking me about lunch? I wondered. I sincerely hoped it was not to invite me to eat with her. "I may work through lunch."

"Well, ring my phone around noon. I owe you."

She smiled while winking. Running her hand across my pencils, Susan looked at the sketch in progress. "Keep up the good work."

She sauntered down the hall, tossing her hair over her right shoulder. As soon as she was out of sight, my head crashed to my desk. *Why does she owe me? Could this lunch date concern Winston?*

With my chin propped on top of my paperwork, I leaned over and called him. I had to know what happened on that date and I had to know right then. He didn't answer and so I attempted to busy myself, made copies of the notes from the morning meeting, and went to Nehri's desk to discuss our project. Minutes later, I was called to answer line 1. I excused myself from Nehri and rushed back to my desk.

"This is Lily."

"You called me?" asked Winston.

"You know why I called you. Don't play coy."

"I'm at work, I can't talk with you about last night. I will say it was nice."

"Apparently, it was so nice, Susan feels the need to take me to lunch to thank me."

Winston laughed. Although I couldn't see him, I

could imagine him leaning his head back and slightly covering his right hand over his mouth.

"Why didn't you call me last night?"

"It was late. I didn't want to wake Carmen. I promise to call tonight. I have to go."

"Yeah, okay."

"Bye," he said with a kiss.

I hung up the phone and contemplated this sticky situation. I could have avoided all of this if only I had been honest. However, it was too late to go back now. If Susan really liked Winston and he didn't ask her out again, she might take it out on me. However, if Winston did ask her out again, I might take it out on her and him. I should never have allowed my personal and professional lives to cross. I saw the large, blinking DANGER flashing in front of my face, and yet I ignored it. I was flirting with a possible train wreck.

As I rose to take the original notes to Susan's desk, my phone rang. With hesitance, I waited to answer on the third ring.

"This is Lily."

"I pray you are not thinking this, but just in case, I did not sleep with her," admitted Winston.

"I wasn't, but thanks."

"I'll talk with you tonight."

"Tonight, bye."

We hung up. I knew Winston did not sleep with her. He was too much of a gentleman to be first date dick. Yet that was sweet of him to call and I had nothing to worry about. I knew how it would play out. He would let her down easy and I would ease her pain, by taking her to lunch next week. We would have quaint conversation about how men are pigs. She'd share her story, I'd share mine, and our girlfriend moment would last all of thirty minutes. I would get across the tracks before the train got within a few feet and avoid all traces of a collision. Without more concern, I spent the remainder of my morning working at my desk. Susan called and canceled lunch because of a conference call and I couldn't have been happier. Nehri and I got together in the afternoon and I left work promptly at five.

Before going to pick up Carmen, I stopped by the market for fresh vegetables, and while I was there, Omar called my cell. Immediately I panicked, for he only called in dire situations. Fortunately, this time he was the bearer of good news. He wanted to spend the evening with Carmen. Therefore, he was going to pick her up from Margaret and take her back in the morning. I was in shock. I quickly called Sarah to get her approval, and once I did, I did a little dance in aisle five and headed home.

Since Carmen was going to her father's house, I would have time to clean and cook lunch for tomorrow. Tired and relieved, I was starting to feel as though Omar was my "baby's daddy" and that was not a good feeling. I loved Carmen, but I was very enthused about her spending the evening with her father. Again, hats off to all single mothers.

I got home, placed my bags in the kitchen, and lit my candles. This was going to be an evening of relaxation. After eating, I slid into a warm bath filled with aromatic lavender bubbles. I was so relaxed that I snoozed a few minutes while in the tub. Suddenly I saw vivid images of Dick rubbing my feet while sitting opposite me in the water. As I giggled at his soft touch, I immediately awakened. I wished he didn't appear every time I closed my eyes. What could I do to get over him? I constantly said that I didn't care in hopes that the words would eventually manifest, but nothing worked. Like herpes, there was no cure for a love hangover; and like herpes, Dick kept coming back.

Wiping the bubbles from my shoulders, I rinsed off, strolled into the bedroom, and slipped into a pair of Dick's boxers. No doubt, wearing his clothing didn't help, but as much as I wanted thoughts of him out of my mind, I also wanted him to remain close. Yes, it made no sense. This was why I no longer questioned it. For love is an arcane, four-letter word that makes the wise man foolish while deranging the sane. And on that note, I slipped my love-crazed body into my bed and cuddled with my teddy. However, before my body heat seeped into the sheets, my phone rang.

"Yeah."

"What a sweet greeting," joked Winston.

Funny, I forgot he was supposed to call. I was so caught up in having a relaxing, quiet evening, Winston and his date with Susan didn't cross my mind and honestly, I didn't care to hear about it at that moment.

"I'm trying to go to sleep, Winston."

"It's only nine o'clock. I want to come over."

"Not tonight. I'm tired."

"Are you still upset about the date? Nothing happened. I am not going out with her again."

"Good, and I'm not upset. I'm bushed and I just want to go to sleep."

"Fine, I'll call you later, bye."

He sounded like he had a little attitude, but I didn't care. I leaned over and quickly hung up the phone because my body was seriously craving sleep. With a long yawn, I turned and continued my passionate slumber. I was not sure what time I entered my first dream phase; however, at 9:50 I was shockingly awakened by a light ringing. Unable to move, because of the sleep monster hovering over my body, I lay there with tensed neck muscles and listened to the incessant ring of the doorbell. Finally, I broke free, sprang out of bed, and rushed downstairs to look out of the window. There was no car in the driveway, yet the bell ringing was relentless.

"Who the hell is it?" I said in my deepest baritone voice.

Suddenly the ringing stopped and I froze. Against the wall in the foyer, my heartbeat increased its pace. Finally, I heard a tiny voice speak from the other side of the door.

"Please don't be mad. It's me, Sam."

"What?" I said, running to answer.

I flung open the door and standing on my step was a frail, teary-eyed teenager. Her sneakers were untied, her ponytail was skewed, and she was clinging on to a tattered piece of blue Kleenex. Before I could say another word, Sam stepped into the house, wrapped her arms around me, and sobbed harder. I closed the door and walked into the living room with her body clinched around my waist. In between the tears, wheezes, and gags, Sam began to speak.

"Please don't be mad. I couldn't stay there. They kept laughing at me."

"Who was laughing and how did you get here?"

"I called a taxi."

"I have to call Ms. Gaither. You cannot sneak out like this. You and I are both going to be in trouble."

"But I want to stay here," Sam wailed.

"Baby, you can't stay here and if I don't call, they will call the police."

I grabbed the phone as Sam began telling me what happened.

"You remember Shannon and Keisha, right? Well, Steve told them that I gave him a blow-job. They told everyone and they all believe it. Now Keisha keeps calling me slut mouth and whenever I pass the boys in the hall, they all make faces and call me names. I was trying to fight smart, like you said, and so I told Keisha to stop but she wouldn't, so tonight when she came to bed, I hit her in the mouth. Mr. Combs broke up the fight and sent me to another room down the hall. So after everybody went back to their rooms, I crawled out of the window, went to the pay phone, and came over here."

Leaning over, I wiped the tears from her face.

"Sam, I am so sorry but you can't run away. It will only make things worse. I still have to call."

"I don't care. I will run away again. You can't make me stay there," she shouted.

"So where are you going to go? Do you have a plan and a place to stay? Do you have an apartment and a job that you are not telling me about?"

Sam looked down and shook her head as I began to dial. Ms. Gaither was on vacation, so I spoke with Mr. Combs, who agreed to let me bring Sam back to the home instead of calling the police.

"Sam, I don't think you realize how serious this is. You cannot do this again. I know you don't like your environment, but if you cause problems and run away, they will send you somewhere you will really hate. You are upset and I know that this one incident is horrible, but I promise to talk with Ms. Gaither about it when she comes back. Give me your word you won't run away again."

"Why can't I just stay with you?" she asked.

At that moment, I really wished she simply could. But currently that wasn't an option.

"Promise me," I reiterated.

Sam didn't verbally promise, but she gave me a hug, poked out her bottom lip, and nodded. I went upstairs, slipped on my jeans and a T-shirt. All the while, I whispered to myself, "Slut mouth? Where do kids come up with these sayings?"

Once we got in the car, I told Sam about the time when I was in the ninth grade and this stupid guy told my classmates that I had given him a blow-job after school before volleyball practice. I remembered being removed from the "cool girl" table at lunch, because I had "penis breath." Naturally, I shamefully left the cafeteria crying.

"Guys tell lies, because they don't know how to express themselves when they like you," I told Sam.

"Well, when I see Steve, I am going to express myself with my fists," Sam griped.

"Is this the same Steve that sits behind you in my class?"

Sam nodded a hesitant yes. "He used to be my friend, but I hate him now!"

"Do not fight him. There are other ways to handle this. If you're patient, he will be exposed."

Sam rolled her eyes and huffed.

"I promise, in a week, there will be a new rumor and this one will be long forgotten. By the way, it is only a rumor, isn't it?"

"Ms. Lily!" Sam shouted alarmingly.

"I'm just checking."

We pulled into the home and greeted Mr. Combs at the door. He asked me to talk with him tomorrow before my class. I agreed, kissed Sam on the forehead, and left.

"If it ain't one thing, it's another," I said aloud.

On the drive home I began to laugh at the entire situation. I totally empathized with Sam. She was as mortified on that similar school day. It happened to all girls at one time or another. It would be so much simpler if boys could just say: "Hey, I like you, will you be my girlfriend?"

But no, they can't do that. They do brainless things like hit you in the back of the head, tell lies, and ask other women to marry them to get your attention. My mind halted in midthought. Swiftly I was tossed back into the ninth grade and this time I was "jilted lover girl formerly known as penis breath." Yet, instead of crying like then, I chose to fight back with harsh words and lies. Suddenly it dawned on me. I started an argument with Dick, because I didn't know how to say: "Hey, I like you, make me your girlfriend, not her."

And he argued back because he couldn't say: "Hey, I miss you and I want to see you."

I swear, we are all a bunch of kids in adult clothing, behaving ridiculously, because of a lack of honest communication. Dazed, I wondered, do we ever leave the stage of adolescence? I started crying over boys at twelve, and eighteen years later they still make me cry. I would have loved to tell Sam that things were going to change, but why lie? The complexity evolves, but through it all we are still girls who cry over boys who do peculiar things to express their affection.

Laughing deliriously, I finally walked into my home and crawled back into bed. Lying here, I thought to myself how I no longer wanted to be an adolescent. I desired to mature to adulthood, and truthful expression was the key. I was going to search within my gut to find it. And I prayed that by the time it made its way through my system and into my mouth, it didn't sour into penis breath.

I arrived at the children's home an hour before class on that Thursday. Mentally preparing for my barrage of questions, I found Mr. Combs's office and firmly knocked on his door.

"Enter," he said sternly.

Without hesitation, I opened the door to greet the concerned eyes of Mr. Combs, Ms. Gaither, and one other female counselor.

"Hi, Lily, have a seat," said Ms. Gaither.

For the next forty-five minutes the counselors questioned me about my relationship with Sam. I assured them that I had not given her any inclination that it was okay for her to run away.

"Sam and I are close, and I am honored that she can confide in me. However, before this week, she never gave me any signs that she was unhappy here. In fact, if it weren't for this incident with Steve, I don't think she would have run away."

"We just want to make sure that she understands the seriousness of this occurrence. She cannot run to you whenever she has a problem," said Mr. Combs.

"I did tell her that she could come to me, if she needed to talk. However, Sam is a smart girl, she knows better. I will reiterate the graveness of her choices," I stated.

After I finished explaining the situation leading up to the night Sam left the home, Mr. Combs dismissed me from his office. Sighing with relief, I leaned my head against the wall next to the door. That was a grueling forty-five minutes. I thought they were going to relieve me of my teaching responsibility. I knew it was only volunteer work, but in it, I found such joy. I had to speak with Sam after class, because she must never do that again.

I walked into the classroom, sat at my desk, and awaited my pupils. Minutes later, eleven of my students slowly strolled in and took their seats. As Steve walked by my desk, I felt the strong desire to trip him just so he could fall on his face in front of the class. Of course, as the teacher, I was unable to do such things. However, it would have been sweet satisfaction and justification for all of the young girls ridiculed and lied upon by the "Steves" of the world. Yet, instead of evil doings, I simply smiled and asked him to take a seat. Sam came in last and stood at my desk.

"I'm not allowed to take your class, I'm on probation," she said.

"Well, there has to be some sort of punishment for your actions."

Sam slowly turned and began to walk from the room. I called out to her.

"Just sit up here with me," I told her.

Sam grabbed a seat and sat by my desk as I started the class.

I sat at my desk, clasped my hands together, and paused while the students settled down. Originally, I planned to have the kids write comic strips using themselves as characters; however, a better idea popped into my head.

"A key to great writing is free expression, and sincere expression comes from good communication.

Therefore, we're going to stand in front of the class and do an improvisational exercise."

After explaining the assignments, I asked each of the students to partner up, and as fate would have it, Steve was the only one left without a partner. Naturally, I volunteered to do the exercise with him and I couldn't have been happier.

"One person starts the conversation by reliving an old situation. The other joins in the conversation and the improvisation between each of you begins. You each have three minutes. Then we will switch and the other person will start the conversation. Does everyone understand?"

For the first half hour, I sat and listened to very interesting stories that ranged from being forced to steal candy from the gas station to divorce to cheating at checkers. Finally, Steve and I rose and began our improvisation.

"Would you like to start?" Steve asked.

"Indeed, I would."

Steve extended his hand and led me to the front of my desk. With a brief pause and a deep breath, I started.

"I can't believe you lied on me," I shouted loudly.

Nervously he answered, "What, what are you talking about?"

"I'm talking about the fact that you told everyone I did certain things with you, when you know I didn't."

"I didn't say anything," he stated, seemingly embarrassed.

"That's not what everyone is saying. You have ruined my reputation. They said that you said I gave you a you know what . . . I can't even say it." I sniveled.

"Ms. Lily, what are you doing?" Steve whispered.

"Stay in character," I commanded.

Steve pulled me to the side of the desk. "Why are you doing this to me? You're supposed to be talking about one of your situations, not talking about something that I did."

Of course by now, we had the full attention of the class.

"I am talking about something that happened to me in the ninth grade. What did you do? Did you lie on someone too?" I said innocently.

Suddenly Steve was quiet. Sam stood up and looked at him.

"All I have to say is I never got over my ninth grade incident and I never forgave the guy. If you did something to someone, you need to make it right and apologize. Not only are you hurting someone, but also whatever wrongdoings you do will come back to you."

Steve folded his arms and leaned onto my desk; however, he was still silent.

"Are you going to be able to continue or do you need to speak with the class?" I asked.

"I might have said something about someone that wasn't exactly true."

"Oh, really?" Sam said loudly.

"Maybe," he mumbled.

Steve turned toward Sam, and quietly mouthed the words *I'm sorry.*

"I can't hear you," stated Sam with her hands upon her hips.

"I'm sorry," he said quickly, and rushed to his seat.

"There is nothing wrong with creative writing on paper or even creating stories onstage. However, creative stories should not be used to boost one's status especially at the expense of someone else's reputation. I don't think I have to explain further. I know everyone here has done something wrong to someone. Therefore, next week we are writing apology cards."

There was a sigh of grief from the class.

"No moans or complaints. I'm letting you go fifteen minutes early. I'll see you next week."

The students gathered their books and strolled from class. As Shannon walked by Steve, she popped him on the head. Steve simply picked up his composition book and walked out of the room without eye contact with Sam or me. Sam gave me a hug.

"Thank you," she whispered, and then rushed from class.

Shannon lingered behind, though, and walked up to me as I was packing up.

"Ms. Lily, can I ask you something?" she asked.

I nodded.

"Can I have Doc's card? I need to ask him something."

"Doc's name is Dr. Winston Fulmore. Is everything okay?"

"I just need to ask him something," she said, looking away.

"Okay, here is his office number, I don't have his card on me."

Taking the number from my hand, Shannon made no eye contact, and hastened from the classroom. With my elbows propped on my desk, I placed my head in my hands.

"I only hope this makes some sort of difference," I muttered.

Leaning over, I grabbed my satchel and placed it over my shoulder. I hit the lights, left the building, and headed home. Thankfully, Margaret was keeping

Carmen tonight because of my class, so I was going to be able to sleep a little later in the morning.

All the while, I keep thinking about Sam. It was funny how pubescent incidents appeared to be life altering. Sure, they hurt, but eighth grade rumors do not ruin a person's reputation for life. Only in the actual moment do they seem to be life lasting. I couldn't underestimate Sam's reaction, but I hoped she'd take the time to realize that there were issues larger than Steve.

Rumors do not shape us into the people we are or the people we become unless we give them the power to do so.

11

Kansas City vs. Emerald City

Sarah came home from the hospital that Friday and I left work promptly at 5:00 p.m. to welcome her home. When I spoke to Sarah she was always in great spirits. Fortunately, she was positive and handling her chemotherapy treatments well. When I arrived at her home, Omar greeted me pleasantly at the door.

"She's upstairs. She was hoping you would come over after work."

"Is she doing okay?"

"She's doing well and I am going to be here a few days to take care of her. My mom will be home next week."

"Good."

I walked into the home overflowing with the aroma from roses and gardenias. Although I adored the smell of fresh flowers, the combination of these two set off my allergies. Upstairs, I found Sarah in Carmen's room sitting in a rocking chair reading to her baby girl. Upon seeing this beautiful sight, I quickly reached into my purse to grab my phone and took a picture.

"Sarah, where is your hair?"

My friend grinned while rubbing her hand against the short spiked stubbles on her head.

"I took your advice and cut it all off. I know it looks crazy, but I've always been a little daring."

"I love it. You look like a young Annie Lennox."

Sarah paused with a scornful look. Then she looked down at Carmen. "I missed her so much."

"Well, we are both glad you are home."

Just then Omar walked into the room and spoke. "Do you need anything, sweetie?"

"Could you get me some water?" Sarah responded.

"And you?" he asked in my direction.

"I'm cool."

He nodded and left the room. Immediately I began to question, "What has gotten into him?"

"Girl, I do not know, but I pray it stays and takes over. He called the hospital every day and he was there bright and early this morning to pick me up. Not once has he complained and he volunteered to stay here and help me out with Carmen. Perhaps God gave him a little wake-up call."

"It's about time," I commented.

I sat with Sarah for about thirty more minutes while she continued to read to Carmen. Once Carmen nodded off to sleep, she decided to take a nap.

"Oh, by the way, we're going to see Meshell N'de-geocello next week. I already got the tickets. This is my thank-you for keeping Carmen."

"You start back to work next week. Do not overdo it," I mentioned.

Sarah nonchalantly waved her hand and closed the door. I kissed her cheek and then left.

I decided to call Tam on my way home. I hadn't spoken to her in a week. Every time we had conversation, she asked me about Dick; therefore, our conversations had become scarce. Unfortunately, she was not home, so I left a sweet message and continued journeying home. My cell phone rang as soon as I pulled into the garage. Reaching down in my purse, I seemed to pull out everything but the phone. Finally it stopped ringing as soon as I got my hands on it.

"Damn! I missed Winston's call," I said, checking the message.

I quickly called him back as I walked into the house.

"Hi, sweetie, I can't believe you answered your office phone, they always have to page you," I said.

"I just called you," he said.

"I'm at home now and calling you back."

"Listen, I don't have a lot of time, but I need to ask you something. I am being honored at an awards' dinner tomorrow night and I want you to be my date."

"I would love to be your date."

"Good. I'm sorry it's last minute. I wasn't going to go, but I just found out about the award. I'll call you tonight when I leave work."

"Talk to you then," I said before disconnecting.

Beaming, I hung up the phone while leaning against the sink. "My baby is getting an award."

My heart fluttered with excitement for him, and then suddenly the flutters took a nosedive. I was sure his family was going to be there for support. It would be nice to think that he didn't invite them, but that was also irrational. I was just not ready for his family to know that we were dating. I couldn't bear to face his mother's expression of shame. She was already one of those women who walked into a room with that aristocratic expression as if she smelled something bad, and I refused to be the stench of her evening. Perhaps, when Winston called back, I would somehow back my way out of his invitation.

I hit the stereo remote on my way to the kitchen and listened to some Tupac. Normally, I listened to jazz in the evenings. I loved old school like Nina Simone and new school like Nnenna Freelon. However, it was Friday night and I was not in the mood to wind down. In fact, I was having rushes of energy. I enjoyed Tupac. His music was great and he was a brilliant poet. And, since I am a writer, I am ardent about lyrical presentation. I need my rhymes to come with clarity, meaning, keen metaphors, and clever analogies. Mos Def, OutKast, Jay-Z, and KRS-ONE are some of my favorites. But when it comes to having all four, Tupac definitely ranks top on my list. Many do not agree, but I am an avid fan of his genius.

While I was cooking, my energy continued to rise. Suddenly I felt the urge to go out dancing. I hadn't been out dancing in about five months and I hadn't been out dancing alone since I moved here over a year ago. However, without much consideration, I decided to get dressed and go out. I was glad I chose to eat light. Placing my veggies and pasta on a plate, I walked into the living room and flipped through the pages of the entertainment periodical. Although many of the nightclubs were listed, I was not sure about the music and crowds at any of these places. However, I refused to give up. I called Sarah to ask her about the happening spots on Friday night.

"Guess what, Sarah? I am going out tonight," I said with enthusiasm.

"With who?"

"With me. I am going out dancing. Where should I go?"

"Are you okay?"

"I'm fine. I simply want to get dressed and go out dancing. Now, where should I go?"

"Well, what kind of music do you want to hear? Pluto's has salsa night on Fridays. That might be fun."

"Yes! I'm going salsa dancing," I shouted zealously.

"Oooh! I want to go," Sarah whined.

"You should have thought about that before you got yourself knocked up. But now you must stay at home with your baby and your baby's daddy." I laughed.

"Well, have fun for me. Call me tomorrow and let me know how it was."

I quickly hung up the phone, finished my pasta, and jumped in the shower. It was only seven thirty and I had plenty of time before the nightclubs opened. However, the one thing I had learned about my body was that if I did not get myself dressed and ready to leave the house, my zeal would quickly die and I would be in my nightgown with hardly enough energy to make it upstairs to bed. It was amazing how the body changed. In college I used to attend parties that started at 2:00 a.m. and ended at 6:00 a.m. All I needed was a disco nap around nine and I would wake up at midnight raring to go. By now disco naps were unheard of, because two-hour naps turned into all-night slumber and I couldn't be convinced to wake up from my sleep to go to a party.

Even if they were giving away money, I would send someone down there on my behalf to pick up my share. This was a different Lily and if this flower didn't leave the house by ten, there would be no blooming.

With my bright pink towel wrapped around my moist skin, I rummaged through my closet to find a sexy outfit. Sexy black dress number one hung slightly off the shoulders, hugged the body, and fell just above the knee. Sexy black dress number two was a jersey cotton V-neck that hugged the body and fell to the shin, with an incredible split on the front of the right leg. Sexy black dress number three was cut on the bias with an empire waist. It was made of silk and definitely a great dress for twists and twirls. Just when I decided on number three, I glanced at option four, hot-red number also made of silk with cut similar to option two's. Upon holding the red up to my body and prancing around in the full-length mirror, I decided option four won, hands down. I had forgotten all about this little red dress and I'd never worn it. Dick had purchased it for me just before I moved here, and as I slipped it on, I imagined Dick standing over my shoulder telling me how beautiful I looked. I could even feel his strong hands on my skin. To rid myself of these thoughts, I put on a choker given to me by Wealth. My ensemble was a hodgepodge of ex-boyfriends, and I topped it off with perfume given to me by Winston. Just then he called.

"What are you doing?" he asked.

"Getting ready to go out dancing."

"Where were you going?"

"Pluto's for salsa night."

"That should be fun. If I weren't so tired, I would join you. Go and enjoy yourself and when you leave, come over and see me. I may be asleep, so I'll leave the key in an envelope in the mailbox."

"Okay, I'll see you later on tonight."

"Good. I can't wait. Bye."

Alas, Winston hung up before I could cancel on him. Once I saw him, I knew he was going to convince me to go, so I started preparing myself. I was sure I was going to have to get a little tipsy to make it through that evening, for the butterflies were already beginning to hatch in my stomach. I knew I'd better have a heavenly time that night, because the next night was going to be hell. I slipped on my three-inch heels, gave a final check in the mirror, and headed downtown to dance away my troubles.

It took me twenty minutes to arrive at the nightclub and I sat in the parking lot for an additional ten minutes, checking out the singles and couples entering the spot. There was an interesting mix of ages and nationalities. Most of the women were in sexy, short dresses and stiletto heels. I glanced down at my shoes, and knew there was going to be plenty of sore, aching feet that evening. After sighing and checking my lipstick, I walked into the club. The line was just forming, and so it only took minutes to get in. I was unaware that women got in free before ten, but I was pleasantly surprised. I hadn't been in a nightclub in a while and it took some time for my senses to adjust to the swirling, colored lights and loud music. I took a seat at the end of the bar, turned my chair to face the dance floor, and watched the couples dance. Entertained, I watch a middle-aged Latino man whirl and twirl his partner all over the floor. He was twisting her in and out of his arms while she grooved her hips to the rhythmic percussions.

"They are really getting down," I whispered to myself.

I salsa very well, but this couple reminded me of the partners competing in the National Ballroom Contests. She was in a tea-length black dress with sequins running diagonally across her body. Their compatibility and dance moves were quite engaging. However, on the opposite end of the spectrum was another couple dancing to the same song yet with a very different rhythm. I was not sure if they were moving to the melody, the horn section, or the words; however, they were definitely not dancing to the beat. The woman towered around five-ten and her partner stood close to five-four. His face was nestled right in between her 38-DD bosom. Every few seconds he came up for air, then grooved his head back into the valley of her peaks. He was holding on to her for dear life and she was spinning round and about. They too were really getting down, but in their own rhythmless nation. I covered my mouth and let out a girlish giggle.

"What's so funny?" I heard a deep voice speak over my shoulder.

As I looked up at the man behind the voice, my chuckle turned into nervous laughter. This beautiful stranger was breathtaking. Without another word, he extended his hand and escorted me to the dance floor. Gently placing his left hand within my right palm, he pulled me close and we danced. As the music sped he pushed my body away, yet still held my hand to maneuver my movements. Once the tune slowed to a sexy tango rhythm, he pulled my body into his and tilted his head slightly so that our ears slightly grazed against each other. Amazingly, subtle body contact was as erotic as sex. With his hand firmly placed within the groove of my lower back, we danced for an hour. Finally, he turned his cheek and spoke softly in my ear.

"Would you like something to drink?"

Slowly nodding with our cheeks touching, I responded, "Water, please."

As he went and got our drinks, I took a seat at one of the small round tables to the side of the dance area. Returning with our bottled waters, he took a seat at the table and spoke.

"Are you Trinidadian?"

I was not sure what possessed him to ask this question and I was even more befuddled as to why I lied.

"Yes," I said.

He smiled and continued conversation. "My name is Thadius."

"Desiree," I replied falsely.

Surely, if I lied about my nationality I would have to lie about my name as well. Quietly, I sat and thought about my next retort. Luckily, my old college friend, Desiree, was actually from there and I perfected her accent. Occasionally, we used to go out and tell people we were sisters; therefore, I had to be able to speak the dialect. However, this was eight years later and I was not the careless college student. It was a little wrong to give fake names and phone numbers, but fake accents and nationalities took the facade to another level, and yet I continued.

"Thanks for the dance," I said in my fake accent.

"I grew up around several Trinidadians and your features are very similar."

I smiled and sipped my water. If he grew up around these people, my accent might give me away. However, if he truly grew up around Trinidad natives, how could he confuse my distinct features with theirs? Perhaps, he was lying too. Regardless, the deceitful club games had begun.

"You dance very well."

"Thanks, Thadius, so do you."

"Please call me Thad," he responded.

Together, we sat and watched the other dancers move about the floor graciously. I carefully inspected Thad from the corner of my eye. Shaded with bronze hues, his skin was freakishly flawless. With high cheekbones, a narrow face, and a strong chin, he sported a perfectly dimpled cleft. His profile was as magnificent as his front, accented with long lashes that curled out from within his deep-set eyes. His strong features resembled the natives from Northern Africa. Thad was definitely caramel eye candy.

"Are you ready to dance some more?" he asked.

Displaying a demure smile, I nodded. Thad rose, took my hand, and led me to the floor. During this dance session, we struck up random conversation. Thad mentioned that he worked in pharmaceuticals and had only lived in Kansas City for a few months. I, in turn, told him that I was a freelance writer who moved to KC for rest and relaxation. There was no need to tell him about my job at Hallmark. He didn't even know my real name and I didn't want him trying to find me. I should have told him my name was Cinderella, because after midnight this salsa-dancing Trinidadian known as Desiree would turn back into the flighty artist known as Lily. My sexy red dress would rag to jeans, and my exotic accent would flux to southern twang. But for the next hour, I served up Desiree and partied until my fairy godmother called me home.

Close to 1:00 a.m., my body was surely showing

signs of fatigue. My arms were weak and my feet were starting to swell. "I have to go."

"Would you like to go somewhere for coffee?" Thad responded.

"I am very tired."

"Well, maybe we can keep in touch."

Walking toward the door, I turned and responded, "I'm in a relationship. You are charming and I have enjoyed this evening, but it has to end here."

"Thanks for being honest," he said.

Of course, that response sickened me, for that was the only honest thing I had said all night. Thad kissed my hand and waved good-bye as I walked through the door. Gracefully rushing across the street, I made it safely to my car and headed toward Winston's home.

Rethinking the evening, I wished I had given Thad my true identity. He seemed very genuine and it would have been nice to keep in touch. However, it was fun to be someone other than Lily for the evening. Laughing, I sang along to India.Arie until I pulled into Winston's driveway. Retrieving his key from the envelope in the mailbox, I cautiously opened the door and walked into the home. Softly, I called out, "Winston. Where are you?"

There was no response. Walking into the downstairs restroom, I washed my hands before heading up the stairs. Checking my reflection in the mirror, I noticed my choker was missing.

"Oh no!" I said, touching my neck.

The beautiful white gold choker with a delicate teardrop ruby was one of the nicest pieces of jewelry I owned. I was aware that lying didn't pay, but the ETA of my karma was quite expedient.

"Oh well, I guess that's what I get."

Glum, I walked out of the restroom and went upstairs. By the fourth step, I looked down and noticed a tiny gold package in the center of the step. Kneeling, I picked up the empty Godiva box. After taking a few more steps, I spotted another empty box. Finally, I saw the trail of boxes. Instantly excited, I anticipated the prize at the end of the path. Therefore, like Dorothy in ruby Louboutins, I followed the yellow box road to my treasure. When I got to the closed door, I took a quick breath and turned the knob. Peering in the room, I saw no one. However, walking in, I immediately noticed the king-sized platform bed covered in gold-foiled Godiva chocolates. I rushed to the bed and tossed the chocolates in the air. As they fell in my lap, I carefully unwrapped my first one. Biting into the splendor of this dark chocolate truffle was heavenly as I fell back onto the huge feather pillows.

"You are so sexy," I heard a voice say.

However, I paid no attention to the man behind the curtain. I was lost in the glitter of the Godiva fields. Suddenly the drapes began to move and a shadowy figure appeared within the candlelit room. Lying in the bed of chocolates, I lifted my lower arm and motioned for Winston to join me.

"I see you are enjoying your treat."

Anxiously, I nodded like a child while eating my second truffle. I watched as he stood at the foot of the bed staring.

"Why are you staring?" I asked.

"If you could see your mocha skin in that red dress lying on silky black sheets covered in golden chocolates, you too would stare."

"Come join me," I responded in my Trinidadian accent.

I figured, why not keep the evening's excitement going? Winston walked around the side of the bed and sat at the head. Kissing my forehead, he fed me my third chocolate.

"What can I do for my island woman?" he asked, playing along.

"My feet, they are sore, please rub," I continued.

"Anything for you," he responded with a smile while giving me another chocolate.

"I can't eat any more. I'm going to be sick."

Winston laughed while pouring a handful of candy over my body. Pulling me on top of him, he kissed my top lip, and then sliding his lips down my body, he removed my shoes.

"Your kisses are delicious, but we are squishing the chocolates," I said.

Rising, I removed the clear empty vase from the nightstand and carefully scraped the candy into the vase. Immediately following, Winston grabbed my waist and tossed me onto the bed. Laughing, we began to cuddle and smooch. Winston's fitted boxers worked their way down to his ankles and he attempted to remove my panties. As tempting as he was, I was simply not in the mood for sex. I just wanted to cuddle and kiss.

"No, no, Desiree just wants to cuddle."

"But I can make Desiree feel so good," he said, pressing his pelvis into my hips.

Okay, convincing him was not going to be easy. I was going to try a different approach.

"But we just met. Desiree doesn't do things like that on a first date," I continued to role-play.

"Oh, I see. What does Desiree do on the first date?"

"I'll dance for you," I said, standing up on the bed.

Winston grinned like a snarling tiger and with a swift motion, hit the stereo remote.

"Let's see your moves," he said, lying back against the headboard.

As my arms crept up my body, I moved my hips from side to side. Soon I was drawn into a full erotic routine. Slowly lifting my dress, I revealed my red panties as I teased him with a quick peek. Winston rose and went to his drawer. Suddenly my feet were covered with five-dollar and ten-dollar bills. In full character, I slowly unzipped my dress and gave Winston a two-minute striptease. As my routine rounded, I stood there in my red panties. With my back faced to him, I looked over my shoulder and winked my eye. His attention was more erect than a private addressing a sergeant during hell week. Winston pulled me from my imaginary stage and onto the bed.

"What are you doing?" I asked.

"Pretend this is the champagne room."

I wasn't sure what that meant, but had a feeling it would lead to something nasty. Hesitantly, I continued to play along.

"No, no, Desiree's body is not for sale," I said, pulling away.

Winston went to the drawer once more. Intently following his actions, I felt my heart begin to pound. Winston walked back to the bed with his hands behind his back. He kissed the top of my feet, worked his way up my shin, and stopped just below my navel. Placing his chin on my stomach, he laid a crisp one-hundred-dollar bill in between my breasts.

"If I can have you for one minute, this is yours. If I can have you for two, this is yours," he said, placing another bill on top of the original.

He continued this proposition until ten portraits of Benjamin Franklin lay smiling atop my breasts.

"Ms. Desiree, all I need is ten minutes," he begged.

Before the period was put on the end of his last sentence, I had a brain freeze. *Wake up, Dorothy, we're not in Kansas anymore.*

Jumping up and completely breaking character, I yelled, "You think I'm a ho!"

Bemused, Winston started to stutter. "Desiree . . . I was just playing along."

"Fuck Desiree, this is Lily and I don't appreciate you acting like I'm some cheap-ass trick."

"You think one hundred dollars a minute is cheap?" he asked, hopping up from the bed.

Grabbing my dress and my shoes, I rushed into the restroom.

"Lily!" Winston shouted, trailing behind.

"You went too far Winston, too damn far!"

Stepping into the bathroom, I slammed the door, yet I could still hear Winston on the other side speaking.

"I thought you were still Desiree. I don't understand. I didn't mean to offend you. We were role-playing, right?"

Putting on my dress, I leaned over the sink and looked at my reflection in the mirror.

"Lily, please come out here and talk to me," he continued.

Still staring at my reflection, I saw a tear roll down my cheek. I knew my outburst was unnecessary; I don't know what happened. Perhaps it was my voice of conscience. I knew Winston did not think that I was a slut. But dating the twin of my ex was doing a number on my subconscious. Had my actions truly been whorish?

*Adults must be very cautious of the games we play, es-
pecially when the rules are not stated in the beginning.*

I gradually opened the door and peered out. Winston, wrapped in sheets, stood on the other side holding chocolates in his hand as a peace offering.

"Lily is my sweetheart, my baby. I would never disrespect my baby. Chocolates?" he said, holding out his
hand.

I melted into his arms as he slowly unwrapped a
chocolate mint truffle and plopped it into my mouth.

"I'm sorry," I said, garbling through the sweet.

"Would Lily like to come to bed?" Winston asked.

Pulling my body away from his, I responded, "Nothing personal but, I'm going to leave."

I began putting on my shoes.

"I don't think you should, it's too late, or shall I say
too early?"

"I'll be okay," I replied.

Kissing his cheek, I walked to the door while holding his hand.

"I'll still see you tomorrow?" he questioned.

Having no energy to discuss my concerns about tomorrow's banquet, I simply nodded and went to my
car. Winston stood in the door with his arm leaning
against the frame. Blowing me a kiss, he tilted his head
onto his biceps. Smiling, I caught his air kiss, placed
it over my heart, got in my SUV, and drove home.

Once home, I dragged my feet into the bathroom
and turned on the shower. The warm water splashed
onto my chest, and officially washed away all traces of
Desiree. After drying, I crawled my naked body into
my bed and pulled the covers up to my neck. Tonight
was quite interesting. I had met a charming stranger

who made acquaintances with an island stranger who stripped for a familiar man with strange reactions causing me to question the stranger within myself.

Looking upon the red dress hanging on the closet door, I whispered, "Thus the effect of the red dress. I cast you back into the closet, forever."

Removing my ponytail holder, I snuggled deeper into the pillow. At the end of a crazy night, my bed felt so comforting. Restful sleep was going to be my friend tonight. I didn't want to talk to anyone, nor write about my experience. I simply wanted to enjoy my bed, alone. Closing my eyes, I clicked my heels together. As I cuddled underneath my covers, my mind replayed one certainty.

"There is no place like home. There is no place like home."

12

Who's That Girl

Still exhausted from the night before, I finally made it out of the bedroom around noon. Throwing on an old Warren Sapp jersey and flip-flops, I walked sluggishly downstairs to start my lazy day. Ordering a pizza, I flipped on cartoons, sat on my futon, and watched old episodes of *Rugrats*. I just loved Angelica and her pranks. Enthused, I curled up on the futon and giggled as I continued to watch. Within minutes of beginning my relaxation downstairs, my phone rang. Luckily, I was prepared with the cordless tucked into the top of my sweats.

"Hello."

"Hi, babe, what are you doing?" Winston asked.

"Watching *Rugrats* and waiting for my pizza," I answered.

I was praying he didn't want to talk about last night,

and thankfully he didn't. Yet he did bring up the banquet.

"Are you driving tonight or would you like me to come and pick you up?"

"Oh yeah, about this evening. I don't think I should go."

"What?" he yelled.

"Well, your family will be there and they may be upset that I am there and this might ruin the night. I don't want to ruin your night."

"Well, maybe I should ask Susan. I'm sure she won't mind if my family is there."

"That's not cool. Why would you say that?"

"Are you coming or what?" Winston was agitated.

After a slight pause, I responded desolately, "I'll see you there."

"The ceremony starts at seven, hors d'oeuvres are served at six thirty. I'll e-mail you directions."

"Bye," I murmured.

A huge grumble started deep within my belly and roared from my lungs.

"I don't want to go!" I hollered, falling back onto the futon. Just then the dryer buzz eclipsed my yell, and so I rose, removed the towels, and put my dark clothing in. While folding my linens, I became more nervous about the thought of seeing Mr. and Mrs. Fulmore with Winston. *What if they think we've been dating all the while? What if they think I cheated on Wealth?* We rode to the lake together that one time. Though I was there to meet Wealth, when he showed up with his ex-girlfriend, I pretended to be with Winston. They weren't going to know what to think.

Walking to the closet to put up my towels, I heard the pizza guy pull into the driveway. Just in time, I was hungry. I gave the guy twelve dollars for my large cheese pizza, and rushed to the living room to partake. Between laundry, eating pizza, and watching television, three hours sped past. When I looked at the clock again, it was a little after five. I hadn't checked the e-mail for directions or prepared my attire for the evening. If the ceremony started at seven, I needed to be there at least by six forty-five. Rushing, I checked my e-mail for directions. The banquet hall was twenty minutes away from my house, which meant I needed to leave my home by six fifteen.

"I only have an hour to get ready," I said in a panic.

Hurrying upstairs while removing my jersey, I hopped in the shower and quickly freshened up. Forgetting to grab a towel, I scurried, dripping wet, into the bedroom closet to dry off while looking for a dress to wear. However, I didn't want to wear a dress. I'd rather wear a pantsuit, but I wasn't sure of the attire requirement, so I called Winston on his cell.

"Hi, sweetie," I said.

"Please don't tell any more bad news," he started.

"What happened?"

"Mom is upset with Dad over some comment, so she doesn't want him to come. Plus, Dr. Yerman was supposed to introduce the guest speaker, but he's stuck in surgery so I'm going to have to do his part."

"I'm sorry. I was just calling to see if the banquet was semiformal, because I wanted to wear a pantsuit."

"Wear whatever you want. I just want you there on my arm," he responded.

"Good. Everything is going to work out and I'll see you soon."

Winston hung up and I jetted to the closet to find an outfit. After careful elimination, I decided to wear one of the few designer suits I owned: a chocolate silk crepe pantsuit by Dolce & Gabbana. The pant leg was wide and unconstructed, yet the jacket was tailored with one medium-sized button for closure. I'd only worn the suit once, but I had had it for close to two years. Evelyn would've gawked at the idea of wearing a designer piece from four seasons ago. However, even on sale, the price of this outfit deserved at least ten wears, and I didn't care if it took me ten years to do it. Pulling the plastic off my dry cleaning, I discovered my mauve blouse looked ravishing against the chocolate brown. These two pieces along with my brown Vivienne Westwood pumps were going to be my ensemble for the evening. Quickly, I applied lotion, moisturizer, makeup, and clothing and left the house immaculately dressed by six fifteen. Although I had directions, I made a couple of wrong turns. Thank God there was no traffic and very few lights on the way; I made it to the banquet hall front door by 6:50.

I gracefully walked to the door, when a distinguished gentleman passed by wearing a polished tuxedo. He opened the door, I nodded thank you, and he followed me in. I prayed we were not going to the same event. However, I began to see more people in semiformal and formal attire. As I came closer to banquet hall C, it became apparent. This was a formal event. Embarrassed, I hesitated to enter the room. My suit was fabulous, but these women were in ball gowns, some of them sequined. This was already going to be an uncomfortable evening, but now I didn't even have my attire to fall back on. Great clothing is such a comfort zone for women. When all else fails, a magnificent outfit helps us make it through the pandemonium. It makes us feel better knowing that although we may feel like shit on the inside, on the outside we look marvelous.

"Are you going in, dear?" asked the woman standing behind me.

As her date opened the door, she motioned for me to walk in.

Slowly placing one foot in front of the other, I made my way into the hall just as the ceremony was about to begin. Immediately, I spotted Wealth. It was easier to tell the twins apart these days, for Winston was finally allowing his hair to grow back. Last summer, he and Wealth both had bald heads and the resemblance was eerie. I walked to the table, but not before stopping by the bar to get a glass of wine. Hopefully, this would calm my nerves and I could make it through the evening without additional embarrassment. Greeting me with a hug and a kiss on the cheek, Wealth spoke softly in my ear.

"You look wonderful. Glad you could make it."

"I'm underdressed. I didn't know it was a formal event," I whispered.

"You're fine. Technically, it's not formal. These people just use any reason to pull out their best wears."

Smiling nervously, I sat in the seat next to Wealth as

I glanced to the stage and saw Winston. I gave him a quick wave as he winked. Tensely, my legs shook underneath the table as I waited for Wealth to ask me about my relationship with his brother.

"Are you okay?" Wealth asked.

"Yes, why?"

"Because you rarely drink, yet you have finished your glass of wine and unless you have a vibrator in your purse, you are shaking like crazy."

"I'm a little nervous."

"What for? Winston already told me he was crazy about you. I messed up and he lucked up. Maybe we were mismatched from the start, but you're a good girl," Wealth said calmly, placing his hand on my leg.

Lowering my head, I gave a tiny smile. Then slightly turning toward Wealth, I responded softly, "Thank you."

He countered with his infamous wink and smile and soon the ceremony began. Just as the welcome started, Mrs. Fulmore appeared from nowhere. One minute Wealth and I were sitting at the table alone; then poof, just like the wicked witch, she was here ogling our every move.

"Where's Dad?" Wealth asked.

She responded with an exasperated huff and took a seat beside her son. Quietly, we sat and listened to the list of awards given for the evening. Finally, Winston received his award for outstanding community service. I never knew that Winston volunteered at the women's shelter every week, giving free exams and checkups to the battered and homeless. He truly was an exceptional man. As he accepted his award, Mrs. Fulmore stood and elegantly clapped her manicured fingertips together to acknowledge her son's excellence. As she sat, she leaned over and whispered to us, "I am so glad that you two came. It's good to see you trying to work things out."

"Oh, she didn't come with me. She is here with Winston," Wealth stated.

Instantly I dug my heel into the top of his foot, causing him to gasp for air. Mrs. Fulmore paused for a second; then tapping her fingers against the table she spoke scathingly. "Funny, when you two were kids, you never liked to share."

Without delay, I rose and went to the bar for another glass of wine. I couldn't believe this. I was standing at the plate waiting for her cunning pitch, prepared with a witty retort and everything. Yet the spin on her curveball still took me by surprise. That old lady was a slick "bitcher." But ashamed and infuriated, I refused to play her paltry game. The evening was almost over, so I remained over in the outfield, until it was time to go home. I listened to the final speaker, and as soon as he finished, everyone began to mingle. I hated to leave before speaking to Winston. But everyone was crowding around the table of honorees to take pictures, so I couldn't get to him. Frustrated, I sipped on my wine as I meandered over to the window and waited. Finally, I felt a soft tap on my shoulder.

I turned but before making actual eye contact, I said, "Congratulations," thinking it was Winston.

However, as I focused on the gentleman behind me, my wine spewed from my mouth and onto his crisp white tuxedo shirt.

"Desiree. I can't believe we meet again," he said.

"Um . . . um," I stammered.

"Thadius, remember?"

I vigorously nodded, but my mouth was welded shut.

"I wanted so badly to see you again and here you are. This could be a sign."

"A sign that all hell is about to break loose," I muttered to myself.

Suddenly I saw Winston making his way through the crowd and heading in my direction. Moving slightly to my left, I attempted to hide behind Thad's slender build.

"I must go," I said to Thad in my island accent.

Abruptly, I skated across the room and posed daintily by the stage. Within minutes, Winston walked up and gave me a hug. As he attempted to pull me over to his family, I resisted by pretending to stumble and hurt my ankle.

"These damn heels," I remarked. "I need to sit right here."

Grabbing the nearest chair, I took a seat at a table several feet away from Mrs. Fulmore. Winston kneeled beside me to take a look at my ankle.

"I'm okay. I'll be right here. Go enjoy yourself," I said in hopes he would go away so that I could vanish into the night.

"I want to enjoy the night with you by my side," Winston said with a smile.

Ordinarily this comment would've warmed my heart, but at that moment the only side I wanted to see was outside. Plus, my three glasses of wine were starting to show their own sides.

"I don't feel so well. Maybe I should go home."

Placing my head on the table, I sensed trouble breathing down my neck.

"Dr. Fulmore, congratulations," Thad said.

Keeping my head on the table, I prayed he didn't notice me. Yet my karma was not going to let me off that easy.

"There you are. I have something for you, don't leave before I can give it to you," I heard Thad's voice ring in my head.

"Have you two met?" Winston asked curiously.

"Why, yes. Desiree does leave a lasting impression," he mentioned before walking away.

"Why did he call you Desiree? Does he know Desiree? How many people have you done Desiree for?"

Immediately, I begin stuttering. "What? I don't . . . he doesn't . . . I have never *done* Desiree for anyone but you. I don't know him."

Suddenly his mother and brother approached the table.

"Winston, I want to make sure the photographer takes a picture with you and your plaque. I must show all of the ladies at the next tea."

"Well, brother, I am about to leave. I am proud of you. Lily, it was good to see you," said Wealth.

Winston gave his brother a hug, just when the photographer came over and asked to take a family picture. Swiftly, I moved to the side.

"Come on, Lily, get in the picture," Winston suggested.

Shaking my head, I motioned for him to go ahead. Conversely, he took my hand and pulled me into the frame.

"The photographer said he wanted a picture of the family," Mrs. Fulmore reiterated, proposing I stay to the side.

"Hush, Mom, and smile," Winston said.

I plastered on my smile for the camera and thought this night could not end fast enough. As soon as the photographer moved from his position, Thadius appeared once more and in his left hand I saw hints of my ruby choker. He must have found it on the dance floor. I lied to Winston, and I was going to be discovered. Taking deep breaths, I could only think of one thing to do. My knees buckled and I suspiciously fell out onto the floor to cause a distraction.

"Lily!" Winston rushed to the floor to revive me.

As I stayed there, I heard the rumbling conversations grow into a fervent commotion. Lying there, motionless, I felt Winston's warm hands against my skin checking for a pulse. Just then, I remembered I was in a banquet filled with doctors. If I lay there long enough, they were going to know that I was faking. Damn! I had to awake slowly from my phony state of unconsciousness. So, blinking uncontrollably, I gradually opened my eyes and focused on Winston.

"Are you okay?" he asked with grave concern.

"I think so. What happened?" I responded faintly.

Thank God, I saw Thad nowhere in sight. However, the choker was lying in my seat, so as Winston lifted me from the floor, I swiftly took my bum and knocked the choker onto the floor and kicked it underneath the table. Luckily, everyone was still so stunned by my incident that no one noticed. Winston was still checking my vitals as I sat with my head leaned against his arm.

"Are you a diabetic? Are you anemic?" he questioned.

I continuously shook my head no.

"That guy went to get you some water," said Winston, referring to Thad.

"Maybe I had too much to drink. I just need some air," I stated, rushing to leave the room.

However, Thad met us at the table before I could take a few steps forward.

"Here you go," he said while handing me the water.

I nodded, took the water, and continued walking away.

"Hold up. Where's the necklace?" he asked.

Confused, Winston continued to escort me out of the room. With his mother and brother following behind, we walked down the hall and stood in front by the parking lot. That was a close call.

I shouldn't have lied; however, I couldn't explain my fake club identity at the doctors' banquet.

"Are you sure you are all right, dear?" asked Mrs. Fulmore.

"I think so."

"Maybe you shouldn't drink so much," she said with an acerbic smile.

I ignore her comment and continued drinking my water. Just as the storm calmed, Thad burst through the door like lightning.

"Here it is."

"Damn it!" I mouthed silently.

Reluctantly, I removed the choker from his hand while holding on to Winston's arm. Everyone was staring at me, and Thadius would not walk away. Suddenly I realized everyone was waiting on me to do introductions. I couldn't be Desiree; the Fulmores would think I was crazy, and I couldn't be Lily, for Thad would call me out. Either way, I was bound to look like a nutcase.

"Desiree, is everything fine?" asked Thad.

"Yes, Desiree, are you okay?" mocked Winston.

"Who is Desiree?" questioned Mrs. Fulmore.

Still, I remained quiet. Finally, Winston formally introduced himself and his family. During introductions, I quickly placed the choker in my purse.

"What was that?" inquired Winston.

"A choker I had on," I muttered. "Thanks," I said to Thad, praying he would just walk away. However, I had no such luck.

"I found it on the floor after you left last night. I put it in the car. Who knew I would see you again tonight?"

"Who knew?" I said as my Caribbean accent slipped out.

In awkward silence, we all stood for two seconds that passed indolently like two hours.

Finally, breaking the silence, Thad remarked, "Well, okay. Desiree, it was a pleasure seeing you again. It was nice to meet everyone. You guys have a pleasant evening."

He just had to keep saying that freakin' name. Finally, Thad turned and walked away. All eyes stared at me. But I gazed off into the heavens and prayed for some sort of divine intervention.

"What was that about?" Winston asked. "Let me see the choker."

While I slowly pulled the jewelry from my purse, Wealth interjected, "I gave you that."

"Yes, I know! I'm ready to leave."

Annoyed by the entire episode, I grabbed Winston's arm and angled my body toward the car.

"Yeah, I'm taking off," Wealth said before walking away.

His mom followed and, giving her son a hug, she once again sang his praises and kissed his cheek.

"You have a good evening," she said to Winston.

Then turning to me, she spoke candidly. "And you, whoever you are. Go home and sober up so that the rest of your weekend is pleasant."

Walking away, she turned back, gave her son another smile, and disappeared just as she had appeared.

"Now is not the time, but you have some serious explaining to do," Winston said.

"I know," I stated simply.

He returned inside to say good-bye to his colleagues, and we mingled in the crowd for a few more minutes before he followed me home.

Once we got into my dwelling, Winston closed the door behind me and stayed positioned there with his back against the frame. I walked through the house and lit a few candles to set the mood for the evening.

"Don't try to create a romantic setting. I'm not sure if I am staying after I hear what you have to say."

"Come sit down, sweetie."

Reluctantly, Winston walked into the living room and sat on the love seat diagonal from the futon. After removing my shoes and turning on some soft music, I began to explain.

"I just met him last night on the dance floor. I didn't want to give him my real name, so I told him it was Desiree. My choker must have fallen onto the dance floor and he was returning it. I didn't think I would ever see him again."

The entire time Winston was shaking his head. I wasn't sure if he believed me or if he thought I was crazy. Nonetheless, I continued. "I'm sorry I lied and said I didn't know him. But I froze up."

"So you passed out because . . ."

"I don't know. I think my sugar level was low. I was so nervous about the situation that I started hyperventilating."

I was coming clean; however, I was not about to admit I fainted intentionally; he really would think that I was insane. As I listened to my own excuse, it did sound like crazy-person behavior.

"And you expect me to believe all this."

Walking over to the love seat, I got on my knees and placed my head in his lap.

"Please," I said, batting my large doe eyes.

Winston leaned over and kissed my forehead. "You are crazy. What about Desiree, you just made that up?"

I nodded vigorously. "She's actually a friend from college. I promise, I have never done that before. I just got caught up in the moment."

"What am I going to do with you?"

"I don't know, but as far as your mom is concerned you might as well paint a scarlet J on my forehead, 'cause she thinks I am a juiced-up Jezebel."

"No, she doesn't," he said.

"Better yet, an M for maniacal, money-hungry minx, or an S for schizophrenic slut," I continued to babble.

"Hold on. I don't think you are any of those things

and I know you don't think of yourself like that. So it doesn't matter."

"Yes, it does. I want to impress your mom."

"Then just be yourself," he said, lifting me off the floor and into his arms. "In the meantime, you need to go to bed. I think you really did have a little too much to drink."

We walked arm in arm upstairs to the bedroom. Winston went into the bathroom and started my bathwater as I removed my clothing. Lighting the candles in the bathroom, he helped me into the tub. After removing his shirt and slacks, Winston leaned into the water and sponged me off. As he wiped the bubbles off my moistened breasts, he began to softly suck on my nipples. With my eyes closed, I leaned back and felt his soft lips against my chest, my neck, and my cheek. Finally, our lips locked. Gradually pulling me from the water, Winston wrapped my body in the towel and drew me into the bedroom. As I reclined down on the bed Winston continued kissing all of my wet spots dry; all but one. He circled my thighs with his tongue, then moved quickly up to my belly button. Soaking wet with excitement, I pulsated waiting for him to lick the moisture in between my legs. However, he continued to move opposite that direction. What was he doing? I wondered. This was the perfect opportunity for oral play, and I was too tired for anything else. I just wanted him to please me, but I didn't know how to ask him. Therefore, I just applied slight pressure to the top of his head in hopes he got the point. Instead, his neck stiffened and it became a tug-of-war between my breasts and my naval.

Finally, he lifted up and asked, "What are you doing?"

Embarrassed, I said nothing. I had been with guys who have tried to push my head into their private areas and I knew how infuriating it was. However, with those men, I made it clear ahead of time that I wasn't going to give them head. Winston had made no such declaration, so why wouldn't he go down on me? I silently glanced into his eyes, then down to my vagina, back up to his eyes, and then back down again.

"You want me to go down on you?" he asked, lifting up from my body.

Turning away, I nodded yes.

"I don't do that. I thought I told you," he remarked.

Baffled, I turned to him and spoke. "What? You don't do that?"

"No. I must be in a serious committed relationship before I have oral sex with a woman. I have only been that close to my ex-fiancée. I don't have random oral sex."

"I'm random?" I said, slowly coming down from my lustful high.

"What I mean is, we have protected sex, right? If I go down on you, what are we supposed to do? I'm not trying to be funny, but I don't know who you are sleeping with and we are not having any kind of unprotected intimacy."

Dejected, I fell back onto the pillow. "Wow."

"I'm not saying I'll never do it. I'm just saying not right now."

I flicked my eyes toward him and poked out my bottom lip.

"Would you go down on me?" he asked curiously.

"Hell nah!" I said with a smirk.

"Exactly."

Turning over, I pulled the comforter on top of my body. Winston enthusiastically tickled me underneath the covers.

"Stop it. Stop it!" I yelled while laughing.

"Come on, baby, you do me and I'll do you," Winston joked.

"Leave me alone."

He rolled himself up in the comforter, almost pushing me off the bed. We faced each other on top of the mattress.

"You're special," he said.

Giving him a twisted grin, I stuck out my tongue and snickered. I reached over and grabbed my journal from the nightstand and began to write.

"What are you writing?" he asked.

"I normally don't let people read what I write, but when I finish you can see."

I finished my page and handed the book to Winston.

"May I read aloud?" he asked.

I motioned for him to continue.

"So few times, we come across men with sexual scruples that when we do, we make them feel like they are the wrongdoers. Not to sound vain, but no man has ever told me no—not sexually, at least. Sure, I have heard I was special, so special that he couldn't wait to have me. Yet never have I heard I was so special that he wanted to wait."

Nevertheless, women should not base their sexual decision on someone else's pronouncement of their importance. We should know how special we are to ourselves and this assessment should be the only reason why we decide to go forth or more importantly to wait.

"Good night."

13

Listen to the Signs

I woke up the next morning, bright and early, while Winston was still fast asleep. I got up and prepared for church. While I was downstairs cooking breakfast, I heard Winston creep down the steps. Sneaking into the kitchen, he snuggled up behind and spun me around. Light-headed and dizzy, I fell into his arms. My head pounded as I attempted to stand upright.

"My head. Don't do that. I can't take it."

Laughing, Winston responded, "You're a wino."

"You know I rarely drink, your family makes me nervous. If I keep dating you, I might as well sign up for AA right now."

"You go sit down, I'll finish this," Winston said while flipping my pancakes.

I went into the living room, sat on the futon, and turned on the television.

"Hey, Winston, did a teenager named Shannon call you? She was one of the girls at Sam's party."

"Nope."

"Well, she's gonna. I think she is looking for a doctor. She says she is okay, but who knows?"

"Okay."

After a few minutes, we sat at the bar and ate pancakes and hash browns. Winston added an omelet to his breakfast.

"You want to go to church with me?" I asked.

"Not this morning, I have to go by the office and review some paperwork."

"You working today?" I pouted.

"Just for a few hours."

An hour later, Winston softly kissed my lips, got in his car, and drove off. I rushed upstairs to finish dressing. While putting on my earrings, I noticed Winston's toothbrush in the bathroom.

"He left his toothbrush over here," I commented sentimentally.

Did that mean we had taken our relationship to the next level? We were obviously at the "leaving personal items stage." First it was a toothbrush, next it would be underwear, and then a full change of clothing. Yes, it was convenient, but it was really just another way of marking territory. Winston kept his hygiene bag in his car, and he left with it this morning; therefore, this little gesture was surely intentional. It was sweet, but was I ready for the next level?

Ironically, the sermon that day was about building and nourishing relationships in a godly manner. The preacher discussed praying for a mate that will complement your attributes and realizing that everything we wanted was not always what God intended for us to have. I hadn't been to church in two Sundays, but today when I attended, the sermon was on relationships. I couldn't help but think God was talking to me. So many times, I knew my relationships were not created from a spiritual connection, but from earthly ties. I was never one to pray for God to bring me a man 'cause I never had problems in that department. Plus, praying for a man seemed so desperate. Isn't that shameful and crazy? How can anyone be embarrassed to show desperation in front of God, who knows the state of all beings even when they don't? This was not to justify my actions; however, I never had time to pray for a man, because as soon as one went away, another was right there to take his place. Never thinking to pray for the right man, I settled for the "right now" man. Which was why my relationships came and went. Further contemplating this situation, I realized that I did want a man who was going to nourish and feed me spiritually. He might not be a churchgoing saint, yet I prayed he was the man the Most High had chosen, instead of the man Lily had chosen.

"Okay, God, I am going to have my eyes open. I will listen to your signs and I will receive the one you have in store for me."

After my little talk with the Creator, I decided to go to Sarah's house before heading home. As I was sitting at the light, my cell phone rang. Rumbling through my purse, I grabbed the phone just before it went to voice mail.

"Hello," I answered hastily.

"Hello, may I speak with Dick?" said the male on the line.

"Who!"

"Dick!" the man repeated.

Baffled, I couldn't respond.

"Hello," he said.

"I'm sorry, you have the wrong number," I stuttered with a lemon-sized lump in my throat.

Suddenly the blaring car horns took me from this sour coma as I saw the light had turned green. Slowly pulling off, I still couldn't believe some guy called my phone asking for Dick.

"Could that have been . . . nah . . . no way."

Pulling up to Sarah's house, I looked out of my window and up to the sky. Not sure what I was looking for, I continued to stare as if some huge D was going to form within the clouds.

"I know I asked for a sign. But how are we supposed to know when it's a sign from God or a sign from the devil trying to throw a snag in the line of communication?" I whispered toward heaven.

Slowly, I walked to Sarah's front door and rang the bell.

"Well, hello, darling," answered Mrs. Richard, Omar's mom.

We hugged immediately.

"When did you return?" I asked.

"Yesterday. Come in. Join us for brunch. I heard you were taking care of my granddaughter while I was gone."

I followed her through the home and onto the patio, where I was greeted by Sarah, Omar, and Carmen. Taking a seat, I made faces with Carmen. Suddenly two hands wrapped around my eyes and I received a sloppy kiss on the shoulder.

"Long time, no see," said the male voice.

Briskly removing his hands, I turned around to see none other than Patch standing over my shoulder.

"Patch. Good to see you," I said with a faint smile.

"Yeah. You look different," he stated, staring me up and down.

"Maybe, because you're looking through both eyes. Where's your patch, Patch?"

Smiling, he leaned back in his lawn chair and answered, "Even God rested on Sunday."

Giving him a mystified look, I mumbled, "I know this man is not comparing himself to God."

I had a hard enough time comparing him to the average man, let alone a higher being; but hey, if you don't have self-love, who is going to love you? I simply smiled at him and poured myself a glass of tea.

"Sarah, I need to speak with you."

Sarah stood and grabbed her glass of water.

"Mom, can you watch Carmen?" she asked.

"I got it," Omar said.

Sarah handed him Carmen and the burping pad. All the while she made eye contact with his mom.

"She'll be okay," his mom reassured her.

Sarah and I walked into the home and sat in the living area.

"You still don't trust Omar, do you?"

"It's not that I don't trust him, it's just that he still has a long way to go. The other day, he let Carmen stay in a wet Pamper for hours. He said he thought we were out of Pampers and now she has diaper rash," she fussed.

"He's learning. He's making an effort, that must mean something."

"Yeah. But I am glad Claire is back."

"I heard you call her mom, that's so sweet," I said, pinching her rosy cheeks.

"Anyway. What's up with you?"

I began telling Sarah about my after-church occurrence. Giggling the entire time, she listened as I explained my prayer and my mysterious phone call.

"What do you think it means?" I asked after finishing.

"It means God wants you to call Dick."

"No, it doesn't," I replied hastily.

"You don't know. It might. Just call him. You know you want to hear his voice."

"But—" I tried to interrupt.

"But, nothing. I know you're dating Winston, but it's okay to call Dick. You guys ended on a bad note, you need resolution."

Placing my head in my hands, I hated to admit she was right. Not one day passed that I didn't think about Dick. I even thought about him at times when I was with Winston.

"I'll think about calling . . . maybe . . . I don't know."

"Until you resolve things, you will not be able to move on. I think he's the one for you. But if you don't, then end it for good and let go."

Hastening from the room, Sarah dashed back to the patio. Returning shortly, she had a crying Carmen in her arms.

"I didn't even hear her," I stated.

"I didn't either. I just knew she was crying. Amazing, isn't it?"

"Yeah, like superpowers," I joked.

"We are in tune. It's just something that happens naturally when you love someone. You know when they need you and you know when they are all right."

Sarah began to feed Carmen as she continued to speak.

"Look, I don't believe there is that one special person for everyone. We meet too many people in life. But I do believe that if we are honest with God, and ourselves, couples can have a special, lasting relationship. I don't know why we meet some of the people we meet. I mean, look at me and Omar. I surely could have done better. But if it weren't for him, I wouldn't have her and she is the best thing that could ever have happened to me. You better be glad this wasn't Dick's baby or I would be breaking down his door to become his wife."

Smacking my lips, I turned away from Sarah, and she handed me a quieted Carmen as she went to use the restroom. Cooing and cuddling, I bounced her on my lap until Sarah returned.

"Well, Sarah, I'm going home," I said, placing Carmen in her arms.

"So soon? You and Patch haven't had any time to talk." She laughed.

"Please."

"Please nothing. God might have sent Patch down here for you."

Slowly turning, I raised one eyebrow and spoke. "If that's the case, then God is going to have to descend and deliver that message in person, 'cause a sign ain't gonna do it."

I kissed Carmen on the forehead and Sarah on the cheek, then began my departure home.

My evening passed quickly and before long it was time to retire to the bedroom. Monday mornings are difficult enough without having a good night's rest. I crawled into bed thinking about my elusive phone call.

"Please give me the strength, courage, and intuition to make the right decisions. I will listen, I promise."

Just then my phone rang. Startled, I froze.

"Is that you, God?" I whispered.

Hesitantly, I leaned over and answered, "Hello."

"Hey, sweetie, it's me, Tam."

Sighing aloud, I was relieved to hear her voice.

"How are you and the baby?" I asked.

"We're fine, I didn't want anything. I just wanted to tell you I love you and that I'm here if you ever need me."

"I love you too."

"Okay, well, it's late. I'm going to call you tomorrow."

"Okay, bye," I said just before disconnecting.

Lying in bed, I stared at the ceiling. I guess that spiritual connection crosses miles and miles.

"Okay, God, I hear you loud and clear. Oh, and one more thing, just in case you did send Patch down here for me. Please, oh please, just break it to me gently."

14

He's Mine,
Now Go Away

I arrived to work early Monday morning. Stopping by Sarah's desk, I placed a welcome-back card in her chair. In her fourth week of chemotherapy, her spirit was still positive and I was extremely proud of her. Walking away from Sarah's desk, I ran into Susan by the coffeemaker. Cordially, we spoke as I tried to avoid eye contact. Unfortunately, before I got out of her eye view, she asked me about Winston.

"Have you heard from Dr. Fulmore lately?"

"Yes, I saw him Saturday," I said, continuing to walk.

Susan turned away to add sugar to her morning addiction. I briskly walked to my desk and buried my head in my paperwork. Seconds later, I saw Susan shadowing over my cubicle. Lurking around my desk, she continued to badger me about Winston.

"Did he mention me at all?"

"Yes, he did."

Still focusing my eyes on my work, I did not look up at Susan once. However, I could feel her temperament change with that response. I should have said no, not at all.

"Well, we had such a great time. I thought he would call. What did you guys do on Saturday?"

Flipping through the pages in my notebook, I answered nonchalantly, "I went to an awards banquet where he was honored."

Susan propped herself on the corner of my desk and crossed her legs. With her left hand holding a coffee cup, she politely closed my book with her right, which forced me to center on her as she leaned in and asked, "Does he have a girlfriend?"

Squinting my eyes while tilting my head to the side, I answered, "I think he is seeing someone."

"Well, why didn't he say so?" Susan remarked.

"Maybe he's keeping his options open," I said before returning to my notebook.

However, as Susan mulled over my comment, I decided to add my statement. "Or he's just a private person and I think it's a new relationship."

Hopping down from my desk, Susan took a sip of her aromatic, hot roasted almond coffee.

"By no means am I desperate," Susan commented. "However, I have learned that you never get what you want by waiting for it to come to you. I know we connected. I'm going to call him and ask him out again."

With a small nod, Susan walked powerfully away from my desk. Without hesitance, I grabbed the phone to call Winston. After seconds of waiting, he came to the line and spoke.

"Hey, sweetie, it's Lily. Listen."

Suddenly, like a jack-in-the-box, Susan popped up in front of my desk with all ears in my conversation. Stuttering, I tried to complete a sentence. "I just . . . want to tell you. Sarah is back at work today . . . so I'll be on time this evening. Okay, bye."

I quickly hung up and smiled at Susan.

"Who was that?" she questioned.

"My friend. We have Pilates tonight. What do you need?" I asked with curtness.

"Don't tell Winston about our little conversation. I don't want to scare him off."

This time she added a wink to her nod and strolled down the hall. As Susan got a few feet away, my phone rang. Knowing it was Winston, I waited until she was out of sight before answering, "This is Lily."

"What was that about?" Winston asked on the other line.

"I can't talk right now. I'll call you at lunch. But expect a call today from Susan."

"Lily, what is going on?"

"Nothing, baby. I'll call you later," I said with sweet overtones.

My day actively got going around noon. By this time Nehri and I were discussing our ideas on "Say it all with one phrase" cards. She thought we should use famous quotes from the scholars and historians. I thought we should make up our own quirky one-liners. Compromising, we decided to do both for our presentation next week. Nehri and I were both talented writers and intelligent individuals, and I felt a tiny bit of competition brewing and as usual, I welcomed the challenge. We were going to display our finest efforts to persuade each other as well as our coworkers on whose idea was the best. The cards must be witty, meaningful, and catchy. My work was surely cut out for me this week. Strolling back to my desk, I stopped by the reception area, but I didn't see Sarah. Therefore, I decided to go to lunch alone. However, as I grabbed my purse, Sarah came rushing from the bathroom.

"Are you trying to leave me?" she asked in her best ghetto-girl stance.

"You weren't in place and I am hungry."

"Let's go," Sarah said, pulling on my handbag.

As we walked out the door, I quickly grabbed my cell phone and called Winston.

"You are not going to talk on that phone the entire lunchtime."

"Aren't you feisty today?" I responded.

Walking ahead of Sarah, I continued to use the phone. Once I finally talked with Winston, he told me that Susan had already called him. She also asked him out. Turning her down, he told her he was on call at the hospital until Thursday, which was true. Finally, Winston said he would call her back later on in the week. I told him about our morning conversation and we both saw that it made no bearing on her judgment to ask him on a date.

"She doesn't care if you have a girlfriend," I told him.

"If she knew you were the girlfriend, it would end all of this crap."

"I'm too far in to say something now. You have to get rid of her."

"I don't like this mess. It's your fault."

"Maybe I'll introduce her to Wealth. She does that nod and wink thing like him," I said.

After a sigh, Winston gave his final remark. "You have done enough. Forget about it. I have to go."

I hung up just as we pulled into the sandwich café. Standing in line, I gazed upon all of the condiments. Watching as the ladies prepared the wraps, melts, and subs, I entertained an intriguing daydream.

The wraps became our friends, the melts our careers, and the subs our mates. The condiments were specific attributes and characteristics. Wheat was wholesome, tuna was healthy, pickles were sincerity, lettuce was wealth, tomatoes were intelligence, olives were dishonesty, and onions were determination. Moving down the line, I continued. Mayonnaise was sex appeal, mustard was vanity, oil was style, but vinegar was domineering, relish was humility, green peppers were wit, salt was loyalty, and pepper was excitement. Smiling, I began to build my perfect mate. Just then, Sarah tapped my shoulder and awakened me from my dream.

"She's talking to you," Sarah said, pointing to the woman with plastic gloves.

"May I help you?"

"Yes, please. I'll have a six-inch tuna on wheat with a little lettuce, lots of pickles, green peppers, and a few onions. I want mayonnaise, but no mustard, some oil but only a hint of vinegar. I definitely want salt and pepper and a small bit of relish."

"Is that all?" she asked.

"Oh no, I want lots of tomatoes, but can I have them on the side?"

"You sure are specific," said Sarah, waiting in line.

"Well, you have to ask for what you want or you will never get it," I commented.

She had no idea that I just ordered the perfect man. Sure, there were many more qualities that I would or wouldn't like, but this was an excellent beginning. I walked to a table by the window and began to partake of my creation as Sarah sat down.

"Why are you eating the tomatoes by themselves?" she questioned.

Thinking back to my daydream, I smiled and responded, "Because they enhance the meal, preparing my mouth for what I'm about to eat. If there are no tomatoes, then why eat the sub?"

"What?" she said with a baffled look. "I don't even like tomatoes."

Giggling, I quietly commented, "That's why you are with Omar."

Other than conversation about Carmen, we ate the remainder of lunch silently. Upon finishing my sub, I glanced over at my last tomato and slowly inhaled each bite. Shaking her head, Sarah resurrected her lunch questionnaire.

"Okay, why did you save one tomato to eat last?"

"It's the icing on the cake, like conversation after sex. It adds value to what you just ingested and leaves you wanting more."

"You're weird," Sarah stated with bewilderment.

"No, I'm not."

"It's just a sub."

"It's a creation," I said while rising to toss my trash.

As Sarah followed, she whispered in my ear, "No, sweetie, it's just a sub."

As we walked to the car, my daydream faded, and soon I realized she was right. It was only a sub. Everything from computers to fast food can be specifically made to preference. Yet when it comes to our mates, we get what we get. I think love and the deli concept need a formal introduction. Because when I say hold the olives, I mean hold the olives, damn it!

Chuckling underneath my breath, I started heading back to work. As we parted our ways to finish the workday, Sarah called out, "Don't forget the concert on Wednesday night."

Nodding, I walked back to my desk to set up for my new assignment. As usual, when I became engrossed in a new project my day passed quickly. Desiring to finish my thoughts, I stayed at work an extra hour and made it home around seven that evening. I decided to wash my hair tonight so that it would look nice and refreshed for the concert on Wednesday. I wanted to do something different. Thus, after flipping through several magazines, I came up with a new and slightly daring hairstyle. Wouldn't Sarah be surprised in the morning when she saw me with my Afro?

Flipping through the channels, I locked in on Joan and Melissa Rivers chatting about Grammy and Academy style and fashion. Although I had never cared much about the stylish and the less than stylish, I watched intently. I found it amazing that people put so much stock in what others wore to red-carpet events. They actually had a two-hour-long episode about it.

Everyone knows that designers live for the fabulous and famous to adorn their bodies in designer originals. It can make or break a designer's career. But what everyday person wears this stuff? The world has many more everyday people than famous people. I wish just one time all the famous people would come dressed in everyday clothing: jeans, T-shirts, and khakis. What a statement that would be! Would it mean they are less fabulous and who would get best dressed? And, on that note, who creates the list for *People* magazine's "50 sexiest people?" Our country holds millions; why is it that the people making the list are famous ones? They should at least search the country and pull some un-knowns into the magazine. To only pull from Holly-wood gives us regular folk unfair expectations. Not everyone can have skin like Halle, legs like Nicole, lips like Angelina, or hips like Beyoncé. What did people base beauty on when there was no Hollywood? I think we need to start celebrating the everyday working mom who has barely enough time to fix her hair or the dad who works two jobs just to support his family. They can be sexy. Why give the credit to those people who already stay in the limelight? This is why our kids are starving themselves and getting implants. I don't know if things will ever change, but we need to be cautious with the message we are sending out to our youth. Although I was teaching creative writing at the youth home, I wanted my kids to learn self-worth. No one had ever told them that they were beautiful, just by being them-selves, and they surely didn't get it from the media. We complain about the situation of our youth today, but when are we going to start being responsible for the bullshit we feed them with? Sure, it does start in the home, but a parent can only do so much when all other glittering forces are saying this is who you need to be.

After finishing my hair, I grabbed my journal and just before turning in I wrote:

> *There is nothing wrong with fashion and certainly nothing wrong with nice things. But they don't make us who we are or define our place in society. It's important we learn this, 'cause if the extravagance ever fades, we wouldn't want our character to vanish as well.*

Good night.

15

Star of My Show

Sarah continuously buzzed my phone on Wednesday. She was so excited about the show; you would think we were thirteen-year-olds going to our first concert without our parents. First, she wanted to know what I was wearing; next, she wanted to know how early we should get there. Her final question was quite unusual.

"Do you think she'll ask a few audience members to come join her in a song?"

"No. Why would she do that? She's not a lounge singer."

"I know. But I have been to shows where the audience participates."

"This is not that type of show. I saw Meshell N'degeocello perform in Atlanta. She sang her songs, played her bass, told a few stories, and that was it. It's a sexy show, but there is no place for audience participation. Sorry."

"Fine. I'll see you at five o'clock," she said, discouraged.

I didn't mean to laugh, but she was so happy to have a night out, she was just beside herself. Motherhood will have a woman excited to simply walk to the mailbox alone, 'cause it is the alone part that causes sheer delirium.

At 4:55 p.m., my phone rang once more. It was Winston.

"You are going to the show tonight, right? So I was calling to ask your breakfast plans. I was hoping to see you in the morning before work. I can meet you for breakfast."

"That would be lovely."

"I can be at your house at six o'clock. We can eat at the café down the street."

"Sounds good."

As soon as we hung up, I saw Sarah whipping around the corner of my cubicle.

"Time to go," she said, tapping her watch.

I organized my desk, grabbed my purse, and headed out the door. With Sarah interlocking my arm she rushed me toward the car.

"Damn girl. The show doesn't start until eight o'clock."

"But the seats aren't reserved. It's general admission. I want to get there early."

"How early?"

"Around six thirty?"

"How about seven o'clock," I debated.

Nodding hesitantly, she finally agreed. After hugging, we parted and agreed to meet at the spot at seven o'clock. Riding home, I started organizing my evening ensemble. I planned to wear jeans and a silky tank top.

Of course, I would have to wear a nice high sandal to pull the look together.

After showering, I danced around the room to Meshell's latest album. As I was strapping up my right sandal, my phone rang. I was sure it was Sarah, and I was correct.

"Yes, dear, I am on my way."

"I can't go," she cried loudly.

"What do you mean? You have to go."

"Carmen is sick. Claire says she has been crying all day and now I think she has a fever. I have to stay just in case I have to take her to the hospital."

Silently, my disappointment showed.

"Why don't you and Winston go?" she continued.

"He's working tonight."

"Well, you have your ticket, please go and enjoy yourself. Tell me how it was."

The fact that Sarah couldn't go took most of the fun out of going. True, I wanted to see the concert, but I was just as thrilled about an evening out with my girl.

"You're going to still go?" she questioned.

"I guess."

"Sorry. I can't leave my baby."

"I understand. I'll talk with you tonight after the show," I responded before hanging up.

Eventually, I wobbled downstairs with my right shoe on my foot and my left shoe in my right hand. I flipped off the radio and walked into the kitchen. Making myself a salad, I ate standing in the center of the living room. All of my excitement had ceased. I might as well sell my ticket. In fact, the more I gave this thought, the more I hoped I could sell the ticket. Finishing my salad, I placed the bowl in the sink, put on my left shoe, and went upstairs to brush my teeth. Minutes later, I got in my car and headed for the theater. It only took fifteen minutes and I was pulling into the parking lot. Grabbing my ticket from the glove compartment, I walked to the front and began my covert ticket-scalping plan. Secretly checking the hands of the people in line, I walked up and down the sidewalk quietly asking if anyone needed a ticket. Most people already had tickets and the ones who didn't were suspicious of me.

"I am never going to get rid of this ticket," I complained.

As the line shortened, I realized that I might as well go in and enjoy the show. I walked into the scenic theater and down the aisle toward the front. Since I was alone, I should be able to find one seat on the end or in between two couples. While glancing down the aisles, I saw a single seat on the third row. Increasing my pace, I headed in that direction. As I grew near, I heard someone calling my name.

"Who is calling me?" I whispered.

With a quick turn, I saw no one, and so I continued to the third row. As I was leaning over to ask the couple if the seat was taken, I felt a pair of arms wrap around my waist. Instantly, my reflex kicked in. Whipping around, I elbowed the man in the stomach.

"Ughh!" he groaned, bending at the waist.

Focusing my eyes on him, I began to feel a pounding ache in my chest as well.

"Patch?" I choked.

"Yeah," he said, gaining his breath.

Grabbing his arm, I helped him stand straight.

"What are you doing here?" I asked.

"Other than getting beat up?"

"Sorry," I said.

"I used to date one of the backup singers. She gave me tickets. Who are you here with?"

"I'm supposed to be here with Sarah, but Carmen got sick, so I'm here alone."

"Not anymore," he said, taking my hand.

As we walked over to his seat in the side section of the fifth row, I slowly removed my hand from his. Patch was truly sweet, but I did not like him. I didn't know what it was, but he annoyed me. As we sat, I couldn't help but think I should have given the ticket away. From my peripherals, I could see him grinning at me with that stupid patch on his eye.

"What's wrong?" he asked.

"I'm upset Sarah couldn't make it."

"But see how God stepped in and now I'm here?"

Turning to him, I responded, "So this was the work of God?"

"Everything is. You know what I'm saying?"

I was hoping we could get through that one evening without that phrase, but so much for dreaming. Making a disgusting face, I slumped down in my seat.

"What's wrong now?" he continued to ask.

Addressing him straightforward, I replied, "The patch. I hate that patch. I don't understand why you wear it, if you are not performing. It's not who you are and you look like a pirate. It's a costume! And costumes should be left for the stage."

Nodding, Patch excused himself and walked away. Feeling remorseful, I sank farther into my seat. I didn't know what had come over me. I had hurt his feelings, when he was only trying to be nice. Closing my eyes, I tried to find the true source of my anguish. Sure, I despised the patch, but I thought it was something greater causing the frustration. Minutes later, I felt a tap on my shoulder. Deep into my zone, I took a few seconds to open my eyes. When I finally looked to my right, I saw the man I know as Patch; however, he was minus the patch and the gold-tooth cap.

"Hi, my name is Donnie Sheffield. Is this seat taken?" he said, pointing at the empty seat to my right.

With a smile, I nodded and pulled down the seat part of the chair.

"I'm sorry!" I said quickly.

"It's okay. I get caught up in the character. Believe it or not, it gets me women."

"You don't say."

"Thanks for the slap in the face."

"Yeah, we all need a little reality check every now and then. Know what I'm saying?"

"Yeah, I know what you're saying." He laughed.

Sliding up in my seat, I began conversation with Donnie. He was quite witty and entertaining. I hated to admit it, but I was enjoying his company.

"Is there an opening act?" I asked, looking at my ticket.

"Yeah, I think it's some band."

At that moment, the girl to my left joined in our conversation.

"SoulTyme is the band and they are really good."

My breath stopped and my gum became lodged in the origin of my esophagus. Beating my chest ferociously, my eyes widened, I looked at Donnie. Without a word, he started pounding my upper back. Tears came streaming down my face. Suddenly my gum passed as I took a deep breath; however, the tears continued to flow.

"Are you okay?" he asked.

Rapidly shaking my head no, I excused myself and

ran to the bathroom. With my head leaning into the sink, my tears finally subsided. My hands shook as I attempted to look at myself in the mirror.

"She said SoulTyme. That's Dick's band. I cannot believe Dick is in this building," I muttered.

I wiped my face with a wet towel, my shaky hands vibrating against my skin. I was flustered. I hadn't spoken to Dick since our argument.

"I know I said I didn't want to be his friend, but he came to town and did not even let me know," I said as I felt my eyes refilled with tears.

Pressing them shut, I tried to pull myself together. Taking a deep breath, I wiped my face and walked out of the bathroom. Once I got to my seat, I assured Donnie that I was okay. Perplexed, he was silent while he softly rubbed my arms to soothe me. However, there was nothing he could do to ease my pain. Unless he could pull out my tainted heart and replace it with a new, unscathed one before 8:00 p.m., this evening was going to be as unsettling as an earthquake. To make matters worse, the chatterbox female to my left continued to go on about the band. She mentioned how gorgeous the lead singer was and how she would do anything to be his "sexy cotton." I wasn't sure what a sexy cotton was, but I was sure she would never be his. My jealousy raged as she talked about my Dick, who no longer was my Dick, but would always be my Dick. I wanted to say something to her, but just as I was about to comment, the lights dimmed and the show began. My muscles tightened as I heard the first drumbeat. The curtains opened and the band, dressed in all white, lit up the stage. Nervously, I looked for Dick, but he was nowhere in sight. I recognized Coffee, the drummer, so I knew this was the band. Maybe Dick decided to skip the Kansas City show. Into the third measure of the first song, I began to relax. My head started to bob to the rhythm and before long I was into the groove. However, just as the song finished, a vision in white linen floated from the right wing and hovered over center stage. In midbob, my head froze to the left as I gasped at his loveliness.

"I told you he was fine," said my neighbor.

She yelled and clapped while trying to jar me from my stupor. Then he spoke and it was all over. The love I had been fighting had knocked me out in the first round. My heart was faint, I heard bells of defeat, and a rematch was out of the question.

"I'm done," I whispered to myself.

As Dick introduced himself and the next song, all I heard in my eardrums was our last argument. In fact, it was not until the fourth song started that I actually began to hear music again.

"They are really good," stated Donnie.

Still unable to speak, I simply agreed with a smile. As the next song commenced, Dick took center stage and the lights dimmed on the other band members. Picking up his guitar, he slowly began to strum. Rambling on in a short story about the next piece, he described a woman who went against the grain of society's image of sexy and his attraction to her. He mentioned how she chose cotton over satin and silk so he referred to her as his sexy cotton.

"This is my song, girl!" chimed the wannabe on my left.

But as he detailed the way he and this woman met and their interaction, I was forced to turn to her and reply, "No, this is my song."

I was sexy cotton. This time when the tears welled,

I could not stop them from rolling. I slowly took my shirt and covered my face. I didn't really know why I was crying, but I couldn't stop. Thank God, it was dark. With my shirt slightly soaked, I continued to listen to the passionate, acoustic ballad. Once I got my tears together, I slowly brought my face from within my shirt. Dick's voice was amazing.

"There is nothing in the world like sexy cotton against my skin, against my heart. I can still feel sexy cotton, for she is a part of me," he finished.

My eye faucets were turned back on. This time, I didn't even bother to hide my face. Donnie didn't know what to say, he simply patted my leg as if I were a child with a scraped knee. Suddenly the houselights came up and I saw Dick peering into the audience.

"Are there any sexy cottons in the house?" he yelled.

The girls went wild. Jumping and screaming, they responded intensely. Even the women cuddled up with other women responded. He always had an affect on the female gender.

"I want a few sexy-cotton women to come up here and dance for our last song," he continued.

Instantly, my neighbor grabbed my hand. Reluctantly, I held back, but Donnie was pushing me to go forward. In a whirlwind moment, I was forced to the stage. Like a Saturday morning cartoon, I could see my heart beating out of my chest. Loudly, the music started and the girls began dancing. I stayed close to the edge of the wing, almost offstage, as I attempted to clap my clammy hands. I couldn't find the rhythm and I looked like a fool. If security were not standing in the way, I would've just danced off into the wings. Especially when I saw Dick move close to each of the girls for one-on-one dance time. With my back to the audience, I kept moving farther away; then I locked eyes with the drummer. His mouth flew open, for he knew what was about to go down. And, just as I was turning to my right, I bumped into *him*. As I froze, like a starstruck groupie, my jaws locked and my joints congealed. Dick forgot his lines and sang a slew of consecutive "yeahs." Turning to face the audience, he jumped back into the chorus. I stopped dancing, moved to the side. At the end of the song, SoulTyme said good night and hastened off the platform. The girls followed for autographs and pictures. I waited nervously at the end of the line. When it was my turn, I stood silently. Looking up into my eyes, Dick spoke while motioning toward the band's eight-by-ten glossy.

"Whom should I make this out to?" Dick said.

"The girl who wants her Dick back." I spoke demurely, attempting to be funny.

"No, seriously, whom should I write this to?" he said without a hint of laughter.

Dick spoke as if I were some stranger.

"That's okay. I don't want your picture."

With my head low, I traipsed back toward the wings to reclaim my random spot among the other arbitrary females. Then just as security was about to escort us offstage, Dick called out, "Hey, you in the tan tank, come here."

Failing to realize he was speaking to me, I continue walking. It was not until the girl in front of me grabbed my attention that I looked up.

"I think he's talking to you."

Slowly turning my head, I saw Dick smirking.

"You forgot your picture," he said, holding it high. My face reeked of pain and I couldn't muster up a smile, yet I slowly walked back to the table and reached for my picture. Dick moved it farther away as I leaned in. Attempting to make me smile, he continued this reach and grab game a few more times, before I snatched the picture from his hand. The security guy held the line, until Dick gave him the go-ahead.

"They can go back," he said, motioning.

As I slowly began to read the message across the bottom of my picture, a smile started from within my belly and tickled its way up to my lips.

"Why does she get to stay back here?" my jealous neighbor called out.

Giggling, I replied modestly, "Because I'm sexy cotton, and I have the autograph to prove it."

In that moment, I whipped around, embraced Dick, and exhaled all of my frustration. He lifted and twirled me in the air, and I became dizzy with desire. As he stopped, my body slowly slid down the front of his chest. For minutes, we gazed into each other's eyes, without saying a word. With our hands interlocked, we walked over to the side of the table and sat.

"The performance was wonderful," I said, beaming.

"I'm glad you enjoyed it."

However, my tone changed as I continued to speak. "I can't believe you were going to come into town and not call me. That is unforgivable."

"Who said I wasn't going to call? We just got here three hours before showtime. I would have called you tonight."

"Yeah, right," I responded, unconvinced.

"Look, the last time I called you were tripping," he said.

"What? You hung up on me," I debated.

"No, I called back in a couple days to apologize, but

you answered the phone saying 'What in the hell do you want?' So I just hung up."

Puzzled, I began to think back.

"I don't remember that, but someone had been calling my phone and hanging up, so I'm sure I thought it was a prank call. I wouldn't have answered like that had I known it was you," I said sincerely.

Dick's right eye squinted, which informed me that he was not thoroughly sold. Yet he was convinced enough to give me a kiss.

"You look good," he said. "You want to go watch Meshell's performance?"

Jumping up, I realized I had left Donnie sitting in the audience. Dick's wondrous presence had given me temporary memory loss. "I'm sitting with someone."

"A date?" Dick asked.

"Not really, more of a friend," I said.

"Well, by all means go back. Perhaps we can link up right after the show," he said, placing a backstage pass around my neck.

Although I desperately didn't want to part from Dick, I couldn't leave Donnie by himself. True, we didn't come together, but I had agreed to sit and watch the concert with him. Plus, I could see Dick afterward.

"Okay. After the show," I confirmed.

After another long embrace, I walked over to the security guy and he escorted me offstage just as Meshell was about to go on. At my seat, Donnie was actively scanning the audience to find me. Once I got his attention, he waved, smiled, and sat down.

"What took you so long? I thought you couldn't find your way back."

"I ran into an old friend."

"Backstage?" he asked.

"Yeah, the band is from Atlanta, I know those guys."

Together, we sat and watched the remainder of the concert. My nervousness had grown into anxious excitement. I couldn't wait until the show was over so that I could spend a little more time with Dick. As soon as Meshell left the stage, the audience started to shout, "Encore! Encore!"

I grabbed Donnie's hand and we proceeded backstage. I was not sure if he would be able to go with me; however, he reached within his pocket and pulled out his own backstage pass. Without hassle, we walked to the side of the curtain and made our way behind the stage. Anxiously looking for Dick, I walked up and down the concrete hallway. Finally, I spotted him off to the side sharing conversation with a very pretty young lady. Stopping for a second, I hesitated to barge in on their moment. Therefore, I waited a few feet away, but definitely in his eyesight. Wrapping up the chat, Dick joined me minutes later. "What are you doing after the show?" he asked.

"I have no plans."

Just then, his cell rang.

"Hi, sweetheart," he answered.

Turning his back away from me, he continued to speak. "Yeah, we just finished the show. We leave here in the morning headed to Indiana. How's your show going?" he asked before turning back to me and raising his finger to suggest one more minute of my patience.

"Okay, see you soon. I love you. Bye."

Quietly he turned and focused on me. Neither of us knew what to say. Luckily, Donnie walked up with his friend from Meshell's band and gave introductions. Afterward, we all agreed to meet at a bar down the street.

"I just need time to pack my things," Dick announced.

Pulling him to the side, I spoke. "I don't expect anything from you and at the same time, I expect everything from you. So if you think coming to the bar is out of line, don't come."

Gently placing his arm over my shoulder, Dick leaned in to whisper, "Thanks for understanding."

"Well, I'm going to go now," I replied, pulling away from his hold on me.

"Okay, you have my cell so call me, but I should see you tonight," he said.

Waving good-bye, I walked away with Donnie. I followed him to the bar down the street. My stomach knotted as I sat nervously in my car. Though I knew Dick had someone else, hearing him speak to her still made me nauseated. I kept replaying the episode when I first found out about Celeste. How I met her with him at the club and how I noticed the ring, before he had the nerve to tell me. One minute he was asking me to move in with him, the next he was giving her a ring. I know I turned him down, but damn, he didn't give me a second to reconsider. Who knew he had someone waiting in the wings to take my place? Part of me knew it was over, but if he didn't come to the bar tonight, it would be confirmation for me to remove any hope that we could ever rekindle our love.

Donnie startled me with a forceful knock upon my window. He stood beside the car waiting for me to get out. I slowly opened the door and walked inside to confirm my future.

Like with most bars, the atmosphere within the dark

hazy space was filled with jovial drunkenness. Donnie and I took a seat near the window at a table for six. He ordered a pitcher of Budweiser and I ordered an iced tea. The back of the bar was lined with old video games such as *Ms. Pac-Man* and *Centipede*, and so Donnie challenged me to a game. He was the *Pac-Man* champion and I was the superchampion of *Centipede.* He didn't win a single game out of four. Shameless, he walked back to our table and finished his ale.

"I have had a great evening. Thank you," I said.

"See, once you get to know me, I'm not half bad, am I?"

Laughing, I agreed.

Thirty minutes after our arrival, the band members started rolling in. Donnie's friend Fiona arrived first along with two other bandmates. A few minutes later, I saw Mike and Rob from SoulTyme straggle behind. Grabbing more chairs, we all sat at the table and shared times as if we were old classmates. As the minutes rolled by, my nerves exploded. I finally questioned Rob on Dick's whereabouts.

"He said he was going back to the hotel," he replied with a careless attitude.

As I sat longer, my mood turned from hopeful to angry to disconsolate. No longer being able to hold a smile, I said my good-byes and left. As soon as I reached the car, I grabbed my cell phone. I held back from calling Dick, although I desperately longed to hear him. I knew why he didn't show, yet I wanted to hear him say it. I was a glutton for punishment. I dialed his area code, then the first three digits of his number.

"Only four more to go," I said to myself.

What was I going to do?

16

It's Over

I sat outside Sarah's home and called her phone. Once she answered, I spat out words at lightning speed.

"I saw Dick. His band opened up. I went backstage. We hugged and kissed. Celeste called him. He said I love you to her. He said I would see him after the show. But he didn't show up at the bar. I told him he didn't have to come, but I thought he would come anyway. It's really over and I don't know what to do."

Loudly and slowly, Sarah spoke into the phone, as if I were hearing-impaired and English was my second language.

"Get in the car and come here!"

"I'm in your driveway," I moaned.

"Then get your butt in the house."

Sarah opened the door, and luckily Carmen was asleep so we had an uninterrupted sob session. I fell into her open arms, and she held me like a lost child who had just found her mommy. On her shoulder, I cried.

"I don't have a futon but I hope the couch will do."

So many times the year before we had dealt with this scene, but reversed. Sarah was running to my house crying over Omar. She would lie on the futon, as I would rub her temples and make her tea. However, this time she was the counselor, and I knew she was thankful to have that role. I tell you, love is no joke and no one wants to be the patient of a midnight sob session. Yet everyone has his or her turn.

"So you saw Dick?"

"His band opened up. He wrote a song about me. See!" I said, pulling the rolled glossy from my purse.

"I see," Sarah said.

"I'm sexy cotton," I continued to snivel.

"Okay."

"Then I went onstage to dance with the other girls and afterward I talked with Dick. He seemed happy to see me and he said he would get with me later, but he stood me up."

I broke out into full bawling.

Sarah frantically ran to the bathroom and grabbed some tissue. I could tell by her reaction that she was stunned. Although I had cried over men before, it wasn't something I usually shared. My girlfriends came to me with their men problems; I rarely went to them. I usually dealt with my issues on my own. But that night someone else's sanity was going to have to reign, because mine was on sabbatical.

"But you know Dick is with Celeste. I thought you were over him."

"I thought so too."

"So why are you so upset?"

Looking at her in complete disgust of how she was handling my breakdown, I knew why she rarely played the part of counselor.

"Because I'm not over him. Somewhere in the back of my mind, I thought there was still a chance. But now I see it's not. He is over me."

"He's getting married. You didn't think he was over you?"

"No! People can move on and still never truly be over someone. I'm supposed to be special!" I yelled.

Quickly grabbing my autographed photo, Sarah placed it on my lap. Softly tapping my shoulder, she spoke. "Look, you are special, you are sexy cotton."

Staring at Dick's picture in contempt, I ripped the photo in half and quickly rose from the couch. "I'm going home. I know you mean well, but this is not helping. It's only making me angry."

"No, don't leave. The tea is boiling," Sarah said, following me to the door.

Snapping around, I responded, "Well, you drink it." Slightly covering my face, I continued to speak. "He turned me down, then stood me up. He fucking stood me up. I could be married to Winston, and I wouldn't have stood him up."

With her index finger, Sarah slowly wiped my lonely tear. Speaking softly, she responded, "If you still loved Dick and you knew spending time with him might jeopardize your marriage with Winston, you just might stand him up."

Frozen at the door, my heart iced as these words sent chills down my spine.

"He's trying to do the right thing," she whispered.

Her words were the dwelling on the ice cap of my body. They left me cold.

"He's trying to do the right thing?" I posed in the same faint whisper.

Slowly, I blinked my eyes to allow the final two tears to run their natural course. Against my cold skin, the salty tears left a trail of warmth. I started to melt as I realized that his not being at the bar wasn't due to his lack of love for me. His decision had nothing to do with me and equally had everything to do with me: such as the contradiction of love.

"Thank you," I said, embracing my friend.

"I did good?" she asked with sincere skepticism.

"You did excellent."

I walked to my car, and Sarah stood at the door with a self-satisfied look on her face. She should be proud. Her growth was inspiring. She was not only an amazing counselor, but was a remarkable friend. Mouthing a silent "I love you," I got in the car and drove home.

Engulfed with thoughts, my mind was racing as fast as the speedometer. I forced my mouth to say two words repeatedly. If I could continue to say these words, surely my heart would get the hint. Yet my heart was often stubborn and she refused to acknowledge the realization that:

"It's over. It's over!"

I said these words so many times that they merged from two familiar words to one that was unfamiliar.

My heart was not going to win this battle. Wrapped as I was within my denial, the twenty miles passed like ten and in no time, I was pulling into my driveway. Yet, as I rounded the corner, I saw a sight that caused my brakes, as well as my heart, to suddenly halt.

"Oh my God, there's Dick," I gasped over my beatless organ.

I attempted to switch gears and pull into the garage, but I couldn't get going. This man had shut me down mentally to the point where I forgot how to drive a stick shift.

After a few failed attempts, I pulled up the driveway and into the garage. In a state of inertia, I sat staring at the dash. Suddenly something told me to look up. Glancing in the rearview, I saw Dick standing behind the car. As he approached, I hurriedly began my chant.

"It's over. It's over. It's over. It's over. It's over. It's over. It's over. It's over. It's over. It's over. It's over. It's over. It's over. It's over. It's over. It's over. It's over. It's over."

Tapping on my window, he tried to interrupt, but I stayed focused. Yet, as the tapping grew louder, the chanting grew softer and soon the assured chant meshed into an indubitable question.

"It's over?"

Turning my head with grave hesitance, I looked at Dick, who had pressed his cheek against my window.

"Please," I heard him say from the other side.

"I need to talk," he continued.

Confounded, my mind wanted to leave him on the outside of my world. In love, my heart wanted to invite him in. With caution, I stepped out of the car.

"Just hear me out," he remarked quickly.

Careful not to make eye contact, I allowed him to

follow me into the house. Slipping off my shoes, I snuggled on one end of the futon and he sat on the edge of the other end. We did not face each other. His eyes seemed to hypnotize and when I was under the spell, he did things—things from which I couldn't recover. Therefore, I focused on a tiny brown smudge left on the wall from a fly's failed attempt to buzz his way into my life. I then imagined Dick as that fly. If only I could take my shoe and smash him into the wall. Then he also wouldn't be able to buzz in and out of my life at free will.

"Are you going to listen?" he asked.

As I gave him one nod, he started.

"I'm sorry I didn't tell you I was coming to town. I didn't think you wanted to see me and I didn't want to put myself out there to be stood up. I was so excited to see you tonight. So happy that for a brief moment I forgot about Celeste."

Just then my heart pushed in the lead and almost convinced me to look into his beautiful brown eyes. Yet I fought to keep my focus as he continued.

"I didn't know what to do. I have made decisions that I must stick with, so I went to the hotel. But as I starting thinking about this whole thing, I kept seeing you. I didn't have your address in my phone and though I came to visit last year, I couldn't remember how to get here. But I called Fiona's room and she gave me the number of her friend Donnie, who you were with tonight. He called Sarah, who called me back and gave me directions. God knew I needed to see you. He led me over here."

Keeping my focus straight ahead, I was compelled to speak. "Are you sure the devil didn't navigate you to my home?"

"I am sure. Lily, I close my eyes and think thoughts of you all the time. It even helps me create."

"Nice to know I am good for something," I said coldly.

By now, my arms and legs were folded in the chair.

"Damn it, Lily! I am trying to do the right thing. But the right thing has become a blur. All I know is you move me and I am struggling to get over that."

Surprisingly, I stayed strong. Ordinarily a comment like that would have melted me right into his arms. Instead, I replied sensibly, "So why try to get over it? Just let it be."

"Because I have made commitments to someone else. She deserves all of me and I can't give her all of me if half of me is still with you."

"Do you love her?" I asked, needing to hear an honest answer.

"I do and I love how she loves me."

Sighing, I made a disgruntled face.

"Love is not enough." Quickly I added, "Does she move you?"

Dick was silent. Still holding on to my focal point, I continued to speak calmly. "Then you are settling."

Ardently, Dick retorted, "She is beautiful and talented and the most sincere person I have met. Celeste is loyal, caring, and intelligent. She treats me like a king. How am I settling?"

Licking my lips, I paused. Finally leaving the central point of the brown smudge, I turned and focused on Dick's pupils.

With a slow-motion blink, I responded, "Because she is not me."

The air stilled and although I didn't check I think the time stopped as we locked eyes and exchanged inaudible words said only with our stare. Surprisingly, these soulful words instantly changed the dynamics of our relationship. I was now in control, not of him or this situation, but of myself. For the first time I no longer saw vulnerability as my weakness.

At last, I realized vulnerability was necessary for growth and once I understood that it was okay to be vulnerable, I could better manage my growth rate.

My mind, still holding strong, spoke to Dick through my dauntless glare.

"Do not touch me," my mind demanded.

Yet my heart, just as determined, also had her say.

"Hold me," she rebelled.

There had been nothing but silence, yet I saw him weighing the options of both my heart and mind. I already knew which one would win. Dick was a creature of impulse, and since the heart often led impetus decisions, she knew to call out to him once more.

"Hold me and don't let go."

And he did just that. Dick's arms leaned across the futon and pulled me into his body. Tightly, we embraced through the night. Holding so close and so long that it no longer felt like the other person was there. Nothing was said, yet everything was revealed. Nothing was resolved but the problem was no longer. There were no explanations for our behavior. However, our actions were completely justified. This was the paradox of love and nothing else compared.

17

Oops!

With a soft kiss upon my forehead in the morning, I gradually opened my eyes, and through my cloudy vision, I saw a man standing over me. My heart warmed, as I thought of my love for Dick and how it felt to wake up by his side. Groggy and still sluggish, my eyes slowly took focus. Funny, Dick looked like Winston.

"You slept on the couch?"

Weird, he sounded like him too. Instantly, opening my eyes as wide as they could go, I panicked. "Winston! What . . . are . . . when did you get here?"

Sitting down on the futon, he held me in his arms. Stunned, I was unable to speak. I knew I was on this futon with Dick last night. So why was I waking up to Winston? Could last night have been a dream?

"You forgot we were meeting for breakfast. Your garage door is open. I came in through the kitchen. You okay?"

Winston stroked my cheek as he spoke. "I told you I would be here around six o'clock."

Looking around the room, I was dumfounded. Did Dick leave? Suddenly I heard a toilet flush. Winston looked at me curiously as I pretended to hear nothing. Quickly rising, Winston rolled me off his lap and onto the floor. Standing in the center of the room, he scratched his chin.

"Don't be upset," I said, making my way off the floor.

My heart throbbed in sync with Dick's pounding footsteps as he galloped down the stairs. Winston's stare was burning holes through my chest. As Dick came around the corner, my eyes shifted in his direction. Startled, he halted.

"Oh! Excuse me," he said, heading back upstairs.

"No, stay," Winston said while motioning for Dick to come sit.

"What in the hell is going on, Lily?"

Dick spoke. "It's my fault, man. I came over—"

Interrupting, Winston raised his voice. "I said Lily!"

Dick quickly crouched in on Winston's personal space, and I rushed in front of him. I was sure they wouldn't fight each other, but when emotions were running high, no one was in control. Extending my arms to each side, I screamed, "Hold it! Winston, please sit down. Dick, you sit over there."

For a brief second we stood in the center of the floor, and finally Dick moved to the chair by the kitchen. Slowly, I moved to the futon, but Winston remained standing.

"Look, Winston, nothing happened between us," I said, pointing at Dick. "His band opened up at the concert last night, I didn't know he was in town."

Folding his arms, Winston argued, "Why should I believe you?"

"'Cause it's the truth," Dick interjected.

"Dick, please!" I yelled. "Just leave us for a minute."

Dick rose and walked out the back door. Reaching forward, I attempted to caress Winston's hand, but he resisted and pulled away.

"Nothing happened! We had a few issues to resolve. The last time we spoke, there was an argument and we hadn't talked since. We both needed to say I'm sorry."

"And that took all night?" he said, still angered.

"No, but the resolution did. I wouldn't lie to you. We were not intimate."

"You are lying. Everything about your interaction with this man is intimate. Maybe you didn't sleep together, but there is something there. He affects you."

His words silenced my argument. Looking at the floor, I couldn't debate his claim. Dick certainly had a profound influence on me. "What Dick and I had is over. Effect or no effect, I am with you and he is with her."

"Whatever." Winston shrugged.

Walking closer and staring me straight in the eye, Winston spoke. "You can say what you want. I saw how he jumped to your defense and how he stepped to me, when all I wanted to do is hear you talk. There is something going on."

"Oh my God, it is over!" I screamed.

"Who are you trying to convince, me or you?" he responded calmly.

Softly, I whimpered, "Why are you saying this to me?"

Moving away from me, and closer to the door, Winston responded, "Why is he still here?"

Walking backward with his focus on me, Winston

opened the front door. "Tell your love supreme, I'm sorry I interrupted his morning."

Pausing, he dropped my spare key on the table by the door, then left. Part of me wanted to go after him, but I didn't have the energy. Plus, I questioned it being for dramatics only. Running after him would not solve a thing, it would only cause a scene and this drama already had too many.

I heard faint knocking sounds off my back window. After taking a deep breath, I open the door. Dick stood at the entrance as I walked back to the futon. Sitting, I watched him walk through my back door while thinking to myself, how symbolic this was of our relationship. When we first met, I was with Romance, and I had to keep Dick a secret. When we were together, we were afraid to commit to each other. When we decided to be friends, Romance couldn't handle it so I lied about our friendship. When I moved to Kansas City we decided to move on with new relationships so we kept our love for each other a secret. Now he was with Celeste and he had to keep his love for me hidden. Our entire relationship had been backdoor.

"And I keep letting him back in."

"I have to get ready to go," hc said.

Sitting on the futon, I brought my legs up into the chair and rested my chin on my knees.

"This is insane," I commented.

"I am so sorry. I shouldn't have come."

"No, that is not the insane part. Why should we apologize for our feelings? If we sincerely care for each other, is that so bad?"

"I should never have started dating you when you were with Romance. We started off on the wrong foot.

We need to start acting more responsible," Dick said while rubbing my back.

Turning to him, I replied, "Responsible in whose eyes, society or human nature?"

Kissing my temple and then my cheek, Dick rose without answering. "I have to go."

Gradually moving off the futon, I walked upstairs to use my restroom. When I returned, Dick was standing in the kitchen by the garage door, reading my old poetry journal.

"Where did you get that?" I asked.

"It was underneath the futon. Do you mind if I read it? I would like to use some of these for song lyrics."

I looked at him with doubt.

"You'll get publishing rights. It could be big money," he said, smiling.

"Fine. I should be published anyway. But I need it back."

He nodded and tossed me my keys, we walked into the garage and got into the SUV. We were silent all the way back to the hotel. I purposely kept my eyes focused on the road while Dick scribbled pictures on a scrap piece of paper. He had this nervous habit where he placed phrases together using pictures, like a makeshift Pictionary. Those were the nuances I missed about him.

As we pulled into the parking lot, something in my heart told me that this was the last time I was going to see him. As the car stopped, I turned and faced him. Realizing I was upset, he nervously bit his lip. Dick never could handle my anguish well.

"You will see me again," he said as if he were reading my mind.

Shaking my head no, I looked out of my window. His

strong hands stroked my hair, slid down my cheek, and lightly turned my chin toward his. After sliding his CD in my hand, Dick kissed my forehead, then my nose.

"You will see me again," he restated.

And at the end of these five foreshadowing words, Dick opened the door and stepped out of my world. Walking away, he waved while speaking.

"Bye, sexy cotton."

Placid was my expression as I simply pressed my left hand against the window and drove away. I never did like the expression "let go of those you love and if they don't come back they were never yours to begin with." On this day, I hated it even more. I knew that if I actively pursued Dick, he and Celeste might eventually break up. However, that didn't guarantee that he and I would be together; plus, it wouldn't be right. Therefore, I must do as the expression says and *let it go!* And man, it hurt.

It was close to 8:00 a.m. and I was in no shape to attend work. I stopped by the office, to speak with Susan. I was praying she allowed me to work from home today or at the very least, allowed me to come in at noon. Like a zombie, I walked through the building and directly into her office. With my eyes filled with water, I requested a day off. Concerned, she inquired about my family. I started to lie, but then the honest bug grabbed hold and an outpour of emotions rolled out.

"My man left me. He's gone and I am barely holding it together," I moaned.

Though my eyes were filled, not a single tear rolled down my face and as I listen to my own words, I sort of sounded like Etta James. Even so, Susan must be a blues fan, because it worked. She permitted me to work from home. Rushing back to my desk, I grabbed my folders and some paper. I hurried out without making contact with anyone, not even Sarah. She and her empathetic looks were more than I could stand. I stopped by the gas station for a Snickers bar, because it was too early in the morning for ice cream, and low and behold if I didn't run into Wealth. Sitting in my car, I attempted to wait until he left the premises, but he spotted me and walked over to say hello.

"I do not want to see him," I whispered to myself.

Quickly, I hopped out of the car, appearing to be in a hurry.

"Hi, Lily," he said as I breezed by.

"Oh, hi. Gotta go, I'm late for work," I said, dashing into the store.

After grabbing my candy, I walked around the back store aisle and peered out of the window. Wealth was lingering out front waiting for me to come out.

"Damn it!" I yelled, kicking into the air.

Finally, I paid for my chocolate and quickly walked toward him. As I approached, Wealth began to speak.

"Can I call you?" he asked.

"What? No."

"I just want to let you know, I have no ill feelings toward you," he hurried.

Slamming my car door, I rolled down my window and spoke calmly.

"Thanks a lot, Wealth. At least now I can sleep at night," I ended with a smile.

Throwing his hand up, he smirked and walked away. I sped from the QuickTrip and went home.

Walking into my home, I tossed my keys across the room and they slammed into the baseboard of the floor. Somewhere in the morning hours, my sadness and frustration had raged into anger.

"I am mad!" I screamed at the top of my lungs.

Flinging my body on my futon, I slouched there in disgust. With my face buried into the cushion, I smelled Dick's body oils, which caused me more anguish. Therefore, I jumped up and hastened upstairs, but my forceful stomps caused me to miss the sixth step and I quickly came tumbling back down the other five. In pain, I lay at the bottom of the stairs. Too angry to cry, I began to scream.

"I hate this!"

I was not exactly sure what I hated, yet I was pretty sure someone hated me, because my day had been hell. As I tried to move, I saw immediate swelling in my ankle. Suddenly I panicked. Scooting my butt across the floor, I reached for the phone.

"Should I dial 911?" I questioned aloud.

The pain was beginning to grow and I couldn't walk. That qualified as an emergency, right?

"I should call Winston," I mumbled quickly.

Temporarily forgetting about our morning episode, I began to dial his number. Abruptly, I hung up.

"Shoot! He's mad at me."

I continued to lie on the floor as the throbbing pain pierced through my ankle.

"Ooouch!" I yelled. "Forget this, I'm calling him."

I dialed Winston's cell, but he didn't pick up, and so I called his office and had him paged. When he came to the phone, I started up. "I fell and I think I broke something."

"Lily, why in the hell are you calling me?"

"Because you're my doctor," I responded.

"I'm not *your* doctor, I am *a* doctor."

I began sniffling softly.

"Call 911, have them bring you to the hospital." He hung up.

Huffing, I dialed 911. Exactly twenty-two minutes later, the paramedics were tapping on my door. Scooting across the floor, down the foyer, I leaned up and let them in. Assisting me onto the futon, they looked at my ankle and decided to take me to the hospital for X-rays.

"Is your other leg okay?" asked one of the medics.

Vigorously, I nodded.

"Okay, then prop yourself up on my shoulder and we will get you to the ambulance," he continued.

In the back of the ambulance, I stretched out on the bed. Slowly, we took off to the hospital. They didn't use the siren; they didn't even break the speed limit. We leisurely drove downtown to the hospital building. Yet while I was riding in the emergency vehicle I felt a sense of transience. In this very spot where I was, so many had lost their lives to gunshots, stab wounds, heart attacks, and strokes. Yet my only concern was a swollen ankle. Suddenly my frustration and anger dissipated, and I found peace in just being alive. Sure, I was in pain, but it was a blessing to take a leisurely ride in an ambulance and not be heading to the morgue upon arrival.

It's sad that sometimes it takes the thought of death to make us appreciate life.

After being wheeled into check-in, I waited in the hallway of wing B for ten minutes. Then a male nurse wheeled me to another room where I waited for the doctor to come see about my ankle. They stuck me in an off-white room in a metal bed with off-white sheets and an off-white curtain divider. This was no place for recovery. Just being in there was making me sick. Lying back, I closed my eyes and tried to relax. However, the excruciating pain was sending shock waves up my leg. Finally, Dr. Meechum came in. Placing his frigid hands tenderly on my ankle, he asked a series of questions. After a couple of "hhmms" and "I sees" he asked the nurse to prep me for X-rays. Handing me an ugly blue gown, they asked me to undress. Minutes later, he returned, helped me into the wheelchair, and took me upstairs to the X-ray room. In the private X-ray room, I waited lying on another metal bed with off-white sheets. At that time, another nurse came in and prepared the X-ray while making small talk, which I despised. It wasn't like they could chitchat the pain away, so why didn't they just hush? She slid a fluorescent blue lamp over my leg, stood back, and clicked a button. Carefully placing my left leg in different positions, she clicked the button five more times before finishing.

"Wait right here," she said before leaving the room.

"Where else am I going to go?" I mumbled.

I reclined on the X-ray table and minutes later another attendee came into the room. I didn't bother looking up until I heard the voice.

"So I guess you weren't joking."

"Winston?" I questioned with excitement. "How did you find me?"

"I'm a doctor and this is a hospital."

"I'm so glad you're here."

Sternly, he replied while keeping his distance, "I'm not staying. I just wanted to make sure this wasn't some bullshit you used to get me to speak with you."

Gasping, I replied, "You shouldn't talk that way to a patient."

"You're not my patient."

"Winston, please. I'm sorry."

"This is not the place. When I'm ready, we'll talk."

Turning away, he left the room, and minutes later, I was wheeled back downstairs into another off-white room, a few doors down the hall from the first one. Leaning over, I grabbed the phone to call Sarah.

"Hallmark, Creative Development," she answered.

"Sarah."

"Lily?" she questioned. "Where are you? I've been trying to call you all morning. Are you with Dick?" she asked with excitement.

"No, I'm in the hospital."

"What!"

I began telling her about my morning. Once I was done, she was laughing hysterically.

"Why is my turmoil the source of your amusement?" I said earnestly.

"I'm sorry. I just have never heard such chaos. Your life is like a soap opera. I can't help but laugh."

"Please let Susan know. I will call her as soon as I get back home."

"Okay. Call me too," Sarah said just before hanging up.

At last, the doctor came in and delivered the verdict. I had a fractured ankle. It was not broken, but it was going to take six weeks to heal. I had to wear a hard cast for two weeks and a soft cast for four. He prescribed me painkillers, gave me instructions, and wheeled me to another section of the wing to get my cast put on.

Approximately two hours later, I was ready to leave the hospital. With a big blue cast from my shin to my toes, I sat downstairs in a wheelchair waiting for a taxi.

If I had known yesterday's events were going to lead me there, I would have stayed at home and listened to the album.

"Is someone coming to pick you up?"

Looking over my shoulder, I saw Winston standing at the reception desk.

"A man in a yellow taxi should be along any moment now," I responded.

He started to walk away, then paused and spoke. "I'm on break, I could quickly run you home."

"I would like that."

Winston grabbed the back of the wheelchair and took me through the delivery wing and out into the parking garage. After helping me into the car, he wheeled the chair back in, rushed back to the car and drove me home. The ride was silent for the first few miles; then I felt obligated to speak.

"I . . . um . . . I care about you," I confided.

"I care about you too," he responded.

Smiling, I leaned over and caressed his arm.

"That is why I'm not going to continue seeing you."

My soft touch turned into a nail-clenching grab. Winston pulled his arm from within my painful grip.

"What?"

"My decision is made. I don't have time for games and I don't have time for distractions. If you're not serious about me and it's obvious you are not, I can't be with you."

Saddened, I turned and stared out of the window. "I'm sorry you feel this way."

Winston helped me into the house and set my leg up on the futon.

"Why didn't they give you crutches?" he asked.

"I don't like crutches, I told Dr. Meechum that I

didn't need them. He disagreed, so I told him I already had a pair."

"Do you?" asked Winston.

"Yeah, in my closet upstairs. But I don't want them, they hurt my under arm."

"You are such a baby. How are you going to walk? You can't put any pressure on this foot for at least two weeks."

Quietly, I sat and contemplated his statement. Unfortunately, he made sense. Yet my mind wandered to something totally different.

"Are you going to be my friend?" I asked.

Winston, baffled, looked at me while shrugging.

"I was just wondering, 'cause I want you to be my man, but if you won't, I hope you will at least be my friend."

"Do you think we can have a respectful friendship?" he asked.

Nodding, I replied, "I know we can."

Winston went upstairs to my closet and retrieved my old crutches. When he returned, he had my journal and a pen. He placed the remote, the phone, and the newspaper by my side and headed toward the door.

"Don't call me, I'll call you," he said.

Not sure whether he was joking or not, I simply said okay and sighed as he slowly walked out of my home.

"Well, Lily, you are alone again. And this time you are crippled."

Grabbing my journal from the floor, I rambled through the pages reading various poems here and there. I could tell my state of mind when I wrote each piece by looking at my handwriting. When I was calm, I wrote in cursive. When I was nervous, I printed. When I was angry, I wrote in all caps. Interesting, there was a nice variety. That day would have been an all-caps day, and that moment I just wanted to escape from everything and everyone. At any given moment, I could easily have flipped out and lost it. No, I didn't break down, but for a second I felt like . . .

CRACKED GLASS

Right now, it's just a nick
A nick in the day is a start
To a part of the unraveling
A tiny chip that spreads
With life's changing temperatures
Soon starts to crack
No turning back
This fracture will soon grow
And grow and grow, and before you know
My pane is broken
And my vision is impaired
One more nick and my shield will shatter
And I will forever be blind

Placing my book aside, I leaned over and grabbed the phone to tell Tam about my latest adventures. She was so excited that I mentioned Dick's name, I think she missed the point entirely.

"So, when are you going to see him again?" she asked.

"Did you hear everything I said? I have a cast on my leg, Winston dumped me!" I yelled.

"Yeah, yeah, I heard. So when are you going to see Dick again?"

"Why do you keep asking about Dick?"

Tam began to exhale noisily as if I already knew what

she was about to say. I could just see her expression although we were miles away.

"Because your leg is going to heal and you are going to get over Winston, but Dick is not going away. So you need to deal with him."

"I don't want to talk about him anymore. I was just telling you about my day."

"Fine, fine. I'm sorry you broke your leg. I'm sorry Winston left you. I hope tomorrow is a better day."

Immediately after Tam rolled off these words in a monotone pitch, I responded in the same manner.

"Thanks for your concern. I'm going to bed."

"Well, I love you. Call me later," Tam said.

We hung up the phone and I stared at the ceiling for hours. Thinking about work, I realized that I needed to call Susan. I couldn't go to work tomorrow. In reality, I couldn't even drive with this stupid cast on my leg.

Picking up the phone, I started to call Winston. Yet I instantly hung up. I couldn't keep asking him to solve my problems. I had to solve them on my own. Tossing the phone on the floor, I flipped over on the futon in an attempt to find a comforting position. However, I had no such luck. I had taken my limit of pain pills for the evening and I was still in agony. This is exactly how addictions start. Yet I already had my compulsions with chaos; to add prescription drugs to the mix would surely secure me a one-room, padded-wall condo.

Closing my eyes, I imagined myself swimming in the beautiful waters of an exotic island and just as I was about to go snorkeling, my phone rang. Slowly turning over, I caught the phone on the last ring.

"Hello," I answered.

"You were on my mind," Dick said softly.

Pausing, I responded simply, "Yeah, I know."

With a quick chuckle, he said peace and hung up. With a warm smile bellowing deep within my gut, my pain seemed to dull. This situation was no longer in my hands; hell, I didn't know if it ever was. But being on his mind gave me a little peace of mind, and that was all right by me.

Good night.

18

Karma from Hell

Bright and early the next morning, I called Susan and informed her of my misfortune. I told her I was able to work, but that I needed a ride. As understanding as she was, she agreed wholeheartedly that I needed to secure transportation and she wanted to see me at work later that day. As soon as we got off the phone, I called Sarah. Hopefully, she was able to pick me up this morning.

"Claire, is Sarah available?" I asked in a rush.

"Hold on."

After minutes of holding, Sarah came to the phone.

"Girl, what are you doing?"

"Trying to get ready for work."

"Listen, I hate to do this to you at the last minute, but I need a ride."

"This morning?" Sarah asked.

"I'm sorry."

"No, no, we'll just be a little late. Leave Susan a message and tell her we'll be thirty minutes late. Oh, and be ready when I get to your house."

We hung up and I sat for minutes staring at my ankle. How was I supposed to get dressed with this stupid plaster on my leg? Grabbing my crutch from the floor, I strategically placed it under my arm and wobbled to the stairs. With my weight on my right foot and my crutch under my left arm, I held on to the bar, struggled up the stairs and into the bathroom. Sitting on the edge of the tub, I ran my bathwater. As long as I didn't immerse the cast in the water, I should be able to bathe. I slowly sat down in the warm water and propped my leg up on the hot water valve. Quickly I bathed before my leg got too heavy, then carefully I stepped from the water and dried my already tired body. I felt as though I had worked a full day. Hobbling into the bedroom, I made my way to the closet. I no longer had a say in what I was wearing; my cast would dictate my wardrobe for the next few weeks. I wanted to wear jeans, but none of my jeans would fit over the horrible cast, and so I had to wear a skirt or a dress. I hopped over to the bed and slid on my long black skirt and went to retrieve one of my knitted pullovers. Yet problems occurred when I realized my pullovers were in my bottom drawer. Tossing my towel to the floor, I carefully slid down onto it, scooted across the floor with the towel, and pulled out a shirt. Huffing and moaning, I leaned against my chest of drawers. Staring in anguish at my crutch, which was clear across the room, I shouted, "This is too hard!"

Sliding back across the room, I found a black pair of Adidas by the bed. I put on my right shoe, fondly kissed the left one as I left it behind, and continued the journey to my crutch. Taking hold of the bottom of the bed's comforter, I crept up the side of the bed and finally made it to the top. With my throbbing ankle, I sat on the edge realizing that I desperately needed some help. The time was 7:43 and Sarah was going to be here at any moment. The only thing I could do was begin my voyage downstairs. Snatching a small pillow off the bed, I placed it under one arm and my crutch under the other. Once I got to the top of the stairs, I tossed the crutch down the steps and took a seat on the pillow. Holding the pillow to my butt, I gently scooted down each step. At the last step, I leaned over, grabbed the crutch, pulled my body up, and hopped across the living room. While I was up, I walked to the front door, unlocked it, and sat in the dining area until I heard Sarah pull up.

"Come on in!" I yelled as she came to the door.

Sarah walked through and took one look at me.

"Ugh, you look . . . not right," she said, frowning.

Suddenly I burst into tears. As I was wiping my face, I happened to touch my lips. They felt enormous.

"What's wrong with my face!" I yelled frantically.

Hopping up, I tried to make it to the bathroom, but Sarah tried to run interference, which made me even more hysterical.

"Come on, let's just get you to the doctor," she said.

Firmly gripping my arm, Sarah pulled me in the direction of the door. She grabbed my purse and together we made it to the SUV. Once she opened my door and situated me in the seat, she ran around to the driver's side. Immediately, I pulled down her visor and looked in the mirror.

"Oh my God!" I screamed in sheer frenzy.

Somewhere between washing my face this morning

and getting ready for work, my lips and cheeks had swollen to enormous proportions. Sarah attempted to calm me; however, I looked like a monster and there was no calming this ogre.

"Don't cry or your eyes will be swollen too," Sarah said sweetly.

However, seeing my face in this condition scared me to pieces and the crying was involuntary. I leaned the seat back and whimpered all the way to the hospital. Once we got in the reception area, I was too embarrassed to get out of the car. Remember Mush Mouth from Fat Albert? Well, if you took him and stuffed his mouth full of marshmallows, then you had me. I looked like a caricature. To make matters worse, my eyes were red and white streaks of tears were dried on my face.

"Don't you have a towel or something?" I asked.

Sarah rummaged through her backseat and came up with a Pamper.

"Yeah, right, I'm going to waddle into the hospital with a Pamper on my face."

Apologizing profusely, she opened my door and helped me from the car. With my face buried into her shoulder, we walked into the hospital. As she sat me down in a reception chair, Sarah ran over to the desk and signed me in. I immediately grabbed the newspaper and buried my face within the editorials. Yet I could feel looming eyes peering through the newsprint. On her cell phone with Susan, Sarah quickly explained why we were not at work. Although my boss was patient, I could hear her tolerance running thin. While nervously patting my back, Sarah sat down next to me.

Thirty minutes passed before they called me up to sign the insurance papers. Then the lady told us it was going to be a few more minutes. To my right sat a little boy, no more than seven years old, who had been staring at me since we walked in. Originally he was sitting diagonally from us; however, he had made his way to the seat next to me and he was still staring. I know his mother saw him and yet she refused to say anything. I don't like kids who stare even on days that I look wonderful. Hence, this kid was really annoying me. As he continued to gawk, I brought my face from within the paper, snapped my eyes in his direction, and let out a sound that would make the trolls under the bridge very proud. The little boy, whose name I learned was Thomas, ran screaming back to his mother. Forcefully pointing and howling, he fingered me as the culprit of his distress. I saw his mother look in my direction. However, I continued to pretend reading. Suddenly, with her terrified son clinging around her body, she dashed over to speak with the receptionist. Sarah covered her face, as she couldn't control her incessant giggling. Instantly, my name was called. I propped myself up on my crutches and hopped to the desk with Sarah by my side. The boy screamed louder as his mom whisked him away from the monstrosity known as my face.

"Is there a problem?" Sarah asked calmly.

"Well, it seems the young man is a little frightened, did you say something to him?" she asked.

"No, I'm so sorry my appearance scares him," I stated, covering my face in shame.

"That's okay, we are going to put you in room 334A and the doctor should be in shortly." Looking up my file on the computer, she continued to talk. "I see you were just in here, it's probably an allergic reaction. You should be fine."

A nurse walked up and escorted us to the room.

"If I had known an episode would get me a room quickly, I would have wobbled in the door making faces and monkey sounds at everyone," I mentioned to Sarah.

She giggled as she responded, "Then they might have put you in a room down there." Sarah pointed to the sign reading PSYCHIATRICS.

Laughing, we walked into the room and waited for the doctor.

"Thank you for waiting with me."

"No problem, I can't leave you like this. You look worse than me and I don't have any eyebrows," she said, making a horrid face, then laughing.

Sarah had been so strong. I sometimes forgot she was in her sixth week of chemo. Here I was, asking her to help me, and I should've been comforting her.

Minutes later, a very attractive male nurse came in to read my chart. My lips were so swollen, I could actually see them protruding past my nose.

"I would get an attractive nurse on today of all days."

"Looks like you were in a fight with Holyfield," he said jokingly.

At least his sense of humor sucks, I thought.

"Well, it looks like you might be allergic to penicillin."

"You think?" I asked sarcastically as drool dribbled from my bottom lip.

He scribbled down a few notes, and left the room. When he returned, he had a doctor trailing behind. Asking me back-to-back questions, they each wanted to know if I had mixed the drugs with any other drugs or alcohol.

"No," I muttered repeatedly.

After looking down my throat, taking blood, and

poking my neck and chest, the doctor gave me a new prescription for pain and sent me on my way.

"What am I supposed to do about my face?" I asked.

"Drink plenty of water to flush your system of the drug and once it is out of your body the swelling will go down."

"What?"

"It didn't swell your throat passage, you should be fine in a few hours," he said calmly.

Of course, he could be calm. He didn't look like a blowfish.

Sarah and I walked to the pharmacy section of the hospital and waited for the prescription to be filled. Unfortunately, there were no newspapers or magazines in this waiting area. I was exposed, impatiently waiting for the next disaster. And it came right around the corner wearing a white lab jacket.

"There's Winston," Sarah mentioned.

Like an owl, I tried to turn my head 180 degrees to face the wall. However, it didn't work. Winston spotted me in a heartbeat. Stopping directly in front of my eye view, he gave a perplexing look. Then from nowhere, he began to laugh, which in turn started Sarah to chuckling. Yet I was still not amused. I know people say that we should be able to laugh at ourselves. But why do that, when our friends are here to laugh at us?

"What are you allergic to?"

"The stupid pain drugs your hospital put me on."

Shaking his head, he walked over to the pharmacy desk and picked up some samples. Sitting down, he looked at my leg, then my face.

"See what happens when you leave me?" I commented.

"Don't put your karma on me," Winston responded.

Sighing with sad, glassy eyes, I placed my head on Winston's shoulder.

"Don't be mad at me," I pleaded.

"I'm not."

"So can I stay with you a few days until I get better?" I asked sweetly.

"No," he said firmly while removing his shoulder from my resting head.

"Fine."

"You are not a child. Your whining and sad eyes don't work for me. If you need help, then ask for it like a mature adult."

"Okay. Winston, I need help. I cannot maneuver around in this cast. I can't drive and I don't know what this new medicine is going to do to me. May I stay with you a few days until I can better handle the situation?" I articulated maturely.

Smiling, Winston paused and responded, "No. But your presentation was excellent."

In disbelief, I sat with my mouth wide open. Rising, Winston said bye to Sarah and nodded bye to me.

"Can you believe that?" I asked Sarah.

"No. But hey, you can stay with us for a week or so, if you like. In fact, if I'm taking you to work, that will work best for us both."

Still stunned, I didn't answer. I simply rose, got my prescription, and left the hospital. Sarah and I stopped by work on the way home, so that Susan was able to see not only my fractured leg, but also my temporarily disfigured face. Sarah assured her that she would be back at work as soon as she dropped me off and I guaranteed that I would be back at work on Monday morning. Then Sarah assisted me with gathering the rest of my folders and notes so that I could work on next week's presentation that weekend. Thanking Susan once more, we headed back to the car. Sarah walked beside me all the while giggling underneath her breath.

"What are you laughing at now?"

"Nothing," she hurried to respond.

"Oh, it's something and I want to know."

Hesitating, Sarah slowly began to comment. "You know the kid from this morning?"

While I was nodding, Sarah continued. "Well, I bet when he goes to show-and-tell he is going to share that he saw a real live *Beauty and the Beast.*" She burst into loud laughter.

"How long have you waited to say that?"

"About an hour." She laughed again.

"You are not funny," I said, smacking her heels with my wooden crutch.

Walking slightly ahead to keep her from seeing my own laughter, I chuckled under my breath at her comment. It did feel good to make light of this karmic tragedy. But if I allowed her to see me smiling, she would call all day and harass me with corny jokes and I couldn't let that happen. We got in the car and soon Sarah pulled up to my home. Once inside, I immediately flopped onto the futon.

"Is the swelling going down?" I asked.

"You want the truth?" Sarah replied.

"Forget it."

"I think you should take a picture like this."

I gave Sarah a confusing look as she continued to speak.

"This way, when you have one of those 'I look like

shit days,' you can pull out the picture and see that you really don't look like shit in comparison to this day."

"It's time for you to go," I said boldly.

Walking back toward the door, Sarah called out, "I'll check on you later. Let me know if you want to come over and stay this weekend."

She strolled out and closed the door behind her. Leaning back on the armrest of the futon, I thought about Sarah's comment.

"Maybe I should take a picture," I stated.

After a few seconds of contemplation, I rolled my busted leg off the futon and hopped into the kitchen. I grabbed my phone and held the camera in front of my face. I begin snapping pictures. I even had the nerve to make funny faces as if I didn't look horrendous enough. I looked like a dog's mess, but it did cheer me up a bit.

Trying to temporarily rid my system of the old drugs before I filled it with new ones, I decided to forgo a couple of days of pain medicine. Consequently, my leg ached, and so I began my heavy breathing relaxation exercises. Right after my second exhale and before my inhale, the phone rang.

"What happened to you yesterday?" said Sam on the other line.

"Oh no, I completely forgot."

"How could you forget about us?" she replied.

"I am so sorry. I had to go to the hospital because I fractured my ankle. Then I had to go back because I had an allergic reaction to the medicine. I am sitting here with a swollen face and a cast on my leg."

Laughing, she responded, "I wish I could see that."

We chatted over a few more things, and then Sam promised to call and check on me that weekend. After hanging up, I started to think how wonderful it would be to have her around all the time. I knew being a single guardian would be more than a full-time job. But I could give her an excellent home filled with adoration and morals. I was seriously considering it. Even the thought, though scary, made me feel very content. Closing my eyes, I dozed off to sleep, and within the first hour of my slumber, I started to dream.

I visualized Dick pushing me on a royal-blue swing set. We were in the backyard of a ranch-style home. Still swinging, I watched him walk to the grill to check the food. He was wearing tattered Levi's with a pale blue linen shirt. The dream was so real, I could smell the food; I think it was swordfish. Yes, that was it. We were grilling swordfish in the backyard of our ranch home. I loved swordfish and this dream was perfect until our company came over with dessert. It was Celeste, carrying a white cake with blue icing. I couldn't believe she was in my dream; she didn't belong there. Yet she seemed to be very comfortable around us. So at ease that she was kissing Dick right in front of me. Dick escorted her over to the swing and she began pushing me. Next thing I knew, Celeste was kissing my shoulders and I seemed to like it. I wasn't sure what was happening to my perfect dream, but it culminated with Dick, Celeste, and myself making love on a royal blanket in the backyard of this ranch home. Afterward, Celeste, wearing only a blue bandana, stood over our naked bodies. She kissed Dick on the lips, me on the neck, then walked away. I was in Dick's arms staring at the crisp blue sky and then everything turned to black, and I could still smell swordfish.

Suddenly I woke from this baffling dream, but the uneasiness kept me from falling back asleep. Sitting up, I flipped on the television. I couldn't believe I'd just had a sexual dream about Celeste.

"And why was everything blue?" I mumbled.

I never really cared for blue and I certainly didn't care for Celeste. In fact, the only sense I could make out of the threesome was the reality that Celeste was Dick's fiancée. I could only have one-half of what he had to offer: half his time, half his mind, and half his heart. Although my dream self didn't seem to mind sharing, my real self did and I had to get Dick out of my mind.

Flipping through the channels, I felt my eyes growing heavier. Soon, I was unable to keep them open. I prayed the dream didn't continue with Winston stopping to share his blue dessert.

"God, help me get it together."

"Help is on the way," I heard in the back of my mind.

As I turned on my side, my body soon became light and I slept like a baby.

19

Peeling Through the Layers

Bright and early Saturday morning, my phone began to ring. Groggy, I answered, "Yes."

"Now, is that any way to answer the phone?" said the criticizer on the other end.

"Mommy," I shouted with the zeal of a toddler.

"How is my baby doing?"

"Not well."

"I got your message and that's why I'm coming to visit. I took a week's vacation and I will be there on Monday."

Pausing, I sat in silence.

"Did you hear me, dumpling?"

"Yes, I heard you. You'll be here Monday. I won't be able to pick you up, though. I can't drive with this cast on my leg."

"That's fine. I can take a taxi from the airport."

"Okay. Are you staying the whole week?"

"Of course, I have to get you healed and back on your feet. Well, I'm going to go, I'll call you on Sunday with details. Love you."

"Love you too, Mommy."

I fell back onto my pillow. When I heard God say help was on the way, I didn't realize it would be in the form of a five-foot-five, curly-haired woman who still referred to me as dumpling. A twitching smile formed in the corner of my lips. I was happy about seeing my mom; however, an entire week of her babying me was not what I needed right now.

Before I could close my eyes again, Sarah called and said she was on her way to pick me up. It was a blessing to have friends and family, yet sometimes I could appreciate the life of a hermit. Solitude was also a necessity. I wanted to spend the day, alone, in quiet reflective thought. The only person who could probably convince me otherwise or change my mood was Dick and unfortunately, I knew he wasn't going to call. Therefore, I lay back down and closed my eyes. As my sleep pattern regulated, I felt a looming presence. I slowly opened my eyes and saw Sarah wide awake, grinning over my weary body.

"I told you I was on my way. Ooh . . . your swelling went down."

"How did you get in here?" I asked.

Over my head, Sarah dangled my "in case of emergency" key.

"Fine, why are you here?" I said in the same troublesome tone.

"Get up. We are going back to my house for lunch."

"I can eat lunch right here."

"You are too heavy to lift, so get up before I roll your ass off the futon."

Reluctantly, I rose and hopped to the restroom. With my crutches and cast, my normal preparation time was tripled, but we finally left the house an hour later. Sarah stopped by the grocery store on the way back to the house. I decided to sit in the car as opposed to hobbling down the narrow aisles of the food store. Unfortunately, she took thirty minutes retrieving her grocery list and I felt like a trapped dog in the car awaiting my owner's return. Finally, I saw her come through the automatic doors and my tail started to wiggle; not from excitement but from the pressure on my bladder. I had to use the restroom with urgency.

As soon as we pulled into the circular driveway, I jumped out and rushed to the bathroom as quick as my one good leg could carry me. Relieved, I started a slower pace to the back patio to make the best of my day with my friend Sarah and her dysfunctional family. Claire greeted me with pillows and tea. She placed the red pillow behind my back and the camel one underneath my foot, which rested on a stool.

"It's so good to see you, Lily. You are welcome to stay with us until your leg heals."

"Thanks, Claire, but I'm okay. Besides, my mom is coming next week."

"Your mom?" Sarah interjected as she walked in with Carmen.

"Yes, my mom. You sound as if I were born in a cabbage patch."

"I'm just surprised she's visiting," Sarah responded.

"I'm not. Moms have to make sure our babies are

all right. No matter how old they are, they are still our babies," Claire commented, taking Carmen into her arms.

Sarah sat as Claire walked back into the house.

"Carmen is going to be spoiled," I stated.

"Carmen is already spoiled," Sarah corrected as she sat and enjoyed the sunshine.

Immediately, I began telling her about my dream with Dick and Celeste. Sarah couldn't contain her laughter.

"It is not funny, why am I dreaming about another woman?"

"I don't know. What was it like?"

Suddenly Claire interjected, "What was what like?"

"Her ménage à trois."

My eyes nearly popped from my head. She had just shared my dream with the grandmother of her child.

"Oh, I remember those back in the seventies."

"I didn't have one, it was a dream," I said with persistence.

Sarah chuckled, while pouring a cup of tea.

"I just wanted to let you two know that lunch will be up in thirty minutes," Claire said before walking back inside.

As soon as she stepped over the threshold, I reprimanded Sarah. "Why did you say that in front of Claire?"

"Please, Claire is so cool. You heard her, she doesn't care."

"But I care."

"Relax. The moment is over," Sarah said calmly.

I quieted down, but with a scornful look I mimicked strangling Sarah around the throat. Just then, a pair of large male hands covered my eyes. As the man brought his face closer to mine, I noticed the distinct smell of Gucci.

"Donnie?" I questioned.

"How did you know it was me?" he said, uncovering my face.

"Your scent is memorable."

He leaned over and gave me a hug. "What happened to your leg?"

"Don't ask."

Sarah excused herself as Donnie sat down. He immediately began playing with my four toes peeking from the tip of my cast.

"I've been wanting to call you. But I didn't want you to get the wrong idea."

"What is the wrong idea?"

"The idea that I want to start dating you. I just want to be your friend. I could use a friend like you."

"Is that so?"

"It is," he stated with a smile.

When that patch was removed, Donnie was a different person. I truly enjoyed his company. He was even cute, in his own hip-hop way.

Upon greeting Donnie, Claire began clearing the table to set the plates. As a gentleman would, Donnie offered his assistance and set the table.

Minutes later, Sarah, Carmen, Claire, Omar, Donnie, and I were enjoying a delectable lunch surrounded by lush greenery and bright-colored patio furniture. As I watched Omar bouncing Carmen on his knee, I felt ounces of jealousy creep in between the valves of my heart. Don't get me wrong, I was ecstatic for Sarah, but her picturesque life was making mine seem gloomy. She had her problems, but her progress to a good family life was phenomenal.

"Is everything okay, Lily?" Sarah asked.

While nodding, I smiled and quietly finished my lunch. Afterward, we retired to the living area and Omar placed Carmen down for her afternoon nap. Sarah rushed into the living room holding a game of Taboo. I could tell she was thoroughly excited about having an evening with adults. The men were so confident about their skills, they decided to team up against the women and challenged us to a game. Max, the chef, joined in on the game just to even up the teams. Poor men, they never knew what hit them. Between the word passes and the stupid expressions, the guys lost with gross embarrassment.

The next five hours passed as the guys went downstairs and played video games, and Sarah and I sat outside and talked. Soon it was time for me to retire home. As Sarah was looking for her keys, Donnie suggested that he take me home.

"Perfect," Sarah agreed.

I could tell by the twinkle in her eye, she would love for Donnie and me to become more than friends, but that was not going to happen. However, I didn't mind him taking me home. I said my good-byes and, me leaning on his shoulder, we headed to his truck.

The ride was quiet and we arrived at my home in no time. Surprising myself, I invited him in and of course he obliged.

"Make yourself at home. I would fix you something to drink, but my leg is aching and I need to put it up."

"I understand. Do you want me to fix you something?"

"No," I replied.

I sprawled on the futon and placed my leg up on the stool in front. Donnie took a seat on the chair directly across from me. The first few moments were filled with uncomforting silence, but eventually we both began to chatter while watching television.

"So how do you like KC so far?" I asked.

"It's cool. It's a nice haven away from the music industry. I can see myself settling down here. I'll probably have to leave in the next few weeks to finish mixing my CD. But after I return, I'm thinking about building a home here."

"Really?" I responded with disbelief.

"You don't like it here?" he asked.

"It's okay. I don't see myself settling down here. But it's cool for now."

Donnie exchanged his seat across from me for a closer view beside me. I immediately felt my body tense up. Not that I was uncomfortable around him, but I was cautious of men in my personal space, considering my state of emotional instability.

"If this is too close, I can move," he stated, obviously aware of my body language.

"I'm fine."

Donnie propped his body against the back of the futon and stared intensely.

"What are you looking at?" I asked defensively.

"I'm trying to figure you out. You act so tough, but you're not. You're soft, like a baby."

"What! I am not a baby. I am tough."

Donnie belted a deep laugh. "I saw you looking at Sarah today. You want what she has, don't you?"

"I don't want Omar," I responded with a grimace.

"You know what I mean."

I looked away, for I hated when people attempted to analyze me. I despised it even more when they were accurate. Donnie scooted closer.

"You don't have to answer. I already know. What I don't know is why you don't have it."

Without looking at Donnie, I answered, "Because I have a knack for driving good men away."

"Not you," he said sarcastically.

Amidst a low sniggle, I continued. "I don't know what comes over me. I meet good men and either I get bored or they anger me, so it ends. Either I talk them into leaving or I make life so unbearable that they can't leave fast enough."

"Why do you do that?" Donnie asked.

Shrugging, I leaned my head back against the chair.

"Do you not want the relationships to work?"

"Sometimes," I responded. "Then there are times when I know it is temporary. For instance, when I dated Wealth, I knew it was fleeting. He was fun, I was single, and we simply started dating. It was a thing for him and a thing for me."

"Okay, we all have moments like that, but what about when you are in love and you want the moment to last? What do you do then? What has been your longest relationship?"

"What is with the twenty questions?"

"I'm curious. I learn a lot from talking to women."

"Good answer. I see you've had lots of practice."

Donnie laughed while he rested on the other end of the futon. "We can stop talking if you want."

"It's okay. My longest relationship was three years. He was Mr. Wonderful at first. But when I started visualizing him as my forever, 'Mr. Wonderful' turned to 'Mr. So-So,' and eventually he turned into 'Mr. I Don't Think So.' Still, I had trouble ending the relationship when all the while I knew it had to be done."

"I've been there. I don't think you drive men away.

I think you are picky. Problem is, you get picky once you fall for them. You need to be picky up front. You wouldn't break so many hearts that way."

"Who said I broke hearts?"

"No one had to say it."

For the next seven minutes, Donnie and I sat quietly. Eventually the silence was broken by three consecutive sneezes.

"Bless you, bless you, and bless you," I stated.

Donnie went to get a tissue from the bathroom, but walking back into the room, he continued the conversation where he had left off seven minutes ago.

"So, have you met Mr. This Is Forever?"

Glancing at him, I smiled. "I don't know, at times I think so."

"So what happened?"

"I didn't tell him in time and he became someone else's Mr. Forever. Ain't that some shit?"

"Don't you hate it when that happens?" Donnie replied with a smirk.

Simultaneously, we gave way to several chuckles. As the mirth calmed, Donnie made a confession of his own. "I didn't tell my Ms. Forever in time either. Now I think it's too late."

As I looked into Donnie's eyes, immediately I knew whom he was speaking about.

"It's not too late," I quickly interjected.

"What are you talking about?"

"You can still tell her. I think Sarah would want to know."

Donnie bit his bottom lip. Finally, he commented, "I'm not into breaking up happy homes."

"Who said you would break it up and who said it was happy?"

"Who said it was Sarah?" he asked quickly.

"The little man inside your heart. I see his reflection in your eyes whenever you're around her. It all makes perfect sense now."

"Do not tell her. I am serious."

"I won't, I promise."

"We were each other's first," Donnie reflected.

"Really, then why is she trying to hook me up with you?"

"That was in high school. We've been good friends ever since. Sarah is always trying to introduce me to good women. We dated in the eleventh grade, but I had a hard time committing. Then my career took off, and I wasn't settled enough to commit to her. I loved her but I couldn't ask her to wait."

"Maybe you should go after her," I said, smiling.

"And maybe you should go after him."

After a few seconds, both of us responded with a soft "maybe." And the next hour was again spent reflecting. As I became sleepy, Donnie prepared to leave.

"This evening has been more than pleasant."

"The same," I replied

"Perhaps if we can't have our forever mates, we can just make the best of forever with each other," he proposed with a grin.

"Good night, Donnie."

"Do you need anything before I leave?"

At first I thought no, but then I reconsidered. "I would love for you to help me upstairs. I want to sleep in my bed tonight."

Donnie kneeled in front of me.

"Hop on," he said, motioning for me to hold on to his back.

Carefully, I wrapped my arms around his shoulders and squeezed my thighs around his waist. Tightly, I held on, begging him to be careful, for it would be disastrous if we both fell down the stairs. Donnie cautiously walked me to my room and placed me on the bed.

Leaning over, he whispered, "You didn't have to lie to get me up here. If you wanted some of the Sheffield, all you had to do was ask."

Sneering, I vigorously shook my head in disagreement.

"The Sheffield?" I questioned. "You call your dick the Sheffield. That is funny!" I laughed so hard tears formed.

Donnie tossed the pillow at my face. After a few laughs, he set my crutch by the bed and said good-bye. "I'll lock the top latch on the way out."

"Thanks. Call me."

"I will," he called from the stairs.

With my leg slightly elevated, I looked at the ceiling. Who knew from that first blind date that Donnie and I would have so much in common? I grabbed my journal and flipped to a new page.

> *Like onions, people's lives have so many layers and the pleasures and pains are often the same: pungent yet flavorful. But once we peel back those layers, it doesn't matter if the shell is green, white, or purple. Inevitably, if we face life straight-on, no matter how tough we are, it can easily make us cry.*

Good night.

20

Second Chances and Second Thoughts

My living room didn't see me on Sunday until around 2:00 p.m. And the only reason I finally made it downstairs was that the kitchen was calling my name.

"Man, I am hungry," I said aloud.

Just then, I heard a cell phone ringing. Yet it was not my ring tone. I hopped back into the living room following the sound of the melodious tune. Just when I reached the futon, it stopped ringing. Suddenly it began to ring again and my cell phone number appeared on the caller ID screen. I quickly picked up the phone and answered, "Hello."

"Why are you on my phone?"

"Why are you on my phone?"

I heard Donnie's deep laughter coming from the other line.

"I accidentally took your phone. Can I come over later and get it?"

"Yeah, and bring me some food, please."

"Oh, by the way, your mom called."

"You talked to her?"

"Yeah, I didn't realize I had your phone until we spoke."

"What did she say?"

"She wanted to know why a man was answering Lily's phone at eight o'clock on Sunday morning."

"What did you say?"

"I told her I was your pimp and my hoes didn't get up until noon."

"No, you didn't," I gasped.

"Yes, I did. I didn't know it was your mom and when she informed me, I quickly apologized and explained everything. I told her you were at home resting and that she should call you this afternoon."

"I'm sure she will call immediately after church. I can't believe you said that."

"I'm sorry. I'll make it up to you."

"You better, I'll see you later."

We hung up and I hopped back into the living room. I felt so trapped and it's not that I wanted to leave the house, but even if I wanted to, I couldn't drive or walk. The next couple of weeks were going to creep by. On the floor, I lay on a pillow and drifted off to sleep. Hours later, I was awakened by the chime of the doorbell.

"Who is it?" I yelled from the floor.

"It's Winston."

On all fours, I crawled to the door, reached up, and unlocked it. I moved to the side and he walked in. Looking down at me, he shook his head in confusion.

"What are you doing down there?"

"Begging your forgiveness," I said sweetly.

Winston kneeled down by my side and kissed my forehead. "What am I going to do with you?"

I softly placed my head on his shoulder and muttered, "Love me?"

"Good try."

Winston picked me up and grabbed the bag placed by the door. As we moved to the living room, I spoke. "Wait a minute. What makes you think you can come by my house unannounced? You broke up with me, remember?"

"I came to bring you some food, because I know you have nothing to eat. But if you want, me and my bag will leave."

"No, you and your bag can stay," I said hastily.

"Good, because I need to speak with you."

Winston went into the kitchen to place our pasta on plates. "How's your leg?"

"A pain in my ass. I never want to go through this again."

Laughing, he returned with the plates. As we began to eat, he immediately started conversation.

"I did try to call you, but you didn't answer your cell and your home phone simply rang and rang."

"Oh, I forgot I turned the ringer off. That's why I haven't heard from my mom. She's coming to visit tomorrow."

"So I finally get to meet the seed from which you bloomed."

"Why do you want to meet my mom?"

"Maybe she can help me understand you better."

"She doesn't understand me. If anything, she will

further confuse you. Why are we even having this conversation, if you don't want to be with me?"

"I never said that. I said I couldn't be with you. There's a difference."

I was trying to stay focused on our talk, but my mind kept wandering off. I was not in the mood to process any deep thinking and I wanted to ask him to come back later, but I knew that wasn't a good idea. And, since I was trying to make nice with him, offending him would not be a good move. Therefore, I concentrated and started listening in case I had to respond.

"I would love to be in an easy relationship at this time in my life. I don't need a woman with emotional baggage and I don't need a woman with commitment issues. I just need someone who wants to have fun, have dinner in the evenings, and occasional weekends away. You are not what I need."

With a baffled look, I replied, "You brought me dinner to insult me?"

"Let me finish. But you are what I want."

"Then what's the problem?"

"I want all of you and if I can't have all of you, then I can't be with you. Naturally, I was upset when I saw Dick over here, because I thought Wealth was my only competition and I knew he was out of the picture. But when I saw you two look at each other, I knew Wealth was nothing in comparison to what you have or had with him."

"But I keep telling you it is over."

"I know. And I didn't want to hear that at the time. But things that are worth having are definitely worth working for."

Nervously, I began playing with my hair. As much as I wanted to be with Winston, it was going to take some serious work on my behalf, to rid myself of traces of Dick.

"Lily, look at me," Winston said sincerely. "Do you want to try to make this work?"

Looking at him, I slowly nodded yes.

"I need you to speak."

"I do."

Winston leaned over and softly pecked my lips. As he kissed me, my heart fluttered with excitement. I might not have been what he needed, but ironically, he was exactly what I needed in my life. Still, as our lips parted, I heard Tam's words ringing in my head.

"If you want to settle, Winston is a great runner-up."

Winston noticed my stray glance. "Are you okay?"

Nodding slowly, I placed my head on his shoulder as he gently massaged my back. We ate dinner and watched television, and the entire evening I thought about the beginning of my new relationship with him. I felt balls of nervous energy in my stomach. I knew Winston was serious this time. Earlier, we were testing the waters, but for him to come back and say this was what he wanted, he was putting it all on the line. I'm not sure if I was nervous from excitement or nervous from the fear of possibly disappointing him. Either way, I was making the decision to move forward with this relationship. Winston and I retreated upstairs as the night fell. He drew my bathwater and assisted me with bathing. As I slipped on my nightgown, I saw he was preparing to remove his clothing as well.

"Are you staying?" I asked.

"Is that okay? I'm sorry I didn't ask."

"Yeah, but I thought you had to work tomorrow."

"I do. I'm staying so that I can take you to work," Winston said with a smile.

I smiled back, even more assured he was what I needed.

I lay in bed, while Winston elevated my foot and covered my legs with the comforter. As he rested beside me, I turned and looked into his eyes. Sticking out my lips, I motioned for him to kiss me.

"I love your lips," he said softly.

Bashfully, I smiled.

"I could kiss them forever," he continued.

"Forever?" I whispered with hidden anxiety.

"You know what I mean."

Winston smiled as he smooched my bottom lip.

"Good night," he said before closing his eyes to sleep.

Again, my heart began to race. Although I was sleepy, I couldn't sleep. If my ankle weren't fractured, I would probably be running for the front door and this was my own house. Instead, I stayed there counting the full rotations of the ceiling fan; I was on ninety-two, make that ninety-three, when I had to get up before I went crazy. Carefully, I slid my hurt leg from the bed, and then rolled my body over to the edge. Unfortunately, my crutch was still downstairs. Therefore, I crept down to the floor and began crawling out of the bedroom. Quietly sliding on my butt, I made it downstairs to the phone. Quickly hitting number 2 on speed dial, I called Tam.

"Hello."

"Hey, girl, are you asleep?"

"Not yet, what's up?"

"We need to talk."

"Why are you whispering?" Tam questioned.

"'Cause Winston is upstairs."

"What have you done now?"

I quickly poured out the entire story as she sighed

wistfully on the other end. After I caught her up to date, Tam responded, "So what do you want me to say? If you think Winston is the one for you, go for it. We both know you are not over Dick, but you have to start somewhere."

"That's exactly what I'm saying. I have finished the last chapter in my Dick book and it's back on the shelf."

"If you've truly finished, just burn the book. That way you won't be tempted to read it again."

"Right, I should burn it," I said with reservation.

"Look, Lily, commitment starts in the mind, then moves its way to your heart. Love and commitment aren't always one and the same. You have made your decision, now make a conscientious effort to abide by it."

"I am. I really am. I just wanted to talk with you."

"Okay, well, I am going to bed. I have a doctor's appointment in the morning."

"Is everything okay?"

"It's just a checkup. The baby is fine and I am fine. I am going to deliver a big, healthy baby this time. I know it."

"I know it too. I love you."

"I love you too, now crawl your tail back upstairs and get in bed before he discovers you are gone. Bye."

Smiling, I hung up the phone. I missed seeing Tam's expressions, hearing her laughter, and being in her presence. I know she cared about my happiness, but she was not going to lie and say that she totally agreed with my decision to be with Winston, but she also knew that, unlike Dick, he was not going to have me running around frenzied. I knew Tam was more concerned about me sticking with a commitment;

hell, she was not the only one. All in all, I knew I made the right decision; I just wanted to hear her voice.

Slowly, I finally made it to the top step. I was at the entrance of my bedroom doorway when I greeted a pair of size-12, caramel feet. Gradually, I tilted my head up and grinned at Winston.

"What are you doing?" he asked.

"I had to go downstairs, I didn't want to wake you."

Tenderly, Winston picked me up and placed me back in the bed. "If you need anything else, just tell me."

"Okay."

Winston quickly returned to his sleep. Gently, I rubbed his stomach as I closed my eyes. No doubt about it, Winston was a wonderful man. I was honored that he wanted me to be his girlfriend. I needed something constant in my life, and Winston provided that stability. He was my friend, we had great conversation, and I cared for him deeply. Falling in love with him was bound to happen. We had all the great makings of a lasting relationship. I knew this for sure. He was not runner-up, he was the prize—my prize. And if my heart couldn't see that, well, Winston was a doctor and I was sure he could recommend a good surgeon to perform a heart transplant. After delicately kissing his chest, I faded off to sleep.

21

Mommy Dearest

My workday that Monday was very hectic. Luckily, I got an early start arriving there at 7:00 a.m. Nehri quickly caught me up on the latest projects. Our last assignment went very well. We ended up using both of our ideas for the "Say it all with one phrase" cards. This week we were finalizing the artwork choices to submit to Susan.

Everyone stopped by my desk to gaze at my leg and give his or her pitiful looks. A few coworkers even asked to sign my cast. Of course, I denied their requests, for it's tacky enough to have a cast, but a cast with writing . . . please. I was a grown woman. Besides, most of them normally didn't speak, and yet they wanted to adorn my leg with their name. I don't think so. Sarah, however, welcomed me back with a bouquet of daisies and mums. She and I sat and conversed awhile when she first arrived. However, my phone began to ring continuously and I unenthusiastically returned to my paperwork.

Engrossed as I was within the piles of artwork, the morning passed quickly and I almost forget about my mother, who was landing at the airport in thirty minutes.

"I forgot to leave her a key."

Hence, she would need to come by work and pick up a key before she went to my home. And before I could get the words from my mouth, the cell phone rang. Instantly, I remembered that I still had Donnie's phone. Just then the phone rang again. Checking the caller ID, I saw that it was Donnie calling from my phone.

"Hey, Donnie. Has my mom called you?"

"Yes. I'm on my way to pick her up from the airport."

"What!"

"It's cool, calm down. She called and said that she was at the airport waiting for a taxi. I told her I was your close friend and that you wanted me to pick her up. Besides, I need to see you anyway to get my phone back."

"Donnie, please be nice to my mom. You aren't wearing that patch, are you?"

"You'll see." He laughed.

"I'm serious. My mom is laid-back, but her ethics are very old school. Bring her here, so that I can give her my house key."

"All right, I'll see you within the hour."

I hung up the phone and nervously tapped my nails on my desk. Sarah came whipping around the corner, walked over, and placed her palm over my jittery hand.

"What's wrong?"

"Donnie is picking up my mom from the airport."

"Yeah! Mom is in town. Is she coming here?"

Quickly, I nodded.

"I can't wait to meet her. Susan said to bring you these."

"What is this?" I said, looking down at the envelope.

"Tickets to our annual charity dinner. It's this Saturday."

Sighing, I uncaringly dropped the tickets onto my desk.

"You have to go. Susan is inviting you to sit at her table. If you don't go, it will be an insult and you don't want to be rude."

Rolling my eyes toward Sarah, I ignored her comment and continued to work at my desk. She eventually walked away while speaking.

"I'll escort your mom to your desk when she gets here."

Immediately, I started thinking about the cleanliness of my home. It was one thing to have dust bunnies and another to have an indication of men lingering about. I didn't want my mom to walk into my home and smell the scent of Winston. I could imagine how that conversation would go.

"Whose house shoes are those? Is he staying here? I thought you said you weren't seeing anyone?"

The questions would not cease. Thank God, I didn't have sex last night, I would have had to fumigate the house. As I continued thinking about my unkempt home, I looked up and Sarah, my mom, and Donnie were headed toward me. Smiling, I leaned onto my desk to stand and give my mom a hug.

"Mommy. How was your flight?"

"Oh, it was fine," she said, embracing me.

"Are you hungry? We can go to lunch or if you're tired, I can give you the key and you go on to the house."

"Are you okay, dumpling? You seem antsy."

Sarah giggled. "Dumpling?"

Cutting my eyes at her taunting, I continued to speak with my mother. "I'm fine. I just want everything to be perfect for you."

"Well, I am a little tired. We can eat when you get home. Donnie, can you run me by the grocery store? I know Lily has nothing in her fridge to eat," my mom stated.

"I sure can, Mama Rachel."

"Why are you calling her that?"

"'Cause she said I could."

With a scolding look toward Donnie, I said good-bye to my mom as they headed toward the grocery store.

"He sure has gotten cozy with my mother on the way over here."

"Girl, that's Donnie, he has no enemies. I keep telling you he's a good catch," she hinted.

"Really, so why don't you go out with him?"

"We're just friends, we are not each other's type."

"Oh yeah, I forgot. You like controlling assholes."

"That's not funny, Lily. No one is perfect and Omar is trying."

"I'm sorry. I shouldn't have said that."

"No, you shouldn't have," she retorted quickly.

As Sarah slowly turned and quietly walked away from my desk, it was apparent that I had hurt her feelings. I swiftly dialed her phone to apologize once more, but she didn't answer. Therefore, I left my apology on her voice mail. Unfortunately, Sarah didn't speak to me the rest of the day. I felt like my good friend didn't want to be my friend anymore and although that sounds juvenile, it hurt. I didn't mean to hurt her feelings; we joked about Omar all the time. But she had just shown me that all jokes about her man were off-limits. I guess she truly loved him. Yet maybe if the remarks weren't so true, she wouldn't take such offense to them. Honestly, I didn't like Omar and I had never held back my feelings about him. Sarah knew she could do better and I prayed she didn't feel restricted to him because of Carmen. She wanted Carmen to have a father figure, but a caring stepfather was better than an abusive blood father any day. As I packed my things, I suddenly remembered that Sarah was my way home from work. I was so wrapped up in the day, I neglected to tell her I needed a ride and now she had left. Winston didn't get off until tonight and so I was left without a ride home.

After a few seconds, I could hear the office chatter grow lighter and lighter. Everyone was preparing to leave. If I didn't find a ride home soon, I'd be stuck here with the cleaning staff. I quickly called Nehri, who was not answering her phone. Then I called Susan, who was still on a conference call. After a few more failed attempts, I realized that I might be hopping home.

"Donnie," I said to myself. "I hate to call him, but hey, I have no other choices."

I quickly dialed his cell number and I heard it ringing in my purse.

"We forgot to switch phones."

Hanging up, I called my number, yet he didn't answer. Of course, he would answer when my mom called and not answer when I needed him. I dialed the number again and then a third time. Finally, he picked up.

"Lily's phone."

"Donnie. I'm stuck at work and I need a ride, can you please come and get me?"

"What's it worth to you?"

"Donnie, don't play."

"I'm not playing. If I pick you up today, you gon' give me some tomorrow."

"I'm never giving you any. Maybe I could cook you dinner or something."

"Why would I want your cooking when I have Mama Rachel cooking for me?"

"What? My mama is cooking for you?"

Suddenly my transportation became a moot point. "Did my mama tell you to stay for dinner?"

"She sure did. I think she thinks I am your boyfriend."

"Oh yeah. You need to come so we can talk," I commented.

"I'll be there shortly."

After hanging up, I hopped into the bathroom. Miserably, this urination process that should have taken only five minutes took close to fifteen. With this horrible cast I couldn't figure out how to pee squatting over the seat. The bathroom was out of toilet seat covers and it was too difficult to turn around to line the seat with toilet paper. So here I was, holding on to the sides of the stall as I squatted on one leg over the toilet. Suddenly the stall door flew open and there was nothing I could do but leave it as I continued to urinate. Unfortunately, I had been drinking water all day and it was taking me forever to finish. I continued to excrete the toxins from my bladder as fast as I could, just when I heard someone walking into the bathroom. Wouldn't you know it, Susan had to also use the bathroom. She strolled by my open stall and stopped to watch me miraculously balance myself over the toilet. As she stood there, I could only wonder why she did not offer to close my stall door, so I kindly asked her, "Susan, could you get the door for me, please?"

"Of course. You know we have an excellent cleaning staff, it's okay if you sit down," she added.

"Thanks."

Yet, I thought to myself, I didn't care how excellent the cleaning staff was. My mother always told me not to sit on public toilets. Plus, I saw a *Dateline Special* on the most germ-infected places and public bathrooms were number two on the list. After that special I didn't go in public toilets for months. As these thoughts circled my head, my bladder was finally beginning to empty. I could now begin the difficult process of wiping, flushing, and exiting this tiny confinement. As I was washing my hands, Susan stood at the counter waiting for me.

"Did you get the invitation to the charity dinner?"

"I did. But my mom is in town and I don't know if I'll be able to make it."

Checking her makeup in the mirror, Susan commented, "There will be people there I would like to introduce you to. It would be to your advantage if you come."

With a taut grin, she quickly exited the bathroom. Looking at my reflection as I washed my hands, I saw the bags underneath my fatigued eyes. I could only imagine how I was going to look by Saturday with my mom here all week. Although I didn't want to attend, Susan made it very clear that this dinner invitation was an obligation. She might as well have said, "Have your ass there or else." Hence, I would be attending the Hallmark charity dinner on that Saturday so that my job would be secure and tension free on the following Monday. As soon as I made it back to my desk, I saw Donnie walking down the corridor.

"You ready?"

Grabbing my purse, I placed my crutch underneath

my arm, met him at the end of the cubicles, and instantly began badgering him about my mom. Before we got to the car, I had rolled off at least twenty questions. I didn't give him time to answer one, before hitting him with another. Donnie tried to keep up, but most importantly he assured me that he hadn't given any unnecessary information to my mom.

"I just want everything to be perfect, you know?"

"It will be. But you must realize that your mom knows that you are not perfect. She is going to love you no matter what you do. I can tell she is that type of parent."

"You're right."

We got home and Donnie helped me into the house and brought in my things from work. When we stepped in the door, I smelled the aroma of barbecue chicken, mashed potatoes, and green beans.

"My mommy's here!" I began to cheer.

Donnie chimed in on my cheering as if he were my brother. Laughing harder, I knew he only meant well.

"You come on in here and sit down. Put your leg up. Donnie, you help her."

"Yes, ma'am."

"I told you about that yes, ma'am, stuff. I don't like it. A simple yes will do."

"Okay, Mama Rachel."

Donnie walked me into the living room and propped my leg up on the futon. Quickly, I reached into my purse and handed him his cell phone. "Give me my phone, before you forget."

"Your mom asked me to stay for dinner, but I will leave if you want some time alone."

"No, stay. I appreciate everything you've done."

Within minutes, my mom was setting the table and calling us to dinner. I almost broke my other leg, trying to rush to the table. Not that I was extremely hungry, but I couldn't wait to have my mom's cooking inside my belly. After Donnie said the grace, I dug in like a famished teenager. Dinner was quiet for the first few minutes; however, Donnie interrupted the silence with breaking news.

"Dick called you."

"What?" I said, nearly choking. "When did he call? What did he say? Did he ask who you were?"

"No. He just said to tell you he called."

"Well, when did he call?"

"Yesterday," he said calmly.

"Yesterday? Why are you just telling me today?"

"'Cause I forgot."

Frowning, I hastily began finishing my food as my mom innocently asked, "Dumpling, does Dick owe you some money?"

"What? No."

"Well, you act like he owes you something."

I ignored my mom's comment and continued eating. But my big mouth wouldn't let it rest. "Who told you to answer my phone anyway?"

Donnie ignored my statement; however, as he gave me a stern look, I could tell he wasn't going to talk about it. I obliged his look; plus, the less my mom heard, the better. I simply held my tongue until after dinner. As soon as Donnie finished, he offered to help clean. My mother insisted that he relax, but Donnie decided to leave.

"Lily, I'll check on you later. Mama Rachel, it was a pleasure to meet you."

"Don't forget to bring me your CD," my mom responded.

"I'll bring it by this week. I promise."

Before he could close the door completely, my mother's comments begin.

"He is such a nice guy. I like him. He said he goes to church and everything. When did you two meet?"

Slowly, I began to give in to the interrogation.

"He is a nice guy, but he is not my man. We are only friends."

"He acts like more than a friend to me."

"But he is *only* a friend. I have a boyfriend, his name is Winston."

My mom was silent as she washed the dishes. As long as she was silent, I was going to stay silent. I knew she was concerned about my life, but I was not in the mood to share. Plus, I had an entire week to enlighten her with the bedlam known as my social life.

"Mom, I'm tired, I'm going to bed early."

"Okay, baby. Let me help you upstairs."

"I'm okay."

As I hopped up the stairs, my mom called out from the kitchen, "Shall I wake you if Dick calls?"

Laughing to myself, I knew this was going to be a long week. "Yes, Mom, wake me if Dick calls. I love you."

"I love you too."

After my bath, I slipped on a T-shirt and slid into bed. In so many ways it felt so wonderful to see my mother. Yet in many other ways her visit was invasive. Although she was my friend, she was still my mother. I knew she didn't expect me to be perfect, but she did have high expectations. In my eyes, it was hard enough to live a life that God would be proud of, but to live a life that would make God and a mother proud was immense pressure for a young woman.

22

Must You Know Everything?

My mom dropped me off at work Tuesday morning at 7:50. Waving good-bye to her with my bag lunch in my hand was very reminiscent of my grade school days. And these traces of puberty lingered throughout this week as I felt the pressure to be a good girl while my mother was visiting.

Upon my arriving at work, Sarah was quick to demand my attention as I approached her desk.

"I am inviting you and your mom over to my home tomorrow night."

"Oh, I see you are speaking to me now?"

"As long as you stop talking about Omar," she exclaimed.

"Okay, but my night was changed and I have to teach at the center tomorrow."

"Well, we'll do it Thursday night, I'm not taking no for an answer."

"Okay," I said as I made my way to my desk.

Quickly, the week was filling. This only left tonight and Friday night for us to be alone. It wasn't going to be as bad as I thought. I got to my desk, checked my messages, and looked over my calendar of deadlines. I only had one project due within the next few weeks, and timing couldn't be better. My creative side had been very active, and I wanted to write on a more personal, emotional level. I found it difficult to write in my journal while I was working on major projects. So I was going to thoroughly enjoy the next couple of weeks and I hoped to write a few inspiring pieces. I began to doodle the time away, for my desire to be here today was extremely low. Unfortunately, days like this seemed to last forever. As the time crept by, imagery of Dick and his beautiful brown eyes continued to flash across my wandering mind. I wondered why he called the other night. We had only spoken once since his visit and our conversation was brief. This time I felt the call had a specific purpose and I planned to call him back tonight to find out his reason. But, in the meantime, I needed to call Winston and see what night he was coming over. After that I needed to call Evelyn 'cause I hadn't spoken with her in weeks. In fact, I was going to spend the rest of my day touching base with my friends.

Around 4:00 p.m., my mom called to find out what time I would be ready to go.

"Come right now."

"But you don't leave until five o'clock," she responded.

"Just come on," I continued to urge.

Once we hung up, I called Winston. We spoke briefly and he invited my mom and me out to dinner tonight.

"I would rather you come over. It's more personal. Plus, she probably cooked dinner."

"Well, if I get out of here in time, I'll come."

"Okay, but call first. Don't just show up."

Laughing, Winston responded, "She really makes you nervous."

"No, she doesn't. It's just manners to call first."

"But I thought we were past that call first stage. You don't have to call first when you come see me."

"Yeah, right. You're never home and I have to call first because I don't have a key."

Winston was quiet. There was nothing like a key exchange conversation to silence the opposite sex.

"Just call," I said, breaking the uncomfortable moment, just before hanging up.

After gathering my things, I walked to Sarah's desk to wait for my mother. We had a quick conversation about dinner Thursday night and then I saw my mom through the front door. Saying good-bye to Sarah, I met her and left.

"How was your day?" she asked quickly.

"Long and boring. I was ready to leave around noon."

"I hope you don't leave early often," she hinted.

"I don't, but since I got this cast, everything I do is difficult. It makes me want to sit at home all day."

When my mother cranked up the car, I heard hip-hop music blaring through the speakers.

"What is this?" I said, very surprised.

"Oh, Donnie dropped off his CD. This is it," she said with excitement.

We continued listening to the offensive lyrics rhyming over an old break beat. The song was about him meeting a girl who only wanted to date him because of his status. After agreeing to play her game, he passed her on to others in his entourage, just so he could tell her how nasty and disgusting she was. I hated to admit it, but the song was hot. Besides an occasional "bitch" here and a "ho" there, Donnie, I mean Patch, was a good storyteller. I looked over at my mom, who was bouncing to the beat, and I realized how backward this situation was. I was supposed to be bouncing my head and she was supposed to be criticizing the music.

"Do you like this?" I asked, bemused.

"I do. It has a good beat," she said, continuing to bob her head.

Maybe I did need to relax more, I thought to myself. Therefore, placing my head against the window, I enjoyed *Bloody Murder Coming at Ya* the rest of the way home.

I watched television, as my mom finished her lasagna. I almost hated to see my mom in the kitchen working so diligently, but she got so much pleasure in cooking for her only child. She insisted she come take care of me and this was how she did it. Plus, her cooking was so delectable, I would be crazy to refuse it. So I sat there like a kid, waiting for my mom to finish dinner. Funny, I felt like I should be doing my homework; just then the phone rang. My mom handed me the phone as I quickly answered—secretly hoping it was Dick.

"Hello."

"Hi, babe. I am on my way."

"Okay, I'll see you when you get here. Mom is cooking lasagna."

Smiling, I hung up and called into the kitchen, "Mom, Winston is coming over."

"Winston? Is that your friend?" she teased.

"Yes, Mom, and be nice to him."

My mom peeped her head around the corner and

smiled. "When have you known me to be anything else but nice?"

Shaking my head, I kept the answer to that comment to myself. My mother was a beautiful woman. She was as sweet as peach cobbler most of the time. But when she was cross, she was walking hell. Not one to curse, but my mother's quick tongue and extensive vocabulary could make anyone feel two inches tall. I'd seen her deliver sentences that made people feel so insignificant that they would've preferred she yelled and cursed and been done with it. I used to find it funny, until I fell victim to one of her tirades. After that, I vowed to never cross that line again. Luckily, I had had much success with staying on her good side. We disagreed, but rarely did we squabble. Overall, we had a great relationship. And, as long as her visits were once or twice a year, it would continue as such.

"Dinner is ready, shall we wait for Winston?"

"I think we should."

Mom agreed, walked into the living room, and sat with me on the futon. At first she was silent, but soon the obtrusive chatter began.

"So what has my baby been doing with her life?"

Timidly, I began to speak as I lifted myself up from my pillow. "Working, writing, not too much else."

"Well, tell me about Winston. How come you haven't mentioned him? Is this the same guy you were dating last year? Wasn't his name Winston?"

"No, Ma, last year I dated Wealth."

At that point I prayed she stopped with the questions, because I refused to inform her that Winston and Wealth were twins. As my mom looked around the room, I could tell she wanted to ask me more questions, but didn't know how to begin. Therefore, I started.

"Winston is a doctor, an obstetrician/gynecologist. I met him last year, but we were only friends. A few months, six to be exact, after Wealth and I broke up, Winston and I started dating. He is very kind and a perfect gentleman. You'll see when he comes over."

"I hope you gave yourself time to heal from the other man. Jumping from relationship to relationship is not good."

"I had plenty of time to heal. It wasn't a bad breakup, we're still acquaintances."

Making a soft humming sound, my mom smiled politely as her mind pondered upon more motherly advice.

"I don't understand all of these dating games young people play. No one is perfect. All you need to do is find a guy with great potential, commit to him, and mold him into a great husband."

"It doesn't work like that. So many men have great potential, but that doesn't mean that a lifetime commitment with that man is going to make you happy. In fact, I am rethinking this whole lifetime commitment thing. How are you supposed to commit to one person forever?"

With an astonishing look upon her face, my mother rose, placed her hands on her hips, and spoke in her reprimanding motherly tone.

"Lillian Drew McNeil, have you lost your mind?"

Shyly, I mumbled, "No," as I looked away.

"Do you plan on sleeping around with different men for the rest of your life?" she continued.

Instantly, my mouth flew open in shock that my mother would even say such a thing. Yet she carried on.

"What is wrong with you? You are a grown woman.

I know you would not have me to believe you are not having sex with any of these men."

"I didn't sleep with Wealth," I admitted quickly.

"Fine. Are you sleeping with Winston? 'Cause, I know you slept with that Dick boy by the way you tense up when anyone mentions his name."

Still in a state of shock, I sat motionless. Every time I tried to speak, my mom opened her mouth with more accusatory chatter.

"Look, I am not trying to come down on you. I know I raised a very mature, intelligent woman. I just don't understand why you would say marriage is a waste, when your father and I have been together for thirty years."

"I didn't say it was a waste. I said I wonder if I can spend the rest of my life with one man and be happy. That's all."

My mom took a seat and placed her hands on top of mine. Looking into my eyes, she gave a tiny chuckle.

"I know things are different. Women have many more options than they did thirty years ago. If we didn't marry by twenty-five, we were considered old maids. But don't give up on the sanctity of marriage. It can be a beautiful thing, but only when both people are ready for it."

Laying my head in my mom's lap, I felt her love radiate through my body. I smiled as she kissed the top of my forehead.

"What are you thinking?" my mom asked.

"How I hate when you call me by my full name."

"If you stop making irrational statements, I won't have to," she said with a wink.

As she ran her hands through my hair, she commented, "And what is going on with your hair? I'm surprised you get a man at all with this stuff thrown about your head, let alone a doctor."

As she tried to wrap my curls into a ponytail, the doorbell rang.

"Leave my hair alone and go answer the door, it's Winston. Be nice."

My mom slowly got up and walked to the door. When she opened it, Winston greeted my mom with a hug and a bottle of wine.

"Trying to get me drunk?" my mom joked as she and Winston walked into the living room.

"That depends, are you anything like Lily?"

"Winston, that's not funny," I responded quickly.

Laughing, he replied, "Your mom knows I'm only joking."

Shaking my head, I showed disagreement.

"Mrs. McNeil, please don't take offense, I'm only joking."

"None taken and please call me Rachel."

"See, I told you," Winston muttered as he kissed my cheek.

Winston helped me to the table and scooted the extra chair underneath my leg. My mom sat to my right as he sat across from me. I prayed we would get through dinner without a lot of controversial conversation. But as talk started, I knew that was not going to happen.

"So, Winston, Lily tells me you are a doctor. I'm sure your parents are proud. Do you have any other siblings?"

Immediately, I kicked Winston underneath the table, just as he called out Wealth's name. His eyes grew large as he tried to get his sentence out, and he could tell by my expression that I wanted him to stop speaking, but it was too late.

"Two brothers, Wealth and Reese."

The next few seconds were silent as I awaited my mother's response and Winston gawked with a confounded expression.

"What's wrong, dumpling, is the food okay?"

"It's great."

"Very tasty," Winston added as he took a sip of his white wine.

I buried my head in my plate and continued digging into my noodles as the phone rang. Quickly, I reached for the receiver, but my mother was closer and offered to answer it for me.

"Hello," she answered pleasantly.

Then, with a differing look, she handed the phone to me while mouthing the words, "We're eating dinner."

"Hello."

"Hi, beautiful."

Carefully, I tried to hold back the bursting smile that suddenly appeared every time I heard Dick's voice.

"Hi," I said quietly.

"Is everything all right?"

"Yes, I'm sitting here eating dinner with my mother and Winston."

"Well, I don't want to interrupt dinner, but I want to speak with you. Can I call you back later tonight?"

"Please do."

"Is ten o'clock good?" Dick asked.

"Perfect."

"Okay, I'll talk with you later."

Quickly, I hung up, smiled politely, and continued eating dinner as if the phone call never happened.

After dinner, my mom rinsed the dishes and placed them in the dishwasher as Winston and I sat and watched television. We all agreed to watch a movie;

however, we were waiting until my mom got out of the kitchen.

"I'm going to kiss you," Winston whispered as he leaned over to kiss my lips.

I obliged with a big smooch, but it still felt awkward to kiss while my mom was close by. And wouldn't you know it, she walked in just as he pulled away from sucking my bottom lip. In hopes of getting a massage, I sat on the floor in between Winston's legs as he stretched back on the futon. My mom sat in the chair across from us. However, by the time the movie started she fell asleep. As Winston and I continued watching the predictable romantic comedy, I found myself constantly staring at the time impatiently waiting for ten to arrive.

"At least the movie didn't end with a wedding. That would have been too Hollywood." Winston laughed as the last scene went black.

Yawning, I agreed.

"You're tired?" he asked.

"Yeah, I've had a long day."

Winston rose and pulled me off the floor. Wrapping his toned arms around my body, he embraced me with love.

"You're lucky your mom is here or I was going to—"

Just then my mom came out of her slumber and stretched her arms high. "Is the movie over?" She yawned.

"You missed the whole thing. Go to bed."

Laughing, she rose as Winston broke from our embrace to say good night.

"It was a pleasure meeting you, Rachel, thanks for dinner."

"The pleasure was all mine. I hope to see you again

before I leave. Or maybe you and Lily can come visit us for the holidays."

"That would be nice," stated Winston.

My mother thought she was slick. Holiday visits confirmed a relationship. After visiting with relatives over Christmas dinner, all parties felt guilty about ending things.

"Good night, kids."

"Good night," we responded in unison.

Winston again wrapped his arms around me and continued to speak. "As I was saying, you are lucky Rachel is here. Because the way I'm feeling, I can go all night."

"Well, I couldn't go ten minutes, I am tired."

"But I could make those ten seem like all night."

With a huge smile, I pushed Winston and his horny demons away from my body. "It's time for you to go."

"I could tuck you in."

"Bye, Winston."

"Okay, okay. I'll call you tomorrow," he replied, giving me one last kiss good night.

I watch him walk down the corridor and leave. Gazing up at the clock, I saw it was 9:33. Man, when I said it was time to go, it really was time for him to go. I had just enough time to get upstairs and prep for bed before my ten o'clock call. Grabbing my crutch, I hopped upstairs to the bathroom, and managed to bathe in twenty minutes; then I got in bed with the clock reading 9:59. Grabbing my journal, I decided to write a little. Plus, staring at the phone waiting for it to ring made me stupid and desperate. In fact, the piece I would write tonight would be about how love can make us feel . . .

STUPID AND DESPERATE

My behavior is irrational
Crazy and insane
No sense can be made of my actions
I crave what I can't have
I crave what I don't need
I crave what I don't want
Yet my desire grows stronger
My system has been injected with a poison
A poison called love
And this toxic has attacked my heart
And it's slowly working on my mind
I could stop its venom
But like the insane, fatality excites
And like the hopeless, I'm apathetic
So I play chicken with love
Just to see who will swerve first
Or just to see who will survive the impact
Now, is that stupidity?
Or is that desperation?

Gazing at the clock, I saw it was 10:42 and my phone had not made a single noise. The reality of my poem was slowly sinking in.

"Oh no, the phone is ringing."

As a test of strength, I needed to not answer it and just let it ring. Nervously, my hands flittered on top of the comforter as the fourth ring went into the voice mail.

"I can't believe I didn't answer the phone," I continued to whisper to myself. "Especially since I've been waiting for this call all night."

Slowly, I slid into the covers, staring at the receiver beside me. I wondered if he left a message. Suddenly the phone rang again. Was I strong enough to let four more rings go by? Of course I wasn't.

"Hello," I answered.

"What's up, beautiful?"

I had to play it cool and act like I had almost forgotten he was going to call.

"Oh, what's up?" I said.

"Are you asleep? I'm sorry I'm calling so late. Practice just got over."

"That's okay. I was just sitting here writing."

"Oh yeah, read it to me."

"No, this poem is not to be read aloud, it's strictly a reminder for me."

"What's it called?"

First I hesitated; then I figured why not tell him? "Stupid and Desperate."

With a sharp burst of laughter, Dick dropped his voice an octave and replied, "A beautiful woman like you should never feel that way."

"Beauty has nothing to do with it. And that sounded like such a come-on line. Cut the small talk, why have you been calling me?"

"I just wanted to talk."

"Well, talk."

After a few sighs, grunts, and sniffs, Dick finally spilled his beans. "I want to see you again before . . ."

"Before what?" I asked quickly.

"You know."

"Say it."

"Before August."

Propping myself up in the bed, I felt my head begin to pound.

"I know, this is wrong. But you have been on my

mind, since the concert. I just want to make sure . . .
I think that . . . if I see you . . ."

"If you think seeing me is going to assure you that
you are making the right decision to marry Celeste,
you are so full of shit."

"Don't get upset. I didn't say it right. I just have
some things I need to say to you face-to-face."

After a quick pause, I began asking a series of questions.

"Were you born male?" I asked.

"What? Yeah."

"Are you HIV positive?"

"No," he answered.

"Have you given me any other disease?"

"Hell no."

"Then we can talk about everything else over the
phone."

Again, Dick was silent. Funny, I couldn't wait for
him to call, but now that I was speaking with him, I was
ready to hang up. I wasn't sure what I was expecting
the conversation to be like, but the fact that he wanted
to visit me to justify his decision to marry another
woman made my blood boil. The longer I stayed on
the phone, the higher my blood temperature rose.

"Dick! You said you wanted to talk, so talk."

"Can I see you or not?"

I said nothing.

"When I'm with my fiancée, I think about you and
she doesn't deserve that. I don't want to hurt Celeste.
I just want to make sure that if I do hurt her, it's for a
good reason—you."

"Listen to yourself, Dick. You sound crazy. I will not
be your scapegoat for hurting Celeste. If you don't
want to be with her, then just leave."

"But I do . . . I think. Then, there is you."

Leaning my head against the headboard, I pressed my face against the phone. Listening to his confusion, I felt I must admit my own conflict.

After a few heavy sighs, I confessed, "I would be lying if I said I didn't love you. I think about you too. But I am in a committed relationship and I am trying to make it work. I cannot leave Winston for you and you cannot leave Celeste for me. We don't need to start a relationship that way. It's too messy."

"But we would not be starting, we would be continuing."

"Same thing."

"Can I come see you?"

"No," I responded hastily.

Dick was silent, yet I heard him softly breathing on the other end.

"You know what? I am having a party the Saturday after my thirtieth birthday. If you are single by then, come see me. If not, let me know where you are registered and I'll send you a wedding gift."

"Don't sound that way," he replied.

"What way?"

"Scornful."

"What do you want me to say? Let's have phone sex like we used to?"

"No . . . not unless you want to."

"Dick, I have to go."

"I'll see you soon."

"Yeah, yeah," I responded before hanging up.

By the conversation's end, I had a pounding headache. Again, I didn't know what I had been expecting to hear from him, but that was surely not it. I was so tired of the back-and-forth bullshit. So what if he loved me, he didn't love me enough to make himself available. And, even if he was available, I couldn't say I would leave Winston. I really liked him and he was good to me. Dick really aggravated the crap out of me. Quickly, I grabbed my journal and scribbled two tiny words in front of the current title, renaming the piece.

"Dick is Stupid and Desperate."

Laughing to myself, I threw the journal onto the comforter and slid back down into the sheets. A few more phone calls like that, and I would be able to get over him a little quicker than I thought.

Closing my eyes, I tried to drift off to sleep; however, I couldn't. The more I thought about Dick's words, the less angry I become, and this decreasing resentment was causing me even more grief. Even his last words, "I'll see you soon," stumped me. Did that mean he was coming to my party? Was he going to break it off with Celeste?

"Ughh!"

Hopping out of bed, I crept across the hall into the guest room to find my mother fast asleep in the bed. Trying not to wake her, I slipped into the other side of the bed and lay still on the pillow. Suddenly I heard her soft voice.

"Is everything okay, dumpling?"

Silently, I nodded into the pillow, for if I spoke, I was probably going to burst into tears, and that would be a dead giveaway that everything was not okay. My mother's soft caress somehow eased my strife. Anyone who says a mother's touch can't heal is simply a big fat liar. I may not verbally share everything with my mom, but we communicate just fine. Though she didn't have the opportunity to use her healing powers as often as she liked, that next morning I gladly reminded her that she still hadn't lost her magical touch.

23

Keeping Secrets

The next day at work slowly slipped by, hour by hour. I managed to do a little work here and there in between the incessant conversations about what everyone was wearing to the annual charitable event on Saturday. As Sarah came back to my desk to deliver the latest gossip and confirm our dinner date on Thursday, I held my notebook in front of my face and pretended I was extremely busy.

"What are you doing?" she asked, knocking down my notebook.

"Trying to work," I replied.

"Whatever, listen to this. I overheard Susan saying that she was going to ask Winston to the dinner this weekend."

"What?" I said, suddenly drawn into the office drama.

"Apparently, she called and left him a message, but

he has yet to return her call. I can't wait to see her expression when you walk in with him on your arm."

My stomach began to toss and turn.

"What's wrong? It's a party, you should be excited."

"This event excites me as much as gray pubic hair."

"Lily!" Sarah exclaimed.

"Look at me! How am I supposed to accessorize this cast? I can't dance. My mother is in town and my boss wants to have sex with my boyfriend. I'm sorry, there are way too many issues for me to be excited about some charity event. And they better not ask me for money."

"Stop being so grumpy," Sarah said with an exaggerated frown.

Playfully, I mashed her on the nose and as she slid her bum off my desk, she commented, "No one likes a sourpuss."

Rubbing my hands over my eyes, I clasped them together in front of my face. As if I was praying, I closed my eyes and bowed my head into my hands. Taking slow breaths, I blocked out the office chatter and my body began to feel light. Meditation is wonderful. I think it should be a required hour within the workday, sort of like the Mexican siesta. Every day around 1:00 p.m., everyone should be required to take an hour to relax and breathe. What a different country this would be, if that were made a law.

After a few quiet minutes, I grabbed my paperwork and my crutch and went down the hall to find an empty room. At the end of the corridor, I saw conference B with no names filled in on the reserved sheet. I placed my things on the desk, closed the door, and took a seat. After closing the blinds, I began to do my work and I stayed in here for the rest of the day.

Around 5:00 p.m., I gathered my things, and like

two young girls, Sarah and I sat outside against the brick wall and waited. Minutes later, my mother pulled up, I waved good-bye to my friend, and promised to see her in school tomorrow. I felt like such a teenager.

"Hi, Mom."

"How was your day?" she asked.

"Great. The teacher used me as an example of a good student today and I made an A on my spelling test."

As we both chuckled, my mom drove out of the parking lot and we headed for home.

We were only home for an hour before we left again to go to my class tonight. My mom took a seat in the back of the room as I prepared my lesson for this evening. As the kids filed in, they eagerly began asking questions about the lady in the back of the room. Once they discovered that the mysterious woman was my mother, the focus turned from tonight's assignment to my behavior as a child. Eventually, I asked my mother to join me at the front of the room and the entire lesson plans were altered. My mom was adopted from a children's home similar to this one. Therefore she, being as candid as she is, openly discussed her experiences growing up and the tribulations she had to overcome. Hands quickly flew up.

"When were you adopted?" asked Sam.

"When I was ten. A couple with another child adopted me and my sister."

"Did you know who your parents were?"

"I knew my mom. She raised my sister and me, but she died when we were four. Her only sister lived on the other coast and she couldn't afford us, so we ended up going into the home."

"Weren't you mad?" asked Karen.

"I was four, a little too young to really get it. But when

I became eight I remembered acting out. I called my aunt and begged her to come and get us, but she never did."

"What do you think would have happened if you'd never gotten adopted?"

My mother sat for a while brewing over that statement. She shook her head and made a funny little noise before answering. "I would have become a stronger person, that's for sure. But who knows what else? The key is that I didn't let my situation dictate the person that I was to become."

This was insight that I never could've given my class; for that reason, I had no problem altering my plans in order for them to have this valuable time. The hour passed quickly and as the kids filed out, I pulled Sam aside and inquired about Shannon's whereabouts.

"Why didn't Shannon come to class?"

"She said she wasn't feeling well."

"What's wrong, does she have a cold?"

"No. She's been sick off and on since the surgery."

"What surgery?"

"You know, the baby."

My voice rose a few pitches, as I got closer to Sam's face. "What baby!"

Sam shut down and looked the other way.

"You've already spilled the beans now, you might as well finish telling me."

Shrugging, Sam leaned against my desk and answered slowly, "Well, she called Doc 'cause she was pregnant and he told her where she could go get an abortion 'cause she didn't want to have the baby. But she didn't want to Ms. Gaither to find out, so don't tell her."

Staring into Sam's eyes, I found her words hard to

swallow. I couldn't believe Shannon was pregnant. Speechless, I leaned against my desk as my mother gathered my things.

"Ms. Lily, are you okay? Don't be mad, I thought you knew. Don't tell her I told you," she added.

"I won't. But tell Shannon to call me if she needs me, okay?"

"Okay."

Sam waved bye to my mom and walked out of the room. Still shocked, I turned toward my mom. "Can you believe that?"

"I can believe anything with the kids these days."

"I can't believe Winston didn't tell me."

I hurriedly grabbed my bag and left the classroom. As fast as I could, I was dialing Winston on the cell phone. Unfortunately, he didn't answer. Hopefully he would return my call as soon as possible, because I want to question him about Shannon's abortion.

"At least he's honorable," my mom commented.

"What do you mean?"

"I'm sure Shannon asked him not to tell you. Plus, there is a doctor-patient oath. Honestly, he is in the right."

"Yeah, well, I just wish I had known. If Ms. Gaither did find out, she could say she got the information from me. She's only fourteen. Who signed the papers for her?"

"Who knows? At least it wasn't Sam."

"Yeah, you're right, but still."

We stopped by the grocery deli for sandwiches and other miscellaneous items. I took a seat in one of the motorized carts with the basket on the end. I had always wanted to ride in those things, and thanks to my fractured ankle, I could. It slightly embarrassed my mom, because she quickly left my side and made her way down separate aisles. But in no time, I zoomed from the bakery section to toiletries. I loved that little motor-powered seat. They should make them for everyone so the grocery shopping time could be cut in half; just grab the item and go—grab and go, grab and go. Finally, I caught up with my mom in the salad section. Together, we got through the checkout lane and went home.

As I was pulling out my clothing for work the next day, my mom came into my room and sat on the corner of my bed. Smiling, I asked her thoughts on her visit so far.

"Pleasant," she said with a half smile.

"What does that mean? I know you have more to say than that."

Leaning back against the pillow, she removed her shoes, crossed her legs, and spoke. "I've enjoyed myself. I like your friends and I love what you are doing at the home. I know you love writing, so your job has to be very fulfilling. But there is something missing."

"Like what?" I asked curiously.

"I can't put my finger on it, but it's something."

As I took a seat in the chair and removed my blouse, my mom continued speaking.

"Are you happy?" she asked.

Pausing, I leaned my head against the wall and grunted. "Of course I am."

"Well, you sure don't sound happy about being happy."

Staring her directly in the face, I became silent. We stared at each other for seconds before she continued.

"Well, I don't want to pry. I just want you to be happy and I am here for you whenever you need me."

"I know, Ma," I said with a soft voice.

My mother rose and grabbed my shirt for work to-morrow. "Do you need anything else ironed?"

Timidly, I shook my head. As she headed out the door, she quickly peeped back in to comment, "By the way, I heard Winston say his brother's name is Wealth. I hope that is not the same Wealth you went out with last year. If it is, I don't want to know."

Then just as quick, she popped her head out and walked downstairs. Chuckling, I thought to myself, she already knew. She just wanted to make sure that I knew that she knew without directly saying "I know what you did."

As I made my way over to my bed, the phone rang. Unfortunately, it was downstairs and I didn't have the energy to go down and get it.

"Can you get that, Mom?" I yelled.

Seconds later, she was bringing the phone to me with her hand over the receiver.

"It's Winston," she whispered. "Be nice."

Now, wasn't that something? The other day I was telling her to be nice, and now she was telling me. With a sarcastic smile, I took the phone and waited for her to leave the room. As soon as he said hello, I asked him about Shannon.

"Why didn't you tell me Shannon was pregnant?"

"Because that is privileged information and you didn't need to know."

"But I gave her your info."

"And I am a doctor. I'm sorry, baby, your mom could be dying of cancer and I still couldn't tell you without her permission."

Quickly, I gasped. "Is that your way of telling me my mom is dying of cancer?"

Laughing, Winston hastily said no. However, I sat on the phone quietly processing this conversation.

"Are you all right? There is no need to be upset."

"I know. I just don't want the home to think I told her where to go to get an abortion."

"I'm sure they won't."

After a few quiet seconds, Winston asked, "Why haven't you told me about the charity dinner on Saturday? Susan called and asked me to be her date."

"I heard. What did you tell her?"

"I haven't called her back."

"Oh," I said softly.

"Don't tell me you are not going," Winston stated.

"I have to go, it's sort of mandatory. Susan asked me to sit at her table."

Winston stirred in laughter. "My dear, you do get yourself into the oddest predicaments."

"It's not funny, Winston."

"It's funny to me. Are you bringing a date or are you going alone?"

"I would like to bring you if you're available Saturday night."

"What? You're bringing me out of the closet?"

"Do you think she will notice that you're not Wealth?" I asked jokingly.

Next thing I knew, I was talking to the dial tone.

"Hello!"

Winston had hung up on me. I was only joking. Quickly, I dialed his number and he answered on the first ring.

"Baby, I was only joking."

"So was I," he said.

"But you hung up on me, that wasn't funny."

"Neither was your joke."

"Point taken. I seriously would like for you to take me to the dinner. With my busted leg, I may not look all that nice, but I promise to be good company."

"Sorry, I have plans," Winston stated boldly.

"What? You made me go through that and you have plans."

Laughing loudly, Winston admitted he was jesting and agreed to pick me up for the dinner around seven o'clock Saturday night. We finally said good night and I hung up the phone just before it rang again. This time it was Sarah. She was upset because she and Omar got into an argument about her and Carmen moving into his place. Omar felt that they should continue staying with his mother and Sarah thought that it would be better for Carmen if her parents lived under the same roof. With him adamantly disagreeing, Sarah thought he was hiding something. Since there was already distrust brewing in the relationship, this spirited conversation had the teapot whistling. I politely asked that we talk about it at work because I had no energy to speak about it tonight. She agreed and I immediately knew lunch the next day was going to be a doozy.

Lying on the pillow, I thought about the hormonal imbalances created by the emotion love. It could take people completely out of character and turn them into new characters. Whether the change happened in a matter of seconds or a matter of years, love, or lack thereof, shapes the people we become. The role of love in our story of life affects how we view others and ourselves. That is some powerful stuff. And as much as I hate the way it makes me feel at times, I couldn't imagine my life without it. As I went to sleep that night, I was thankful for all of the love I had received, the love I had lost, and the love I would find.

There is no doubt in my mind that God is love, 'cause nothing else could have such a magnanimous power over mankind. It's amazing . . . simply amazing.

24

How Do I Like Me …
Let Me Count the Ways

At lunch today, Sarah divulged her so-called brilliant plan to spy on Omar.

"I will tell him you and I are going away for the weekend. Then we'll follow him around town to see if he is seeing someone else."

Covering my face with my hand, I lowered my head and said nothing.

"What is wrong with you?" Sarah asked.

"No, my friend, what is wrong with you?"

"Nothing. I'm trying to find out if Omar is messing around."

"Then ask him. Or, if you don't trust him, take some time away from him. But we are not sneaking around town like a couple of sleuths, better yet, a couple of crazy teenagers."

Sarah frowned while stuffing her mouth with fries. After a few bites, she began to complain. "It's not fair. If you wanted me to spy on Winston, I would."

I looked away from Sarah, because I couldn't bear to see her shed tears. It was distressing that she was so unhappy in her relationship and I wished she would leave Omar altogether. However, this was the father of her child and unfortunately that was a tie that binds. I looked back at her reddened eyes and tried to help her with a solution.

"Sarah, does he ever go out on the weekend?"

"Yeah, he goes to this club uptown on Friday nights."

"Okay, I will beg Winston to go to the spot and check out his behavior. He may not go, but if he does and says that Omar was not messing around with any ladies, you promise to let this go."

Sarah was quiet as she contemplated my suggestion. Finally, after finishing the last bit of her sandwich, she agreed.

Since we took a late lunch, we only had two more hours left at work and I spent that time working on anniversary greetings with Nehri. At the end of the day, I stopped by Sarah's desk to confirm dinner at her house tonight, but it seemed that Claire was not feeling well, and so Sarah decided to cancel plans for the evening, which gave me more time to spend with my mom. True, I was hesitant about her visit at first, but after day two, I was so glad she came.

We stopped by the grocery store to get strawberries, pineapple, and mangos because tonight I was making fruit smoothies with whipped cream. My house phone was ringing as I walked in the door at six o'clock.

"Hello."

"Hi, Ms. Lily, it's Shannon."

"Well, well. It's good to hear from you. How have you been?"

"You're mad at me, aren't you?"

"Should I be mad at you?" I asked.

"I know you know about the baby, but I couldn't tell you. I knew you would be really upset."

"What I don't understand is how did you get pregnant with all of the birth control that's out there? Why are you even having sex?"

"I don't know."

"That is not good enough, 'cause if you don't know, you could get pregnant again."

"I'm not going to get pregnant again, I promise."

Quietly, I sat, gripping the phone.

"Ms. Lily, did you hear me?" Shannon questioned.

"I heard you. Do you have a boyfriend? Does he live at the home?"

"I have a boyfriend, we go to the same school."

"Who signed for you to have this done?"

"My older cousin."

A few more seconds passed in silence before Shannon asked, "You don't like me anymore?"

"It's just the opposite, Shannon. I want you to take care of yourself and think about things before you do them. I don't want to see anything happen to you. What if you had contracted HIV instead of a child? What would you have done then?"

I heard nothing but silence on the other end.

"Do you hear me?"

"Yes, ma'am."

"I know Sam is technically my little sister, but if you want to talk to me before making rash decisions, I'm here. Please call me or talk to Ms. Gaither. Again, you shouldn't be having sex. You are a child."

"Okay, okay, stop yelling at me."

"I have not raised my voice."

"Ms. Lily, I want to go now. I just wanted to call."

"Okay," I responded quickly.

Shannon didn't hang up immediately, she waited for me to disconnect first.

As I turned around, I saw my mom standing in the kitchen smiling. "What are you grinning for?"

"'Cause my baby is grown and giving advice to another baby. It makes me want grandchildren."

Making a disgusting face, I fell back onto the futon. My mom swiftly came into the room to pinch my cheeks. Laughing, she helped me into the kitchen and we began making smoothies.

Mom had a headache so she turned in early; therefore, I decided to do the same. However, I awoke around 3:00 a.m. Unable to go back to sleep, I went to the window to gaze at the full moon. Moving my desk lamp, I pulled out my journal and began to write. Normally, I used the book as a poetry journal, yet I didn't feel like writing poetry tonight. As I stared at the empty pages, I began to analyze myself. Eventually, the page filled with positives and negatives about Lily.

LIKES	*DISLIKES*
sense of humor	*indecisive*
determination	*short tempered*
dedication to friends	*judgmental of strangers*
confidence	*leery of love*
leader	*too demanding of others*
intelligence	*won't quickly confront serious issues*
nurturing	*must have my way/spoiled*
my smile	*my knees*

As I was writing I saw a shadow looming over my right shoulder. I quickly turned around to see my mom peering over me attempting to read my journal.

"What are you doing now?" she asked.

"Writing," I responded nonchalantly.

"Let me see."

Suddenly my mom snatched the journal from my hand and rushed over to the bed.

"Give it back!"

However, she began reading the "Dislikes" column aloud.

"Don't read it! It's not fair. I can't walk."

Hobbling back to bed, I attempted to pry my book from my mom's hand, but she was putting up a good fight.

"Stop playing," I fussed like a toddler.

"Stop whining," she retorted in the same manner.

Huffing, I sat against the headboard and let her have her way. As she finished, she commented, "I like your smile too."

Of course, I couldn't help but grin.

"In fact I agree with everything on this list."

"You aren't supposed to agree with the dislikes."

"Why, if they are true? It's good we recognize our flaws, that way we can fix them. Which one are you going to work on first?"

"It's too early for this conversation. Why aren't you asleep?"

"Why aren't you asleep?" she questioned.

"Mommy."

"Well, let's see, you can't do anything about those ugly knees of yours, so let's start with number three. Why are you judgmental of strangers? I didn't raise you that way."

"My knees are not ugly, why would you say that?"

My mother simply laughed as she sat on the foot of the bed.

"Oh, Lily, I'm just joking." She closed the journal and turned her head in my direction. Before she could get a word out, I heard her thoughts and responded to them immediately.

"Yes, Mom. I am happy."

"What? I didn't say a word."

"You didn't have to, I can hear your thoughts."

Smirking, she continued to comment, "I wasn't going to ask you that. I was going to ask you if you were lonely here in Kansas City."

"Not really, I have my friends. What are you getting at?"

"Why are you leery of love?"

I knew it was coming. I didn't know how soon, but I knew it was close. "I don't know, I don't want to get hurt, I guess. I mean, I love my friends and family. I even love some of the men I have dated. But I don't want to be so in love that I lose myself in the relationship."

"You don't have to lose yourself to be in love. I love your father and I am very sure of myself."

"I know, but if he decided to up and leave one day, you would be devastated."

"I would. But I would eventually get over it and move on. Anything can happen. People are here one day and gone the next. You being afraid of losing yourself in a relationship has nothing to do with your fear of someone leaving, does it?"

Quietly, I shrugged.

"Okay, let's take Winston. He seems like a nice guy. He would provide a nice life for you and a family. What's wrong with him?"

"Nothing, he's perfect. He's the type of man that would stick with a relationship through thick and thin. He would make a great husband."

"Great, so fall in love with him."

"I can't make myself fall in love," I replied.

"But you can make a commitment."

"But I want that head-over-heels, 'this is never going to end' type of love."

"Good luck. Love is what you make it. If you want it to be that, it will. But magical love doesn't fall from the skies. It's great in the beginning, but making it last takes work and it's no easy task. Trust me. I love your father, but there were plenty of times I wanted to walk out and never look back. But I didn't, 'cause I made a commitment not to, and his love and commitment make me fall in love with him all over again."

Leaning over toward my mom, I began to massage her feet as she continued to talk.

"So, what about that other boy, the one who calls and gets you all upset?"

Laughing, I said, "Dick? What about him? He's a musician, he's sweet and I like him. No, I love him. He and I have a special relationship. But we can't be together."

"Why not?"

"'Cause I'm with Winston and he is about to marry Celeste."

"I see. It's good that you and he are upholding your commitments."

"What made you ask about him? You don't know him."

"I don't have to, I know you."

Sighing, I placed my head on her shin, but her silence prompted me to defend my stand on Dick.

"Dick and I dated awhile, but he wanted me to

move back to Atlanta and I wasn't sure so I turned him down. Then when I was thinking about changing my mind, it was too late, 'cause he was already with Celeste. But he did visit when he came in town for a show and since then he's been calling."

"And you call him as well?" she asked.

"Yes. It's strange, we keep saying we are only friends, but it's more."

"Well, I can't tell you any more than you already know."

"Sure you can, you've been telling me stuff my whole life."

"And apparently you haven't been listening."

Laughing, I spitefully pinched her pinky toe. I had never asked my mom for advice on love before, but I decided it was time. "What should I do about Dick?"

Pausing briefly, my mom lifted her upper body off the bed, and caressed my hair. "It sounds like a cliché, but follow your heart. But, since we are talking about a man who is committed to someone else, I don't know what to say."

"That's not good advice."

"Well, how about this cliché? If you can't be with the one you love, love the one you're with."

"I don't like that advice either."

"Well, it's difficult to give good advice to such a hard head."

Other than a tiny grunt, I stayed silent. Soon, my mom continued.

"If you stay committed to Winston, will you be happy? If so, there's your answer. Winston is a good man, you said so yourself, but that doesn't mean he's the man for you. That doesn't mean Dick is the man for you either."

"That's all?" I asked.

"You just want me to say what you are already thinking, simply for justification. But I don't have to, you already know what you are going to do."

"The only thing I know is that I am never giving you a foot massage again, 'cause your crusty feet are causing my hands to blister."

Laughing, I moved my mother's feet away from me as she attempted to rub them against my face. Seconds later, she rose and retreated to the door. Yet, before leaving, she responded, "A man who is truly committed doesn't visit the house of his 'special situation' girl and he surely doesn't call her after eleven."

"He does if he's a dog," I griped.

"But is he?"

And on that note, my mother silently walked back into her room, closed her door, and went back to sleep.

Placing my journal beside my bed, I got underneath the covers. As I replayed the conversation in my head, my adoration and respect for my mom was growing more and more. I was so glad she came to visit. When I asked for help, I hadn't expected my mother to be the one for assistance. Neither had I expected her aid to extend beyond that of my fractured leg.

It's amazing how we ask for one thing and sometimes get another. And if we are patient enough to see the outcome, the very thing we receive is what we really needed in the first place. I guess the race is not always given to the swift.

"Love the one you're with."

I never cared much for clichés, for they always start with "They say." Who are they? If I don't know who they are, how can I be sure that they know what's right?

I decided to start with number three on that list.

25

Like Mother
Like Daughter

Saturday's charity dinner and dance filled the office chatter. You would think this was the Oscars, the way my coworkers were talking about their hairdos and designer dresses. I wished I could be more excited, but I honestly could not care less about going.

"Boo!" Sarah scared as she walked up behind me.

"Are you just getting here? It's almost noon," I said.

"Yep, Carmen had a doctor's appointment this morning."

"She okay?"

"Yeah, it's just a checkup."

Sarah rubbed her nearly bald head against my arm. Grazing her peach fuzz, I simply laughed and she gave a quirky smile. I was simply amazed at her strength.

"This is my last week of chemotherapy. Can you believe it has been eight weeks?"

I nodded and rubbed the peach fuzz atop Sarah's head. Her hair had thinned out, but she never went completely bald.

"I'm thinking about keeping my hair this short for the rest of the summer. What do you think?"

"It's cute."

Sarah rubbed her head before placing her hands on her hips. "I'm so glad it's over, but now I have to go back to shaving my legs."

"How do you feel?"

"I feel okay. Some mornings I feel a little sick and I have no strength to lug Carmen around, but other than that, I feel okay."

"Well, you are inspiring."

"I do have moments throughout the day when I think about my death, and what would happen to Carmen if I died, or what would happen to me if I died."

I didn't say anything, I only thought about what she was saying as she continued.

"I know Claire would take care of Carmen, so I wasn't that worried, but I really want to see her grow up."

"And you will," I said.

"You don't know that."

"No one knows, that's the scary thing about life."

"Yeah, but we know people die from cancer every day."

"People die in car accidents every day, so again, we never know."

"You're right. I have a lot of things left to do. After I get completely well, I think I'm going back to school, and I'm going to take a foreign language, and travel. I have to be able to give Carmen every opportunity I wasn't given."

"You are a great mother, that is very precious in its own right."

Sarah reached over and gave me a hug. But as soon as the sentimental moment had settled, she dove right back into the office gossip.

"Susan still doesn't have a date for tomorrow."

"And . . ." I replied.

"Are you and Winston still sitting at Susan's table?"

"I guess. Do I have a choice?"

Sarah shrugged, before peeping down the hall again. "What are you going to say when Susan asks you about Winston?"

"Maybe she won't notice."

Sarah burst into sharp laughter. "I want to sit at your table, maybe she won't notice me either."

"Get off my desk and go to work."

Sarah moved off the corner and walked beside my chair. "Listen, I'm wearing a maroon dress and a long brown wig."

"A wig?" I commented, making an awkward face.

"Yeah, a really long one. Like Cher in the seventies," Sarah said with a huge smile.

"You are crazy."

"What? It will be fun. I haven't had real long hair since I was a little girl."

I simply laughed, 'cause I absolutely loved Sarah's carefree spirit.

"What are you wearing?" she continued.

"Go back to work," I said, pushing her away.

Sarah slowly moved away from my desk and began to stroll down the hall. As she left, I pondered her question.

"What am I going to wear?" I said to myself.

As the day went by, I finished my paperwork and turned in my latest project. Thank goodness I only had thirty more minutes of work. I walked into the bathroom to wash the chalk off my hands, only to hear more chatter about tomorrow's event. Quickly, I exited just before I was wrapped in the gossip. However, as I was walking out of the door, Nehri inquired about my date.

"He's an old friend," I responded, before exiting.

Swiftly, I walked back to my desk and outside to meet my mom. Thankfully, she was there early; therefore, I went home.

Once home, I rummaged through my closet to start preparing tomorrow's attire. Propping myself up on my crutch, I began tossing clothing right and left until my room was cluttered with textiles of all colors.

"Come eat your dinner," my mother called from downstairs.

Using the end of my crutch, I quickly swept the clothing aside. As I smelled the baked chicken, I started to loathe my mother's departure on Sunday. This week had spoiled me, and I didn't want to go back to cooking. I wanted a chef, like Sarah.

"I'm coming," I called from the stairs.

I made it down to the kitchen and rapidly sat down.

"What were you doing up there?" my mother inquired.

"Trying to find a stupid outfit to wear to the charity dinner tomorrow. I don't want to go," I griped.

"I see."

"How am I supposed to go to a dance with a cast on my leg? Plus, it's your last night here."

"Don't you even put me in that equation. I don't

know why you don't want to go, but I am sure it's not 'cause of me."

I stared at her while poking out my bottom lip.

"Just eat your food. I don't want to hear it."

Laughing, I continued eating, savoring every bite. During dinner, the phone rang three times. Surprisingly, we both let it ring, without glancing in the phone's direction.

"You should come visit me more often," I mentioned.

"I should. I can get away every few months to come here."

"Not that often." I giggled as my mom rose for more juice.

We finished dinner and I sat in the kitchen talking to my mom as she rinsed off the dishes. Then she came with me to the bedroom to assist in my clothing decision. Upon checking the messages, I saw that Tam, Winston, and Sarah were my three missed calls. However, Winston was the only call I returned, because I was not in the mood for girlfriend chat this evening. My mother and I narrowed my event attire down to two choices: a long black gown with a halter neckline and an asymmetrical hem and a long crimson, strapless dress with tiny sequins scattered throughout the fitted bodice and full bias bottom. Both were beautifully tailored dresses.

"Why do you have so many long gowns?" questioned my mom.

"Last year, Wealth and I used to go to society events every other weekend. I had to constantly buy new dresses to wear. I guess they added up to what you see here."

"And Wealth is Winston's brother?" my mom inquired slyly.

"I thought you said you didn't want to know."

My mom simply cut her eyes at me while placing my other dresses back in the closet. While her lips stay closed, her eyes spoke volumes. Hence, once again I was forced to defend myself.

"I really like Winston, I only liked Wealth a little."

Still, she said nothing.

"If you met Wealth, you probably wouldn't have liked him either."

Suddenly my mom chuckled aloud.

"What's so funny?" I asked.

Moving over to the bed, she spoke. "I dated your uncle the year before I started dating your father."

"Why are you whispering?" I murmured.

"I don't know." She laughed. "I just find it cute that we both did the same thing."

"I can't believe you left Uncle Andrew for Dad. Uncle was fine back in the day and he played pro football too."

"That was the problem. He knew he was fine and he thought he could have any woman he wanted. Your father was obviously the better choice and when Andrew messed up, he stole me right from under his brother's nose."

Gasping, I responded, "That's exactly what happened with me."

We both fell out laughing.

"Why didn't you ever tell me this?"

"Why should I? This all happened before you were born."

Suddenly my laughter stopped.

"What's wrong?" she asked.

"My middle name is Drew. What does that mean?"

"I know you are not insinuating that Andrew is your father." Her tone changed. "You know you were named after your grandfather Andrew."

Squinting my eyes I stared closely at my mother.

"Girl, what is wrong with you? I ended things with Andrew three years before you were born. That man is not your father. Alvin McNeil is your father. There has never been a question about that," she said while rising off the bed.

"Okay," I stated simply.

Pointing her long skinny fingers in my direction, she remarked, "You are batty, I would never go back and forth between brothers. You have been watching too much daytime television."

I thought to myself, if only she knew daytime television was nowhere near as taboo as my own soap opera life. I might as well pack up, move to Pine Valley, and become best friends with Erica Kane, 'cause drama was my middle name. Thankfully, my mom left the room before any more of the script was revealed. The longer she stayed, the more I saw we had in common. Fortunately, her vacation was rounding, 'cause the similarities were becoming eerie.

After preparing for bed, I reached into my drawer and pulled out my journal. However, as I stared at the blank page, I kept visualizing Uncle Andrew and my mom. Ironically, when I was growing up, I used to wish he were my dad. He drove a Cadillac and always had money. It was nothing for my uncle to give me a twenty every time he saw me. He used to always say, "Andrew keeps a pocketful of Andrews."

I remembered thinking he was the coolest man in the world. Sure, a twenty doesn't go far these days, but this was 1985 and to a five-year-old, two twenty-dollar bills meant you were a millionaire.

My mom was funny, she let her true self slip out every now and then. Even so, I had never wanted to be like her while growing up. I wanted to be like Diana Ross or Jodi Watley or even Farrah Fawcett (long story). But my mom is a remarkable woman and I am so proud to be a little like her.

She walks with grace
She talks with understanding
She never boasts
She doesn't have to
She is an example of beauty
She is an example of love
Her smile is contagious
Her peace is obvious
Her voice is heard
Without a yell

I long to walk
I long to talk
I long to teach
I long to smile
I long for wisdom
Like her

As I placed my book on the nightstand and slid under the sheets, I couldn't help but wonder if my mom ever had a "Dick" in her life. I made faces even as I thought of Dick and my mom in the same sentence. Even worse, what if her "Dick" was my father, "Alvin"?

"Yuck!" I said aloud.

No matter what role my dad played in my mother's

early years, they had managed to make it work and I thought their love was beautiful. Closing my eyes, I began to pray quietly.

"Maybe one day I will be delivered an Alvin to fill every role in my sitcom. Hopefully, my drama will turn into a situation comedy and maybe one day, a family program. I know we will have *Different Strokes*, but through the *Good Times* and bad let us remain *Friends* and lovers for all of the *Days of our Lives*. Most importantly, let us forever be in syndication."

Amen.

26

Out of the Closet

"Wake up, dumpling, it's Donnie," my mother said as she stood over my bed and handed me the phone.

"Hello," I answered with very little excitement.

"Are you still asleep?" he asked.

"Yeah, what time is it?"

"Around ten o'clock."

Moaning, I sat up and stretched my arms. "I didn't sleep well, I had crazy dreams all night long."

"Well, what are you doing for lunch?" Donnie inquired.

"Nothing, I'll probably eat something around here."

"I have to talk with you, I'm taking you to lunch."

"But my mom is leaving tomorrow. Can we exchange lunch for dinner and do it tomorrow after she leaves?"

After a few sighs, Donnie replied, "I guess. But don't cancel tomorrow, 'cause it's important."

"Is everything okay?"

"We'll talk tomorrow. Are you going to that dinner tonight?"

"Yeah, why?"

"Just wondering," he answered.

"Are you sure everything is okay?"

"Yeah, I'll see ya tomorrow. Is seven good?"

"Yeah, just come over."

We hung up and I slowly moved my body from the bed and hobbled downstairs to join my mother.

"You want breakfast?"

"Nope, my stomach hurts. I just want some ginger ale."

"Don't try to play sick. You are going to that dinner, it's part of your job responsibility."

"I'm not playing, my stomach really hurts," I said while going to the fridge for a drink.

After I got dressed, my mom and I went to the movies just for some last-minute girl time. Afterward, we grabbed a few subs and headed home. As soon as I walked into the house, the phone began ringing.

"I know that's Sarah. She's been calling my cell all day, I just didn't answer," I said to my mom.

As I picked up the receiver, I could hear Sarah on the other end, yapping.

"Where have you been? I've been trying to call you all day."

Calmly, I responded, "I spent the day with my mom. I didn't answer the phone, because we were at the movies."

"Oh, I hope you had a lovely time," she replied sincerely before turning caustic. "But what if I had an emergency? I have to be able to get in touch with you."

"Sarah, you have Claire, Donnie, and Omar. They are also your emergency contacts."

"Claire is at the spa, I am not speaking to Omar, and Donnie is my emergency. I kissed him last night."

"What!" I yelled.

"Don't be mad. I didn't mean to do it. It just happened. I know you like him."

"Girl, I do not want Donnie, I assure you."

"I don't know what to say, it's weird. And now I don't have a date, 'cause I am not taking Omar."

"Well, take Donnie."

Sarah was silent.

"Did you hear me? I said ask Donnie."

"I can't."

"Why not?"

"'Cause."

"Look, I have told you what to do. We only have three hours before this thing starts and I have to take a nap, then get dressed. Are you going to be okay?"

"I guess," Sarah responded despondently.

"You and Donnie are friends, have a great time at the dance and talk about the kiss afterward. It's a good idea, I promise you."

"Okay," Sarah agreed softly.

As soon as we disconnected, a huge smile popped onto my face. The smile grew into a robust, sharp laugh.

"I knew it!" I shouted with my arms in the air.

Gyrating my body, I moved around in place while chanting the phrase, "I knew it, I knew it, I knew it."

As my mom exited the restroom, she inquired, "What did you know?"

"I knew Sarah and Donnie would eventually link up. They kissed last night."

Frowning, my mother replied, "Why are you happy about that? She is with that other boy, Carmen's father."

"But we don't want her with him, we want her with Donnie."

"Oh, we do? I don't understand y'all. She needs to be with that baby's father. Why is she kissing on Donnie? I thought he liked you."

"I told you we were just friends."

Shaking her head, my mother mumbled a few undetectable words and went upstairs. I soon followed, retiring to my bedroom to take a catnap before this evening's events.

An hour and ten minutes later, I turned over and looked at the clock and griped about the fact that it was time for me to get ready for the event. Slowly, I moved to the edge of the bed and stared into the closet, where my dress hung on the door. I began to chuckle thinking about Sarah in her long Cher wig. I hoped she and Donnie did get together.

"I don't like Omar," I said to myself. "I don't like him at all," I repeated as I made my way to my bathroom.

Looking at myself in the mirror, I lit up with an idea.

"Hey, Mom!" I yelled downstairs.

Slowly, she walked up the stairs while answering, "Yes, dear, what can I help you with?"

Peering out the door, I poked out my lip. "You don't sound excited to help me."

"What do you need?" she reiterated.

"Well, I want to straighten my hair for this evening and I need help with the hot comb."

Perking up, my mother hastened up the stairs, reached underneath the sink, and blew the dust off the iron hot comb.

"You should have said something earlier, we could have done this before you lay down. Now we have to hurry."

In no time, my mom had the comb heated and I was sitting in between her legs as she pressed my hair straight.

When she is done, I had a headful of straight, shiny hair that fell a few inches below my shoulders.

"Turn around and let me see," my mother said, beaming.

Slowly, I turned and winked at my mom.

"You look so pretty."

"Are you saying I don't look pretty with my hair all curly?"

"No, dear, I am not. But the change is nice. I need to clip your ends, though."

She walked into the kitchen and grabbed some scissors.

"Don't cut too much."

Surprisingly, she did a great job and I was quite pleased.

"I do look different," I said, looking at my reflection. "No one here has ever seen me with straight hair. I hope Winston likes it."

All of a sudden, the phone rang. But before I could turn to get it, my mom was bringing the receiver to me.

"Hello," I answered.

"Hi, babe," said Winston.

"Hi, have I got a surprise for you!" I responded.

"Well, I've got bad news. I am not going to be able to take you to the dance."

"Oh no! Why?"

"One of my patients just went into labor."

"Can't someone else pull the baby out?" I asked.

"Her case is special. She's having triplets. We were going to deliver them C-section on Tuesday, but she can't wait. I have to do the C-section in about an hour."

"Well, I really don't want to go now. I just started to get excited."

"What kind of surprise do you have for me?"

"Never mind, it doesn't matter."

"Listen. I will come as soon as the surgery is over. If all goes well and there are no complications, I should only miss the first hour."

Pouting, I sat silent.

"Lily, I'm sorry," Winston apologized.

"It's okay."

"I will try to make it there before it's over. My tuxedo is in the car."

"All right." I sighed. "I'll see you there."

"Cheer up. I can't wait to see you."

Dejected, I sat down on the cold closed toilet seat while leaning my head against the wall. Abruptly, the phone rang again. I looked at the ringing phone as I held the receiver in my hand. Finally, it stopped ringing, only to start again seconds later.

"Hello," I answered irritably.

"What time are you and Winston coming?" Sarah questioned quickly.

"Winston has to deliver triplets. He says he's going to meet me there. So I guess I'll get there when my mom drops me off."

"Donnie and I can pick you up. He can swing through and get you before me," she responded anxiously.

"Don't you two want to be alone?"

"No," she interjected quickly. "I'll call him right now and have him call you. Go get ready."

"How do you know I'm not already dressed?"

"I can tell by your voice. Now go!" Sarah said before hanging up.

Slowly, I removed my body from the bathroom, went upstairs, and prepared myself for the evening. With my mother's assistance, I was dressed and ready by 6:30 p.m. Although the dinner was going to start at seven o'clock, we didn't want to get there until seven thirty. I was rooting for eight o'clock, but Sarah and my mom agreed that an hour late was too tardy. Therefore, I sat downstairs across from my mom as she stared at me with a big smile.

"Please stop looking at me."

However, she continued to stare until the doorbell finally rang. Grabbing my cane, I wobbled to the door to meet Donnie. As I opened the door, his mouth flew open, but no sound came out.

"Will you close your mouth!"

Donnie rubbed his hand against my hair.

"Stop, you're going to mess it up," I said with a girlish giggle.

It's amazing how a new hairdo can give you an entirely different personality.

"You look so good."

"Even with the cane?" I asked.

"Where's your crutch?"

"It's right here," I said, removing it from the side of the door. "I want to try the cane, but I'm taking the crutch as a backup."

"Cool, you ready?" asked Donnie.

Suddenly my mom popped into the hallway with a disposable camera in her hand. "I should take a picture."

"C'mon, Mom, this is not the prom."

Placing his arm around my waist, Donnie concurred with my mother. "That would be a great idea, Mama Rachel."

Frowning at him, I moved closer to appease my mom before hurrying out of the house.

As soon as the front door closed, I yelled, "I knew it! I knew you and Sarah were going to hook up."

Bashfully, Donnie replied, "We only kissed. And it shouldn't have happened. She was very embarrassed, which made me self-conscious, and now I don't know what's going to happen."

"Well, she called me, just as confused as you. But I say go with the flow. Follow your heart."

"I can't believe you're saying that. Not the one who keeps her heart in the castle, behind the locked iron door, across the moat with the lifted bridge."

"I'm not that bad."

"You're kidding. You protect your heart like they protect Fort Knox." Donnie laughed.

"Whatever, this is about you and Sarah, not Lily and Lily's heart."

"Fine, but we agreed not to talk about it tonight, so do not mention it once Sarah gets in the car. We just want to have fun like old friends. 'Cause that is what we are."

"Okay."

The next few minutes were spent listening to Saturday jazz on the radio. However, Donnie broke the silence and confessed, "I really like her."

Smiling, I simply responded, "I know."

That evening, no more was said about the infamous kiss. In no time we were at Sarah's home. And, after she finished her rounds of oohs and aahs over my straight hair, we arrived thirty minutes late to the formal affair.

Although my seat was set at Susan's table, I walked over to the table where Sarah was seated. Grabbing a chair, I sat and sparked up chitchat with the others, while Donnie mingled at the bar with the other men.

"You better go over to your table," Sarah commented.

"I will a little later. Look over there, no one cool is at Susan's table. I don't have anything in common with those people."

Sarah glanced over at Susan's table placed strategically in the center of the other round, lavishly decorated tables.

"You're right. You are sitting at the pretentious table. Too bad," she said sorrowfully, patting my back.

"I only hope Winston hurries and gets here."

"You are going to be in so much trouble, Susan is going to hate you."

"Hush," I said as Donnie approached.

Extending his hand, Donnie asked Sarah to dance. Politely, she welcomed his invitation.

"No, don't leave me!" I whispered loudly.

However, Sarah paid me no attention as she trotted arm in arm to the dance floor with Donnie. I sat and watched them for a few minutes, then finally made my way to the pompous crew at table 22. Luckily, most of them were up mingling, and so I didn't have to make unwanted small talk. Sipping on my tea, I sat back and watched the others dance until Susan walked up behind me. Complimenting my look, she quickly sat and energetically began to talk.

"So, where's your date?" she asked.

"He had an emergency, he may not make it," I said, looking toward the door.

This could be a blessing in disguise. Perhaps I could leave before Winston got here. At least then, I wouldn't have to explain anything to Susan.

Just then, Susan looked at her watch and responded, "Yes, I am expecting Winston any moment now."

I turned to her so sharply, I almost threw my neck out.

"*You* are expecting Winston. My Winston?" I asked with widened eyes.

"Yes. I asked him several weeks ago. But when he returned my call, I missed it. Then, as you know, I left town," she rambled on.

Tuning out all of the words in the middle, I eagerly awaited the finale where she confirmed Winston as her date. Finally, I couldn't wait any longer, so I interrupted. "So when did you talk with him?"

"Well, I didn't. I called his secretary this week to see if he was available and she checked his calendar. Then she informed me that he had the Hallmark Charity dinner on his calendar for Saturday and he just had his tuxedo cleaned." Susan beamed as my stomach turned.

"But—" I attempted to interrupt but failed as she continued.

"I confirmed the time with her and left him a message that I couldn't wait to see him. We're so busy, we keep playing phone tag. I didn't want to bring another date, when I found out he was planning to meet me here. He's such a sweet man."

"So you came here without talking to him?" I asked slowly.

"I know it sounds crazy. But if he couldn't make it, it would be fine, 'cause I am so busy entertaining. Plus, I am speaking. Honestly, I really don't need a date. But when she read that he was planning to come, it felt good. I knew we connected, that was just confirmation."

Just then, an elderly gentleman tapped her shoulder and whisked her away. Dumbfounded, I sat alone at table 22, waiting for the next bomb to drop and blow me out of here. My disturbing blank stare prompted Sarah to dance her way over to my table.

"You okay?" she asked.

Dazed, I shook my head from right to left.

"I feel sick," I said, holding my stomach.

"Let's go to the restroom," Sarah said, lifting me from my seat.

Slowly, we walked from the banquet hall, down the carpeted hallway, to the brown door marked WOMEN'S. Quickly, I began explaining my dilemma. Yet Sarah found nothing but humor in the entire story.

"This makes no sense. How could you plan to come to dinner with someone without talking to them?" I stated as I peeped under each stall door.

Sarah only had one response to give. "This is going to be so funny."

Propping my body against the counter, I placed my hands over my face.

"I'm sorry. I'll stop laughing," Sarah apologized.

Spreading my fingers, I peeped through the small crack of my index and middle appendage as she continued to talk.

"You'll have to stand outside the door and warn Winston before he comes in. You may even be able to leave."

"Good idea, let's go."

Sarah and I hastened from the bathroom and walked back into the banquet area. We each stood outside the room and peered down the hall. Winston was nowhere in sight. Therefore, Sarah grabbed my arm and together we both walked in. However, once we were two steps inside the room, we immediately came to a standstill.

"I guess the triplets are healthy," said Sarah as she

and I stared at Winston walking through the center of the room.

"What am I going to do?" I said slowly.

"You better grab him before Susan sees him."

Sarah quickly pushed me in that direction, but then realized I could only go so fast with the cane. For that reason, she zoomed past me, grabbed Winston's arm, and escorted him out of the room all in a matter of seconds. She even managed to tell Donnie to distract Susan just in case she saw Winston walking out the door. Before I could make it out the door, Sarah was explaining. I quickly interrupted by stepping in front of her and picking up in the middle of her sentence.

"Although you didn't call Susan back, she thinks that you are here as her date."

Speechless and looking askance, Winston stood with his right hand placed against his right cheek.

"What should we do?" I asked innocently.

"Yeah, what should we do?" Sarah echoed.

Winston looked inside the banquet hall, then looked at the two of us. "We should go in and explain."

"Bad idea," I interjected quickly.

"No, good idea. This way everything will be out in the open once and for all. If we don't say something now, she will still think I want to date her. I'm so ready for this thing to be over."

Laying my head on his chest, I let out a tiny whimper.

"Well, I'm going back to my date," Sarah said, patting me on the shoulder just before she walked back into the main room.

After running his fingers down my back, Winston grabbed my hand and we slowly walked through the doors to face the truth. Although my palms were sweaty,

Winston's tight grip was ensuring that I didn't slip away from him.

"Where's our table?"

Pointing across the room, I focused on table 22, where I saw Susan standing talking to several distinguished gentlemen. My feet became paralyzed.

"I need you to move with me," Winston urged.

"We need to get our game plan together. Who's going to talk first? Maybe you should let go of my hand."

"I'm not letting go of your hand and I will speak first. I'm going to tell her that I am your date and she will deal with it however she deals with it," Winston replied.

Nervously, I felt that it was not going to go as smooth as Winston explained. Yet I slowly put my one good foot in motion. As we came closer, Susan focused on Winston and a big smile stretched across her face. She immediately halted her conversation and made a beeline in our direction. Within a blink, Susan was standing before us.

"Winston, you made it," she said, beaming.

Immediately, my muscles tensed up and locked around his hand. Consequently, Winston had to greet Susan with a cordial left-handed handshake.

"Lily, thank you for bringing him to me," Susan commented.

Other than a slight nod, I was numb.

"Winston, there are so many people I want to introduce you to," Susan said as she attempted to grab his left side and pull him into the crowd. Unfortunately, I was still attached to his right and we looked like partygoers trying to start a conga line.

"Susan, we need to speak," stated Winston.

Susan, still beaming, turned and placed her hand on his left shoulder. "Well, we have all night."

"No, this is important."

"Okay," Susan said with some concern.

Funny, she still hadn't asked why Winston and I were holding hands and my heartbeat was increasing by the minute. I knew she couldn't fire me over this, but she sure could make my job very unbearable. Winston was so sweet to agree to speak with her, but I needed to step to the plate and play the game I started. I looked up and saw Sarah from across the room. She motioned for me to tell her.

"Winston, I'll speak to her," I said boldly, while removing my hand from within his.

"What is this about?"

"It's a simple mix-up. Let's walk out in the hall."

"I don't want to walk out to the hall, just tell me here," Susan said slowly and very articulately.

Stepping in between Winston and Susan, I gently placed my hand in the curve of her back and slightly nudged her in the direction of the door. Nodding back to Winston, I assured him that I could handle the situation. Then, leaning back, I whispered in his ear, "If I'm not back in five minutes, call security."

Finally Susan and I made it to the door and I immediately began explaining.

"This is going to be weird. Um . . . Winston is my date. He offered to take me before you asked him."

With her hands placed on her hips, she leaned against the wall and responded with a puckered brow, "Interesting."

"It is," I snapped with a spontaneous burst of laughter.

For a few seconds we stood staring at each other, then she finally spoke again.

"So, why didn't Wealth bring you?"

"I don't date Wealth," I responded, hoping she didn't take this line of questioning any further.

"But you did date him, right?"

"Kind of . . . for a little while last year."

Again, she was silent while looking down the hall to acknowledge mingling guests.

"So that's it?" she asked, moving back toward the banquet room.

"Yeah, I suppose so, sorry about the mix-up. It's embarrassing."

"Not a big deal," she said with a fake smile. "Nothing wrong with a friend taking his dateless friend to a work function," she replied, emphasizing the word *dateless.*

"Yeah," I mumbled.

"You should have said something."

"I know. Again, sorry."

Susan with her plastered smile began walking into the room, but not before she looked back and commented, "But if I play my cards right, our evening will continue after this event is over." She winked before walking in the door.

"He's got a girlfriend," I blurted out.

Whipping her body around, Susan confronted me. "A what? Winston never mentioned seeing anyone."

"I asked him not to."

"Why?" she asked, now more frustrated than before.

"'Cause, I'm the girlfriend," I finally confessed.

Susan stood in the doorway and brushed her long hair to one side. Looking me up and down, she simply repeated her favorite response. "Interesting."

Then she walked back into the dinner to socialize. Relieved, I leaned against the wall and let out a huge breath. Although the charade was over, I felt the travesty just beginning. I picked myself up and made my way toward table 22, where Winston awaited.

"I take it everything is okay?" he asked, before I could sit.

Shrugging, I responded casually, "I guess."

We participated in light conversation with a few more of the guests, and then dinner was served fifteen minutes later. The conversation at table 22 was filled with nothing but boring corporate talk. Between the "stocks are up and stocks are down" phrases, I couldn't get a word in edgewise. Susan sat to my right, one seat over from Winston, but she didn't include us in any of the conversation. I assumed she no longer wanted me to meet the important people she had mentioned earlier. It didn't matter, however, because Winston and I engaged in our own entertaining discussion.

Following dinner, Susan walked to the platform to speak. After a brief blurb about the company and its commitment to the community, she introduced the host for the silent auction.

"I hate these things," Winston murmured.

"Me too. I wish we could leave."

"We can," he said.

"But we have to wait. Everyone is sitting. They will see us. We're sitting in the center of the floor," I commented.

Winston sighed before replying, "We'll wait a minute and then someone else is bound to stand."

After the host announced the winning bid for a series of Dickens-signed hardbacks, the banquet servers came around to the tables to gather plates and bring desserts.

"Go now!" Winston exclaimed.

As if I were committing a jailbreak, I swiftly rose and

hobbled my way in between white jackets. Once on the outside, I awaited my partner in crime. Minutes later, I felt a warm touch on my shoulder and I turned thinking we were home free only to see Sarah, bright-eyed and smiling.

"Where are you going? What happened?"

"Why are you out here?"

"Looking for you," she responded honestly.

"Well, we are leaving as soon as Winston gets out here."

"Good, I want to leave too, let me go get Donnie."

Grabbing her arm, I stopped her in her tracks. "You can't leave now, we are leaving now. It would cause a scene. We are sneaking out."

"Fine. We'll sneak out behind you. Don't leave the building."

Sarah rushed back in just as Winston came out.

"You ready?"

"No, we have to wait for Sarah and Donnie," I said, placing my arm within his. "Let's walk down here and wait."

Winston and I walked to the end of the corridor close to the outside entrance and killed time until the two of them arrived. Once we got outside the building, small laughter bubbled over to sheer amusement.

"Now let's go have some real fun," Sarah said, tossing her wig to and fro.

"And do what?" I asked.

Confused, we looked at each other with odd expressions. Suddenly, Donnie shouted, "I know. You guys follow me."

We walked across the street to the parking deck, then followed Donnie and Sarah to a western saloon on the other side of downtown. After we parked, Winston and

I sat in the lot staring at the neon sign that said WELCOME COWBOYS AND COWGIRLS. Donnie knocked on the car window, startling us both.

"Come on!"

Slowly, we removed our bodies from the car and walked over to the bar.

"Don't you think we are a little overdressed?" I asked Donnie.

"Yeah, but who cares? It will be fun."

"They have karaoke," Sarah added with enthusiasm.

What happened when two skeptics and two karaoke fans, all dressed in formal attire, waltzed into the country-western bar? We were about to find out.

As if a tornado whisked through the door, all heads snapped in our direction as soon as we walked in. As suspected, we stuck out like men in the Miss America Pageant. Donnie walked near the tiny wooden stage in the front of the bar and cleared off a table. We took our seats and a petite blond waitress came over and placed a pitcher of beer on our table.

"Good to see ya, Patch," she said with a country twang.

"These are my friends, Lily, Winston, and Sarah. This is Katie."

"Hi," we all said in unison.

She placed four glasses by the pitcher, squeezed Donnie on the shoulders, and walked away. Baffled, we all stared at Donnie for an explanation.

"I come here when I'm recording late nights. It's the only place near the studio that stays open late. It's a cool spot."

Looking around the lantern-lit saloon with horse-shoes and saddles adorning the wall, I cynically responded, "I bet it's a blast."

Suddenly the music was turned up and Clint Black was blaring through the speakers. The dance floor crowded and a line dance formed.

"That looks like fun," I said, surprising myself.

"It's like the electric slide," said Donnie.

"But for white people," Sarah added.

Winston, who had been silent the entire night, finally made a comment. "I know how to line-dance."

We all turned in his direction and awaited the rest of his story.

"I liked a girl once who was a line dance instructor. I took a few of her classes to get her number and ask her out."

"This evening has been so full of surprises." I giggled.

"Speaking of surprises. What did Susan say to you?" Sarah inquired curiously.

"She responded with her favorite word. Other than that, she didn't say much."

"What's her favorite word?" asked Donnie.

"Interesting," Sarah and I both mocked in our best Susan voice.

We all laughed as Donnie poured himself another glass of beer.

"Winston, let's go dance," said Sarah.

At first he denied her request, but upon her constant coercing, he agreed and the two of them hit the dance floor. Donnie brought his chair around the table for a better view.

"Wow, he really can line-dance," I said, watching Winston show Sarah the steps.

Donnie and I could do nothing but laugh as we watched Winston in his tuxedo and Sarah in her long gown with a long brown wig maneuver and jig their way in between the Levi's and spurred boots.

After Sarah's dance lesson and a few more beers, we were all ready to leave. Upon saying our good-byes in the parking lot, we parted ways. We rode in the car for minutes, before I realized that Winston was taking the long route home.

"Where are you going?" I asked.

"To your house," he responded.

"Why this way?"

"I don't want the evening to end just yet."

Smiling, I wrapped my fingers around his and laid my head on his arm as we drove down the street. With the top down, I closed my eyes as the breeze cooled my skin.

"Why don't you stay with me tonight?"

"I can't. You know my mom is in town. She leaves tomorrow."

"So, we'll take her to the airport tomorrow, when I bring you home."

Although I would have loved to stay with Winston tonight, I just couldn't. I faced Winston with a frown. "I have to go home. I can't stay out all night. It's not right."

"I'm sure Rachel knows that you stay at my house sometimes."

"Probably, but I'm not doing it while she's in town."

Winston said nothing. He only accelerated his speed and hastily got me home. I think he was a little upset. But he would just have to wait until the next night to be alone with me.

As we pulled up to the driveway, I attempted to soothe him. "Let's do something tomorrow night."

"I have an early morning Monday. Tomorrow is not good," he said with curtness.

"Well, I'll see you next week."

Winston walked me to the door and kissed my cheek just before I walked in.

"You're welcome to come in," I encouraged.

Winston simply waved bye and left. I walked in and quickly went upstairs to my bed. Minutes later, my mom peeped her head in the door. From my bed, I motioned for her to enter. She sat on the foot of my bed as she asked about my evening.

"It was decent," I replied.

"That doesn't sound like fun."

"Well, the dance was not, but then we left and went to a western saloon. That was different. But I think Winston got upset with me when I wouldn't stay with him at his place."

"You didn't want to stay?" she asked.

"I don't know. Not with you here. I feel it's disrespectful."

"Honey, you are grown. As long as I know you're safe, I'm okay."

"I don't know if I really wanted to stay, I just wanted to come home," I admitted.

Rubbing my shoulders, my mother giggled.

"What are you doing up? It's after two a.m."

"I was up reading, I couldn't sleep," she said, walking toward my door.

"Well, I'm going to bed."

My mother threw her hand in the air as she walked back into her room. Then she meticulously stepped in again, displaying half of her body in the door frame.

"Dick called," she said with a curious smile.

Tossing my pillow at her, I shrieked, "Why are you messing with me?"

"What?" she asked innocently as she disappeared into the hallway.

I finished removing my clothing just before I lay across my bed. Of course, my energy was roused up from just hearing Dick's name. Tossing and turning on the bed, I wondered what this particular call was about. Then sighing, I buried my head underneath the pillow.

"I wonder what Susan is going to say to me on Monday?"

Well, the truth was out and it felt good . . . sort of. It's not that I was embarrassed to be with Winston, but now that people knew, it really made us an official couple.

When a relationship is covert, there is much less pressure. No one inquires about the status or future plans. But once it is out there, invitations come in his and her name and if either party attends a function without the other, questions arise. And sometimes those questions tend to make the individual question the relationship. Again, I was glad the truth was out, but with the strangeness hovering over my connection with Winston, I was going to be gawked at all next week at work, and I just didn't want to go through that.

I needed to have a speech prepared to reel off every time someone asked about my date. Grabbing a piece of paper, I attempted to write my retort of witty dialogue. However, in no time, sleep crept into my body and I didn't have the energy to write or get up and put on nightclothes. Thus, I stretched across my bed in my panties and fell asleep.

"The truth may set you free spiritually, but realistically, it's a pain in the butt. I'm spent."

27

Daughter by Blood,
Friend by Choice

The loud ringing of my cordless startled me first thing in the morning. Slowly turning my head, I stared at the clock while wiping the sleep from the corner of my eye. Leaning over, I grabbed the phone.

"Yes," I answered heatedly.

"Wake up," said a chipper Donnie on the other line.

"Why are you waking me up?"

"What time are you going to the airport? Do you need a ride?"

"Her flight doesn't leave till two o'clock. It is now eight twelve," I grumbled.

"If you need a ride, I can take you. I'm on my way home now. But I can be at your house around eleven thirty."

"Fine, great. I appreciate it."

"Well, I'll see ya then."

"Hold it!"

Donnie was silent.

"Did you say you were on your way home? From where?" I asked.

After letting out a small chuckle, he responded, "From Sarah's but it's not what you think. We stayed up so late talking last night, I stayed in one of the guest rooms."

"Whatever you say," I said in a tone to suggest doubt.

"Seriously."

"I'll see you when you get here."

I hung up and tossed the phone back on the bed. Then crawling toward my headboard, I slid my body underneath the covers and attempted to go back to sleep. However, seconds later my mother was knocking on my door.

"I'm asleep," I called out.

"Well, wake up," she said, walking into the room.

I pulled the comforter over my face and held it in place as my mom tried to pull it away. Finally, she gave up and removed the covers from the base of the bed, which exposed my bottom half. Flinging my good leg in the air, I tried to discourage my mom from waking me. Unfortunately, I accidentally kicked her in the face.

"Ouch!"

Quickly, I sat up and comforted her. "I'm sorry. I'm sorry. I was playing."

My mom sneered at me as she covered her left eye. Removing her hand, I inspected the damage.

"It's okay, it's not red or anything."

"Not yet," she responded. "Wait until I tell your father you kicked me in the face."

Gasping, I retorted gravely, "You know I didn't mean to kick you."

My mom cut her eyes at me as she stood to leave the room.

"Don't be mad, Mommy. I'm sorry," I called as she disappeared.

"I'm not mad, I'll see you when you get downstairs," she responded from the hallway.

I stared at the ceiling and realized that my morning was over. I needed to get up and enjoy my last few hours with my mother. Especially since I almost caused her an eye injury.

Moments later, I was sitting at the kitchen counter enjoying a cup of tea across from my mom, who was ending her conversation with my dad.

"Did you tell him I said hello?" I asked as she hung up.

Nodding yes, she asked, "Why don't you and Winston come visit next month?"

Shrugging, I responded, "Maybe, if he can get some time off. We'll see."

Tapping her nails against the wooden kitchen table, she nodded and smiled. "I'm glad I came."

Smiling, I responded, "So am I."

Placing my hands on top of hers, I looked into my mother's eyes and saw my future. I hoped I was as cool as she was twenty-five years from now.

"Stay right here," I said while rising from the table.

Hastily, I hopped into the guest bathroom and returned shortly with a tin can filled with nail products. "I can't let you go home with your nails looking like that."

My mom spread her hands on the table and looked. "They could use some work."

I took her right hand and cleaned off the chipped pale polish. Displaying five different colors between the hues of brown and burgundy, I asked, "Which color do you want?"

"This one," she replied, pointing to Revlon's Cherry Wine.

Grinning, I began to polish my mother's nail, something I hadn't done since I was a child. At least this time, she wouldn't have polish all over her hands.

"I know this may be none of my business," my mom blurted out.

"If you preface the sentence with that remark, I'm sure it's not your business."

Laughing, she responded, "Whether it is or not, I'm saying it. I try to stay out of your love life. However, I know there is something between you and Dick. And if you're not ready to be in a relationship with Winston, you shouldn't be in one."

"But I am ready," I said.

"Dick is more than a friend, and something tells me you two have unfinished business. All I'm saying is closure is important in order for you to move on. If you are ready, then fine, but if not, take the time, trust me."

Staring at her, I nodded and then said, "I love you."

My mother winked and replied, "I know."

With a tiny chuckle, I wrapped my fingers around hers and kissed the top of her hand.

After I finished her nails, she gathered the remainder of her things and before long, Donnie was ringing the doorbell and it was time to go to the airport. We stood at the security gate giving hugs and kisses as my mom prepared to go to her gate.

"Call me as soon as you get home."

"I will."

"It was so great to meet you, Mama Rachel. I hope to see you soon," Donnie commented.

She gave him a kiss on his cheek and took her bags from his hand. Donnie and I stood there as she placed her things on the ramp before walking through the scanner. Blowing kisses, she waved bye and disappeared into the crowd of people. Donnie and I walked back to the car and I prepared myself to hear about his all-night episode with Sarah. However, to my surprise, Donnie was silent for the first ten minutes of the ride. Finally, after the suspense got the best of me, I asked him about his evening.

"What is going on with you and Sarah?"

Innocently, he smiled and responded, "Absolutely nothing. It was late, we stayed up talking and it got later, so I spent the night."

I was silent.

"Sarah and I are, and will always be, good friends. I have accepted that."

Looking out of the window, I responded casually, "If you say so."

We rode home and I spent the remainder of my evening preparing for my unnerving day at work tomorrow. I called Tam around eight o'clock to catch up with last week's news. We hadn't been able to talk since my mom had been in town. Thankfully, she and the baby were doing fine. Stan was out of town at a principals' conference and Evelyn had been over almost every night for dinner. I asked to speak with her, so Tam put her on the phone.

"Hey, girl, I hear you and the island man are still going strong."

"We are, can you believe? I'm so happy."

"I didn't agree at first, but I'm happy for you. Are we talking marriage?" I hinted.

"Maybe," she said. "He'll be here next weekend."

I could hear her smiling through the phone.

"Call me later," she said before handing Tam the phone.

"Tam, she seems really happy."

"At least she has the guts to go after what she wants," Tam cut in.

"Tam, don't start," I quickly interjected.

"Start what?" she asked.

"This is why I don't call you."

"Whatever, you call me all the time."

"Well, this is why I'm going to stop calling," I jested. The conversation fizzled until I admitted, "He called last night. But I wasn't here."

"Have you called him back?"

"Nope."

"Okay, well, I'm getting off the phone, I'm tired," said Tam.

"Fine, I love you, bye," I said just before disconnecting.

Hopping upstairs to prepare for bed, I couldn't help but laugh at Tam. I knew she truly wanted me to resolve things with Dick, but she just didn't understand. If he wanted me, he had to show it. And staying with Celeste while calling me in the middle of the night was not enough.

I pulled out my journal and counted the few pages left. I went through these things like crazy. I began to write:

I've seen so many relationships where the man or the woman doesn't have the courage to stand up for what he or she truly wants. They would rather settle for the easy or safe course all the while questioning if the other path was the one they should have routed. I refuse to spend my life wondering "what if." I have to keep forward on my path and be at peace with each of my decisions. The next time I speak with Dick, I will tell him that he needs to make peace with his choice to be with Celeste, especially since she is going to be his wife. It's okay to choose the safe route, over the risky, more adventurous one. Hell, I should know. But we both need to look onward and not back, because driving ahead with your attention in the rearview mirror is sure to cause an accident. And I don't know about him, but my heart is not insured.

Good night.

28

Repercussions of Deceit

As I walked through the workplace corridors, I could feel the office eyes gaze in my direction. Immediately, I walked toward Sarah's desk; however, she was not there. After waiting a few moments, I decided to meander to my desk and start my day. Yet, minutes after sitting, Susan called me into her office. Although she didn't mention Winston, I knew the pending conversation was about him. Pensively preoccupied, I sat in thought for another ten minutes, until Susan buzzed my phone once more. Finally, I went down to her office. Although she greeted me with a pleasant smile, I saw through her facade. I too watched the Discovery Channel and I knew it was normal for lions to sneer at their kill just before attack. Therefore, I returned her smile with a quick grin, leaned back in my chair, and prepared for assault.

"So, did you enjoy yourself this weekend?" she started.

"I did."

With her eye on me, Susan shuffled through the folders on her desk and pulled a bright yellow one from the stack. "You should read this. It's a new idea I've been toying with. I want your input."

"Okay."

"Are you all right, Lily?"

"I'm fine," I answered just as succinctly.

Susan leaned back in her chair with her arms folded. Looking across the room, she sighed.

"Is that all you need with me?" I asked, in haste to leave her office.

Nodding, Susan whimpered a soft yes. Thus, placing the folder underneath my arm, I grabbed my crutch and headed toward her office door.

"Oh yeah, I need to leave around four o'clock today, so that I can have the hard cast removed and replaced with a soft one. I hope that's okay," I said before leaving.

"Just have some notes on that before the day is over," Susan said, pointing to the folder.

Smiling, I opened the door and exited her office.

As soon as I got back to my desk, I waited for my heart to stop racing, but it didn't. The tension in Susan's office was as thick as the rain forest. Yet she didn't mention Winston or the dance. Unfortunately, this still left me on pins and needles. I wished she had gotten it out in the open instead of leaving it as a lingering thought. This situation was just like several of my childhood episodes. Whenever I would do something bad, my mom or dad wouldn't castigate me right away, they would make me wait an entire day, sometimes longer, before reprimanding me. The anxiety alone would unnerve me, because I knew it was coming, I just didn't know when and where.

As soon as I opened my folder and tried to get some work done, Sarah called me on the phone.

"I just got in, has Susan said anything to you about Winston?" she asked with zeal.

"You are the nosiest person I know."

"Then, indulge me."

Laughing, I continued. "No, she hasn't, Sarah, but she did ask about your whereabouts."

"No, she didn't," Sarah stated quickly.

"Yes, she did."

Quickly, Sarah defended herself as her voice hit an earsplitting pitch. "I told her Friday that I would be late. I had to take Carmen to the doctor this morning. I even wrote it down."

"Calm down, I'm only joking." I laughed.

With a small grumble, Sarah calmed only for a minute before fussing about Omar. I hastily interrupted.

"Look, girl. I have to go to work. I get this stupid cast off today, Donnie's coming to get me at four o'clock."

"Okay, bye," Sarah said quickly, and then hung up.

Although I tried to get some work done, every so many minutes someone came by my desk, to tell me how nice I looked at the dinner. Even though they complimented me, I felt they were trying to work up the nerve to ask about the mix-up. I wasn't sure who knew, but I was sure they were having secret talks about the whole thing. Hours into the day, I got a pleasant phone call. It was Dale, my old writing partner. I hadn't heard from him in months. He called to see how everything was going. Of course, he had no idea of the circling gossip, but I guessed his sacred connection with

Hallmark was still very strong. Hence, when I told him about the night's events, he hollered.

"I miss you guys. How's Sarah?" he asked.

"She is wonderful. Carmen is growing. You should come visit."

"I think I will."

"In fact, I'm having a birthday party next month and you should come."

"E-mail me with the details and I'll check Terry's schedule to see if he can come too."

"That will be great. I'm excited," I responded.

"How's Nehri, that's her name, right?" he asked.

"She's still cool. We get along, but she's no Dale."

"Oh, we are trying to adopt."

"Really!"

"Yes, if all goes well, we may have a baby girl by the end of the year."

"Wow!" I said, surprised.

Other than that exclamation, I wasn't sure what to say. I knew times were changing, but sometimes the pace amazed me. I remember when it was extremely difficult for heterosexual couples to adopt. Homosexual couples were out of the question. I had always agreed that children need love, no matter where it originated from. Yet it was still a mind adjustment. I knew Dale and Terry would be wonderful parents. Yet I wondered what kind of effect it would have on a child to grow up with two loving fathers; maybe none, but then who knows? All I knew was that everyone was moving in the direction of settling down. Hell, even Evelyn said she could marry Pierce.

"Lily, you okay?" asked Dale.

"Yeah, you will make a great father."

"Keep your fingers crossed."

"I will. Look, I have to get back to work." I felt Susan was about to pop up at my desk.

"Don't let them get to you. Keep creating. I await your e-mail."

"Okay, sweetie. Bye."

"Bye."

Smiling, I hung up, and finally I got back to work and had an uninterrupted work session until lunch. I ate at my desk during lunch and thank God no one came to bother me, not even Sarah. I loved her, but sometimes peace and quiet was what I needed.

As I looked at the clock, I saw it was close to four. I grabbed the folder and headed toward Susan's office. I prayed she was not in so that I could slip it in her tray by the door and just leave. In fact, I decided to slip it in the tray even if she was in. I dreaded having to see her face again today. However, she was prepared for me, with her door wide open. Susan never left her door open; therefore, I knew something interesting was brewing. As I got in her eye range, she motioned for me to come in. I stood by her desk and handed her the folder. As she read over my ideas, she spouted a few "Interestings" and "I sees."

"You understand all of the side notes, I hope."

With a cutting eye, she responded, "Of course I do."

"Good, well, I'm going to go now," I said, heading toward the door.

"Could you wait a minute?" Susan asked with a harsh tone, while still reading the notes.

Impatiently, I wobbled my leg as I looked around the room.

"You can sit," she offered.

"I'm good."

As she continued to read, her tone changed and

she asked an intriguing question. "What do you think of me?"

I looked around the office before answering the question, as if someone else were in the room other than the two of us. Not sure if this was some sort of trick question, I hesitated.

"I think . . . you are a good boss?" I stated.

Susan still looked down at the notes and continued to speak. "So you see me as your boss, before you see me as a person."

"Sometimes, not all the time."

"Why couldn't you just be honest with me, Lily?"

I knew it was coming. I could only avoid this talk for so long. Gradually, I moved to the chair and took a seat. Finally, Susan removed the folder from shielding her face and looked me square in the eyes. Suddenly I wished the folder were guarding my expression.

"Me not saying anything had nothing to do with you. I didn't mention Winston because everyone knew I dated his brother last year. I didn't want to look bad."

Susan clasped her hands in front of her and placed them on top of the folder. "Well, you don't look good now."

Silent, I didn't know how to take that response.

"Lily, if you had been honest with me from the start, it would have kept both of us from looking like fools. I don't know why Winston didn't mention it, but I could only assume he thought you would. Either way, I can't help but think you were laughing at me behind my back."

"No, I wasn't. I was truly embarrassed that you would look down at my behavior. I know it sounds crazy, but I do respect you as a woman and as a superior."

"Well, I thank you. I respect you as an artist. I think

your talent is wonderful and I see great potential. But I have to admit, as a woman, my respect for you is waning."

Another low blow, again I was silent. This time I gazed out of the window away from her judging eyes.

"I'm not so disappointed in you about this situation, but more so at what you just told me."

"Why?" I asked, still rudely looking away.

"Well, you have strong leadership abilities. I see a lot of me in you. Perhaps this is why I could let my guard down enough to discuss personal business with you. However, if you are so concerned about others' opinions of your character, then I wonder if you can lead a team."

Susan was quiet for a second. So I adjusted my focus back in her direction. Looking at the clock, I saw it was now four o'clock, but I dared not ask to be excused.

Finally, she continued. "I know what people say about me and frankly, I don't care. 'Cause at the end of the day, I have done my job and I've done it well. As long as I am okay with my character and behavior and I'm not hurting anyone in the process, what others say or think matters not."

"That is a wonderful quality about you," I admitted.

"I am a woman running the creative department for a multimillion-dollar company, which bases its finances on its creativity. Do you know how much has been said about me?"

Shyly, I rapidly shook my head from side to side.

"Well, a lot. But once I decide on something, I stick to it. I uphold it, like it's the best thing ever. Even if I doubt myself, I never show it, 'cause I must convince everyone else that I am assured and certain in my decisions. If I were afraid to tell people things because I worried about their opinions, nothing would ever get accomplished."

"But that is business, this is personal. I am very confident about my work and work decisions."

"You may be, but if you can't be proud of your personal decisions that deal directly with your character, how can I be sure you will be proud of the business ones? Especially when you have to make them under pressure when everyone is against you. You can't be swayed by disapproving eyes."

The talk was starting to feel like an after-school special. I wished she would get to the point, 'cause I was ready to go. I got it already . . . I should have been honest. The more she talked, the more I felt like a non-listening, rebellious child. Finally, I saw her rising, which I hoped meant she was culminating this laborious lecture.

"I don't care about who you date, that has nothing to do with the good work you do here. I hope you know that."

"I do. At least I do now," I admitted.

"I hope so, 'cause if you are going to lead this new project, I don't want to be disappointed. Especially since I've told my superiors you had the talent."

Suddenly my ears and eyes perked up. "What new project?"

"This one." Susan slid the folder back across the desk. "You can pick a team of four to work with you. But you are responsible for their daily activities and progress. I'll monitor it weekly and I expect updates on every Friday. In four weeks, I want a complete draft of the entire line."

Beaming, I didn't know what to say. Susan was a wonderful woman who had my utmost respect. Not because she entrusted me a project, but because she could let go of pettiness, for the betterment of business. Many women, take that back, many people, couldn't have done that.

"Thank you for this," I said, taking the folder. "And I thank you for the maturity in which you handled this situation."

"Well, we are adults."

"Yes, we are. Although I feel like a child with this horrible cast on my leg," I hinted as a reminder that I needed to leave.

"We'll talk next week. I'll have some notes for you in a couple days."

I stood, shook her hand, and left her office. As I hastened past Sarah's desk, I saw her and Donnie talking.

"Where have you been?" she asked.

"With Susan," I said, holding up the folder.

"Walking papers?" Sarah questioned.

"No, girl, you have her all wrong. C'mon, Donnie, we have to go. I don't want another minute in this plaster."

Donnie escorted me to the car. Although we were late, the doctor made me his last appointment. Finally, my leg, though very hairy, was able to breathe again.

Sitting on my futon, I propped my leg up in the chair and stared at my feet. Why, I was not sure. All I knew was that an hour seemed to pass and all I did was stare. In my head, I kept replaying my conversation with Susan. Stunned at how she handled the situation, I needed to pay more attention to her to learn a few things. I owed her a big thank-you. Still, I was unsure why I was so concerned about how she would look at me if I told her about Winston. Why was I so concerned about how his family might look at me? If I was happy and proud to date Winston, it shouldn't matter if others thought it to be inappropriate. What was wrong with me?

I reached my arm under the futon and pulled out my recent journal. Flipping through the pages, I looked for the page that held my "likes" and "dislikes" about myself. As I kept reviewing these eight dislikes, I decided this was the year that I would change. My thirtieth birthday was next month and these were issues I refused to carry into my future years. Yet there were so many, to tackle them all at once was too demanding. Again, not knowing where to start, I used an old surefire method to decide. Closing my eyes, I slowly moved my fingers across the page; after a few Braille glides, I stopped. When I opened my eyes my hand was close to the top of the list. It was between the words *leery* and *love*. Unfortunately, this was exactly the one I didn't want to start with.

"I want a do-over," I said to myself.

After a few sighs, I realized that it might not be so bad to start with that one. I was giving love a chance to rear her head in my relationship with Winston, where the old Lily would never have given a relationship with such great potential a chance. But I had to admit the other night when he said he could kiss my lips forever, I felt unrest in my heartbeat. People used the word *forever* too loosely. How did he know he could kiss my lips forever? What comes over a person to make him think that he would want to kiss the same pair of lips forever? I had never gotten that feeling in my life and he just blurted it out like it was no big deal.

I moved away from that page and began to write and read aloud.

"My problem with love is this. People in the state of love sometimes say and do things that they can't possibly live up to. Disappointments are inevitable and this sheer premise makes me leery. If I only give so much and hold back the rest, then I have some sense of stability when the love boat rocks. I do want to go into the ocean, but I need the anchors lowered, so that I don't just float away into oblivion. I've seen people out there, just swimming away until a storm comes along and turns that peaceful love stroke into frantic flapping. Before long, they are underwater, helpless. Personally, I believe drowning has got to be the worst way to die. Your lungs fill with water, you can't breathe, and then your chest cavity implodes. I have never talked to a drowning victim. However, I have talked to many broken-heart victims and the end results sound tragically similar."

I flipped back and stared into the page of "dislikes" and daydreamed about my life with Winston. We were living in a mansion with our two smart kids; I even had a chef. Everything was perfect. We were smiling and playing in the yard. It was a sunny day and it looked like something out of a storybook.

"Could this really happen?" I asked myself.

Suddenly the phone rang, jarring me from this surreal life.

"Hello," I answered.

"Hi, girl, what's up?" said Tam on the other line.

"Nothing. What's wrong?"

Tam was silent.

Suddenly my heart caved. I could feel my heartbeat triple and it plummeted to my stomach.

"Evelyn's mom had a heart attack. She's still living but she is in critical condition."

Although it took a few seconds, my breathing subsided and I was able to speak.

"How is Evelyn doing?" I asked.

"Not well. She thinks her mom is going to die. You can't have a conversation with her without her breaking down. You know I'm already emotional with the pregnancy. Honestly, I can't take it."

"Do you think she's gonna make it?"

"I don't know, it can go either way. The whole thing has me depressed. I started thinking about my mom, who's doing well now, but you never know with cancer. I just need to see you."

"I would love to come home, but I just got this big project at work and I don't know if I can get away."

Suddenly, Tam burst into tears.

"Oh my God! Stop crying. What's wrong, what's wrong?"

"Nothing . . . I just . . . I don't know. Life is so short. We prepare sometimes for things that never get to happen. Should we just live day by day? What is all of this for?" she rambled through the wails.

Of course, my tears immediately began to fall, for I was already two steps from crying over my list of "dislikes"; all I needed was to hear my best friend's sadness to set me off.

"I just really want to see you," she said.

"Okay, okay. I'll try to come next weekend. It's okay, baby, please stop crying."

Eventually, Tam calmed her wails to a low whimper. In between the sniffles, she continued. "I'm so sorry to call you like this. It's just that every time I get upset, Stan thinks it's about the miscarriage. He tries to cheer me up by saying our baby is going to be healthy and strong, but it's more than that. What if something happens to me and I don't get to raise my child, or what if something happens to my child?"

"You can't think like that. We all know that tomorrow is not promised, but we are here now. And, in this moment, we have to find enough pleasure and peace to know that whatever happens, everything is going to be all right."

"But what if everything is not all right?"

"It's never going to be perfect, we just have to pray and find strength to make it through. Plus, what is perfect anyway? Perfect is what we make it, right?"

Still whimpering, Tam let out a soft response. "I guess."

"Your life is wonderful. You have so many blessings. Go to sleep and dream on how they are going to multiply."

"I'll try. I still want to see you, though," she mumbled.

"I know, baby. I'm going to try my best to come."

"Okay."

"I love you, girl," I said.

"I love you too. Good night."

"Good night."

Wow, that was a first. Tam never got that emotional over anything. Even when her mom was diagnosed with cancer, she handled it so calmly. To hear her in a tizzy was almost unbelievable. It had to be the pregnancy. She was actually having a "Lily" moment and Tam didn't have "Lily" moments.

"I have to go home and see about her," I commented aloud. "I need to check on Evelyn too."

Slowly rising, I walked into the kitchen to look at my calendar. I didn't know if this project was going to require weekend work, but maybe I could sneak away next Friday evening. We'd see. Grabbing my journal, I made my way upstairs to prepare for bed. Although I didn't speak with Tam that long, the conversation exhausted me. After I took a shower, I was going to call Evelyn. I wasn't sure if I had the energy to talk long, but I wanted her to know that she was in my prayers.

I guess sometimes we all fear life's uncertainties. Most of my fright was in the department of love, yet that was a major part of life. I guess my foremost step to striking my first "dislike" was to listen to my own advice. I must find enough pleasure and peace in love that no matter what happened, I knew everything would be all right. Like life, love is not always idealistic or perfect, and I wanted to experience the true beauty of the sea. I assumed I would have to lift my anchor in order for that to happen. If I could enjoy the sea's beauty and respect the exquisiteness of its nature, not only would I be better prepared to handle the storm, but also I would look forward to sunnier days.

However, my anchor was very heavy. I might need to call Winston to come over and help me hoist. No doubt, he worked all day and I was sure he was tired; however, with him and me pulling together, I was confident we'd eventually get it up. No pun intended, of course.

29

They're Running Rings Around Me

Work was beginning to become extremely busy. I organized my team of coworkers for the new project. I picked Nehri as one of my writers and Stix as my main artist. I admit I was a little hesitant about Nehri. She was a great worker but she was a bit of a control freak. Especially when she had a good idea. Nehri would not stop until everyone had listened and agreed that her idea was best. Yet she did have great ideas and I knew her pattern of thinking would be an asset to this project. Stix, on the other hand, was a shoo-in. I had wanted to work with him on a project since last year. Not only was he a talented sketch artist, but also his eye for small detail was amazing. But Stix was chosen because of another minute issue. He wore orange socks every day. No matter what color clothing, no matter the outfit, if he was wearing socks, guaranteed they'd be orange. Sounded crazy, but his odd behavior intrigued me. Anyone who had the nerve to wear orange-colored socks with everything either didn't give a damn about what others thought or was completely out of his or her mind. Either way, that's the eccentricity of a genius artist and I needed his ballsy brilliance on my team.

This new project was a line of romance cards, but the sayings would be one or two short phrases. Something like "I like you—no, I take that back. I love you." This was one of Susan's examples. We, as a team, had to develop the artwork, the size and shape of the card, phrases, and the line name. The market age was twenties to thirties; therefore, the pictures needed to appeal to young adults. I was excited about the challenge. I had pulled together a talented team and if we could work together without too much aggravation, we were going to have a dynamic product line.

We called our first meeting to discuss line concepts. The meeting lasted an hour and by the meeting's end, we had at least twenty good phrases to start the drafting process. This meant I could go to Atlanta that weekend without worrying about the start of next week. I would take some of the work on the plane with me to look over. However, I didn't want to think about this project or work once I landed. I wanted to see my girls and relax.

After work, Sarah and I decided to go to dinner. We went to this very chic restaurant with superb spicy tuna sushi. The décor was dim, almost gothic. It certainly didn't go with the Asian-inspired cuisine, but the food was excellent. Immediately, Sarah and I began chatting to catch up on the last day's episodes. Before Carmen was born, Sarah and I used to dine out at least twice a week. It was cut down to twice a month, if that. Consequently, when we did have girl-friend time over dinner, it was yap, yap, yap until we finished our last bite.

"So, what is going on with this project you're lead-ing? When did Susan give you this?" asked Sarah.

"Right after she spoke to me about Winston."

"I can't believe she wasn't mad."

"I think she was a little mad. But her demeanor and style in which she handled everything were impres-sive. I took notes."

Sarah laughed while diving into her salad.

"I'm serious. She told me how she didn't appreci-ate my dishonesty and said that she believed in my talent and hoped that I would be more professional when overseeing this new project."

"I guess that's why she is the boss."

"I guess so," I agreed.

"'Cause I wouldn't have given you a damn thing." Sarah chuckled. "If you embarrassed me like that, every idea you brought to the table would be vetoed before it was even discussed."

With a grin, I replied, "This is why you answer the phones."

"I do more than that," Sarah said.

"I know you do, honey, I'm only joking," I said, pat-ting her hand.

Sarah had already admitted she sometimes felt in-ferior to the others in the office. Although her title said administrative assistant, she did so much. Multi-tasking was surely her strong suit and I needed to be more mindful when joking about her position.

We each took a few more bites into our salad, as Sarah struck up more conversation.

"So, you're working with Stix? He's so talented and easy to get along with. You'll like him."

"He seems cool. I still think he and the orange sock thing is crazy."

"He has over fifty pairs, you know."

"No. How do you know?" I asked.

"He told me. Plus, we dated for about a month when I first started here."

"Get out! You never mentioned that."

"It wasn't a big deal. We went out on a few dates. Eventually, we slept together, but that was months after we stopped dating."

Making a funny face, I stared at Sarah, begging for details.

"You and Stix did it?" I questioned.

"I know. It was weird. Good, but weird. He kept his orange socks on the whole time."

Laughing aloud, we finished our salads as our main course was served. Within the next hour we discussed our workplace, love life, family, friends, and weekend department store sales. Sarah snatched the check before I could take a look at it and gave our server her card.

"You do not have to pay."

"Sure I do. I still owe you for keeping Carmen while I was sick."

"That was months ago and you don't owe me. It was my pleasure. She is my goddaughter."

"I know. But it's too late, I already took care of the bill. You can get the next one," Sarah said while signing her name on the receipt.

As we slowly walked to the car with our origami swan-shaped doggie bags, Sarah paused and looked into the star-filled sky.

"What's wrong?" I asked.

"Nothing. Remember how, as kids, we used to wish upon a star?"

"Of course," I said, joining her stargaze.

"I used to believe that my wishes would come true. I wish I still had that kind of faith."

"Is that faith or ignorance?" I asked.

Shrugging, Sarah didn't vocally respond.

"Try it. God knows your heart is in the right place," I continued.

Sarah closed her eyes and faced the heavens. I joined in, praying that her wishes came true. We solemnly stood there for at least a minute in the well-lit parking lot. Finally she tapped my arm and I opened my eyes.

Giving me a hug, she asked, "When you get to Atlanta, are you going to see—"

"Nope," I interrupted, knowing she was asking about Dick.

"Okay. Well, tell Evelyn she and her mom are in my prayers."

"I will."

We began walking to our cars in silence. I stuck my key in my SUV door and tossed my bag in the front seat. Looking over the top of Sarah's car, I called out, "I love you, girl."

"I love you too," she responded.

We got in our vehicles and drove home. Of course, I thought about Sarah's somber moment all the way there. I wasn't sure exactly what her wish was, but I was sure it was concerning Omar. She really wanted the three of them to be a family. Unfortunately, I didn't know if that was ever going to happen. Although Omar was active in Carmen's life, he still wanted to be single. He still lived in his own place and he probably still dated other women. One part of me wanted to tell Sarah to give up the fairy tale, and the other part was praying she could have it, 'cause everyone deserves a happy ending. But could there be a happy ending, if the beginning and the middle were so messed up? Omar was not good for her, bottom line. I didn't know what it was going to take for her to move on, but I prayed the stars spelled out a new future for my friend.

Immediately, I got home and crashed. Thankfully, I had already packed and cleaned the house. Therefore, after my shower, I rushed to the bed and snoozed. Unfortunately, I woke up around four o'clock in the morning and couldn't go back to sleep. Tossing and turning, I finally got out of bed and minutes later I was watching old game shows on television. Sucked in into *Let's Make a Deal*, I began chiming in with the audience to pick door number 3. I never understood that game show. Why did everyone dress in costume and what did that have to do with the show or its concept? Furthermore, if there was a five-legged cow behind the unfortunate picked door, was the audience member truly expected to take home that bum prize?

Finally, after bombarding myself with senseless questions, I flipped through the channels and landed on SOAP TV. Now, this was comical. I began watching a rerun of *Dallas*. I couldn't believe the story lines and terrible delivery. Moreover, I couldn't believe my mom and her friends used to sit home on Friday night and watch it. The whole country did for that matter. People may be ashamed to admit it, but during the year of 1980, the world tuned in to see who shot J. R. Ewing. There was even a chart-topping song about it. This thought made me laugh aloud and this chortle must have triggered some dysfunction in my brain, because

I suddenly grabbed the phone to call Dick. Yes, it was four-something in the morning and I had no business calling him at all, especially at this time. Yet I still called to let him know that I was coming to Atlanta. By the third ring, the cell-phone voice mail picked up.

"What's up, Dick? Just called to let you know I will be in your town this weekend. Call me if you get a chance. By the way, do you know who shot J.R?"

Quickly, I hung up, then stared at the phone, praying he didn't call back, for I wouldn't know what to say. Even worse, what if Celeste called back?

"What was I thinking?" I said, tapping myself on the forehead.

I couldn't do that ever again. I had to keep reminding myself that he was getting married to someone else. Plus, I had Winston, my loving, respectful boyfriend, who should never be tucked so far away in my brain that a reminder was necessary. I needed to take my behind to bed.

Tossing the remote, I went back upstairs and attempted to sleep. After a few tosses and turns, I drifted off. A couple of hours later my phone rang. Gazing over at the clock, I saw the time was 6:23 a.m. Half awake, I leaned over and fumbled to answer the phone. "Hello."

"Hi, sleepyhead," said the deep voice.

At first, I was quiet as it took moments for the voice to register in my head. Subconsciously, I knew it was Dick.

"Are you there, beautiful?"

Sighing, I slowly responded, "I'm here, Dick."

"Is everything okay?"

"Yeah."

"So, you're coming to town."

Sitting up in my bed, I gathered my thoughts and

cleared my throat. "It's been a minute. I'm surprised you called back."

"Yeah, well, I figured if you were calling me that time of the morning, it must be quite important."

"No, not really. Just thought I would let you know I'd be there."

Dick was silent.

"I shouldn't have called, I'm sorry," I continued.

"Well, I'll be in Canada this weekend. You know I'm still on tour."

"I figured as much."

We both sighed and remained silent. Finally, after a few seconds, Dick questioned, "Is that the only reason you called?"

"Um, yeah. Why else would I have called?" I stated, undoubtedly unsure, and yet it was obvious.

"Only you can answer that."

Again, we remained silent as the conversation filled with subtle tension. Dick and I didn't know what to say to each other.

"Lily."

I weakened when he spoke my name. My molecular structure simply broke down to mush.

"Yes, Dick," I replied, soft and sweet.

"I miss you."

"I miss you too."

There, we said it. Why did it take so many words and so many arguments just to say those three words? And why did those words lift the vulnerability quotient up five notches? Ranking just behind "I love you," that phrase was the second top risky phrase in a relationship. It was an expression that didn't require a reply, yet one was always expected.

"I need to talk to you."

"I'm right here, talk."

"I can't right now. I've been up all night. We did a show and I'm so tired. I just wanted to call you before I went to sleep."

"Where are you?"

"On the bus, headed for Philly, we just left New York."

"Well, I'm going to let you go."

"I hate that I won't see you this weekend. Why are you going home?"

"Tam needs to see me and Evelyn's mom had a heart attack."

"Oh no. Is she all right? How is Evelyn?" he asked.

"Her mom is finally stable, but she still has breathing complications. Evelyn is losing it and driving Tam crazy. With the baby and everything, she is really emotional. She broke down crying the other day just thinking about insane uncertainties."

"Yeah, pregnancy can do that. I am not looking forward to it."

Suddenly my heart caved. "Is Celeste pregnant?"

"Hell no," he replied quickly.

I slid down into the bedsheets as I heard Dick laughing on the line.

"What's so funny?" I asked.

"You are. Why do you always ask if she is pregnant?"

"I don't know. Maybe because then I will know it's official. There's no turning back once you have a family."

"Once you get married, that is your family," he responded.

"But kids are different. I wouldn't . . . well let's just say if you had kids, I wouldn't call you at four in the morning."

"If I had a wife, would you call me at four in the morning?" he asked, being cute.

"If you had a wife, would you be so quick to return my call?" I rebutted.

After a small grunt, he replied, "I don't know, Lily, I guess we will see, won't we?"

I didn't have an expected response, but that definitely wasn't what I wanted to hear.

"You and I will talk soon," he added.

"Yeah, soon. Call me."

"I will."

"Bye, Dick."

"Bye, Lily."

Neither of us hung up immediately. We stayed on the phone like teens waiting for each other to hang up first. Finally, I burst into laughter.

"Hang up," I said between the giggles.

"Okay, I'm hanging up. I'll call you."

"Okay, bye."

This time we both ended communication. I snuggled in my sheets with a big smile on my face.

"Why does he do this to me?" I asked aloud.

A moment later, my phone rang again. Hastily, I answered, "Yes."

"Kristin, she shot J.R.," Dick said, chuckling on the other line.

"Who was she?"

"The sister-in-law."

"What? I don't even remember her."

"Were you even born? How do you remember the show?"

"I watched reruns, but how do you know that?"

"I Googled it," he said, chuckling. "Good night, beautiful."

"Good night, baby," I responded.

Melting like warm butter on hot toast, I felt tingles

shoot through my body. Beaming, I pulled the sheets over my face. Just then, the alarm went off. I came from within the sheets, and glanced at the clock, which read 7:00 a.m. It was time for work. Surprisingly, I was not sleepy. Perhaps the excitement of leaving for Atlanta had me hyper. Then again, it could've been the lasting effect of Dick on my brain.

As soon as I got to work today, I began preparing for my departure to Atlanta. I called Tam to confirm my flight arrival. Next, I spoke with Nehri and Stix about Monday's meeting, since I would not be into work that weekend. Finally, I met with Susan to give her an update with the project. She seemed pleased; however, whenever I came within a few feet of her she squinted her eyebrows and crossed her arms. Although I gave her a thank-you card, this was a direct sign that her guard was up. I knew I embarrassed her, but I was going to have such a dynamic product that she would have no choice but to embrace my warmth. I was a likable character, and I was utterly determined to make her like me. By the time I got back to my cubicle, it was almost 1:00 p.m. Rushing to my desk, I called Winston on the phone.

"Are you on the way here?" I asked briskly.

"I'm about ten minutes away."

"My flight leaves at three o'clock."

"I know. You will be there on time," he said before hanging up.

Seconds after I sat down, Sarah popped around the corner.

"What time are you leaving?"

"As soon as Winston gets here, which should be in fifteen minutes."

Sarah walked around and took a seat on the corner of my desk. "I wish I could go. I just want to get away."

"Next summer, I promise we will take a vacation, just the two of us. By that time, Carmen will be walking around and you'll feel better about leaving her with Omar."

"No, I won't," she quickly negated.

I looked at her and nodded as she repeatedly shook her head no.

"This is not a vacation anyway. I'm going to comfort Evelyn and check on Tam. I'll be right back here Monday morning."

"Good," Sarah said, and she patted my arm.

Just then, I noticed the diamond ring on her right hand. Snatching her arm, I held her hand in the air. "What is this?"

Gazing upon the ring, as if she hadn't noticed, Sarah replied dismally, "I think it's supposed to be an engagement ring. I don't know."

"You don't know? Omar gave this to you?"

"Yeah."

"When?"

"Two days ago," she replied with the same lackluster expression.

"What! Why didn't you say something last night?"

Sarah shrugged as she continued to look at the diamond that had to be at least three carats. Shocked, I sat staring at her blank expression. If Sarah had three bowel movements in one day, she felt the need to tell me, yet she had kept this sparkling secret for over forty-eight hours. Something, other than the obvious, was terribly wrong.

"Let's go outside and wait for Winston," I said,

grabbing my purse with one hand and her arm with the other.

Rapidly, we walked toward the front door. Purposefully, I spoke to no one as I was leaving. The last thing I wanted was to get wrapped up in small talk about my weekend. As soon as the front door closed behind us, I grilled Sarah.

"What is up with this ring?"

"Omar came over the other night. Actually he's been over almost every night. But last week, he started talking about us getting married for Carmen's sake."

"What did you say?"

"I said that I agree she needed a mother and father, but getting married just for the child never works."

"Good answer."

"Then I talked with Claire and she said that Omar really wants to make things right and that I should give him a chance. Then Monday night when we were watching movies, he paused the movie and told me he had something for me."

"The ring?" I questioned with anticipation.

"No. He had a piece of paper with a jeweler's name and address. He told me to go to the man and pick out the ring I wanted."

"You're kidding!" I said with my mouth wide open.

"No. He had everything arranged. So Claire and I went a few days ago and picked this one out."

Sarah stuck her hand out again. I was silenced by her story. I didn't know whether to be happy or not. Every girl loves a ring, but the man attached to this ring was Omar.

"The way it happened was blah. He didn't propose or anything. It's not supposed to be like this," she complained.

From the corner of my eye, I saw Winston's car pull up to the curb. "You and I have to talk. I have to go now. I'm calling you this weekend. Try not to get married before I get back."

Sarah chuckled before giving me a hug. I rushed to my SUV and grabbed my bag from the back.

"You have a good weekend," she called out just before I reached Winston's car.

Blowing her a kiss, I waved good-bye, then took off with Winston. Leaning over, I kissed Winston on the cheek.

"I missed you," I said.

"Missed you too," he grumbled.

"What's wrong?" I asked.

Winston looked at me and sighed, yet didn't answer. I wasn't sure what that meant, but it must have been something serious, 'cause he rarely got grumpy. Silently, I awaited his response. I knew not to push too hard, 'cause it would only perturb him further. Finally, after minutes of silent riding, he talked.

"My mother is leaving my father."

Gasping aloud, I was stunned. I couldn't believe the perfect TV family was having troubles.

"Dad thinks she is having an affair."

This time my gasp was more like a shrill as I took both hands and covered my mouth. "No way!"

Winston sadly bobbed his head. Inside, I was bubbling over that little Mrs. Perfect Fulmore had been screwing around. Yet I was disgusted at the fact that Mr. Fulmore, whom I adored, had to go through this. Plus, this was difficult for Winston.

"Baby, I am so sorry," I said, leaning over to kiss his cheek again.

Winston didn't say a thing; he quietly got on the

expressway and headed toward the airport. I, in turn, didn't know what to say, and so I remained quiet until he pulled up to the check-in curb. We both got out and he went into the trunk to pull out my suitcase.

"Thanks for the ride."

"Are you sure your SUV will be all right at work?"

"I'm sure."

Placing both hands by my face, he kissed me. As his hands slid from my face down to my shoulders, I put my head upon his chest and tried to comfort him.

"Everything with your parents will work out. Every marriage has its kinks."

Winston kissed the top of my head.

"You better go." He spoke softly while handing me my bag.

"I'll be back Sunday night. I'll call you."

He waved bye as I walked up to the check-in counter. Looking over my shoulder, I watched him somberly walk back to his car, get in, and drive off. I almost hated leaving him.

My flight was only an hour and thirty minutes, and I closed my eyes and rested the entire time. While I was making my way through the airport, my cell phone started to ring. Rummaging through my purse, I finally grabbed it, just as it went into voice mail. I was sure it was Tam; therefore, I called her back.

"What do you want?" I said as she picked up her phone.

"Are you here already?" she asked, surprised.

"Yes. Where are you?"

"I'm on the way."

"Tam! Did you forget the time?"

"No, I just don't move as fast as I used to. Just take a seat in baggage claim. I'll call you when I get there."

"Didn't you just call me?"

"No, why?"

"Never mind. I'll see you soon."

I hung up and scrolled through my list of calls to retrieve the last number. As the number came onto the screen, I froze like a deer in headlights.

"It's Dick," I said to myself. "Should I call him back?" I continued to babble.

I decided against it, dropped the phone in my purse, walked over to baggage claim, and took a seat. Grabbing my book from my bag, I began reading as I waited for Tam to call. Of course, I kept thinking about Dick. If I just called him back and got it over with, then I could finish reading, I thought.

"If it were important, he would have left a message," I said underneath my breath.

Softly, I banged the book against my face. I was trying to knock some sense into my head. I walked to Starbucks, but with Dick still on my mind, I nervously tapped my teeth as I looked over the variety of coffee bean products. Perusing the interesting names, I decided to change my normal drink of choice and go with something different, yet when I approached the counter, I froze up. Although I wanted to branch out to foreign taste buds, what if the experience wasn't savory? If I went with what I knew, I had nothing to lose. So with an agonizing smile on my face, I finally spoke to the woman behind the counter.

"I'll have the . . . um, a café mocha, with whipped cream and chocolate shavings."

"What size?"

"Take that back, I'll have the caramel frappuccino, tall," I said, nodding to confirm.

As she poked an additional five to eight buttons to

correct my order, I quietly apologized and move to the right. I hoped I wouldn't be disappointed, I thought to myself. It's difficult to change eating and drinking habits.

I used to be angry when people in fast food lines would stare aimlessly at the menu trying to make a decision. I would think, what are they doing, the menu has not changed in years? Just order the damn burger already. But what if those people were having that moment in life where a burger no longer satisfied their craving? What if they were trying to make that change to the chicken sandwich, but didn't want to risk a possible upset stomach? Today I understood their dilemma.

"Caramel," the drink mixer called out.

"That's me," I responded, handing her my ticket.

I grabbed the drink and headed out to the curb to wait for Tam. While pondering my fear of change, Tam called.

"Where are you now?"

"Parked right behind you."

Quickly, I turned around and saw her waving out of the window of a new SUV. Waving back, I accidentally spilled some of my drink down my arm.

"Thank God for change. If that had been my mocha, I would've been burned. Everything has its purpose," I said to myself as I reached her SUV.

Tossing my bag in the backseat, I quickly hopped in, reached over, and gave Tam a big hug. Rubbing on her belly, I hugged her again just before she drove off.

"Look how big I am."

"You're pregnant, and you so look good," I said, smiling.

Tam rubbed her belly.

"I really want this," she commented with a huge smile.

"I know. Before you know, there will be a beautiful baby running around and you will be calling me saying, 'Is this really what I wanted?'"

Laughing, Tam left the airport terminal and got onto the highway.

I gazed out the window staring at the downtown cityscape.

"I miss it here," I admitted.

"Good. Come back, 'cause it misses you too."

Pressing my forehead to the window, I continued to gaze in silence. Poking my shoulder, Tam broke the calm.

"I can't wait until your party."

"You're gonna come?" I asked with excitement.

"Yeah. The doctor said it's okay. Stan and I are getting our tickets this week."

"Stan is coming too?"

"And I think Evelyn is coming."

Clapping, I turned up the radio, began dancing in my seat and singing.

Tam joined in and we sang radio-play tunes until we got to her house.

As soon as we walked in, Tam rushed me upstairs to get changed for dinner. "Hurry, I told Evelyn we would meet her at seven. It's almost six."

I quickly changed into nicer clothing, and rushed back downstairs. Other than small talk about the baby, Tam was quiet on the way to the restaurant. I knew she wanted to ask about Dick, but she hadn't so far and I was glad. It would be nice not to talk about Dick all weekend. Especially since I was not going to see him.

"You all right?" Tam asked as we walked in.

"Yeah, why?"

"You've been quiet. Just checking."

"I'm fine. Let's go see about Evelyn."

We immediately saw Evelyn at the bar waiting for us. She ran over and hugged me as if I were her long-lost best friend. Shocked, I needed a minute before I could wrap my arms around her and return the hug.

"It's good to see you. I missed you," she said with an endearing expression.

"Good to see you too, Evelyn," I responded while eyeing Tam over Evelyn's shoulder.

We were seated and I immediately began perusing the menu. "I am so hungry. What's good here?"

"I don't know," Tam responded quickly. "I've never been here."

"I've only had the steak and you don't eat steak," replied Evelyn.

"How is your mom doing?"

"I think she's going to die," said Evelyn with a matter-of-fact expression on her face.

Looking up, I glanced over at Tam, who was staring blankly at me. We glimpsed at Evelyn, who was looking at her menu, and then I spoke.

"How can you say that? It's disturbing. What are the doctors saying?"

"They say she may be able to pull through. Her condition is serious, but her heartbeat is strong."

"Then why would you say that she's going to die?"

"Well . . ." Evelyn started to explain as she placed her menu on the table. "I go talk to her every day and she's just not herself. She keeps saying she's tired. I don't know if she has the strength to pull through."

"But she may. Words are powerful, you have to watch what you say."

"If she doesn't pull through, I have to start accepting it now. If she does make it, then that's wonderful," Evelyn stated just before she raised her menu to continue checking out the meals.

Tam tapped me on the hand and whispered softly, "I told you."

Shaking my head, I glanced across the room as the server brought water to our table.

Eventually, we all ordered and within twenty minutes colorful dishes were decorating our table. Conversation lightened and soon we were joking and laughing over none other than the men in our lives.

"So, how is baby boy?" I asked Evelyn.

"Pierce is fine and don't call him that."

"She is sensitive about her man, be nice," Tam said.

"Fine. When did you last see him?"

"He was here a month ago."

"Things are serious, I see."

"He's talking about having kids."

"With you?" I asked with a frown.

"Of course with me. What, you don't think I would be a good mother?" she asked sincerely.

"No. You would be a good mother. It's just so soon to talk about kids."

"Not when you know it's right. We're good together, you'll see. We'll be at your party."

"He's coming too. Everyone is going to be there. It will be so much fun! Do I need to make hotel arrangements? 'Cause y'all aren't staying at my place."

"Ain't that a bunch of nothing," Tam commented. "You just don't want us staying at your place 'cause you might have company."

"What kind of company?" Evelyn asked.

Tam rolled her eyes away from the table while

making a cooing sound. "I'm not having company. I just don't have room for everyone."

"We were getting a hotel anyway," said Evelyn.

"And you, Ms. Tam, cut it out," I said, tossing my napkin in her direction.

As we finished our meals and I was looking throughout the restaurant, I noticed a young lady staring at our table. In fact, she had been staring at our table the entire time.

"Don't look right now, but the girl two tables over to my left has been staring over here. Do you know her?"

Immediately, Evelyn turned and looked. Thankfully, Tam was slicker with her glance as she rose and walked to the restroom.

"She looks familiar, but I don't know her," Evelyn said.

"No need to whisper, you damn near entered a staring contest with the girl. She knows we are talking about her now."

"Maybe you should go ask her," suggested Evelyn.

Shaking my head in disagreement, I quietly waited for Tam to return. Once she did, she admitted that the girl also looked familiar but she couldn't put a name to the face.

"Well, I want to know why she is staring at me like we're old schoolmates."

"Maybe she likes you," mentioned Evelyn.

Making an awkward face, I just shook my head at Evelyn's comment.

"What? She's a cute girl, but she could be a lesbian. There are a lot of lipstick lesbians living here."

"She is a pretty girl, I even like her taste in shoes, but she's not staring like she wants one of us. She's looking like she hates one of us."

"Well, I think she's coming over here, you can ask her," said Evelyn as the mystery woman approached our table.

As she got to the table, she smiled and looked over at Tam.

"Are you Stan's wife?" she asked.

"Yes, why?" Tam questioned.

"I'm Stacy," said the woman as she pleasantly stuck her hand out to greet Tam.

However, Tam still confused, hesitantly returned the handshake.

"I'm sorry, Stacy Wright-Williams, Romance's wife."

Immediately, my water spewed from my mouth and across the table into Evelyn's face. I began to choke and forcefully beat my chest as Tam flustered and Evelyn squealed, while wiping water from her face and silk blouse. Stacy softly patted my back as Tam tried to make sure I was okay.

"Are you all right?" asked Stacy.

With my eyes watering, I furiously nodded, assuring them that I was all right.

"I'm sorry to interrupt. Ro and I saw you two shopping one day, but you were too far away to speak. Ro talks so highly of Stan, I just wanted to come introduce myself."

"I'm glad you did. By the way, this is Evelyn and Lily."

Still stunned, I tried to gather myself to speak.

"You're Lily? The Lily?" she asked as I saw her making the connection.

"The one and only." I grinned with teary eyes.

"Oh," she said, shifting the chaos to silent awkwardness.

Finally, her girlfriend came over to the table. Quickly,

she introduced me. Forgetting my two compadres at the table, I was now the focus of the conversation.

"Tameka, this is Lily."

Tameka looked at me and replied with the same empty expression, "Oh."

Seconds later, she continued. "Nice to meet you. I'm her sister," she said with a tight-lipped grin.

"Same," I responded with no grin.

"So, when did you get married?" Evelyn asked, trying to break the weirdness.

"Three months ago. It wasn't here, it was in Detroit, that's my home. We had a reception here, though."

"I got your invitation," Tam chimed in as my eyes switched focus. "I'm sorry we weren't able to come."

"That's okay, maybe we can all get together for dinner. I'll have the men set it up."

"That would be nice," said Tam.

Shocked, I stuck my finger in my ear to remove some of the wax that was hindering my hearing. I knew Tam was not making nice with Stacy Wright-Williams.

"Well, we're going to go, I just wanted to speak. Lily, nice to finally meet you," Stacy said, extending her right hand to shake mine.

Trying to sneak a peek at her left hand, I purposely extended my left hand, in hopes she would switch hands, but she didn't. Instead our fingers danced around each other as we ended our awkward and un-expected meeting in a nod. Smiling at the others, Stacy Wright-Williams and her sister, Tameka, gracefully walked away. Immediately, I looked to Tam for answers and she quickly delivered.

"I didn't think you cared to know."

"What? Why would I not want to know?"

"'Cause you are not with him and you don't care about him."

"I do care. I want him to be safe and if something bad happened to him, I would want to know," I commented.

"Well, nothing bad happened, he just got married, that's all."

"I can't believe you didn't tell me. You called to tell me about Dick and his engagement party—"

"Which, by the way, was fabulous," interrupted Evelyn.

Flaring my nostrils in her direction, I continued speaking to Tam. "But you didn't think I would want to know about Romance and Stacy Wright-Williams. And did you hear her call him Ro? What's that about? I came up with that name. How come she doesn't come up with her own name for him?" I continued.

Tam didn't answer; she quietly mulled over the bill.

"What if he gave her my engagement ring?" I added.

"Oh, that wasn't your ring," Evelyn interjected.

"How do you know?"

"I saw it. Your ring was two carats, princess cut, right?"

"Right," I answered.

"Her ring is oval and close to three carats."

Disgusted, I bit my lip to keep from cursing at Evelyn.

"Let it go," said Tam as she handed the server the bill.

Tam and Evelyn rose as I sat and pondered what had just happened. Finally, Tam grabbed my arm and pulled me from my chair. "We're leaving."

Sluggishly, I rose and walked out of the restaurant, leaving my pathetic pride to be bused with the dirty dishes. As we got to the parking lot, I continued to talk about her like a high school rival. I knew it was childish before I opened my mouth to speak, but it came out nonetheless.

"You're right. Why should I care that Romance married some ole ugly girl? She has man hands and hairy arms anyway," I added.

Tam simply pushed me into the SUV as I tried to say good-bye to Evelyn.

"I'll visit the hospital tomorrow. I'll see you," I stated.

Evelyn hugged Tam and trotted to her car. Once Tam got into her SUV, she rapidly spoke.

"We are not going to discuss this all night. You have exactly two minutes to say what you have to say and then it is over." Tam glanced at the clock. "Your two minutes start now."

Sighing, I decided it was best to purge for my two minutes, even if it were childish. If I talked fast, I would be able to get in at least three more Stacy insults while I complained about Ro.

"I can't believe he's already married someone else, it's only been a year and a half. Where did she come from?"

"Detroit," Tam interrupted.

"Right. And did you see how she casually waltzed over to the table? She knew who I was. I'm sure she has seen a picture of me. We were together for almost three years. Ro has a lot of pictures of us."

"Stan said he got rid of them all."

"Anyway, I came up with Ro. He should have come up with a new nickname after I left. She seems fake with her news commentator voice. I don't like her."

I looked at Tam, waited for her to interrupt with an agreeing comment, but she did not.

"You don't like her, do you?" I asked.

"I don't know her. Stan mentioned her once or twice. She seems nice."

Making a horrible face, I rolled my eyes away from Tam.

"Hi, I'm Stacy Wright-Williams," I mocked.

Tam began to laugh. "Your two minutes are up."

"Fine. I'm done anyway."

We rode a few more minutes, and then I had to speak on the situation once more. "One more thing."

"No more things," Tam commented with a chuckle.

"No, really, this is serious. If you and Stan start hanging out with Romance and Stacy Wright-Williams, they could become your married couple friends. Just in case this does happen, don't stop calling me."

Tam pulled up to the stoplight a few blocks from the house and looked at me. "You are crazy. You really are crazy."

"What?" I asked innocently.

"I'm not going to stop calling you. I'm not even justifying this conversation with a comment."

Tam turned back around and waited for the light to turn green. I, in turn, also sat and waited for the light to turn green and that was the end of that. I met the woman living the life I could have had. It was a visit from the ghost of relationship-past. I didn't know why it even bothered me that Romance had moved on. I had expected him to do so. Stacy had her a good man and though she seemed too prissy for him, it must be what he wanted. He surely wasted no time in making it legitimate. Yet I wasn't surprised, he was always the marrying type. He talked about marriage with me the first year. I'm the one who pushed it back a couple of years. I couldn't be upset that while I was searching for rubies, someone found the diamond I tossed aside.

"I know you're thinking about it."

"I'm making peace with it. I hope they make it."

"Good, he deserves love and happiness."

"He does."

"And so do you," Tam added.

I quickly reached in my purse and grabbed my cell phone. "I forgot to call Winston to let him know I made it in okay."

I dialed his home but he didn't answer, and so I left him a text letting him know I was okay.

Tam and I walked into the house and passed the new baby room. As I peeped in, I saw she had repainted and put up new wallpaper.

"You redid the room?"

"Stan did it. He thought it was best. We did keep the furniture, though. I didn't want to shop for new things. Go in and look."

Tam pushed open the door. I walked in and saw all of the baby gifts and boxes against the wall. The bassinette was packed with diapers and Pampers. "Where did all of this stuff come from?"

"The stuff in the boxes is from last year. All of the Pampers are from Stan's mom. She sends us a pack every week."

"The room is going to be so packed, the baby isn't going to have anywhere to sleep. You still don't know the sex, right?"

"No. The little monster won't uncross his or her legs. I think it's a boy. I think Stan does too, but he won't say."

From nowhere, I was overwhelmed with joy for Tam. I rushed to hug her as she stood in the center of the room. Not sure what had come over me, Tam slowly wrapped her arms around me and embraced me.

"I'm so happy for you," I bellowed as tears started to roll down my face.

"Are you okay?" Tam questioned as she patted my back.

Nodding my head onto her shoulder, I mumbled, "Yeah."

We stood clutched together in the center of the diapers, Pampers, blankets, and soft-squishy toys. Seconds later, Stan knocked on the door to say hello. As I wiped my face, I quickly went over to greet him. From the corner of my eye, I could see Tam making a strange face to warn him of my highly emotional state.

"Good to see you," he said, giving me a quick friendly hug.

"I'm so glad you love my friend," I stated in an octave higher than normal.

"I'm so glad your friend loves me," he said, walking over to Tam.

They kissed as Stan rubbed her belly and I had a complete meltdown. Rushing to the bathroom, I closed the door, sat on the toilet, and cried. I didn't know what was wrong with me. One minute I was fine and the next I was in the bathroom crying like my prom date stood me up.

"Lily, what is wrong with you?" I heard Tam say from the other side of the door.

"I'm fine. I'll be out in a minute."

Slowly, I got up from the toilet and went to the sink to wash my face.

"Get it together," I said to my reflection. "You came here to support Tam, not let her support you."

After wiping my face with cold water, I made my way from the bathroom. I saw Tam in the living room waiting for me. Slowly, I walked into the room and took a seat on the sofa beside her. "Where's Stan?"

"In the bedroom playing video games."

"He plays video games?" I asked, surprised.

"He's a man," Tam said, making a funny face.

We both laughed and then after a couple of sighs, Tam spoke. "All right, girl, talk to me."

"About what?" I questioned.

"About your little breakdown. I know you are not that upset about Romance."

"I am not at all upset about Romance and Stacy Wright-Williams."

Tam quickly butted in. "Stop calling that girl by her full name and tell me what is wrong with you."

Leaning my head onto the sofa cushion, I responded, "I don't know. I really am happy for you and I wanted you to know. But then those happy feelings turned wacko and I became upset. Not because you're happy, but . . . because everyone is happy."

"What are you talking about?" Tam asked, sounding more confused than before.

Pouting, I sank farther into the cushion pillow and tried to explain. "I started thinking about how you have Stan, Sarah has Omar, Evelyn has Pierce, and now Romance has Stacy Wright-Williams."

"And you have Wealth, I mean, Winston," Tam commented.

"I know. But Winston and I are far from married."

"But you don't even want to be married."

"Yeah, yeah. I know," I said. "I just feel everyone is so engrossed in their family life, it's like time is moving on for them but standing still for me. Everyone is graduating and I have to repeat the twelfth grade. I want to graduate too."

"How can you say you aren't moving forward? Your career is growing."

"But what's really important? Family is, and everyone is getting one or is close to having one, but me."

"Oh, I see. I understand now."

I quietly cut my eyes at her as I continued to lean against the cushion. "I don't want to talk about this anymore. Let's change the subject."

"Fine. Let's talk about Dick."

Abruptly, I sat up in the chair and directly faced Tam. "You know what? You always want to talk about Dick. Tonight we will talk about him. What do you want to know?"

"What is it about him? Why do you compare every man to him?" Tam immediately started.

"I constantly think about that. Dick encompasses so much of what I want in a man. He is confident, intelligent, witty, artistic, and incredibly sexy. When we're together, he makes me feel beautiful. I love that."

"What about Winston, how does he measure up?"

"Winston is a good man. Honestly, he has most of those characteristics and when we're together, it feels good, but it's nothing in comparison to the magic I feel when I'm with Dick. It's almost indescribable."

"The magic?" Tam queried.

"Yeah. I love magic shows. I love the anticipation of the act, the exhilaration, and the suspense is exciting. Then once the trick is over the aftermath is just as thrilling 'cause you spend the next hour trying to figure how it was done. It's stimulating. It's moving. Dick moves me like that. When we part, I spend hours trying to figure out what has happened. When we are together, I'm floating and I never want to come down."

"Well, I haven't been married for that long, but eventually gravity takes hold of that floating feeling."

"I know, but when I'm with him, I want to be so

much more of a woman. He unlocks something inside me. No one else has been able to do that."

"So why did you let him go?"

"'Cause I'm a fool," I said with a quick chortle.

Agreeing with laughter, Tam nodded for me to go ahead.

"Well, first we started off all wrong. We were so caught up in the sexual aspects of our relationship, I felt he wouldn't respect me in the ways I wanted and deserved."

"But did he ever disrespect you?"

"Well, there was that time he thought I was going to have a threesome, but he didn't know. He was only being himself. Other than that, he was always respectful. And as we spent more time together, we learned a lot about each other and the respect grew. I felt like a princess around him."

"So why didn't you move back here with him?"

"I just didn't want to drop everything, to go back and shack up with Dick. I mean, why did he want me to shack up? Princesses don't shack up. All of a sudden, I went from Diana to Camilla."

"Well, Camilla eventually got her man."

"But people don't respect her like Diana."

"Maybe he wanted to get to know you better. Did you want to marry him?"

"I don't know. We never talked about it. He told me he couldn't see himself getting married. So when he gave Celeste the ring, I was thrown. Then, when you said he was getting married, I couldn't believe it. Like I wasn't good enough to marry, but she was. It's the whole cow and milk theory."

"The what?"

"Why buy the cow, if you're getting the milk for free?"

"Oh yeah," Tam said, nodding.

"Yeah, and that heifer probably held out on the dairy and now look, she's getting purchased!"

"So you think that if you hadn't slept with Dick, he would have asked you to marry him."

Shrugging, I tilted my head to the side and rolled my pupils into the corners of my eyes. "Who knows?"

Reaching over, Tam began to stroke my hand to comfort me. However, the sentimental touch was making me more emotional and I just didn't feel like crying again. So I removed my hand from hers and walked to the restroom, while she spoke.

"I know you don't want to hear this, but maybe you and Dick weren't meant to be."

Calling from down the hall, I answered, "You're right. I don't want to hear that."

Forcefully shutting the door, I walked into Tam and Stan's brilliant blue bathroom. Sliding down the back of the door, I sat on the hardwood floor and stared at the toilet. I didn't have to use the restroom, I just wanted to leave the room and this was my poor escape plan. I wasn't sure what devoured my brain, but the consumption must have taken a while, 'cause I was startled minutes later by Tam knocking on the door.

"Are you all right?"

Bumping my head against the doorknob, I called, "Ouch. Yeah, I'll be out in a second."

Slowly, I rose and opened the bathroom door and I saw Tam on the other side looking just as glum as I felt.

"What's wrong with you?" I asked.

"My friend is upset and I can't help her."

"It's okay," I said, passing her as we walked back into the living room.

Quietly, we sat and listened to music for at least an

hour. As the CD approached the last song, Tam spoke. "You love him?"

With my dazed focus straight ahead, I slowly nodded my head up and down. After three bobs, I placed my chin against my chest and closed my eyes. Leaning to my right, I placed my head on the sofa's arm and Tam lifted my feet into the chair.

"You want me to put the CD on repeat?" she asked quietly.

"Yes."

Grabbing the chenille throw from the back of the sofa, I draped it over my feet. Tam tussled my hair and headed to the bedroom. "Holler if you need me."

"Thank you. Love you," I replied.

"Yeah, yeah, I know." Tam giggled as she walked down the hall.

Again, I had to get myself together. I was here to cheer up my best friend, not add worries to her plate of headaches. Why was this so difficult? I didn't understand why the great man I had was not helping me forget the good man I didn't have. I was happy with Winston, so why was he not satisfying? If I let it all go and forced myself to commit to Winston, would I ever be satisfied? Commitment isn't something that should be forced, it should be a desire and honestly, it was. I did want to commit to him; at least my mind did. But Dick had my heart and the impulses it was sending through my system were overpowering my brain waves. As much as I loved being a woman, times like that made me long for a pair of testicles and a heap of testosterone.

Women are emotional creatures and at times, I hated it. No matter how deep we try to bury it within our careers or independence, in due course it creeps out.

I reached in my bag and pulled out my journal. After staring at the blank page for a few minutes, I finally wrote:

> *I have a strong mind, but I sometimes underestimated the organ that keeps it all going: the heart. Tam and I are always talking about love and commitment, its origin and its differences. Obviously, people can commit without love and people can love and never commit. However, I was determined to have both and I knew it was possible. I just needed to figure out how to snatch my heart away from Dick and carefully deliver it to Winston. Even better, retrieve it from Dick, and hold on to it until further notice from the Creator. The heart is the lifeline, it can't be handed over to anyone, for his or her hands may be dirty.*
>
> *Thus, allowing people to touch the heart is a dichotomy. One never knows if the warm hands are bearing fortification or contamination. Yet if the heart is never touched, it is sure to grow cold.*
>
> *Now that this double-edged sword has cut me, I don't know whether to bandage it or just let it bleed until it heals itself. Which comes first, the chicken or the egg, love or commitment? Does any of it really matter? I simply want peace of heart to complement my peace of mind, because chaos cannot be divine.*

Good night.

30

Is She Is or
Ain't She His Baby?

Bright and early the next morning, I heard Stan in the kitchen cooking breakfast. As I sluggishly rolled off the sofa, I walked into the kitchen with the throw tossed over my shoulders. Slightly bent at the waist and my hair tossed about, I wobbled on my good foot. I'm sure I looked like someone's granny.

"Whatcha cooking?"

"Omelets and grits."

As I peeked over Stan's shoulder, Tam snuck up behind me. Unfortunately, she scared me and I accidentally bumped Stan and he knocked over the pot of grits, burning his arm in the process.

"Damn!" he yelled while shaking the grits off his arm.

"I'm sorry, I'm sorry," I yelped as I frantically looked for a cloth. Tam rushed to the sink to wet a rag and quickly handed it to Stan. In this process she slipped on the grits and almost fell. Thank God for Stan's quick reflexes. He caught her back and pushed her onto me. I, in turn, fell forward onto the counter and Tam landed on my back. Once the pandemonium was over, grits were everywhere, my chest was slightly bruised, Tam was panicked, and Stan had given up on breakfast.

"Is everyone okay?" asked Stan.

"I'm okay, baby," said Tam as he lifted her off me and walked her into the living room.

"Yeah, I'm okay too," I said to myself as they left me in the kitchen.

"Lily, I got the mess, don't worry about it," Stan called out.

"I got it," I stated while wiping the counter. "Again, I'm sorry."

Minutes later, Stan came into the kitchen to help me finish the cleaning.

"Tam all right?"

"Yeah, just a little shook-up, she's lying down. I'm going to take her an omelet."

With my appetite ruined, I decided to go upstairs, take a shower, and get dressed. Tam and I had plans to go see Evelyn's mother before the afternoon. Therefore, I knocked on her door once I was dressed to see if she was ready.

"Come in."

I slowly walked in and saw Tam sitting on the edge of the bed as she put on her earrings.

"You ready?" I asked.

"Yeah, let me get my shoes," she said, walking to her closet.

I went down the hall and waited for Tam. While waiting, I called Winston to check on him. He didn't call me back last night after I paged him and that was not like him. Today, he answered his cell on the first ring.

"Hey, baby."

"Hi, Lily."

"Winston?"

"No, this is Wealth. Winston went to the store."

"Why are you answering his phone?"

"Nice to talk with you too."

"Sorry, Wealth. It's good to hear your voice. How have you been?"

"Well, if you called more you would know. I've been sick."

"No. What's wrong?"

"Stress, they think. I've been having chest pains and migraines. My tests show no signs of real danger, but my blood pressure is up."

"Wealth, please slow down. I don't want to come visit you in the hospital."

"How sweet, you would come visit me?"

"Of course I would. I do care about your well-being."

Wealth remained quiet, and Tam tapped me on the shoulder. We walked to the SUV while I continued speaking with Wealth.

"You okay?"

He smacked his teeth.

"Wealth Fulmore, stop simpering and say something."

"You're a cool lady. My brother loves you and I understand why. I hope you two really make something happen."

This time I was the one silent. I wanted to ask about his parents but I didn't want to get into a long discussion and I knew Wealth, unlike Winston, would want to dialogue.

I finally responded, "Thanks Wealth. I'll talk with you when I return."

"Maybe we can do lunch."

"I don't know. Just tell Winston I called. Don't forget."

"As soon as he and Angela get back, I'll tell him."

"Oh, he's with Angela. She sure does get around, doesn't she?" I said, sneering, never really liking Wealth's girlfriend.

"No more than you, my dear," he sniped back.

"Good one. Real good one," I responded.

"Glad you liked it."

"Good-bye, Wealth Fulmore."

"Good-bye, Lily McNeil."

As soon as we hung up, Tam started.

"Why are you talking to Wealth?"

"'Cause he answered Winston's phone."

"Don't you feel weird talking to him?"

"Not really. It's almost like we never dated. He said he wants Winston and me to be together. I don't know if I completely believe him, but I just go with it."

Tam made a funny face and continued driving. In no time, we pulled up to the hospital. As soon as we got to the fourth-floor B wing, we saw Evelyn standing at the desk yelling at the receptionist. We hastened to the problem.

"What's wrong?" Tam and I asked in unison.

Moaning, Evelyn turned to us while griping, "They moved Mom to another unit and now she is in a room with someone else when we pay for her to be in a single unit."

"Where is she now?" Tam asked.

Evelyn pointed down the hall.

"Okay, I'll stay here and get this straight, you and Lily go see about your mom."

Hesitantly, Evelyn escorted me down the hall, and as soon as we walked into the room, my heart started to ache. I'd only met Evelyn's mom once; however, the last time I saw her she was a vivacious, healthy woman swapping exchanges on the tennis court. To see her lying weak on this bed with tubes in her veins was a dose of unwanted reality. I rushed to her side and gently kissed her hand.

"Mom, this is my friend Lily, you remember her?" Evelyn asked softly.

Mrs. Schaffer softly bobbed her head.

"How are you feeling today?" I asked as I sat by her bedside.

"Better than yesterday, worse than the day before."

"Well, I need you to get better so that you can still teach me to play tennis like you promised."

"Tennis?" her mom questioned.

"Yes, the last time I saw you, you were spanking Mr. Schaffer in a game of tennis. I told you I needed some pointers and you agreed to assist me."

Squinting her eyes to recall the memory, Mrs. Schaffer began to smile. "Oh yes, I remember. A very handsome gentleman accompanied you. I recall him standing behind me and showing me a few tips on my serve." She beamed brighter.

"That's right, I was with Dick."

"Oh yes, he was mighty fine and strong. I do remember," she said, slightly lifting from her lying position.

Again, Dick's affect on women was amazing. This woman was lying here suffering from heart failure, yet when she recalled seeing Dick, she began to smile and sit up as if her attack were mere heartburn.

"Is he with you today?" she inquired while attempting to brush her hair away from her face.

"Calm down, Mom. Dick is not here."

Laughing, I quickly saw where Evelyn got her overzealousness for men.

"I tell you what, once you get better and get home, I will tell Dick to come visit you," I said with a wink.

"Ooh, a little motivation to get home quicker."

"What about Dad?" Evelyn asked.

"His worrying me is probably what gave me the heart attack in the first place," she teased.

"Don't say that," said Evelyn.

We heard a slight tap on the door, and then Tam peeped in.

"What did they say?" asked Evelyn.

"They said they will get her in another unit by tomorrow morning. Her condition is stable now, so they had to move her over here."

"But—" Evelyn started.

"But they have no single rooms over here until the morning."

"Are you still fussing about the room, Evelyn?" her mom asked.

"Yes. This is not what we are paying for."

"*We* aren't paying for anything, your father is. I'll be fine."

Evelyn quieted down and we sat and talked with her mother for another forty minutes. We left when the nurse came in to check her blood pressure and run a few other tests.

"I have to leave town tomorrow, so I may not be back to see you this trip, but I'll be back before the year is out."

"Okay, dear, tell Dick I said hello."

"I sure will."

Evelyn kissed her mom. "I'll see you later today."

We closed the door and walked into the parking deck.

"Evelyn, your mom is not dying," I commented.

"Well, she looks better today than the other days."

"She'll probably be going home soon," said Tam.

"I hope so," Evelyn added.

Evelyn walked with us to the SUV and Tam and I looked at her peculiarly as to where she was going.

"Where is your car?" Evelyn asked.

"I'm going with you two."

"Do you know where we are going?"

"No, but wherever it is, I'm going too."

Tam chuckled and responded, "Let's go eat. I'm hungry."

We piled into Tam's SUV and headed toward Peachtree Street.

"Let's go to Justin's," suggested Evelyn.

"How is their lunch menu?" I inquired.

"It's all right," Tam answered.

Quietly, we rode down the street while listening to the radio. Seldom did the three of us ride in silence, but today our minds were filled with our own concerns. Issues still so foggy, the density had us mulling instead of bantering. Within ten minutes, Tam was handing the valet her keys and we were walking into the exquisite restaurant named after Sean Combs's firstborn. With no wait, we were immediately escorted to our table. Tam quickly looked over the menu and put it down.

"I know what I want. You guys ready?" she asked.

"We just sat down. Give me a minute," I requested.

The server came over and took our drink order, which turned out to be three iced teas without lemon.

Finally, I decided to have the pan-seared trout with rice and vegetables, Evelyn settled with a fried chicken salad, and Tam got the shrimp. As soon as we ordered, Evelyn's phone began vibrating. While she spoke to her caller, Tam and I had our own quiet conversation.

"Thank you for last night," I told her.

"Thanks for coming to see about me."

"I don't know why you're thanking me. I came to cheer you up, instead you end up advising me."

"I miss that. Maybe that's what I needed," Tam said with a smile.

Interrupting our conversation, Evelyn happily interjected, "My brother is going to have lunch with us."

"That's nice, I thought he already left for New York."

"He decided to stay through the weekend."

"I thought your brother lived in Europe," I remarked.

"My oldest brother, Marcus, lives in Europe, the one under him lives in New York."

"You don't talk about him too much. In fact, you don't talk about either one of your brothers."

"That's because I'm eight years behind Vinny and nine years behind Marcus. They were away in school when I was growing up. We only spent summers together."

"I wish I had brothers. I don't like being an only child."

"Me either," I agreed.

Tam and I sipped our drinks while we discussed only-child syndromes, babies, and families. Minutes later, our food was being brought to our table. Our server, Nicole, set the tray to her left and carefully placed each hot plate before us.

"Smells good," said Tam.

Evelyn and I agreed with quick head bobbles.

"Do you need anything else?" asked Nicole.

"More napkins and then we're good," said Tam.

We quickly said our grace and dug in. However, just as Nicole moved away from our table after dropping off our napkins, this six-two, light-skinned figure swooped into the table and lifted Evelyn from her seat. She clung to his muscular arms and held tight.

"You seen Mom today?" she asked.

"Not today. You?"

"Yeah, we just left," she said as he turned around to acknowledge us.

Just then, my dark brown eyes locked into his hazel greens. Evelyn slid back down to her seat and my mouth, filled with food, flew open.

"Lil?" he asked.

"Luv?" I muttered.

"You two know each other?" asked Evelyn.

Tam, engrossed in her lunch, barely looked up to speak before diving back into her plate of shrimp. Evelyn's brother quickly took a seat.

"You're Evelyn's brother?" I questioned, still stunned.

"Yeah, he's my brother. How do you know him?" she inquired defensively as she held tight to his arm.

"We went to grad school together," he answered, staring into my eyes.

Bashfully, I looked down at my plate and continued chewing.

"So how have you been?" he asked, reaching over to stroke my hand.

"Fine, and you?"

Nervously, my leg shook underneath the booth. As it brushed against Tam's leg, she finally came from within her pile of shrimp to notice the sparks flying across the table.

"So, when is the last time you saw Vinny?" Evelyn asked.

"Years ago. At least seven."

"At least," he commented with a smile.

"What happened to your hair? Where are your locks?"

Laughing, he rubbed his hand against his clean bald head. "Wall Street and old age."

"You look good," I said, admiring his close-shaven beard with hints of gray.

"And you look . . . beautiful."

Clearing her throat, Tam broke the sparks by asking me, "How do you know him again?"

"If you could lift your head from your shrimp, you would have heard him say grad school. Luv, I mean Vinny, and I went to Southern together."

"Why do you call him Luv?" Evelyn asked with a frown.

"That's just what I used to call him."

"I don't remember you talking about a 'Luv'?" Tam frowned.

"Remember M and M?"

Tam's eyes widened as she slid her fork from her lips.

"He's M and M?" she stated as if he were not sitting directly in front of us.

Puzzled, he questioned me about the double *M*s. Embarrassed, I began to explain.

"I used to refer to you as a married man."

Chuckling, he scratched his beard and smiled. "Well, now you can refer to me as S and M. Because this single man has been divorced over three years."

Smiling, I felt his leg gently brush against mine. The table was silent. Yet all focus was on me as Tam nudged my elbow. Luv softly glided against my leg and Evelyn stared disapprovingly. Thankfully, Nicole came over to take Luv's order and broke the stillness.

"I'll have a glass of chardonnay and the same order as this young lady here," he said, pointing to my plate.

"Excuse me," Tam said, poking my left side so that she could get out of the booth. I slid over and out of my seat. As Tam scooted out, she grabbed my wrist and pulled me with her.

"Excuse us," I hastily commented before she forced me off to the ladies' room.

As soon as we got into the room, and the door closed, she cornered me with questions.

"You never slept with M and M, did you?"

"Nope. He was married. You know I don't do that."

"But you two liked each other."

"Our relationship was very intimate. We just never had sex. I really liked him. It went on for a year."

"You sure you didn't do it?"

"I would remember. I am sure. We kissed, flirted, and held hands. It was the closest I ever came to having an affair with a married man and I felt like shit. Finally, I called it off. He graduated and moved to New York, and that was that."

"But he's not married now."

"I know, but my man-gumbo is zesty enough, I don't need to add any more spice. I don't even want to think about it."

"Good. I just wanted to see where your head was," Tam said before entering the stall.

"My head is on straight and though he looks good, very good, I'm going to have to let Luv go."

"Good girl," she called from the stall.

Once we returned to the table, Nicole was bringing

Luv his lunch. Tam, Evelyn, and I sat quietly and finished our food. Other than a few stares and a couple of foot rubs, the rest of lunch went smoothly.

After we finished, Tam and I decided to walk through Buckhead and check a few of the new shops. Evelyn rode with her brother back to the hospital to get her car. She said she might meet up with us a little later. But I would rather spend the afternoon alone with Tam. As we stood in the parking lot saying our good-byes, Luv pulled me to the side to speak with me in private.

"I want to see you tonight," he said.

"I'm spending time with Tam this evening," I replied, trying not to be swayed.

Luv took my hand and pulled me closer to his side. "I have to see you before you leave."

He softly kissed my cheek and I felt myself getting weaker. As the light brown flecks of his irises sparkled from the sun's light, I could almost see through his hazel eyes. It was too late, he was drawing me in.

"Maybe tomorrow," I said, quickly looking away.

Luv turned my cheek to face his direction, leaned over, and kissed the corner of my lips.

"Definitely tomorrow," he said, handing me his card. "Make sure you call me tonight."

I took his card and we quickly embraced. Luv slid his hands from around my shoulders, down my back, and rested them just above my rear. As he slightly tugged on my shirt, he added, "You are a vision of wonderful. I can't wait until tomorrow."

I returned his compliment with a smile and slowly walked toward Tam. As I passed Evelyn, she said good-bye and joined her brother at the car. I jumped in the SUV while keeping my focus straight ahead. I dared not look into Tam's criticizing eyes.

"Looks like someone's head is starting to unravel."

"We are only hanging out one day. He's an old friend."

"An old divorced friend."

"I'll be good."

"That's what I'm worried about and what he's counting on," she simpered.

We continued to ride up the road, found a great space by a two-hour meter, and parked. Tam and I got out and started our afternoon of shopping.

"I want a new purse and a pair of new shoes. That's all," Tam admitted.

"A new purse would be nice. I definitely don't want to shop for clothing, at least not in Buckhead."

"I could go for something vintage, maybe we can go to Decatur tomorrow."

"I'm supposed to hang out with Luv tomorrow."

"I'm supposed to hang out with Luv tomorrow," Tam mocked.

"Stop mocking me."

"It's already starting."

"What is starting?"

"You're going to get all gooey over him."

"No, I'm not."

"I hear it in your voice."

Ignoring Tam's statement, I made a sharp turn and went into J. Blue. However, while looking back at her, I accidentally bumped into the Amazon beauty walking out.

"Sorry," I said quickly as my eyes moved up toward her face.

"Lily?"

I froze as Tam bumped into my back.

"Celeste . . . hi."

"Celeste," Tam joined in.

"How are you two doing? Lily, have you moved back here?"

"No, just visiting," I answered as Tam and I stepped from the doorway and into the store.

Celeste stepped in to continue the conversation.

"Lily, you look different," she added.

"It's my hair, it's straight."

"It looks good," Tam quickly commented as she saw my confidence wavering.

"Yeah, I like it."

"What are you doing out here, shopping?" questioned Tam.

"Just killing time. I have a spa appointment in about an hour."

"Oooh, the spa, that's what we should have done today. Let's go get pedicures."

"Oh, they do great pedicures. You have to have an appointment, though," Celeste said as she lightly tapped my arm. Just then, I noticed a very important item missing from her hand: specifically, her ring finger. She was not wearing the infamous diamond ring. Where was it? I wondered. Quickly, I cut my eyes at Tam to see if she noticed, but she did not. As Celeste started to chatter about the sale up the street, I began to stare at her hand and become obsessed with speculations. Tam, completely oblivious, wandered throughout the store. Tapping my nail against my teeth, I thought vigorously. It would be inappropriate to ask about the ring, but I really must know. Where was Evelyn and her crassness when you needed it? Not only would Evelyn have noticed the missing jewel, but also she would have asked its whereabouts and gotten the full scoop by now. Finally, Celeste wrapped up her random conversation, waved good-bye to Tam, and left the store. During this entire exchange, not once did she mention Dick. Something was awry. I rushed across the store to Tam.

"Celeste wasn't wearing her ring," I whispered loudly.

"Okay," Tam said, unconcerned.

"What does that mean? Are they still together?"

"I guess so. I don't know. You talk to him more than I talk with her."

"But he never mentioned breaking off things with her."

"Then they're probably still together. Don't get excited. I don't see anything in here. Let's go."

We walked a few blocks up the street and I could no longer contain my anxiety.

"I have to know," I exclaimed.

Grabbing my cell, I hastily dialed Dick's number. Nervously patting my arm against my leg, I waited for him to pick up. Of course, he didn't, and so I left a message for him to call back.

"Why didn't you just ask him in the message?" inquired Tam.

"'Cause I want to catch him off guard. If I leave the message, it gives him time to come up with a clever response, which may not necessarily be the truth."

"You've got this all figured out, haven't you?"

"I hope so."

"Don't get too excited," Tam replied as we went into another store.

My appetite for shoes had turned into an appetite for information. I couldn't have cared less about shopping. I simply wanted to hear from Dick. I pretended to peruse through the store until my phone rang. Quickly, I hastened out the door and onto the

sidewalk. Glancing at the caller ID, I saw that it was not
Dick, but Winston. Although this was not the expected
phone call, I was still thrilled to speak with him.

"Hey, baby," I answered.

"How's Atlanta?"

"Hot."

"How's the gang?"

"Everyone is good. I saw Evelyn's mom today and she
is doing much better. I'm shopping with Tam right
now. You sound better."

"Yeah, Wealth and I have been hanging out. I'm
trying not to worry about Mom and Dad."

"Good. They're going to be all right."

"When are you coming back?"

"Monday morning. My flight arrives at nine thirty.
You can still pick me up, right?"

"I got you. I'll see you then."

"Okay. Bye."

"Bye."

As soon as we hung up, Tam tapped my shoulder.

"Who was that?"

"Winston."

She wrapped her arm within mine and pulled me
back into the store.

"Look at this purse," she said as we walked in.

We spent the next few hours shopping, walking, and
talking. Tam bought two purses and a hat. I bought
nothing. I couldn't find anything more exciting than
Celeste not wearing her ring. That unexpected, stag-
gering news filled my desire for new shoes. Offhand,
I couldn't think of anything that filled the longing for
a new pair of shoes. I certainly didn't wish unhappi-
ness and despair on anyone. However, if Celeste and
Dick were separating, the gap was about to widen,

'cause I was stepping my five-foot-five, 125-pound frame into it. Wrong or not, I saw this as an opportunity and I was taking advantage of it.

We arrived back at the house around six and Stan was prepared to take us to dinner. Unfortunately, I was still filled from lunch. Tam, being five months pregnant, was hungry again. I assured her that I was okay being left at the house and that she should go to dinner with her husband, and after a couple of persuasive arguments, she was convinced and I was left alone.

With my mind filled with conjectures about Celeste and theories as to how to approach Dick, I had no choice but to call him again. Still, he did not answer. This was driving me insane. I made my way up to my room to take a nap, the only thing that was going to calm me. We had mentioned going out tonight, but I doubted we are going anywhere since it was almost eight o'clock and I hadn't heard from Tam or Evelyn. This was what happened when girlfriends settled down. No one wanted to go out and meet new people. Tam was blissfully happy, Evelyn was romantically involved, and I . . . well, I was content. If Dick were to tell me he and Celeste broke things off, my entire situation would instantly be turned upside down. I couldn't drop Winston like a hot potato, that would be wrong, not to mention foolish, but I couldn't just pretend I didn't care if Dick was single. Honestly, I didn't know what I was supposed to get from all of this.

Fingers that were once bare now were dressed with rings, and fingers that were once dressed with rings were now bare. What was really going on? The last few days had been like a bad reality show.

"Welcome to this could have been your life, but you messed up and everyone has moved on but you."

Yeah, yeah, it was a long title, but it was a work in progress.

"What if Dick broke it off with Celeste and he wants me back?" I said to myself before drifting off to sleep.

Well, mind, I hope you are equipped for battle, 'cause if that is the case, my heart has already primed her troops and it's about to be a war.

31

Tainted Luv

Around six the next morning, I woke up and sat straight up in the bed. Glancing at the clock, I couldn't believe the time. I must have been tired, 'cause my nap turned into an all-night slumber. Still lethargic, I wiped my eyes and slowly rolled from the bed. While using the restroom, I heard a soft knock on the door.

"Tam, is that you?"

"Yeah."

"Come in," I responded as I flushed the toilet and proceeded to wash my hands.

Tam handed me the phone, turned around, and walked back out of the restroom without saying a word. I looked at the receiver before placing it to my ear. Finally, I put the phone to my earlobe and listened.

"Hello," I heard the voice say.

"Hello," I answered with hesitation.

"You were supposed to call me last night, what happened?"

"Oh, Luv, I fell asleep."

"Well, are you up and dressed?" he asked anxiously.

"No. It's six in the morning."

"I know. I'll be there in twenty minutes. Get dressed."

Shocked and dazed, I stood in the bathroom staring at the phone.

"Twenty minutes?" I said to myself in the mirror. "It's six in the morning, is he crazy?"

I was waddling back to the bedroom when the phone rang again. Quickly, I answered it, for I did not want to awake Stan and Tam once more.

"Hello," I said rapidly.

"Twenty minutes. I hope you're ready. We're going to have fun. I promise."

"Why so early?" I asked.

"You'll see," he said.

"No. Tell me now, or I'm not going."

"Fine. I was going to take you to Savannah."

"Are you crazy? I'm not going with you to Savannah. We can go to dinner or have lunch and that's it."

"Just be ready."

"I'm not—"

Luv hung up.

Moaning, I fell back onto the bed and stared at the ceiling. As far as Luv was concerned, I could take him or leave him. Yes, I was gaga over him back in the day, but that was then. He looked fine, I admitted, but his energy was very overpowering. He had always been a bit of a bully. A full day of him and I was sure to be worn out. On a good note, though, if we started early, I should be back here in time for dinner. I grabbed my clothing and headed to the bathroom to shower.

Exactly twenty-two minutes later, I heard a car pulling up into the driveway. I hurried downstairs, only to bump into Tam as I rounded the corner.

"Where are you going?" she asked sternly with her arms folded.

"I love him, Mom! You can't keep us away from each other!" I said in my best distressed-teenager voice.

Tam burst out laughing. "Don't make me laugh. I'm serious."

"Girl, he was trying to take me to Savannah. I told him no, so I guess we're going to breakfast. I should be back here this afternoon," I commented.

"Call me," Tam requested.

Throwing my hand in the air, I waved a quick good-bye and walked to the car to start my day with Luv. As soon as I hopped in, he took off down the street.

"Well, good morning to you."

"Good to see you this morning," he stated, focusing on the road.

"Where are we rushing off to?"

Luv didn't answer.

"Luvinious, where are we going?"

"Oooh, I remember that tone. When you were angry you always called me by my full name. We are going to breakfast."

"Good. Was that so hard to say?"

I leaned my head back against the leather seat and closed my eyes. Although I was not sleepy, I was still a bit sluggish; plus, it was too soon for conversation. Yet, when I opened my eyes again, we were pulling into the parking deck of the airport. Lifting myself up, I loudly commented, "Why are we at the airport? I told you I was not going to Savannah. You said we were going to breakfast."

"We are. Breakfast in Savannah."

"No, Luv. I have to leave in the morning, and I came to spend time with Tam."

"Our flight returns tonight. We're only spending the day there. I already have the tickets."

"I don't care. You should have asked me first."

"The girl I know would have loved this."

"Well, the woman you don't know does not."

"I wanted to surprise you."

I refused to get out of the car and our bantering went back and forth for another fifteen minutes. Finally, we agreed to go back to have breakfast at the Four Seasons, where he was staying.

During breakfast we caught up on the last six years. He told me how he and his wife tried to make it work for years, but that they were unequally matched. They married young because of their daughter and through the years grew further and further apart. He showed me pictures of his daughter, who was now fourteen and lived with his ex-wife in Maryland. We reminisced about our days at Southern and how we used to sneak off and spend days by the river having picnics. Luv and I took economics class together and I abhorred that subject. Fortunately, he excelled in it, and agreed to tutor me and that was how our bond started. We started seeing each other almost every day and economics was hardly the topic of discussion. We talked about love, life, satisfaction, bliss, and other life essentials. I must admit, I quickly fell for him, but I refused to be the other woman. Still, our escapade lasted almost a year.

"I know you thought my wife and I were never going to separate."

"I knew you weren't happy, but it would have

been foolish of me to wait around until your marriage collapsed."

"We had so much fun."

"We did," I concurred while smiling.

After breakfast, we hopped in the car and drove to the park. The day was absolutely gorgeous. I leaned my chair back and placed my crossed legs up on the dash. With my shades on and my hair blowing in the wind, I felt as though I were in a movie. We spent three hours talking and walking in the park. Once I got tired of the sun, we hopped back into the car and headed back. I thought we were going back to Tam's house, but we went to the hotel instead.

"Why are you even staying at a hotel instead of your parents'?"

"I like my privacy," Luv said.

"Then why are you bringing me back to the hotel?" I asked.

"Relax, it's okay," he said, patting my leg.

We pulled into the hotel, and Luv gave the valet the keys. As he swaggered across the lobby, I could see the confidence bouncing off his smooth complexion. I always liked a confident man.

"He is a tall drink of water on an arid, sunny day. Quite refreshing."

We went into the suite and talked for another hour. The memories were so marked that I became that twenty-two-year-old graduate student being romanced by that thirty-year-old M&M.

"Remember our cartoon?" I said with excitement.

"Of course I do, *Luv and Lil*. I still have the book."

"Really? Send it to me."

"Okay. You used to write the funniest dialogue. I'm so glad you are using your writing talent."

"Yeah. I love it. Of course, I would love to be writing more independently, novels and whatnot. But for now I'm in a good place.

"You don't draw anymore?" I asked.

"No. A financial analyst by day can't be a cartoonist by night. I gave that up a long time ago. My daughter, though, seems to have picked up the skill. I'm definitely going to encourage her."

"You should."

I closed my eyes as I stretched across the foot of the bed. In no time, I drifted into a light siesta. However, two soft lips pressed against my forehead woke me. Slowly, I opened my eyes and I saw Luv. He softly kissed my lips. Smiling, I wrapped my arms around his neck and pulled him down on top of me. He turned over so that I was on top to deliver dozens of tiny kisses all over his body. With his knees pressed tightly around my waist, he began to slide my pants down to my ankles. He wrapped his large hands around the base of my face and passionately delivered kiss after kiss after kiss. Within moments our clothing was off. Just then, I felt warm hands around my neck. The grip was comfortable at first; however, it got tighter as each second passed. As my air passage got smaller, Luv gently yet forcefully entered me. I gasped for air as I took my tiny hands and placed them around his strong arms. With might, I attempted to pull his hands from around my neck; however, he grinned as if this was all a part of the plan. Meanwhile, he was still stroking. He flipped our bodies over and my head sank into the large down pillow. I gasped, only taking in short breaths of air. Luv was pressing himself deeper inside me and my body caved inward with every thrust. The thrill was exciting and at the same time frightening, like a roller-coaster ride. The peaks almost made me climax and the dips took my breath. Suddenly my body stiffened. I didn't know if I was having an orgasm, a heart attack, or both.

"Lily, Lily," I heard faintly in the background.

Again, I felt soft lips upon my forehead. Slowly, I opened my eyes and saw Luv hovering over my body. I began choking.

"Babe, you okay?" he asked.

I looked down at my body, which was fully clothed; then I glanced at his chest. Dazed, I felt my breathing subside and begin a normal pattern. I slowly sat up, realizing the sexual roller coaster was only a dream. Brushing my hand against his close-shaven beard, I smiled.

"I had a crazy dream."

"About what?" he asked curiously.

Embarrassed, I nodded demurely and looked away. Sliding close beside me, he turned my head.

"C'mon, tell me."

"You were trying to choke me to death."

Luv rolled onto his back. Placing his arms behind his head, he began to laugh.

"What is so funny?"

"Were you enjoying it?"

I didn't bother answering his question.

"Why did we run into each other again after all this time?"

Slowly sliding his chest from underneath my head, Luv placed his face in front of mine.

"So that we can do this." He gently kissed my lips. "And this."

This time he passionately kissed me while pulling my body on top of his. "And this."

"No, no. I can't do this." I pulled away and lifted myself from the bed.

"I have protection," he commented.

"It's not that—" I attempted to remark, but Luv silenced me with another ardent kiss.

Again, I moved away from his body, but accidentally rolled off onto the floor and scraped my injured leg on the corner of the bed. It began to bleed. Luv looked at my leg, rushed to the bathroom, and came back with some tissue.

"Do you want me to go down and get some Band-Aids?"

"Yes, please."

"That's what you get for running from me."

"Just go," I stated, pushing him toward the door.

My leg started bleeding again, so I wiped and then began rummaging through his bag for ointment. I found keys, his wallet, sunblock, and an extra pair of shades. I ran my hand across the bottom of the bag and came across a tiny plastic bottle. Pulling it from the bag, I saw it was some prescription medicine. Dropping all of his things back into the bag, I realized he had no ointment. Yet as I sat there, curiosity got the best of me and I dug my hand in once more and pulled out the medicine again. I just wanted to see what kind of meds he was on. It had been seven years, who knew, he could be a depressed, maniacal sleepwalker or a nervous insomniac.

"What if he is on Viagra?" I giggled while reading the prescription.

Unexpectedly, my throat dried and my eyes bulged as I read the three infamous letters on his prescription.

"Or what if he is on ATZ?"

My breathing subsided into heavy panting. I only knew one reason why a person would be on this medication and it had nothing to do with lack of erectness.

"Luv is HIV positive?"

I heard him opening the door. Quickly, I dropped the prescription back in the bag, tossed the duffel on the floor, and sat on the corner of the bed. Not exactly sure of the best way to handle this, I prepared myself for the truth. I thought I would bring up testing in conversation. He came over with two bandages and fixed my leg.

As I smiled and thanked him he commented, "I should at least get a kiss for this."

I simply frowned, but he continued.

"I know and you know this has been a long time coming. Are you saying you don't want me?"

"That is exactly what I'm saying," I said with a very serious expression.

"What's wrong?" he inquired.

"We need to talk," I said, hesitating to jump to conclusions.

"Let's talk afterward," he said, attempting to smooch.

I saw he was leaving me no choice. I stood, pushed him off me, and blurted out, "Have you ever had an HIV test?"

Slowly dragging his hand across his face, Luv rose and looked me dead in the eye.

"I have," he said with a grave expression.

"And?" I asked, anxiously awaiting the truth.

Luv moved down toward the edge of the bed, but he didn't answer. I guessed that was proof enough. No one dithered around when their test results were negative, especially when they were trying to get laid. I didn't know if he was trying to come up with a lie or find a way to tell me the truth, but he needed to tell me something.

"Talk to me, Luv."

"Come here," he requested, motioning for me to move closer.

With my eyes squarely set upon his, I walked over and sat at the top of the bed with my legs folded. Luv turned around to face me.

"I am positive," he said.

By my staid expression, he assumed I already knew.

"Evelyn told you?" he asked.

"No. I was looking for some ointment for my cut when I saw your medicine in your bag."

Luv simply shook his head and looked away.

"When were you going to tell me? Were you going to tell me?"

"I was."

"When? After we had sex?" I asked with a hint of anger.

"So we were going to sleep together?" he asked.

"What? No."

"Then why are we having this conversation?"

"Because you were trying to sleep with me without telling me that you were positive. Protection or not, you are obligated to tell someone you are planning on sleeping with that you are positive," I said while rising from the bed and walking to the balcony.

My temper was slowly rising and I was trying to remain calm. However, the thought that he was actually going to try to sleep with me and not make me aware of his condition was appalling.

I turned and said, "And you kissed me."

"And . . . do you check everyone's HIV paperwork before sleeping with them?" he asked.

"Are you making a pathetic argument? If so, you need to shut up right now, 'cause your actions are not acceptable."

"Listen to me," he said, walking over to the window. "I just wanted to rekindle some of what we had. I didn't want to get into a long taxing conversation about the disease. How and where I got it and if I had AIDS."

"Do you have AIDS?"

"No. I found out I was positive two years ago and that is all I want to say about it."

"Fine," I said with frustration.

Luv began massaging my shoulders. "Condoms protect against the spread of the disease. I won't give you anything."

I turned around so quickly, my head instantly began to ache. "I know you won't. 'Cause you are not touching me. You are dishonest and sneaky."

"Dishonest? I could have lied and come up with an excuse about the medicine."

"You could have not tried to be intimate with me or told me the truth up front, without me confronting you. I'm really disappointed in you, Luv."

"'Cause I'm positive?"

"No. 'Cause you made the decision to put me at risk."

"I would never have slept with you without protection."

"Condoms break."

"Then you make the decision to put yourself at risk every time you sleep with someone," he responded boldly.

I paused silently upon hearing these daunting words. Finally, I turned toward him and spoke.

"You're right, it's a scary thought. But I would hope

that someone who cared about me wouldn't intentionally put me at risk. Take me back please."

Grabbing my purse from the nightstand, I walked out the door. As I looked within my purse for my cell phone, I realized I didn't have it.

"No wonder it's been silent all day," I said to myself.

Other than Luv singing along with the radio, the ride back to Tam's house was silent. I always adored his singing voice, and so I sat, listened, and reminisced about that time and place that was no longer. Luv and I said nothing to each other until we were pulling into the neighborhood.

"I would not do anything to intentionally hurt you. I want you to know that."

"Hurt, by design or not, is still hurt. However, I do forgive you."

Luv's tough exterior slowly gave way to a grin. He leaned over to kiss my forehead. Quickly, I interjected, sternly holding up my index finger.

"I still don't trust you."

Empathetically, Luv gave a relaxing nod. While walking me to the door, he stopped and gave me a hug.

"It was so good to see you again," he said.

"Same here."

"You take care of yourself. Is it okay if I call you now and then?"

"No, not really."

"Well then, be good," he said before turning to walk away.

"Good-bye, Luv."

"So long, Lil."

Standing on the step, I waved good-bye as he pulled away. As I turned and approached the door, I saw that it was already cracked open. As soon as I stepped in,

Tam peeped from around the corner, staring at me, her eyes filled with anticipation, almost fright. Immediately, I knew that she knew.

"I didn't sleep with him."

Her eyes looked deeper into mine, but she said nothing. It was as though she was trying to pull the truth from my soul's window.

"Really, I didn't sleep with him."

"Do you know?"

"I know. He told me."

Sighs of relief filled Tam's chest. She rushed toward me.

"I tried to call you. You left your phone here," she said, hitting me on the arm.

"I'm sorry. It was by accident. I can't believe you thought I would sleep with him."

"Y'all have history, plus one or two mimosas and you never know."

Tam pulled me over to the sofa to get the full scoop.

"Evelyn called me about ten this morning. When she found out you two went out, she knew he might try sleeping with you and thought he might not tell you," Tam quickly rambled off.

"He told me only when I confronted him. It was crazy. What if I had done it with him?"

Tam simply shook her head, looked away, and commented, "You still would have used condoms."

"But still. Anything could have happened."

Tam still sat on the couch dazed.

I turned and asked her, "Are you all right?"

"He was so fine," she said, speaking about Luv.

"He still is fine. He's just positive," I responded.

"And you would never know."

Walking up the stairs, I repeated, "And you would never know."

"I want to go get some flowers for the backyard in about an hour."

"Okay, I'll be in the room resting, just come get me when you're ready."

After checking my phone and returning a few missed calls, I reclined on the bed and pulled out my journal. It never ceased to amaze me how life could take major turns for better or worse in a split second. It only takes a second to get into a car accident. It only takes a second to get pregnant. Something like a second seems so minuscule compared to the hours in a day and the days in a year. Yet each second of the day, someone's life is dramatically changing and time doesn't stop for that certain someone to get it together. As powerful as we humans think we are, we are mortals in every sense of the word, especially when it comes to the phenomenon of creation and existence. We are often unmindful of the sixty tick-tocks in each minute. Yet it's amazing that every second has a purpose in the grand cipher of life.

My day that once seemed so peaceful had shifted to disturbing. I was no longer upset with Luv, but the thought that I could easily have slept with a man who was HIV positive had tainted me with a sea of questions. "What if this, what if that" kept resonating in my head.

It wasn't long before Tam was ready to go to Home Depot. She'd set aside a specific area in her backyard for flowers but didn't plant the seeds months ago when she should have. Hence, she decided to buy a few perennial plants and plant those instead. While we were out, of course, she brought up Luv.

"Do you think he got it from his wife?" she asked me.

"I don't know."

"Evelyn never said, she just wanted to make sure you knew."

"Not to be funny, but you would think her brother's status would keep her from sleeping around."

"She doesn't sleep around now," Tam said.

"But she used to, remember last year when she was trying to get me to switch boyfriends, so that she could sleep with Dick?"

"Oh yeah, I do."

We shopped for a while before continuing. This time I started up.

"What if I've already slept with someone who's positive?"

"You've been tested, right?"

"Yes, but what if it just hasn't shown up yet?"

Tam didn't respond right away. She asked that I grab two gardenias, and then walked down the aisle and picked up a barberry. Afterward, we proceeded to the checkout. While waiting in the line, Tam continued the conversation.

"I'm so glad I'm married."

"Gee, thanks," I replied.

"You're not positive, but you have to be very careful."

The rest of the day was peaceful. We went to the grocery store and back home. Tam and I stayed in the rest of the evening. We watched television, and talked. Around ten o'clock, she got tired and went to bed.

After my shower, I sat on the bed and scrolled through my phone. Immediately, I began deleting old numbers of people. The day still wasn't sitting well with me, and I couldn't help but think about my various sex partners. I'd been lucky, 'cause I hadn't always been careful.

Just before I went to sleep, Sarah and I talked about my weekend. I didn't tell her because I knew it would turn into an hour-long conversation. We spoke about her and Omar's weekly argument. I was tired, and I wanted it to be brief; however, after listening to her rant and rave for forty minutes, I was extremely bushed. I crawled underneath the covers and dreaded leaving Atlanta tomorrow. I missed it here, and this trip made me want to move back.

Gazing at my silent cell phone, I longed to call Dick. Though the day had thrown me for a loop, I still wanted to hear that he and Celeste had ended things. Though I wasn't sure what I would do with that information, I still wished it were so.

32

Body Language

Bright and early, Tam and I arrived at the airport. The weekend had flown by.

"I don't want to leave," I said.

"I'll see you at your party in a few weeks."

"Okay, love you," I responded before walking into the building.

Tam stood by the car with her left hand placed upon her belly and her right blowing a kiss. I don't have a sister; however, if I had one, I would want her to be just like Tam. She was one of the most beautiful people I knew and whenever she was in my space, she delivered happiness and peace.

As soon as I got to my seat on the plane, I closed my eyes and began planning my week at work. We had a presentation that Thursday, and thankfully, my team was already prepared. I set our deadline for Tuesday so that Thursday would be a breeze. Fifteen minutes into the flight, I felt myself drifting off to sleep. Although I was tired, I didn't want to fall asleep. The flight was not long enough to get any rest; it was only long enough to tease, and since I had to go straight to work, I did not want to go into work lethargic. Because of this, I made a conscious effort to stay awake.

As planned, Winston greeted me at the curb when I landed. After the surprise-filled weekend, it was a relief to be back to normalcy. As he greeted me with a passionate kiss, I saw he felt better than he did when I left.

"I missed you this weekend," he said.

"Good. Maybe I should go away more often."

Softly rubbing my face, he took off toward my job.

"You're in a good mood."

"I am. I really missed you," he reiterated.

Smiling, I answered, "Well, babe, I missed you too."

"Let's do dinner tonight. My day should wrap around six o'clock."

"Sounds good."

Winston placed his hand on my leg and stroked my thigh. Although he was often affectionate, this infamous thigh stroke meant he was in the mood. Either subconsciously or purposely, he was letting me know that he wanted some tonight. I enjoyed the way lovers communicated. Little nuances here and subtle signs there, it was so sexy. I placed my hand on top of his and slightly grazed my nails back and forth atop his hand. As he looked at me, I winked, and then he let out a small chuckle while biting the corner of his lip. In lover language this meant that I agreed to give him some and foreplay was not necessary. His chuckle and lip gesture assured me that it was going to be really good. The remaining car ride was quiet, for our minds were already ten steps ahead imagining the great sex we were going to have approximately twelve hours later. Winston pulled up to the job. I leaned over and kissed his cheek.

"I can't wait," I stated just before getting out of the car.

He let out a tiny growl. I wasn't sure what that meant, but I was definitely game. I grabbed my bags and walked into work, just in time for the chaos. Before I could put my things down, Nehri rushed over to my desk.

"I have a great idea, but Stix won't draw it out. If we are supposed to be a team, he needs to cooperate."

"Slow down, let's go to conference room two. I'll be there in a minute."

Sighing, I put my things down and called Sarah. "I'm back, but I have to go into a meeting."

"Okay, come see me after."

Gathering my folders, I organized my notes, and walked into the maroon conference room. As soon as I walked through the door, Nehri started arguing.

"I gave Stix two ideas that I needed him to sketch out for me. All he had to do was pencil them out, it would have only taken an hour or so. I needed them done by today so that I could show you and we could incorporate them into the presentation. But he didn't do it and he acts like it is no big deal."

I looked over at Stix, who was staring into the blank maroon wall.

"Look at him. He doesn't care about this project."

Stix slowly turned around to address Nehri. "On the contraire, I don't care about you and your demands. You are not the project leader."

"Okay, Stix, state your side," I said, trying to calm the tension.

"We decided on the twelve cards for the presentation on Thursday. I was finishing the sketches for these when Nehri told me, not asked me, to do two more."

"I asked you. You were done with the others, it's not like you were busy."

Stix stood and raised his voice. "This is exactly what I am talking about. You don't know if I was busy or not. You need to learn how to talk to people and stop acting like the top bitch in charge."

Suddenly Nehri stood and yelled, "I will not work with him!"

She stormed out of the room and slammed the door. Stix quietly sat back down and apologized.

"I'm sorry, I can't stand her. She talks down to everyone she feels can't assist her with a job promotion."

"I know Nehri has some issues with communication, but she is talented."

"Talented or not, I can't work with someone like that. She even talks about you," he said, defiantly trying to persuade me to his side.

My defense stopped there. Although I was sure Nehri had said a word or two behind my back, I didn't want to hear the details, I only wanted this mission complete.

"I just want this project to go on without complications. Plus, I don't want this mess getting back to Susan."

"I'm sure she's running to Susan right now, blabbering about me calling her a bitch."

Quickly, I gathered my things and rushed to the door.

"Look, I'll try to take care of this. Just work on the things we discussed Thursday and I'll call you around four o'clock."

Hastily, I rushed to Nehri's desk, to halt the growing

snowball steadily approaching the valley of Susan's office. However, she was nowhere to be found. I peeped my head in several offices asking her whereabouts, but no one had seen her. Thankfully, I ran into Susan, who had also not seen or heard from her. I smiled and Susan smiled while mentioning the excitement about Thursday's presentation. I assured her she would be pleased. She could not know about the internal power struggle, because I did not want her stepping in and taking over the project. Well, I was officially in the nucleus of messy Corporate America, as the drama unfolded between the jealous backstabbers and the lying ladder climbers. I did not long to be a part of this cast; I simply wanted to write. After giving up on Nehri, I made my way to the restroom, but as soon as I entered, I heard crying coming from stall number three. Something told me that it was Nehri, and I had no energy to console her. I was much more comfortable dealing with her on a bitch-to-bitch basis.

"Please don't let her be a sensitive bitch with feelings," I muttered.

Slowly, I walked over to the stall and knocked on the door. "Nehri?"

She quieted, and within seconds, she slowly opened the door and faced me with a pitiful, teary-eyed expression.

Knowing she could still be the enemy, I walked toward the counter and kept my distance during consolation.

"I hope you're not crying over the incident with Stix."

"I was only trying to help. I really thought these ideas would add to the presentation."

"I think your approach was wrong. You should have come to me first."

"But you were gone, this was late Friday."

"It could have waited. Nevertheless, you need to learn how to talk to people. Your tone can be overbearing at times."

Nehri walked over to the sink to rinse her face as I continued talking.

"I will look at your ideas and we can add them to the final presentation. It's just important that this confrontation stays within our group. I don't want Susan to think we can't handle this."

"It will."

"Good."

Sniffling, she added, "I don't understand why he had to call me a bitch. That was uncalled for."

"I'll speak to him, but don't worry about Stix. We are a team and I'll make sure this doesn't affect our project."

She looked up at me, still teary-eyed and sad. "He makes me sick."

As I looked at her expression, I suddenly realized this blowup had little or nothing to do with creative differences. I could recognize that scornful idiom from miles away. It was the look of love gone awry. My empathy caused me to move in closer to comfort. No, I didn't completely trust Nehri; however, as a woman, I knew she needed a little reassurance.

"Men don't like to take orders from women. Especially strong, assured women like us. You struck a chord with his manhood."

Her tears began to subside as she nodded in concordance. I continued to give her the food she needed to make it through this day.

"You have to slip him ideas and let him develop his own twist. It may not seem fair, but as long as your idea is represented, you will get credit. Furthermore, we are a team."

"You're right, we are a team," she said, tapping my shoulder.

"You'll be fine."

Again, she nodded. Nehri checked her makeup in the mirror and headed toward the door. As she turned to thank me, I gave her one more boost of positive energy.

"Plus, he's crazy. Orange socks, think about it," I said, laughing.

Nehri laughed as she threw her tissue in the trash and walked out. That was just the lift she needed. For women, there is nothing better than hearing that the man who just hurt your feelings is a fool. Of course, it doesn't dawn on us that we are crazy for fooling around with fools. It's just a great temporary fix, like glue, and we sometimes need a little Elmer's to help us through the day.

Sighing with relief, I leaned my head against the towel dispenser. Patting myself on the back, I was proud of the way I disengaged that bomb. I was determined this thing would go off without a hitch.

"Nehri and Stix?"

He and his orange socks were making their way around the office. I wondered whom else he was sleeping with. Although I wouldn't let Nehri know that I was aware, I would confront him. If they did have something going on, I needed it to cease until this project was done. Project partners make for bad bedmates. Working together and sleeping together was a definite mistake. I quickly used the bathroom and headed for cubicle 12. As I came around the corner, I saw orange socks stretched across a desk as they peered from underneath a pair of pinstriped, brown pants. Without missing a beat, I forcefully walked up to Stix, leaned over, and commented, "I don't know what is going on between you and Nehri, but it smells personal and I don't want your personal shit stinking up my project. If you are sleeping with her, stop now. Send her flowers and be sweet to her for two weeks. At that point, this project will be done and you may resume with sex."

"What did she say?" he said with guilty eyes.

"She said nothing, she didn't have to. If I am mistaken, I apologize."

Stix said nothing while looking down at his paperwork.

"That's what I thought. I don't care what you do and who you do, but you will not mess this up. I will take both of you off this project and I mean it."

"Did you tell her this?" he asked, still looking at his desk.

"She knows nothing about this conversation. I don't like mess. Do this, and it will stay between us."

Stix slowly looked up at me and extended his hand.

"Deal," he responded.

"Deal," I said, clasping his hand.

Swiftly, I turned and walked away as forcefully as my approach. I was so glad my hard cast was off, it just wouldn't have had the same "smooth bitch" effect if I'd had to hobble away.

"All right, Ms. Lily, you did that," I said to myself.

As much as I disdained the supporting role in this corporate drama, I thought I had found my niche. Nehri could talk about me all she wanted and so could Stix. It didn't matter, 'cause I handled the situation and my presentation was going to be wonderful. As I laughed to myself about their love quarrel, Sarah popped her head over my carpeted divider.

"Where have you been?" she asked with a huge smile.

"Busy with this project. What's the smile for?"

"No reason," she responded quickly.

"I know you're lying, but I don't have time to question it. I'm busy, I'll call you later."

Sarah waved bye and disappeared down the hall. The remainder of the day, I organized my boards and checked with the two other teammates to ensure that everything was ready. These final three hours passed like thirty minutes. In no time, I was leaving work. I called Winston to confirm dinner plans and we agreed to meet downtown at my favorite Italian spot. I didn't have time to go home, and so I went ahead to the spot and waited for Winston. As soon as I walked in the door a man with a familiar face was walking out, pleasantly greeting me. We both stopped to speak; however, neither one of us remembered the other one's name.

"I'm so sorry, I forgot your name."

"I'm Lily."

"Bruce," he responded.

"Yes, the math teacher. How are you?"

"Good, and you?"

"I'm good."

We both stepped aside to allow the other guests to enter. Bruce lightly pulled me to the waiting area to speak.

"You never called," he said.

"I apologize. I did say I would call. I'm not going to make excuses. I just didn't do it."

Bruce and I awkwardly smiled at each other.

"Do you dine here often?" he asked.

"Maybe once a month. The food is excellent."

"I'll let my partner know you think so."

"You know the chef?"

"I'm a silent partner in this restaurant. Myself and three of my fraternity brothers own it."

"Wow. Well, it's one of my favorite spots."

Again, Bruce and I were quiet as we smiled at each other. He then reached in his pocket and pulled out a card.

"If I give you another card, will you call this time?"

Admiring his smooth face and deep dimples, I thought to myself, *He is absolutely adorable.*

However, I had a boyfriend who was just as adorable and was also coming through the front door.

"I'm seeing someone. I wasn't then, but I am committed now," I said as I started moving out of his personal space.

"I understand," he said, still handing me the card.

Winston saw me standing in the lobby and quickly made his way to my side.

"Hi, sweetie," I said, kissing his cheek.

He gave me a hug and hastily acknowledged the man standing directly in front of me.

"Winston Fulmore, this is Bruce . . ."

"Bruce Banner," he answered.

Suddenly, a jolt of laughter leapt from my mouth.

"Bruce Banner, isn't he The Incredible Hulk?" I asked.

Embarrassed, Bruce shook his head. "Yes, and I have heard every joke in the book."

Winston and Bruce cordially shook hands.

"We have reservations, did you check in?" Winston asked me.

I quickly shook my head. Therefore, Winston excused himself and walked to the host.

"Well, Bruce. It was a pleasure seeing you again."

"Same here, still feel free to call," he said with a handshake that suggested much more.

"I better go."

I swiftly made my way to Winston and we were seated at our table. Within minutes we were having light conversation over drinks and perfectly toasted garlic bread.

"Well, Dad moved out," Winston admitted just before dinner arrived.

I was silent. I covered my mouth with my fingers and stared at my plate. Glancing at Winston, I saw he was waiting for me to respond.

"I'm sorry to hear that. I'm sure they need time to filter everything out."

"Mom admitted to the affair, but she says it's over."

I stared at him in disbelief. No, I was not surprised at Mrs. Fulmore's behavior. She was always on my suspect list. However, I was stunned at Winston's unconcerned expression. When I left, he was distraught over the possibility and in one weekend, he seemed to have dealt with not only the idea but the obvious result.

"I don't know what to say."

"There is nothing to say. My mother's behavior is inexcusable. My father has given her everything. I don't know how he could forgive her."

"There are two sides to everything."

"You are not trying to defend her, are you?" he said, placing down his fork, and frowning in my direction.

"No," I said, quickly filling my mouth with food.

I certainly had no plans to defend his mother. I hadn't liked her since she commented on my kinky hair during last year's fishing trip. Furthermore, I didn't want to get Winston in a tizzy, for he might get upset, ultimately changing his mood, and I'd been thinking about sex with him all day long. I was not about to let Mrs. Fulmore ruin my ecstasy, especially when she was off getting her own twisted fantasy fulfilled.

"As I said, her affair is indefensible. If my father does forgive her, he is a better man than I."

I nodded silently and continued eating. I heard the disdain in his voice when he spoke; hence, it was best to let that situation alone. I would not mention it anymore unless he brought it up. Quietly, we ate our meal. Although the conversation about his parents was brief, it still had an affect on dinner. I could tell it was on Winston's mind and I never could think of a follow-up conversation to adjust the tone. At the end of dinner, I softly stroked his arm in hopes of stirring up our morning hand dialogue.

"You finished? Do you want dessert?" he asked.

"Not here," I flirted.

Winston grinned and got the server's attention to ask for the check.

As she approached, she said, "It's been taken care of."

Winston looked at me as I shrugged.

"What do you mean?"

"Bruce says it's on the house," she said before walking away.

"Really?" Winston uttered while looking at me.

Smiling, I responded, "He's one of the owners. That was nice of him."

Winston left a hefty tip while giving me a peculiar eye. He rose and walked with me to the door. After a quick hug, we parted and he followed me to the house. As soon as I got in the door, I flipped on the television and walked upstairs.

"I have to take a shower, I'll be back down in a minute," I said to Winston.

He took a seat and I rushed upstairs to the restroom. Sitting on the toilet, I removed my nylon leg brace. I was so over this stupid Velcro contraption. My leg felt fine, I didn't know why the doctor insisted that I still wore it. However, I was trying to be more orderly and less rebellious and so I had promised Winston I would keep it on until my final checkup, which was the following week. I was ready to be back to normal. My designer heels missed me and I desperately missed them.

I stepped into the shower and washed away the dirt and grime from today. Suddenly I felt a breeze. Pulling back the shower curtain, I looked at the door. Surprisingly, I saw my naked boyfriend posed against the door frame.

"What are you doing?"

"I feel dirty," he said with a peculiar grin.

Smirking at his corny line, I motioned for him to join me. Poor Winston, he tried, but he just was not smooth when it came to romancing with sexy dialogue. Unfortunately, that was the one thing he and Wealth had in common. He stepped into the shower, pressed me against the tile, and delivered beautiful kisses from my neck to my breast. Yet what he lacked in dialogue he made up in action. He was certainly passionate. I continued to lean back with my eyes closed as he adorned me with smooches. He softly bit my side just above my navel, and my stomach cringed with excitement. He continued to move farther down and just when I thought he was on his way back up, Winston surprised me by moving down farther. His lips were just at the top of my vagina. I was not sure where he was going with this, but I dared not ask. He made it clear that he didn't feel comfortable having oral sex and we hadn't discussed the issue since. However, as the tip of his tongue slightly crossed the border of my clitoris, I gleefully welcome him into oral country. I pressed my body against the steamy tile for balance. On his knees, Winston spread my legs with his shoulders.

"Oh my God," I moaned in between the sighs.

This felt incredible. My legs buckled as I began to quickly climax from excitement. I could no longer stand. Slowly, I began sliding down the back of the tub. Winston seductively caught me. With one arm underneath my legs, he placed his other around my back.

"Hold on," he said.

Carefully, he rose out of the tub and carried me into the bedroom, where he continued to please me. Uncontrollably, I shook my body completely dry. What an experience. Winston slid his moist body up against me. We were now face-to-face. He softly rubbed his nose against mine and pressed his lips to me. Normally, I preferred not to taste myself during a session of love, but he had me so intoxicated, I sucked his lips as if my juices were chocolate icing. I licked every drop. More unexpected, I began sliding down his body. He slightly lifted to give me room to maneuver underneath. I could feel his veins pulsating. As I was still under his influence, my jaw movements became more rapid and his hands tightened around my neck and shoulders.

"I'm coming," he stuttered.

And just like that, my lustful inebriation quickly sobered. As if he were shooting acid, I rapidly moved my head away from the spewing body part. I was indeed caught up in the moment, but not high enough to swallow his babies. Sperm had no business lining the walls of my esophagus. It just didn't belong there. So, with my head placed beside his thigh, I glanced at him and removed my sticky hand from his still erect penis. I chuckled silently as he lay there whimpering and quivering.

What was it about orgasms that rendered us helpless and made our actions infantile? I am sure there are all sorts of scientific reasons, but truly I think it's God's quirky sense of humor. He gave us something that feels so great that we act crazy to get it, look crazy while doing it, and look even crazier afterward. Sex simultaneously sets off every involuntary reflex we have. There is nothing else we do that makes us look as stupid, yet there is nothing else we'd rather do. We even watch others doing it. Sure, not everyone is into sex flicks. However, if we catch a couple in the middle of having sex, something compels us to look just a little longer than necessary even if we are appalled. You know why? Because it gives us something to laugh at later in the day and that is exactly what God is doing. However, we have become a sex-filled nation and have taken acts to new, unscrupulous heights and God is surely not laughing at that. But that is a different subject altogether.

Winston finally roused from his trance and softly rubbed my head. Smiling, I rose and went to the bathroom to retrieve a towel. Before I finished cleaning his body, Winston was asleep. Again, I laughed to myself. Once I returned from the restroom, I cuddled beside him. I knew he was sleepy, but I wanted to know what possessed him to go down on me, especially when he was so adamant about not doing it. In fact, he said he would only do it if he were in a serious, committed relationship. I guess we had shifted from exclusively dating to seriously committed. As I snuggled underneath his body, Winston softly rubbed my shoulders, let out a small moan, and wrapped his arms around me. This was lovers' dialogue for, "I truly enjoyed that. Now let's not ruin this moment with conversation," Winston whispered in my ear.

And there was the big difference between man and woman. We preferred verbal dialogue after sex and they preferred silent discourse. That night I gave him his wish. We both knew what we had was special and our hearts didn't need words for confirmation. I held his hand while kissing his fingertips. Winston pressed his body closer. This meant I was going to get some more that morning, so I best rest up.

33

Overnight Express Opportunities

Around 5:00 a.m. I felt Winston's erectness firmly poking me in the back. Although I was tired, thoughts of him inside me were like ginseng and they gave me a sudden boost of energy. He crawled over my body, went into my nightstand, and pulled out a condom. Before I could get the sleep out of my eyes, he was inside me.

"Oh my," I moaned lustfully with his first deep thrust.

He scooted my body to the edge of the bed, took my legs, and wrapped them around his neck. Immediately, I began to orgasm. It was something about watching him move that turned me on. Toward the end of my climax, I saw Winston's body begin to stiffen. I guess it was good for him too. His body caved over mine as he let out a loud moan. Heavily breathing, he leaned over and kissed my forehead. A good quickie in the morning, along with Cheerios, is a great way to start the day.

"Oh no," he stated quickly while pulling out.

My body tensed. "Oh no" are words one never wants to hear during sex.

"What happened?" I lifted myself up and looked at Winston's body. Oddly, he seemed to be staring into my vagina. My eyes shifted down toward his penis.

Hastily, I commented, "You're dripping on my floor. Where is the condom?"

Winston, still silent, lowered his head in between my thighs.

"What happened to the condom?" I frantically asked.

"It's still in you," he replied calmly.

I began flinging my legs in the air. "Get it out! Get it out!"

"Stop moving, be still," he said, placing his hand on my stomach.

Huffing, puffing, and whining, I was still as Winston carefully reached into my orifice in search of the missing Trojan.

"You feel it?" I asked nervously with my head propped up.

"Not yet," he said, sliding his hand deeper inside me.

Groaning, I continued to let him delve. He was a doctor and I supposed he knew what he was doing. Yet it was taking an awful long time.

"It's probably stuck against the walls of your uterine canal."

"What?" I said with irritation. "This is not a pelvic exam. Stop being technical and just get it out!"

After another twenty seconds, Winston finally wrapped his fingers around the latex and pulled it from within my opening. "I got it."

Sighing with relief, I hopped up and rushed to the bathroom to take a shower. Laughing, I heard Winston singing in the other restroom as he showered. I wondered if it would be like this, if we were married. Suddenly I pictured Dick. Every time marriage entered my mind, Dick was the one person I thought of. I pulled my clothing out for the day and I involuntarily continued this thought.

"This has got to stop," I said to myself.

"What has to stop?" Winston said as he snuck up behind me.

Startled, I turned and wrapped my arms around him. Stammering, I attempted to answer him. "This pondering over what old clothing to wear. I need a new wardrobe."

"You've got plenty to wear," Winston commented, running his hands through my hangers.

"But it's all old. I haven't purchased anything new in almost a year."

"You just got some shoes last month."

"Not shoes, clothes. I have plenty of shoes."

Laughing, Winston left the closet and resumed dressing. Sitting down in the center of my closet floor, I gazed at the boxes of shoes. I didn't want to go to work. However, there was no way I could call out this week or the next, so I needed to get it together because the day had started. I got dressed and met Winston downstairs in the kitchen. Sipping on a cup of coffee, he leaned against the counter in his slacks and undershirt.

"Now, see, that outfit looks practically new," he mentioned.

"Whatever."

I poured a bowl of cereal, and as I was sitting down

to eat, Winston spoke. "Do you think it will be like this when we are married?"

Shocked that we were having similar thoughts, I stated, "I was just upstairs thinking the same thing."

Smiling, we both shrugged and I continued eating. However, as I took my next bite, my brain replayed his comment. Suddenly I realized we did not think the same thing at all. His statement held one very important word that mine did not.

Turning around in his direction, I commented, "You said *when* we are married."

"No, I didn't."

"Yes, you did."

Casually, he replied, "Well, maybe I did. When, if, whatever."

"There is a big difference. 'If' means the possibility is there. 'When' means plans are being made."

"Lily, you're making a big deal of this. It was a slip," he said as he walked over and kissed my shoulder.

Winston grabbed his shirt and walked toward the door.

"But if you must analyze everything, I do think about marrying you. You would make a good wife."

I followed him to the door. Of course my heart was melting on the inside. No one, other than Tam, has ever said that I would make a good wife.

"I am so lucky to have you," I said, wrapping my arms around him.

"Have a good day. I'll call you later."

"Okay, bye."

He opened the door, just as a courier was approaching.

"It's mighty early for a delivery," said Winston.

"I know," I answered, signing for the package.

Winston left as I stood in the doorway and began opening my mail. I was leery about opening it because I didn't recognize the name. Slowly, I walked back to the living room and pulled out the smaller envelope inside the big envelope. As I read the front of the small red envelope, a smile as big as the sun radiated the room.

"Beautiful," I said, reading the black script written across the envelope. "It's from Dick," I yelped with excitement.

Quickly, I tore into the envelope as a plane ticket fell out. In awe, I stared at the ticket, which lay on the floor. My heart became increasingly heavier. Slowly, I kneeled, picked up the ticket, and began reading the letter inside.

Hi, Beautiful, I hope this letter finds you well. Sorry I haven't called. I wanted to speak with you, but the phone just didn't seem like the right way to communicate. I must see you. We will be in Lexington, Kentucky, this weekend. If you don't come, I have no choice but to respect your decision, but please consider it. Things need to be said and they need to be said face-to-face. Honestly, more than that, I want to see your gorgeous smile. I miss you, Lily. We are staying at the Airport Marriott. I will have a key waiting for you. Please show up.

Love Always, Dick

Immediately, I fell back onto the futon. Covering my face with the pillow, I began screaming, "What does this mean! Oh my God, what does this mean!"

Gasping and shrieking, I grabbed the phone to call Tam. She was going to flip out. Glancing at the time, I saw that I only had thirty minutes to grab my leg brace, shoes, and continue to prepare for work. However, I couldn't make it through the day without talking to Tam. After three rings, she finally picked up.

"Oh my God! You are going to flip out," I yelled through the receiver.

"What is going on!"

"Dick wrote me a letter and sent me a ticket to come see him this weekend."

"What!"

"Yes. He said he missed me and that he had to speak to me face-to-face."

"You talked to him?" she questioned.

"No. He said it in the letter. I still haven't spoken with him."

Tam was suddenly quiet, which caused me to be silent.

"You can't go," she responded abruptly.

"What?"

"You can't go. You don't know if he is still with Celeste."

"Why would he send me a ticket if he is still with her?"

"C'mon, Lily, you know Dick."

"But I want to go," I whined.

"I know, baby. And you probably will go, but I don't think you should."

I sat quietly on the other end.

"Lily, you are with Winston. I thought you finished the last chapter in the Dick book. You were supposed to burn it, remember?"

"I was," I continued to gripe.

"So what happened?"

"I couldn't. It was just too great a read."

Tam began to chuckle. "If you go, this is it. If he

tells you he is getting married, you can never, I repeat, never, go see him again."

"Okay," I said quickly.

"This is serious."

"I know. But what if he and Celeste ended things and he wants to be with me? What then?"

"Then I would hate to be in your shoes," she answered softly. "If you don't go, the decision is already made for you."

"But I have to go," I responded assertively.

"Then go."

Motionless, I sat on the edge of the bed where I had just made love to my boyfriend. I could ask anyone, including myself, and we all would agree that visiting Dick was asinine. Winston was a dream man. But that didn't change the fact that Dick was the man of my dreams. I fell back onto the bed and stared at the ceiling.

"I know, God. I know."

This was one of those moments when you're sure you are about to go do something you will regret. Yet you are going to go do it anyway.

"I might as well ask for forgiveness ahead of time."

Glancing at the clock, I finally made my way out of the house. I had class tonight at the home and my day was not going to get any shorter by lying here contemplating this issue.

I walked by Sarah's desk when I first arrived at work; however, I decided against telling her the news until later in the week. The workweek was going to be turbulent enough, without her incessant comments and questions. I stayed at my desk most of the day. Of course, I check with Nehri, Stix, and the other team members just to make sure all was well. Everything was set and ready for Thursday's presentation, and so I sat quietly and began working on marketing ideas. Though marketing was not my department, I thought it would be an additional perk if we added some ideas to the presentation. Plus, there was no way I could do any real work today. My mind was too cluttered with Kentucky. Quickly, the day passed and I rushed out of work as fast as I could. On my way to teach, Winston called.

"How's your day?"

"Fine, and yours?"

"Look, what are you doing this weekend?"

I was silent.

"Lily?" he called out.

I didn't know what to say. I didn't want him making plans for the weekend. Yet if I told him I had plans, he was going to want to know what they were. I couldn't say anything. Therefore, I told him I had to call him back and quickly ended communication. I turned my phone off and threw it in the seat. Yeah, it was messed up, but the situation was already becoming disordered. I was just out of town last weekend and now I was going to be out of town the next. Winston was not going to be pleased. I had to call him tonight and tell him that I was going to Kentucky with Sarah. Suddenly a lightbulb popped into my head.

"I'll invite Sarah to Kentucky with me, so that it won't be a lie."

She'd been saying she wanted to go home. Plus, her father had never seen Carmen. He wasn't too happy about Omar being black, but at least she and her father were on speaking terms. That was it. Sarah and I were going to Kentucky.

I walk into my classroom and my students were already seated and ready to begin.

"Well, well. What a pleasant surprise," I commented while placing my things by the desk.

"Does one of us get to teach today?" asked Sam with excitement.

"You remembered. I guess I can let someone teach. Who would like to start?"

Almost every hand in the room went straight to the ceiling. The room was filled with "pick me, pick me" and "right here." However, I looked over in the corner and Delvin was sitting quietly with his elbow on the desk and his hand slightly raised. This was a first. Delvin never wanted to participate. He hardly spoke. I had to beg him to take part. He was very shy and the kids picked on him because he was missing his two front teeth, which caused him to have a lisp. They were knocked out in a fight and the home had no dental insurance to replace them.

"Delvin, would you like to teach?"

Shyly, he nodded as I motioned for him to come to the front of the class.

"No, not him!" yelled Stephen.

"Hush, Stephen. I have made my decision."

As Delvin approached, he handed me a piece of paper with his idea on it. As I read, I looked back at Delvin, who looked down at my desk.

"This is fine. In fact this may be a good idea. A bit morbid, but let's see what happens."

I began moving away from the desk as Delvin grabbed my arm.

"You'll be okay. I'm going to take a seat. This is your class now."

I turned and gave a stern warning toward the students. "Delvin is in charge, but I am still here. You will respect him and you will behave or you will be escorted out."

I walked over to the chairs and sat beside an excited Samantha, who was saving a seat for me. Delvin slowly told the class about our writing assignment.

"We will write eulogies," he said.

"What!" Stephen groaned.

"Eulogies," Delvin reiterated.

"What's that?" asked Stephen.

Quickly Samantha interjected, "It's what people say at your funeral, stupid."

"How are we supposed to know what people are going to say?"

Finally I cut in. "If everyone is quiet, Delvin will continue to explain."

Delvin explained and after a few gripes, notebooks were opened and everyone began writing. The assignment was to write our own eulogy. This seemed a bit much for a class of teenagers, but these kids had seen and done so much, I thought they could appreciate a full life as much as any adult. As I looked across the room, they seemed to be doing well; I was the only one staring at a blank sheet of paper. Why was I finding this so difficult? What do I want people to say about me after I am gone?

I slowly began jotting down words. *Sincere, joyful, helpful, spiritual, loving,* and *great mother* led the pack. Gradually, I began putting my eulogy together. Although I wanted to be remembered for being loving and spiritual, I wanted to be honored most for making others smile. I would like people to say that I added some sunshine to their life. Whether it was through kind words, helpful advice, or corny jokes, I wanted to make a difference in the lives of people I encountered. If someone said that at my funeral, I would know I had served my purpose. As I wrapped up my eulogy, I spoke about being a great mother. That was important. I looked at these kids and all of them were products of poor parenting. It was so important that we instilled enough goodness in our kids that they could go on and continue that process.

"Well, that wasn't so bad," I said to Samantha.

"You finished?"

"Yeah, you?"

Suddenly from nowhere, Delvin appeared in front of us. "I take it you two are finished, since you're back here talking."

I looked up at him in astonishment.

"Yes, I'm done. I'll be quiet so that the others can finish," I said politely.

Delvin smiled and took my paper. I gave him a tiny wink as he turned to take Sam's paper.

After he collected the papers, he mixed them up and we all read them aloud. Again, I was amazed at the voices of these kids. Some of them wanted to be remembered for their courage and someone said they wanted to be remembered for their medical invention that cured cancer. However, as Shannon read the last paper, I was taken aback at the words coming from her mouth.

"If only one person remembers that I existed at all, I am grateful. I'm sure their memories will be fond. I lived a great life and I was kind to those who were not always kind to me. I led by example, not by words. I want my spirit remembered. As long as I am not forgotten, I will always live."

I stood and asked, "Who wrote that?"

Everyone looked around, but no one claimed the paper.

"The papers are anonymous," said Delvin.

"I know, I know. But I want to know who wrote that."

Still, no one claimed the paper. Finally, I sat and let Delvin dismiss the class. I give Delvin a hug, and congratulated him on an excellent assignment. The kids piled out and I gathered my things and walked out behind them. Sam and I talked as we walked down the hall.

"How are you and the doc?"

"We're fine. And you, stop being so nosy."

"Fine," she answered quickly.

"Who are you dating these days?" I inquired.

"Ms. Lily," she said bashfully.

"See how it feels?"

Sam and I both laughed. She gave me a hug and slipped a tiny piece of paper into my hand.

"What's this?"

"It's for you, but don't open it until you get into the car."

"Okay. You behave. I'll talk with you later this week."

"Bye," she said before trotting to her room.

She turned back around, made a funny face, and spun back in the opposite direction. Shaking my head, I thought to myself, *I really love that little girl.*

I had started researching foster parent information, but I didn't have anything concrete. I needed to move forward with that soon. I cranked up my SUV and headed home. When I was halfway there, my cell phone rang. Before I looked at the caller ID, I already knew that it was Winston. I had to tell him something, and so I picked up and answered.

"Lily, are you all right?"

"Yes, sweetie, I'm fine. I had class tonight."

"But I've been trying to call you since this afternoon."

"My phone went dead and I left it off to charge. I'm sorry."

"Well, call me when you get home."

"Okay. I will."

We hung up and I quickly called Sarah. As soon as she answered, I started. "Guess what we are doing this weekend?"

"What?" she answered enthusiastically.

"We're going to Kentucky."

Sarah was suddenly mute.

"Did you hear me? We are going to Kentucky."

"No, we aren't."

"Yes, we are. I am going and you are going with me."

"Look, I can't talk right now. I'll call you later."

"Fine. But we are going to Kentucky. Tell Omar to get you a ticket. We leave Saturday morning."

"Bye," she said.

We hung up and I tossed the phone into the seat. I desperately needed her to go along with my plan. Plus, we'd have fun together in Kentucky. Glancing down at the phone, I saw this yellow notepaper folded into a triangle. In the chaos, I forgot about the note given to me by Sam. As I was pulling onto my street, I unwrapped the tiny paper and focused on the scribble. Squinting, I read aloud.

"If something were to happen to me, I would want you to deliver my eulogy. I know you would never forget."

I drove down my street doing five miles an hour as I stared at these words. My eyes watered and within seconds the tears were streaming down my face. I looked up and saw that I was headed for my neighbor's mailbox. Abruptly, I jerked the wheels back into the lane and drove into my garage. As I stared at the paper, my tears continued to flow.

"Of course I would never forget," I said, wiping my face.

Suddenly my phone rang, jarring me from my empathetic moment. I leaned over and grabbed the cell.

"Yes," I answered while sniffing.

"Girl, what is wrong with you?"

"Nothing, Sarah."

"Fine. Why are you going to Kentucky?"

"I'll call you when I get into the house."

I walked into the house, placed my things by the door, and scurried to the restroom to wipe my face. Removing my shoes and my brace, I stretched onto my bed. Grabbing the phone, I called Sarah. I told her all about Dick and the ticket. She screamed with excitement. As much as she adored Winston, she was still rooting for Dick. She agreed to go with me, and promised to get her ticket tomorrow. She was going to bring Carmen along and visit her father. Of course, that idea took a little more convincing, but she knew it was the right thing to do. As soon as we hung up, I called Winston to tell him about my weekend plans. He was given tickets to a play and he thought we could go together, but once I told him about Kentucky, he decided to give the tickets to Wealth. We agreed to see each other on Thursday, said good night, and disconnected.

With my body sprawled diagonally across the bed, I finally began to rest. Still, I couldn't believe Sam, her eulogy and her request. I desired that people remembered me as a joyful, giving individual while she wanted to make sure that she was simply remembered. To me, it was a given that people would remember me, at least in some way. I had too many loved ones to be forgotten about altogether.

"Wow, the things we take for granted," I uttered.

I continued lying on the bed thinking about Sam. Her writing was so eloquent and beautiful. I thought she had a hidden talent, and was definitely a special kid.

"Anyone who has met you would remember you, Sam," I said aloud to the ceiling.

As I was thinking about my eulogy, I wondered who would deliver it and I wondered what they would actually say. Of course, we all had a wish list of what we would want others to say about us after we were gone, but the best way to have those wishes granted was to live life the way you want to be remembered in death.

If I want people to say I was sincere, joyful, giving, and loving, then I have to live accordingly. It's that simple. 'Cause after life there are no more chances to get it right. Besides, who says you can't live the life you dream? You can and I am. Plus, I think Sam should too. I closed my eyes and pictured myself as a mother. As scary as the thought was, it was just as wonderful.

"I will be a great mom," I said to myself before drifting off.

"I'm going to see Ms. Gaither tomorrow."

34

Getting Lucky
in Kentucky

My presentation went so well on Thursday that I took my teammates out for lunch. Susan loved all twelve ideas; now we only had another twelve to pull together for the entire line. We chose linen paper for the cards and adorned the front of each with charcoal sketches, compliments of Stix. The inside greeting was written in script, but with a calligraphy flair. It was a very sexy line of cards.

I spent that Friday brainstorming with Nehri about new phrases for the line. Although she, Kate, and I had a very good start, I didn't think I was helpful at all today, because my mind was miles away. Sarah and I had a late lunch, but all she could talk about was how nervous she was about bringing Carmen home to meet her father.

However, in between the conversations about Carmen, she was steadily asking about Dick and me.

"What if Celeste is gone?"

"I don't know," I responded

"What if he wants you back?"

"I don't know."

"What if he says he loves you?"

"I don't know."

"What do you know?" Sarah asked.

"That I have a ticket to Kentucky and I'm going. That's all I know."

Sarah nodded and continued eating her sandwich. All of her questions had made me nervous. I was just ready to go to Kentucky and get it over with.

We only had two hours left in the workday once we returned and those two speed by. I stopped by Susan's office to make sure she didn't need to speak to me before I left. Again, she told me how much she loved our ideas and that she looked forward to the entire line. I thanked her for the opportunity, grabbed my bags, and headed home to pack. Winston and I didn't get together Thursday like we'd planned, but we are going to see a movie that night. Although I wanted to be honest, I still hadn't mentioned Dick. Sarah and Tam said that I shouldn't. Tam said there was no need to say anything until I resolved my issues with Dick, and I agreed. This was why I suggested a movie over dinner. This way, we wouldn't have time for plenty of conversation. The less Winston and I talked, the better.

After the movie, he was exhausted. Thank goodness. I was praying that he wouldn't want to come over. I was staying at Sarah's home that evening since we had an early flight and we were riding together to the airport. I rushed home to shower and finish packing my things. Flipping on the television, I checked out the weather channel. It was going to be great weather in Kentucky, high seventies.

In an hour, I was leaving the house and headed to Sarah. Although it was only 11:00 p.m. when I arrived, Sarah was already asleep. Therefore, I walked to the guest room and lay across the bed. I felt like a kid on the day before Christmas. I was so anxious that I couldn't sleep. Tossing and turning, I moved about the bed in at least twenty different positions. Finally, I rose, got my journal, and began writing. All I can think about was:

WHAT IF HE'S THE ONE?

What if he's the finest man I've ever seen
What if there is no such thing
Sure, it's not about the cover but the content of the book
But what if he's the best book I've ever read
What if I can't get him out of my head
He gives me everything I ask for
Before I can inquire
I enjoy everything he gives
He fills every desire
What if he totally understands me
And still loves me unconditionally
What if he keeps me laughing
What if he keeps me loving
What if I run out of "what ifs" to ask
Great friends will we continue to be
Great lovers loving effortlessly

What if I just give in
What if I let him win
I can't believe I'm saying
What if he's the one

As I closed my book, I kept thinking about my feelings for Dick. There was no such thing as "The One." He was simply one of the ones. He just happened to be the most appetizing one. I was not sure what the divine plan was, but I really needed a glimpse of the life map because I was at a crucial crossroads. Perhaps I should've turned around and backtracked down the path instead of proceeding forward. Clearly, I had missed a sign or two along the way.

I snuggled into the thick, fluffy down duvet. However, as I was closing my eyes, I heard Carmen crying. I lay there for a few minutes while she screamed waiting for Sarah to calm her. However, no one was tending to her and her whines were growing louder and louder. Finally, I walked down the hall and peeked into her room and accidentally bumped into Sarah, who was leaving her room.

"Is she okay?" I asked, concerned.

"She's fine. She just wants some attention. She'll eventually cry herself back to sleep," Sarah said, seemingly unalarmed, as she strolled back into her room.

"Aren't you going to stop her from crying?"

"No, she'll stop in a while," Sarah said, crawling back into her bed.

I stood at Carmen's door peeping in and then I looked into Sarah's room. She had easily crept back into her sleep. Slowly, I began walking back to my room; however, as I heard Carmen's wails, I was compelled to comfort her. I tiptoed into the room and picked her up. Immediately, she quieted.

"You are spoiled," I whispered to Carmen while making faces.

She giggled and cooed, knowing I played right into her hand. I walked with her into my room and turned on the television.

"I guess since we are both awake, we'll watch a little TV."

Carmen released a few more giggles and together we watched movies for the next couple of hours. She drifted off to sleep and somewhere in the early morning hours so did I. Yet, before my first sleep phase was complete, Sarah was tapping me on my shoulder. Startled, I popped up like toast.

"What time is it?"

"Time to go," she said with her hands on her hips.

I looked to my left, with a half-asleep, dazed glance.

"Carmen is downstairs with Mom," Sarah answered intuitively.

Slowly, I rolled from the bed. Since I had showered just hours ago, I tossed on my jeans and T-shirt. While brushing my teeth, I heard my phone ringing in the bedroom. Quickly, I rushed into the room, to catch it before it stopped ringing.

"Hello," I said, garbling with the toothbrush in my mouth.

"I miss you already."

"I miss you too," I said, rushing back to the bathroom to spit.

"I wish I could go with you."

Staring at my reflection in the bathroom mirror, I said nothing. I hoped this wasn't the part where I was supposed to say, "I wish you could too."

Finally, Winston spoke again. "You enjoy yourself, but the next weekend you decide to get away, I am coming with you."

"That will be nice," I said, looking upon my guilty image.

"Call me."

"I will."

We hung up as I continued to stare into my lying eyes. As soon as I heard a dial tone, I knew exactly what signs I had missed down this jagged road. I wasn't sure how, but along the journey, I missed the bright orange sign that said DETOUR: FOR THOSE NOT READY TO COMMIT TO A SERIOUS RELATIONSHIP. Furthermore, I didn't bear left when I saw the bridge of doubtfulness up ahead. Even when the bridge was lifted so that the boats filled with lingering love and late-night phone calls could pass, I waited to cross instead of turning around. I really thought I could move on with my passage to starting over. But currently, I felt like my course, which was supposed to lead me out of the bushes of confusion, had landed me deep into the jungle of disorder and deceit.

"Are you ready?" asked Sarah as she walked up behind me.

Quietly, I nodded yes.

"What are you looking at?"

I slowly moved my index finger up to the mirror and pointed, my appendage to my reflection's nose. Sarah moved in closer and we both stared.

"I need direction," she said, still gazing.

Sarah placed her head on my shoulder and closed her eyes.

"I need closure," I continued.

"We all do," she replied.

After a few seconds of stillness, we left the house

and headed for the airport. Before noon, we were
landing in Kentucky, both of us unsure about why we
were there, yet both of us certain that it was a necessary stop in order to proceed with our journey.

As soon as we boarded, Sarah talked about her and
Omar. He still was beating around the bush about her
moving in.

"But he gave you the ring," I mentioned.

"I think it was Claire's idea, or it was just to shut me
up. Either way, he said that we could try it, but he
didn't want to make anything permanent. I'm sure he's
seeing someone else."

"Again, you don't know that."

"I don't care anymore. I'm done with thinking this
can be anything more than it is."

I reached across and held her hand, but she assured me she was fine. Thankfully, Carmen slept the
entire flight. To occupy her mind during the flight,
Sarah started drawing animations to complement the
Luv & Lil comic strip, which I had dug out of my old
keepsakes.

"I never knew you could draw. This is good. Maybe
we should send it in and try to get it published," I said.

"I don't know. Maybe I will."

Taking the notebook from her hand, I looked at
her work. "No, seriously, these are good."

She grinned, but as soon as she saw we started exiting, Sarah's nerves turned her smile into a grimace. As
comfort, I decided to wait with her before catching the
shuttle over to the hotel. After thirty minutes or so, we
saw a bright blue Ford pickup pulled up to the curb
beside us. Quickly, Sarah perked up. She passed
Carmen to me and rushed over to the young lady,
whom she resembled. They tightly embraced and

squealed with excitement. Sarah brought her look-alike over to meet me.

"Lily, this is my favorite cousin, Elizabeth. We call her Lizzie."

"Hi, Lizzie," I said, extending my hand to greet her.

Quickly she pulled me to my feet and gave me a hug, squeezing Carmen in the center.

"I've heard so much about you. Oh my God, is this Carmen?" she said, removing her from my arms.

Sarah stood back and nodded with pride.

"She is so beautiful," said Lizzie while rubbing Carmen's curly red locks.

Shuffling around in Lizzie's arms, Carmen began to become unnerved. She looked around and immediately began to cry. Hastily, Lizzie handed Carmen back to Sarah.

"She's got some lungs on her too."

Sarah took Carmen while Lizzie and I placed her things in the truck. I stepped back from the curb as Sarah placed Carmen's car seat in the truck.

"Where are you staying?" Lizzie asked before getting in.

Pointing across the street, I called out, "The Marriott."

"Why aren't you staying with us?"

"Because she is meeting her love supreme," Sarah interjected hastily.

Lizzie and Sarah began to coo like two adolescent teens.

"Okay, okay, that's enough. Sarah, call me."

"I will," she said as Lizzie put the truck in gear.

I waved good-bye to Carmen as they pulled off.

* * *

With quivers steadily growing in my tummy, I walked down to the airport shuttle and got on. Within minutes, we arrived at the hotel, and I stepped into the plush lobby and slowly walked over to the counter. Part of me wished that Dick forgot to book the room. This way, I could be upset with him and spend the weekend with Sarah. Another part wished he were eagerly waiting in a room filled with candles and flowers. Smiling at the receptionist, I gave her my name.

"Lily McNeil, I should have a reservation."

As she typed in my name, my nerves continued to escalate. Smiling, she leaned over and handed me a key and a note.

"You are in one of our penthouse suites. You will need to use your key in the elevator in order to access that floor."

"Thanks," I responded.

"I see here you are scheduled for a massage at three o'clock. Would you like anything brought up before then?" she asked pleasantly.

Hesitantly, I responded, "I don't think so."

"Well then, have a great stay."

Smiling back, I nodded and walked toward the elevators. When I got to the door of the room, I paused. Leaning against the wall, I opened the note and read softly aloud.

I will be there around 5:00. Enjoy the massage and order whatever you want. Glad you came. Can't wait to see you.

Love, Dick

I opened the door and walk into the massive suite with ceiling-to-floor windows.

"This is so gorgeous. I feel like *Pretty Woman*," I said, falling back onto the king-sized bed with thick down covering. As I closed my eyes and began to daydream, a jolting thought came to mind.

"*Pretty Woman* was a whore," I yapped.

I sat up and looked around the room. I never knew what Dick had up his sleeve and this premise alone always made me suspicious of his actions.

"Is he doing all of this, just to tell me he is marrying Celeste, but that he wants to have one last fling with me?" I questioned.

Rising, I walked toward the window and admired the great view of the city. Gazing, I whispered, "What am I doing here?"

Looking at my watch, I saw I had a few hours before my scheduled massage. There was no need to keep wondering about Dick, I would find out soon enough. I might as well enjoy the city while I was there. I took a shower, put on fresh clothing, and walked down to the lobby to get a taxi. I didn't know anything about Lexington; consequently I had the driver drop me off downtown. Like most downtown cities, it was filled with office buildings, small sandwich shops, and boutiques. After grabbing a bite to eat, I walked into a jewelry store. Upon trying on several pieces, I decided to buy a silver ring with an oval tiger's eye stone. I was going to get the necklace to match, but I never wear matching jewelry, so I figured it would be a waste of money. I continued walking along the city admiring its clean streets and beautiful architecture. Lexington was not all what I had expected. It reminded me of Charleston, South Carolina. I lost track of time as I walked and window-shopped. Before I realized it, it was close to three o'clock and I had to make my way back to the hotel. Fortunately, I had asked for the cabdriver's number, and within five minutes he was picking me up and whizzing me back to the hotel. Since it was 3:10, I stopped by the desk to make sure I hadn't missed my massage. The attendant told me that my masseuse would be up to my room in five minutes. I rushed upstairs to get ready. As soon as I walked into the room, I saw the blinking light on the phone.

"What do you want, Dick?" I said aloud.

Other than Sarah, he was the only one who knew my whereabouts and she would have called my cell. I went to the phone to retrieve my message. Of course, it was Dick saying he'd see me around five o'clock and not to make dinner plans. As soon as I heard his voice on the phone, I weakened. Without failure, he did it to me every time. I fell back onto the bed and closed my eyes; however, as soon as I saw darkness my masseuse knocked on the door. I opened it and invited this petite woman into my suite. Upon introducing herself, she strolled in rolling a massage bed, handed me a robe, and asked me to put it on while she prepared.

"Which fragrance do you like?" she asked, displaying her oils.

I leaned over and smelled the four different aromas. "I like this one."

"This one is Lillies," she responded with an Asian accent.

"That's my name," I stated.

Lying down, I let her tiny hands go to work. With my deep breaths, she smoothed out each kink in every muscle. Her hands felt amazing.

"Is this too much pressure, Lillies?"

I laughed softly at the fact that she had pluralized my name. "No, the pressure is fine."

The more she loosened up my muscles, the more relaxed I became. Soon my heartbeat slowed and I fell into a state of inertia. When she was complete, I was so lethargic I could hardly move my body. Thankfully, her table was set close to the bed. I rolled from the table onto the fluffy comforter, and with my face sunken into the supple, feather pillow, I softly said bye.

"Good-bye, Lillies," she said before closing the door.

Again, I chuckled. I was not sure why I didn't correct her; I suppose it was not that important. All I wanted to do was lie there and drift off to sleep. Closing my eyes, I did just that. Expensive bedding makes such a difference, and that bed felt heavenly. I didn't toss and turn, I didn't even dream, I only slept. The entire experience felt like a fairy tale. The next thing I know, Prince Charming was standing over me delivering a magical kiss to awaken me from my slumber. Although I was partially asleep, I smelled the distinct scent of myrrh, Dick's favorite oil. Slowly, I opened my eyes and saw one of the most handsome men I'd ever met, leaning over my body. A smile widened across my face.

"Hi, beautiful," he said before giving me another kiss on the nose.

I extended my arms toward his body. Dick leaned over and embraced me. With my feet lifted from the floor, we hugged each other. Dick spun our bodies around, finally landing on the foot of the bed. As I sat on his lap facing him, our bodies were so close that the tips of our noses practically touched. With gooey-eyed smiles, we stared into each other's eyes.

"Why are you smiling?" I asked.

"You know," he said, smiling wider.

Again, we embraced. Wanting to ingest every ounce of this man, I softly laid my head onto his shoulder and sniffed. Dick wrapped his arms underneath mine and caressed the base of my neck. For minutes, we remained silent in this position. It was obvious that we wanted to soak up the splendor of each other. Finally, after I felt a tingling in my leg, I adjusted positions and moved beside him. Anxiously, I was ready to begin conversation, yet the mood was so wonderfully calm, I didn't want to erupt with turbulence. Therefore, I sat and made small talk until I couldn't stand it any longer.

"Why am I here?"

"'Cause I wanted to see you."

Frowning, I looked unpleased by his answer.

Dick chuckled, rubbed his hands against his mustache, and spoke. "I got your messages and I wanted to talk with you about them."

Standing, I walked toward the window to brace myself for disappointment.

"Well, talk," I said, gazing out into the cityscape.

"Right now?" he asked, walking up behind me.

As he placed his arms around my waist, I leaned my head back onto his chest.

"Over dinner," he said, kissing my temple.

"Depending on what you say, I may or may not stick around for dinner."

Dick leaned over my shoulder and tried to make eye contact.

"Are you serious?" he said in disbelief.

I nodded yes.

"Where are you going?"

"I know people here. I was not coming all this way, have you act up and me not have anywhere to go."

"No one is acting up. Just let me take a shower. Then we can go eat."

Dick walked into the bathroom and started the

shower. I grabbed a seat by the window and stared into the sky. Already, I felt disappointment seeping in, and doubling knots in my stomach. There was no way I was going to be able to enjoy my dinner. However, when I heard the water stop, I walked into the bedroom, changed clothing, and prepared for my anticipated evening.

We arrived at the intimate restaurant close to 7:00 p.m. We only had to wait a few minutes before the hostess sat us. Hand in hand, Dick and I walked toward the booth in the back. As soon as we sat down, he attempted to make small talk. I responded curtly to all his questions while reading over the menu. Of course, Dick didn't stand for this too long before asking curiously, "Is there something wrong with you?"

I cut my eyes above the menu to face him. Staring into his eyes, I said nothing. Seconds later, I changed my focus back to the menu, still silent. Dick took his hand and pushed the menu flat down on the table.

"I'm talking to you. Don't act juvenile."

"Fine," I said crossly, sliding the menu to the side. "Please continue."

Dick now stared at me in silence. He lowered his head and softly clasped my hands within his. Already, I prepared myself for upsetting words.

"You want to know why I sent you a ticket to come?" he said.

I looked at him with a matter-of-fact expression.

"Well, I wanted to see you. And I wanted to talk to you face-to-face."

"Dick," I interrupted.

However, he placed both of our hands, still clenched, to my lips to silence me.

"Listen. I know you saw Celeste. And yes, we are still together."

The hope built up in my throat quickly sank to the pit of my large intestine. Interestingly, I was not as upset as I thought I would be. I think I was expecting it. The server came to take our order. Dick continued to hold my hand while he explained.

"I still care for you and the closer we get to the date, the more I feel I am making a mistake."

"Dick, we have been over this."

"I know. I just needed to see you so that we could talk about our feelings."

"Why didn't you call?"

"Because I never know when you are telling me the truth these days. But your eyes, they give you away."

I quickly looked in the other direction away from him.

"What do you want me to say?" I asked softly.

"That you want to be with me, like I want to be with you."

I faced his sincere eyes and we stared in stillness for seconds. Finally, after a couple of sighs, I spoke. "I can't do it."

Dick slid his hands from atop mine. "I really do love you, Lily."

"And I love you."

"So what's the problem?"

"Love's not enough," I muttered while lifting his chin toward me.

"If I were single would it make a difference?"

"Perhaps. Except I'm not single."

"Do you love him?" Dick asked.

"I care a lot about Winston, but this conversation has nothing to do with that. This is wrong," I said, pointing back and forth between us. "We are sneaking around, meeting each other. Lying to our partners. This is no way to start anything. Would we be able to even trust each other if we started dating?"

With grief, Dick placed his face within his cupped hands. Mumbling, he spoke through his fingers. "I think you and I were supposed to be together, so why can't we get it right?"

Shrugging, I responded, "Maybe we're supposed to be good friends."

Peeking through his hands, Dick was quiet. The server brought our plates. After saying grace, we began eating while continuing conversation.

"As lovers, we are good together, too great to simply be friends," he said, picking up where the dialogue last dropped.

"So we should just leave our significant others and run away together? Is that what you're suggesting?" I asked curiously.

"I know that wouldn't be right."

"Exactly, it wouldn't be. Honestly, I was hoping that when I got here you would tell me that Celeste was out of your life. I was so excited when I saw her without the ring."

"What if I had told you that?"

"I don't know," I said with despair. "I don't know."

We continued eating dinner as the jazz band started their first set. Nothing was resolved, but at least I knew that he still wanted me. Truthfully, I felt that if I told him to leave Celeste, he would. For how long, I don't know. However, if I had to tell him to leave, it completely spoiled our beginning. We already had enough to work through without a sour start. Not much more was said during dinner. We finished, took a taxi down to the riverboats, and strolled hand in hand along the boardwalk. The first few minutes were quiet; then I finally broke the mood.

"Again, why did you send me a ticket?" I said, laughing.

"So we could do this. My boy told me that this town was very romantic. Immediately, I thought, I want to share this with Lily."

Shaking my head, I sneered. "Immediately you should have thought, ooh, I want to share this with Celeste, my fiancée."

Dick said nothing; thus we strolled a few more feet before I commented, "If you were unattached and pursuing me, I would go with you in a hot minute."

"Oh yeah?" Dick responded.

"Yeah. But this is crazy. How long are we going to do this back-and-forth thing? Till one of us gets married?"

Dick smirked, and with his hands cupping my cheeks, he leaned over and kissed me. I was surely not one for public displays of affection; however, we kissed for close to a minute. When he pulled away, I was light-headed.

"This is not crazy," he said before walking over to a bench and taking a seat. I continued to stand at the railing in front of him. Sighing, I looked out onto the river at the lights reflecting sparkles into the water. With my chin propped on the cool railing, I began to pray. I really did love this man, but I refused to be with him as long as he was with her. Ring or no ring, he was still planning on marrying her and it was just not right. I was setting myself up for hurt. Opening my eyes, I glanced over at a tormented Dick. He was just as befuddled. He didn't want to hurt her, but again I was not about to be his scapegoat for leaving. Slowly, I strolled over to Dick and sat on his knee.

With my face buried within his broad chest, we snuggled. I began to hum a tune as we cuddled up closer.

"What are you humming?" he asked.

"Don't laugh. I'm humming Sonny and Cher, 'I Got You Babe.'"

Immediately, he laughed.

"I said don't laugh. I like that song. The phrases and verses are very simple yet so significant."

"But Sonny and Cher didn't even stay together."

"Yet you always got the feeling that they had each other's back. Even once they separated. Hell, even at his funeral, you could tell that she'd lost a true love."

Dick laughed again.

"Forget it, you don't understand."

Dick held me closer and whispered, "Yes, I do."

We stayed like that for an hour, and then finally made our way back to the hotel. By this time, I had decided that I was not going to sleep with Dick. Though we both said we wanted to, we both agreed that making love would only complicate the issue. Therefore, Dick slept in one room and I slept in the adjoining one. Yet we left the door open and talked to each other nearly all night. He caught me up on his music and I told him all about Samantha, Sarah, and my job. Through jokes, sexual innuendos, laughter and confiding, I realized that it was not sex with Dick that I missed most. I missed him; my friend. Sure, last year we did romp in the sack a lot. However, we had some amazing after-sex talks, breakfast banter, and intelligent conversation. Maybe this was why I couldn't shake him.

Finally, slumber hit and I began drifting off when I saw the sun coming up through the sheer curtains. Glancing at the time, I saw that it was close to 6:00 a.m.

I rose, walked into Dick's room, and kissed his temple. Then cupping my hands around my mouth, I yelled into his ear, "Wake up!"

Dick jumped up, accidentally bumping his forehead into my eye.

"Ouch!"

"What are you doing?"

Laughing uncontrollably, I couldn't answer, and Dick picked me up and slammed me on the bed. Immediately, we began pillow-fighting. However, with one big blow, he knocked me off the bed and onto the floor. Although I was not hurt, I stayed still as though I were. He leaned over the bed and spoke.

"You're not fooling me." He went to the bathroom.

I continued to lie still pretending to be injured. Finally, Dick came from the restroom and saw me still lying on the floor. I heard his breathing as he cautiously leaned over.

"Lily, get up. Stop playing."

Still, I said nothing. Finally, he started to believe that something was truly wrong. He picked up my limp body and placed it on the bed. I chuckled inside as I heard his breathing become heavier. From the corner of my eye I saw him pacing back and forth.

"Lily, for real, stop playing," he said with a hint of panic.

Dick sat on the bed and placed his hand and head on my chest. I then took both hands from my side and grabbed a handful of his hair. With his head in my hands I wrestled him to the floor. Rolling with giggles, Dick and I playfully grappled on the carpet until we found ourselves in the missionary position. With our eyes fixed on each other, the laughter quickly stopped.

"What are you thinking?" we said in unison.

After a few beats of silence, Dick responded, "I'm thinking I should make love to you."

Nervously, I began to stutter. "I . . . I think—"

Suddenly my phone rang. "I have to get that," I said softly, pushing him off my body.

I rushed to the bedroom and answered the phone and wouldn't you know it, Winston was calling.

"Hi, sweetie," I said innocently.

"Hi, babe. How are you?"

"Fine," I answered as Dick came into the room trying to play.

"How's Sarah?"

"She's fine. I'll be home tonight," I said, hoping to quickly end the conversation.

Just then, Dick grabbed my foot and pulled me off the bed.

I angrily made a face and pointed vigorously to the phone, indicating for him to stop. He grumbled and waited at the door for me to finish. As I continued talking to Winston, I rose and closed the door, with Dick standing just at the other side. The next few minutes I had a quaint conversation with my boyfriend while feeling guilty about the man I desired on the other side of the door. We disconnected after making plans to see each other later that night when I returned home. As soon as I opened the door, I fussed at Dick, who sat like a child at the edge of the bed.

"Why were you doing that? You knew that was Winston."

"I didn't know who that was," he said defensively.

In disbelief, I walked back into my room. However, he followed.

"You going with me to sound check today?"

"I don't know," I sighed.

"What's wrong?" Dick said, pulling me into his chest.

"I feel bad about lying to Winston. He is a good man and he really likes me."

"I'm a good man too and I really love you."

"And you have a good woman who loves you," I said, pulling away.

Walking over to my bags, I began pulling out fresh clothing for the day. Although I got no sleep last night, I was not tired.

"Lily."

Freezing my motions, I turned and looked at him.

"We all fall short and I don't take any of this lightly."

Slowly, I walked back to him and spoke. "Dick, you are still with her because that is where you want to be. No one is making you stay. Whether you love Celeste or just don't want to hurt her, you are still with her by choice."

"But if I weren't with her, would you—"

"But you are with her and I am with him and neither of us seems to be doing anything about it," I interrupted.

"So are you saying we are both where we want to be?" he said, slow and uncertain.

"I guess so."

Upon kissing my forehead, Dick embraced me.

The rest of the day, Dick and I went to lunch, to the movies, then to sound check. We enjoyed the day as platonic friends and there wasn't another sentimental moment until I prepared to go to the airport. Sarah came over to the hotel around seven o'clock, so that she could see Dick before his show. Dick immediately became enamored with Carmen and he played with her for minutes before acknowledging Sarah. Around seven thirty, his manager rang the room to inform him of the 7:40 lobby call. Our flight left at 9:35 and since his show didn't start until nine o'clock, we gave our complimentary tickets to Lizzie. Dick gave Sarah a hug, grasped me by the arm, and pushed me into the other room. He sat me on the edge of the bed and kneeled between my knees. With his hands in my lap, he spoke.

"Thank you for coming."

"Thanks for inviting me," I responded cordially.

We sat staring at each other, both carefully thinking about our next response. It was astonishing how a still moment could speak volumes. Finally, Dick remarked, "I don't know how this is going to play out but—"

"We'll see," I interrupted.

Gently placing his hands around my neck, he continued. "You know you're the one."

With a wink, I responded softly, "I know."

Dick and I both leaned in to kiss and though it was quick, it was one of our most passionate moments. I could feel his adoring energy and it gave me an instant high. We embraced one last time and he left for his show. Moments later, Sarah and I hopped on the shuttle and headed to the airport. We got there early; however, she wanted to sit in the coffee shop and discuss my entire weekend. After oohing and aahing her with a play-by-play, we boarded the plane and arrived home a couple of hours later.

I was supposed to see Winston, but I just wanted to go home and sleep. I hadn't slept in a day and I was one step past exhaustion. I called and talked with him on the way home, and we agreed to link the next day. I hoped by then, I would have showered away most of my remorse. I walked in my door and could barely make it upstairs to my bed. Before reaching the bedroom, I was almost naked. I didn't have the energy to shower. I just wanted to get in my bed, pull back the comforter, and snuggle in. Just before I set the alarm clock, I said a little prayer for clarity. I was still not sure why this weekend had happened. However, I was thankful that I didn't sleep with Dick. Hence, I was making progress. Although intimacy was still cheating, I prayed I could let that go and move forward with Winston. Dick was simply a pothole in the road to my stable future and God was testing my driving skills. Sure, I could ride the pothole, at the risk of damaging my car. But it would be best to circumvent the rut altogether and get through this journey intact.

I tell you, when God decides to test us, He pulls out all the stops. But I was going to pass. I just wanted to do right.

Quickly grabbing my book from my nightstand, I scribbled:

Wouldn't it be simpler
If we had no choice
If we had no voice
To speak ill or wrong
If only we were like the angels
With no option, but to obey
Wouldn't it be best if
We had no say

Yet we are free
To choose wrong from right
We've been given the sight
And with ignorance we view
Are we wise enough to choose
Are we too cocky for clues

When our egos win
Do our souls eventually lose
Freedom

Good night.

35

Go, Lily,
It's Your Birthday!

The next couple of weeks blissfully went by as I planned for my big birthday bash the coming weekend. Winston's schedule lightened and we were able to see each other almost every day. Our friendship and love were growing, and though I would be lying to say the passion was as strong as I would like for it to be, I saw progress and each day he became more attractive. I hadn't heard from Dick since the Kentucky trip. I assumed he was still with Celeste and they were continuing with wedding plans. Although it hurt at times, I knew it was the best thing. Currently, I had no complaints personally and professionally. Life was good and I was happy. Susan and the board were thoroughly pleased with our presentation of the new line, which we ended up titling "Impulse." It wasn't my personal choice, but the team unanimously agreed and Susan went bananas over it. I didn't see what the big deal was; however, when I received a bonus in my check, I finally had something to go crazy over. I used the money to buy these wonderful Jimmy Choo shoes I had been admiring. They were my birthday gift to myself. As for the party, Claire took care of the catering. I left the menu up to her, so I didn't even know what we were eating. Up until the week of, the party was supposed to be at my house. I wanted to have it in the backyard, because my downstairs was too sectioned off to house a lot of people. However, the forecast called for rain, and so Sarah suggested her house, which really wasn't her house anymore, since she had been spending many of her days and nights with Omar. Yet Claire loved a party, and when Sarah made the suggestion she jumped in with ideas. Other than Sarah's baby shower, she hadn't had a party in two years and everyone was keyed up. I took off from work that Friday, so that I could get Tam, Stan, Evelyn, and Pierce from the airport. This was the first time my friends had come to visit and like a kid, I was overwhelmed with joy.

Checking the time, I saw that I had an hour before Tam and Evelyn's flight arrived. Aimlessly, I rode around town trying to kill some time and ended up at Marshall's searching for bargains. I certainly had nothing to shop for, but what better way to pass the minutes? Therefore, close to an hour later, I was leaving the store with two pairs of twenty-dollar jeans, a fifteen-dollar sundress, and five pairs of new panties. I tossed my bag in the back and drove to the airport. As soon as I pulled up to park, my cell phone rang. I scrambled through my purse to answer it, but before I could say hello, I heard Tam fussing on the other end.

"Is this how you treat your guests? Where are you?"

"Where are you?" I asked.

"We are at the Delta curb waiting on you. We've been here almost twenty minutes."

"But your plane landed at seven forty-two."

"Our plane landed at seven twenty-four," she corrected. "Are we dyslexic now?"

"Hush. I'm pulling up now."

I turned around in the parking deck, circled the airport, and went back to the drop-off curb.

"There are my friends," I began to chant as I saw them standing on the corner.

Quickly, I whipped in and hopped out. After I gave them all huge hugs, we dumped the bags in the back and drove away. Though it was still early they were all tired, so after eating dinner everyone retired and agreed to meet the next day.

I woke up early Saturday morning and got to Sarah's house to prepare. However, when I got there, Claire had done everything. Better yet, she had hired someone to do everything. I swear money was such a valuable tool. Claire was sitting on the balcony with a checklist in one hand and a mimosa in the other, while men and women in white jackets were setting up tables, chairs, and tents. What had started as a simple backyard bash had magically turned into an elaborate birthday extravaganza. We had a live band, a DJ, centerpieces, and trays upon trays of food. As soon as I sat down, Claire commented while lifting her glass in the air, "It's going to be fabulous. You just relax, have a mimosa, and enjoy the party."

Grinning, I sat with her and watched my party evolve. While I was relaxing and chatting with Claire, Omar walked in with Carmen. He handed her to his mother, gave me a light tap on the shoulder, and walked back through the house.

"Where's Sarah?" I called out.

"Don't know," he responded from inside.

"Sounds like they are at it again," said Claire, sighing.

Exhaling with her, I asked, "What is going on with them?"

"Your guess is as good as mine," she replied while playing with Carmen.

Though I came prepared to work, there was nothing for me to do. Feeling helpless, I walked back onto the balcony.

"Are you sure there is nothing I can do?" I asked Claire.

"You can pour me another glass," she said, smiling.

I took her glass and emptied the carafe. "Well, I guess I'm going to go. Tell Sarah to call me."

"The band will start up around eight o'clock. Is that too soon?" Claire asked.

"I guess not. I'll be back around seven o'clock."

I left the home and immediately called Sarah. She didn't answer her phone. Therefore, I called Donnie. He answered right away, and told me Sarah and Omar had another argument. She came over to his home that morning around four and that she should still be there sleeping. I didn't know when Sarah was going to realize that she and Omar had a very unhealthy relationship. Although she was still wearing that ring, I hoped she was not seriously thinking about marrying him. If they couldn't get the boyfriend-girlfriend relationship right, the husband-and-wife liaison was surely not going to work.

I called my friends and made plans to head their way. Tam wanted to meet Sarah, Evelyn wanted to go shopping, and the guys wanted to eat. While the discussion was growing, Donnie called back to see if I had eaten lunch. I told him that my friends were in town and of course he wanted to meet them. Hence, we all decided to meet at my home. Donnie, Stan, and Pierce went to eat food and shoot pool. The girls and I decided to go boutique shopping. We all agreed to meet back at the house around five o'clock and prepare for the party that night.

Once we broke away from the guys, the discourse quickly turned from mature dialogue to girly, adolescent yak. Evelyn and Tam started tag-teaming me about Dick and Winston. Although I told Tam I had abstained while I was in Kentucky, she now acted as if she didn't believe me. Evelyn, completely oblivious of the entire Kentucky trip, was steadily trying to catch up with details and put her two cents in. On the way into town, we passed the exit for the children's center. I wanted to introduce Tam to Sam, and so we decided to stop by. Plus, this would ease the love-triangle banter for the moment. Although I had been keeping it a secret, I decided to tell Tam about my conversation a week ago with Ms. Gaither.

"I might have the opportunity to become Sam's foster parent. Who knows, it could lead to adoption."

Tam was quiet, yet Evelyn seemed to be elated.

"That's wonderful. Isn't it, Tam?"

"I guess it's wonderful," she said with little enthusiasm.

"What's there to guess about?" I asked defensively.

"For starters, are you ready? Secondly, adopting a teenager from a home is not like having a baby. She's coming with her own set of issues that you have no control over."

"I know this, Tam. I also know I can make a difference. This little girl is part of my journey, how dare you try to spoil this?" I replied with a bit of anger.

"I'm not spoiling anything. I just know you. You jump in the pool with your eyes closed and then you realize it's been drained. I'm saying look before you leap this time."

"I have been looking. I have always wanted to adopt. The opportunity may be here and I'm going to take advantage of it."

Evelyn quickly cut in. "Let's not argue, please. Let's just go meet Sam and have fun today."

Tam and I silenced. Both of us, still perturbed, said nothing until we got to the home's driveway and got out.

"I haven't mentioned it to Sam yet, so don't say anything."

As soon as I pulled up, the girls in the front yard came running up. Shannon pulled me into the yard, untied the ropes from the fence, and handed me the cords.

"Turn the ropes, Ms. Lily."

Slowly, I began twirling, trying to remember my double Dutch days.

"You're doing it too slow," said one of the girls.

I began flipping my wrist faster, as Evelyn walked up and whispered, "Which one is she?"

Looking around the girls, I didn't see Sam, so I answered, "She's not out here."

Tam eventually made it over to the girls while Evelyn tried to jump in. Although the girls kept encouraging her, she kept messing up.

"I never learned how to do this," Evelyn complained.

"You never learned how to double Dutch? Ain't you black, what's wrong with you?" one young girl called out.

Evelyn, once again tripping over the flying jump ropes, remarked, "I don't know. Lily, what's wrong with me?"

Laughing, I responded, "We don't have enough time in the day to answer that one." Evelyn pouted and moved over to the side in order to let the girls continue. I handed the ropes to Keisha and asked Sam's whereabouts. The girls pointed inside; therefore, Evelyn, Tam, and I walked inside the home. Immediately, we walked toward the game room. If I knew Sam, she was inside playing video games. We walked by the office and I introduced Mr. Combs to Tam and Evelyn. He mentioned my talk with Ms. Gaither and gave me a smile. Afterward, we walked down the hall to find Sam. Following the cheers and upsets of teenage voices, we found Sam and a couple of the others in the game room sitting by the television. We stood at the door for a moment before any of them noticed we were there. However, once Sam saw us, she tossed the game down and ran over. Hastily, she began telling me about their video game tournament and how she had made it to the final round. She spat out her words so fast, her breath was having a hard time catching up. Finally, I got a beat in between her sentences to introduce Tam and Evelyn. Sam gave each of them a hug and started conversing with Evelyn about how she looked like her baby sister.

Suddenly Sam's video cohorts called for her.

"I'm coming," she yelled.

She invited us in, but we declined.

"I just wanted them to meet you. We have to go."

"Isn't your birthday party tonight?" asked Sam.

I answered with a nod.

"No kids allowed, right?" she said with a quirky smile.

"Right."

"Okay. I have something for you." Sam rushed down the hall and came back moments later. She handed me a gift.

"Don't open it now," she said swiftly before giving me a quick hug and retreating to her tournament.

We all said good-bye, left the home, and headed uptown to shop. There was still some tension between Tam and me, and so the shopping conversation was rather quiet. We each looked through individual racks, left, and went to check out another spot. The only person who bought anything was Evelyn. Afterward, we ate at a small café downtown and again, conversation was minimal. Finally, I decided to say something.

"This is not good. Why are we not talking?"

Evelyn and Tam both shrugged and kept eating.

However, I continued. "Tam, are you mad at me?"

"No," she said curtly.

"Then why are you so quiet?"

"I don't know. I'm just tired. I want to take a nap."

"I'm just quiet 'cause you two are quiet," added Evelyn.

"Fine. Maybe everyone needs a nap," I said with an attitude.

We finished lunch and headed toward my house where the guys were waiting for us. They went back to the hotel to rest and change for the evening. I spoke to Winston about the night and lay down for a quick snooze. I wasn't sure what was wrong with Tam. However, I hoped her funky mood dissipated during her nap. Just before I slept I opened Sam's gift. It was a picture of us taken when she was at the house for her birthday. The frame was black with hand-painted writing on it. The words, written in what looked like fingernail polish said *best friends*. It was the most precious gift I'd ever received. I placed it on my dresser and then lay across my bed.

I must have been more tired than I thought because when I awoke it was close to seven o'clock. My house ringer was muted and my cell phone was downstairs; consequently, I couldn't hear it ringing. I was sure people had been trying to call me. Grabbing my phone off the couch, I saw that I had eight missed calls. Two from Sarah, one from Winston, one from Tam, one from Wealth, one from Donnie, one from my mom, and one hang-up. Rushing back upstairs to the restroom, I began returning my messages. Sarah was at Claire's waiting for me, and Donnie agreed to pick up the crew from the hotel and bring them to the party. Winston and I were going to meet there because he would be rushing from work. I didn't call Wealth back; however, Winston informed me that Wealth wanted to come to the party. At first, I thought it was not a good idea, but then I figured why not? The more the merrier. Plus, Claire's place was so huge and the way the guest list was growing, I probably wouldn't even see him. All of my team from work was attending and the engineers from Donnie's studio were also coming. I even think Claire invited some people. Laughing to myself, I thought, *This party is going to be the gala event of the summer.*

As I jumped out of the shower, my stomach began to cramp.

"Oh, please tell me my period is not about to start," I said aloud. I walked into the bedroom to look at my calendar. However, as I began counting, my days were not adding up. Again, I counted the square boxes on the date book. My period should have started over a week ago.

"I'm almost two weeks late," I gasped.

I was never late. My cycle was as regular as sunrise. How could I have forgotten about it? Panicking, I began to think about my sexual episodes with Winston. We always used protection and I hadn't slept with any one other than him. On my fingers, I began recalling each time we'd had sex over the last month. That is when it hit me.

"The condom was stuck. Oh no," I began chanting around the room.

Immediately, I started jumping up and down as if I could make my period work its way down my uterus and out of my body. Suddenly the phone rang. Answering it, I responded to Sarah's immediate question.

"No, I haven't left home yet."

"What is taking you so long?" she questioned.

"My period."

"Oh no, sweetie you got your period."

"No, I missed my period," I stammered.

Sarah yelped.

"What if I'm pregnant?"

"By Dick?" she questioned.

"No. I told you I didn't sleep with him!"

"Winston?"

"Yes."

"But you guys use protection."

"But there was this one time and the condom came off. Look, I'll be there in a minute."

We hung up and I swiftly dressed for the party. I no longer wanted to wear my off-white tank dress. I would much rather wear something black just in case my period did start. Yet I couldn't decide on anything and I really wanted to wear my new shoes. Hence, I kept on my tank dress, grabbed panty-liners and tampons, and headed to my birthday party.

As soon as I got to the house, Sarah accosted me at the door. She grabbed my hand and led me to her bedroom. Running her hands through her very short curly hair, she paced back and forth.

"What are we going to do? What are we going to do?" she repeated.

Sitting on the edge of her bed, I simply shrugged and kept quiet.

"If you're pregnant, Winston is going to want to get married. That could be good, right?"

"Could be."

"But are you ready?" Sarah asked.

"Don't know."

"But what if he wants you to have an abortion?"

"He wouldn't want that, and I couldn't do that."

"Well, we have to find out. We have to find out!" she screeched.

An abrupt knock at her door startled us both. We jumped about the room as if we were hiding stolen jewels.

"Come in," Sarah said, poised by the wall.

Claire came to the door and told us that the first guests were arriving.

"Thanks, Mom, we'll be right down."

Claire smiled while commenting, "Lily, you look so pretty. You have a glow."

As soon as she closed the door, Sarah jumped over to the bed. Frantically pointing and whispering, she began chanting as if I were *The Last Dragon*. "You got the glow. You got the glow."

Calming her, I grabbed her hand and placed it over her mouth. "Hush! No more baby talk. We have to go downstairs. I'll take a test tomorrow."

We walked down to the party to greet the arriving guests. I was astonished at the presentation. The theme was diamonds and pearls. Therefore, everything was white, silver, or iridescent in color. The appetizer table was decorated with oyster shells, filled with faux pearls. The wine had faux diamonds draped around the necks of each bottle. The room was filled with iridescent and silver balloons and the place was covered with white tulips. Surprisingly, the weather was beautiful, and so the party was able to spill outside by the garden. On the green, Claire had set up ten round tables with huge diamond-cut glass vases. The vases were filled with faux pearls that draped over the top. Silver painted roses were scattered on each table. This party looked absolutely regal. Searching through the small crowd of people, I looked for Claire. Upon finding her in the back, I rushed to embrace her.

"Everything is so beautiful."

"I'm glad you like it. Go have some fun."

I mingled in the growing crowd, acknowledging my guests and the guests of others. Finally, I met with Sarah again, who was talking with Wealth and his date. As I walked up he introduced her and gave me a hug. Whispering in his ear, I asked cynically, "Where's Angela?"

"Would you like me to invite her? I can call her right now."

Lightly punching his chest, I pushed him away. He handed me a tiny gift, wrapped in aqua paper.

"Does that say Tiffany and Company?" I asked.

Wealth simply winked and walked away with his date to enjoy the party. Quickly, Sarah eyed my gift.

"He got you jewelry?" she asked.

"I don't know," I said curiously.

We both intriguingly looked at the little box as if it were going to magically open itself.

"You think Winston will be mad?" I asked Sarah.

"I know Omar would," she responded.

"Should I give it back?"

Again, we continued to look at the box, and then unanimously responded, "Nahhh!"

Sarah took the box from my hand and commented, "We can put the gifts in my room. I'm sure you will get more throughout the night."

As soon as she walked away, Donnie, Tam, and Evelyn walked up. Evelyn immediately started raving about the decorations. The theme was right up her alley; she and Claire would have so much in common. Tam pulled me aside to speak in private. Right away, we both apologized for our earlier demeanor.

Tam admitted, "I don't want you rushing into anything because you feel that everyone is moving on except you."

"I'm not."

"This decision will permanently affect Sam's life. You can't just decide you don't want her anymore because you're busy. Don't do this for selfish reasons."

"I'm not!" I kept repeating.

Tam looked at me carefully, smiled hesitantly, and then gave me a hug. "Okay, then. If this's what you want, I will support it."

"Good," I said, embracing her support.

Yet, as we parted, I felt compelled to tell her about

my missing monthly. Leaning over, I whispered in her ear, "Guess what?"

"What?" she answered, just as covert.

"I missed my period, I might be pregnant."

"What!"

Quickly, I attempted to quiet her down. *"Shhh!"*

Suddenly Sarah popped her head into our conversation. "You have two gifts now. Some guy gave me another box on the way to my room."

"Sarah, this is Tam. Tam, Sarah."

Like old friends they began squealing and bouncing up and down.

"Does she know?" Tam mouthed while hugging Sarah.

Nodding yes, I inadvertently just gave my two best friends permission to discuss my pending predicament. While they began chatting rapidly, I turned and walked away. Yet I swiftly twirled back to remark, "Don't tell Evelyn."

"Don't tell me what?" Evelyn said, staring over my right shoulder.

Sighing, I already saw this thing snowballing.

"Why are you keeping things from me? I want to know."

"Fine. Whatever. But this is it. No one else can know," I said, walking away.

Of course, Evelyn stayed behind to hear the gossip as I went to mingle. An hour later, Winston arrived. He walked up behind me while I was talking to Stix. Wrapping his arms around my body, he spun me around and gave me a kiss. "You look beautiful."

"Thank you, baby."

Taking my hand, he led me to the dance floor set up in front of the band. Tenderly, we danced for a few songs while the party crowd continued to grow. Glancing to the side of Winston's shoulder, I saw Pierce and Evelyn also dancing.

"I want to introduce you to my friends."

We glided to the left beside the two and introduced Winston. We finished the dance and moved to the side for conversation. Yet, as talk began, Pierce made a comment that jump-started the exhilarating evening.

"Happy birthday."

"Thanks, Pierce. My actual birthday is Monday."

"Well then, I'll just say congratulations on the baby," he remarked while patting my stomach.

Immediately, Evelyn snatched him away.

"Sorry, Lily," she called out.

Like an owl, Winston gave a piercing stare. Quickly, I responded, "I'm not pregnant."

Still, he was stationary.

"At least, I don't think I am."

At last he stuttered, giving some sign of life. "What . . . when . . . you and me?"

"All I know is that my period is late, really late."

"But when?" he asked, still scrambling to form a sentence.

"Remember that time the condom got stuck?"

"Stuck?"

"Inside me, remember?"

Covering his face with his hands, Winston was taken aback.

"I'm sorry, baby. I don't know how he knows. I wanted to tell you later tonight. I'm going to take the test tomorrow."

Winston was silent. He stared into my eyes. I couldn't figure out his expression. Somewhere between contempt and compassion, his stare was disturbing. I didn't know what to say next. Jarring him from this stupor, Wealth walked up and patted his brother on the back.

"Excuse me, Lily. Winston, there is someone I want you to meet."

Winston slowly blinked, took a deep breath, and excused himself from my presence. As soon as he walked away, I began scouring the party for the three big-mouthed culprits. Weaving in and out of the crowd, I finally spotted all three hovering outside by a far right table. Forcefully, I walked to them and began scolding.

"I told you no one was to know. I don't know who told what to whom, but now Winston knows. I can't believe this! What do you have to say!"

All three girls were silent.

"Damn it, don't you hear me! Do not tell anyone else. This is how rumors start."

"But, Lily—" Sarah started.

"No, I'm serious. No one! I don't want this night ruined. And I don't want any more surprises."

Again all three girls were silently staring in my direction. At first, I thought they were gawking at me, but then Sarah began to blink, Tam started to nod, and Evelyn joined in with a wink. Curiously, I gazed at all three of them. However, when I said nothing, their ticks began moving faster and all I knew was that Winky, Blinky, and Nod had better say something quick or I was putting them back in their boat and sending them the hell on their way.

"What is going on?"

Finally, Nod mysteriously spoke. "Turn around."

Immediately, my heart pounded faster. I didn't know what lurked behind me, but I was hesitant to look. "What?"

"Turn around," she repeated.

Slowly, I rotated my body to the left and glanced over my shoulder; however, I saw nothing or no one. Turning back around, I looked at all three girls, who now seemed to be smiling as if they were pageant contestants.

"What in the hell is wrong with y'all?"

Suddenly I felt a touch on my right shoulder. The strong hand pressed down, giving me a caressing squeeze. My heart skipped three beats as a short gasp left my mouth as a hiccup. I recognized this touch from one hundred others. The flutters in my stomach worked their way up through my throat, and out of my mouth came the one name that always turned me to mush.

"Dick."

He walked around, placed both arms on my shoulders, and gave me a tight squeeze. I, feeling helpless, left both arms at my side and limply waited in his arms.

"Hi, beautiful."

I couldn't believe this. Someone had found the key to my secret closet and every skeleton I had was floating around this damn party. I softly mumbled something resembling the word *hello,* but my jaw muscles were not quite working. I was in shock.

"Hi, Dick," the girls chimed in harmony.

Giving them each a kiss on the cheek, he spoke before turning his attention to me. Still, I was unable to speak. Thankfully, Tam spoke for me.

"Dick, what are you doing here?"

He looked at Tam, then back at me as I motioned for him to answer.

"Lily, we need to talk."

"Well, talk," Tam continued.

Again, I nodded for him to carry on. At that moment, I really needed my girls there for support. I didn't know what Dick was going to say. However, if need be, Sarah could run interference with Winston, Tam could curse Dick out if he said something stupid, and Evelyn could catch my fainting body, if he said something wonderful like:

"Lily, I want to be with you."

My breathing pattern halted as these words interrupted my thoughts.

"But we talked," I said, short of breath.

"And you said we were both where we wanted to be, but I wasn't. But now I am."

Evelyn positioned her hand in the small of my back.

"I got you," she whispered.

Suddenly Sarah cut left and dashed across the yard. I assumed she was the tackle running interference on this right sweep that had left me without defense.

"But, Celeste," I murmured.

"That's done. I want you. I need you and I came here for you."

I tried speaking, but only short gasps of air crept out. I was beyond speechless. The lump in my throat was blocking my flow of oxygen and my head felt light.

"I have to go," I said faintly.

"You shouldn't have come," said Tam to Dick as she pushed me away.

Speedily, I went upstairs to Sarah's room. Tam followed, leaving Evelyn and Dick standing in the center of the garden. Tam remained positioned by the door as I slowly paced the floor like a zombie.

"Oh, Tam," I whimpered like a broken-down Mary Tyler Moore.

She, just as stunned as I, repeatedly shook her head back and forth.

"I can't go back down there," I continued to moan.

"We could leave."

"We could leave, couldn't we?" I said, perking up.

"But then the problem will just continue at your house. Eventually, you have to face it."

Suddenly there was a knock on the door and we heard Sarah's tiny voice on the other side. Tam cracked the door and let her in. Her eyes were three times larger than normal as she took her position next to Tam. Together, they looked pathetically over at me while shaking their heads. I felt as if I were some poor squirrel who fell from the tree. I was so close to having that big acorn, until a gust of wind came along and blew me from my shaky branch, and now I just lay there on the ground with my legs stiff in the air. I wasn't dead, but I was incapable of any activity.

Glancing at my onlookers, I whispered, "Just put me out of my misery."

"I can't believe Dick is here," Sarah said.

"How did he know we were here?"

"He already knew about the party and you left the directions on your voice mail," Tam answered calmly.

"I don't know what to do."

"You can either leave or go enjoy the rest of the party. I'll tell Dick to leave and you can talk to him later. Sarah can keep Winston occupied while you get yourself together."

"That sounds good," said Sarah, excited to be part of the plan.

She quickly clapped her hands and turned away as if we were breaking from a huddle. I really hoped this pass play worked, 'cause it was the fourth down and my heart was too faint to run for it.

"I'll be down in a minute," I said, walking into the restroom.

I stared into the mirror and commenced praying.

"God, please let this night go by effortlessly. I just want to make the right decision and do the right thing. I don't want to hurt anyone. I know I slip up, but I have been trying to do right, please just help me through this."

After a few sighs, I reapplied my lipstick and headed downstairs. However, when I got to the garden, I saw chaos and disorder had erupted. Men were running toward the garden and women were hollering.

"What's going on?" I asked.

Quickly, I ran to the center of the disturbance and saw Donnie and Dick fighting Omar. Sarah was nowhere in sight and three other men were trying to break up the fight. Tam rushed over and grabbed me. Holding her pregnant belly, she began telling the story.

"I was trying to find Dick, but I ran into Winston instead. He asked me about Dick and while I was hammering out a response, I saw Omar shaking Sarah in the garden."

Tam very dramatically acted out the scene, grabbing my shoulders and vigorously shaking me back and forth.

"He saw Sarah and Dick drink from the same glass and he went crazy. Donnie saw Omar's hands on Sarah, took off running, and punched him in the face. Then Dick jumped in."

As Tam was belting out the play-by-play, the fight was disbanding. Omar, still yelling and swearing, was being carried away while holding his bruised and bloody face. Dick was brushing himself off and one of the gentlemen was pushing Donnie away from the commotion. Tam and I rushed over to Dick.

"You need to go," I said to him.

"He put his hands on Sarah."

"I know. But you need to go. This is too much right now, Dick, I can't take it."

Dick handed me a tiny card from within his pocket. "This is where I'm staying. Come see me tonight."

Staring at the card, I hesitated.

"Tonight?" I questioned.

"Promise me, tonight," he said, stepping away.

Nodding yes, I mouthed the word *tonight* silently. He walked away. I turned and watched him walk through the party. Suddenly Winston walked up from behind and startled us. I swore this party needed more light.

"What was going on?" he asked.

"Long story."

"Lily, I need to see you," he said, pulling me away from Tam.

I continued looking at her as he whisked me away. She crossed her fingers and plastered a stupid grin on her face. Frowning, I turned and faced the looming question.

"What was Dick doing here?"

Poised and straightforward, I answered, "I casually invited him months ago. I didn't know he would actually show up. He's gone now. We can continue to party." I motioned with my hand, inviting him onto the dance floor.

Winston, however, didn't move. He looked at me and remarked, "I don't know what is really going on, but I will say this. If we are committed like we both say we are—"

"And we are," I interrupted.

"Then he has no business coming around. I don't like it and it's disrespectful."

Winston stared intently, as he continued. "If you are pregnant, we need to discuss our future. My intentions with you are true. Do not start wavering on me."

"I'm not," I said, gulping down my irresolution.

"Good," Winston said, kissing my cheek. "I have something for you, but I'll give it to you later."

Smiling, like a child I asked, "A gift?"

"Yes, a gift," he said, taking my hand.

We passed Claire on the way across the floor. She apologized profusely for Omar's behavior, and I assured her that it didn't ruin anything and that we should continue on like nothing had happened. I could tell his behavior deeply disturbed her, yet she felt it was out of her control. As we walked away, Winston leaned over and commented, "Omar should get some help."

"He's supposed to be in classes. I guess it's not helping. Where is Sarah?"

In all of the uproar, I forgot to look for her. "Winston, I have to go talk to Sarah."

"Where is she?"

"Probably upstairs."

I left him and rushed up to her room. There, I found Sarah lying on the corner of her bed, talking to Evelyn. Once I walked in, Sarah rushed over, hugged me, and whimpered, "Lily, I'm sorry."

"It's okay. This is not your fault. Omar is crazy. You have got to leave him alone."

"I know. I know," she said, burying her head on my shoulder.

Evelyn left quietly as Sarah and I sat and comforted each other. After fifteen minutes or so, I rose to leave. Sarah stayed behind while commenting, "I'm going to stay up here. I'm too embarrassed to come back down."

"You sure?" I asked.

She softly said, "Yes."

"Okay. I'll check on you later," I stated before leaving the room.

Man, this party had had more action than a summer blockbuster. Tapping my hand against my chest, I felt the piece of paper given to me by Dick. I'd placed it in my bra right after he walked away. Turning away from the crowd, I removed it and read. He was staying at the Residence Inn, downtown. Again, he told me to come see him tonight.

"There is no way I can see him tonight."

I balled up the card and tossed it in the trash.

I continue to meander throughout the crowd. Another half hour passed while I mixed with some people from work. A little after midnight, Winston and I linked. He was ready to go and so was I. However, I didn't know if it was appropriate to leave the party while guests were still mingling. He and I walked over to Claire to ask her opinion. She held up her finger, reached behind the bar, and pulled out her bell. Funny, I forgot about the infamous bell. I hadn't seen it since Sarah's baby shower the year before. Claire walked over to the stage area and rang it into the microphone. The crowd slowly quieted as Claire spoke.

"First, I would like to thank everyone for coming. I hope you are having a wonderful time. Secondly, I would like to bring the birthday girl to the stage as we all sing 'Happy Birthday.'"

Claire rang her bell once again to start off the song

while Winston pushed me to the stage. Embarrassed, I stepped up to the microphone just as the song was finishing.

"Thanks, everyone, for coming. It's so wonderful to see all of my old friends mixing with my new friends. I am so blessed to have people, like Claire, who love me enough to throw me such a wonderful party. Everyone give Claire, our host, a hand."

The crowd, now gathered around the stage, clapped.

"Again thanks for coming out and, um . . . enjoy. Good night."

Claire quickly hopped to the stage.

"Excuse me," she said, ringing her bell once again to simmer the crowd.

"I would love to keep this function going all night, but old ladies like me need to get their beauty sleep. The band will play one more set and after that we'll start to wrap things up. Before you leave, please grab a party favor from the basket by the door. Men, your basket is on the left and, women, yours is on the right. Make sure everyone has a designated driver and be safe getting home. Good night."

Claire exited the stage.

"You two can leave, the band is only going to play a few more minutes and then we're clearing this party out."

Laughing, I gave Claire a hug. "I just love you."

"I love you too. Just take care of my girl for me. I know she is having a rough time," Claire said, pointing upstairs.

"I will."

Claire hugged Winston and disappeared into the crowd. I mingled at the door a few more minutes saying good-bye to some of the exiting guests. Winston walked up and handed me a party favor.

"What is it?"

"I don't know. Don't you know?"

"No. The party favor idea is all Claire's."

Rapidly, we both began opening. In Winston's silver sack, there were a pair of silver cuff links. In mine, there was a gorgeous piece of costume jewelry.

"I can't believe it. This is too expensive."

I rushed back through the crowd to find Claire. I saw her standing by the band. Holding up the jewelry, I commented, "Claire, this is too much. I have to help you pay for this."

"Please. I had them donated. Didn't you see the jeweler's name on the bag?" she asked, holding the bag in my face. "Go home. Have a good night."

Laughing, I waved good-bye and went upstairs to say good night to Sarah. Lightly, I tapped on the door, but she didn't answer. I slowly opened it and looked in to see Sarah asleep on the bed. I tiptoed in and kissed her forehead. She slowly opened her eyes.

"You okay?" I asked.

"Yeah," she answered softly.

"Well, I'm about to leave. I'll call you tomorrow."

Sarah nodded, then turned over to continue sleeping. I grabbed my bag of gifts and walked back down to meet Winston and the others. He had gathered the crowd up and they all were waiting at the door. Donnie had already left. As a result, I had to take the others back to the hotel. Winston insisted I stay with him tonight. Thus, I agreed to come there after I dropped off my friends. We all gathered and left my thirtieth birthday party extravaganza; and what a show it was, one that I would never forget. It only took fifteen minutes to arrive at the hotel. Immediately Stan and Pierce jumped out to leave the girls alone to talk.

"Are you going to see Dick tonight?" asked Evelyn.

"No. She is staying with Winston," answered Tam.

"Both of you, get out," I ordered.

They stopped badgering and gazed at me in silence.

"I'm serious, go inside with your men. I'm tired, I'll call you tomorrow."

"Is that all you have to say?" Tam said with her hands on her hips.

"That, and where's my birthday gift?"

Tam quickly shut the door without answering. Evelyn kissed my cheek good-bye, hopped out, and caught up with Tam. I laughed as the two of them walked up the sidewalk. I drove up beside them and rolled down my window.

"I know you're talking about me."

"Ain't nobody talking about you. Go on home to one of your men," Tam said with a grin.

I rolled up my window and drove off. I decided to take the long route to Winston's home, because the quickest route took me directly past the Residence Inn. If I turned onto the street, I knew I would find myself wandering up to Dick's room. And if I got in his room, that was it, I would not see Winston tonight. And if I didn't stay with Winston, our relationship was over. I turned on my cell phone, thinking I might have a message from Dick, but I didn't. I wanted to call him, but I was afraid. In my mind, I heard Winston's promising words. *"My intentions with you are true."*

As they rang repeatedly in my head, I swiftly made my way to his home across town. As soon as I pulled up, the garage door opened. This meant he was anxiously expecting me. I walked past his cars and into the kitchen, where he sat up drinking a cup of tea.

"Want some?" he offered.

"No, thank you," I said, sitting down at the table.

"You had quite a few gifts there."

"I know. I like gifts," I said with a childlike demeanor.

Winston chuckled and placed a decorative envelope on the table. "Well, here's one more."

Looking at him, I slowly open the envelope filled with hundreds.

"I know money may not seem like the most thought-ful gift, but this is to start the new wardrobe you wanted."

Immediately, I began to cheer up.

"Money is good. I like money a lot," I said, jumping up to give him a hug.

Winston kissed me as we moved from the kitchen to the living room. Usually, our kisses were quite pas-sionate; however, tonight everything inside me was conflicted and he picked up on this right away. He pulled away and asked, "What is it?"

Sighing, I looked away.

"Lily, talk to me. Are you worried about the preg-nancy?" he asked.

Still looking toward the window, I nodded.

"Well, come to the office on Monday and we can take a test. There is no need to stress yourself, until you know for sure. Even then, there is nothing to worry about. We'll be fine."

Again, I nodded in silence.

"Is there something else?" he asked, sounding as if he already knew.

I couldn't look at him, knowing I should just tell

him the truth, yet also knowing that I was not going to. Sitting there, I watched my heart, covered in armor, leap from my body, say adios, and walk out the front door. She was just as tired of the conflict as I. For this reason, she had decided to give up and exit the situation altogether. I couldn't blame her. I guess the mind was most powerful after all. I turned and stared at Winston with a blank expression.

"Let's go to bed. I'm exhausted."

I retired to the bedroom. He took a shower and joined me moments later. We lay in bed and held each other. We attempted to kiss and cuddle, but the intimacy was off. The groove between us had been disturbed. Although neither of us confronted the obvious, we both knew that exhaustion was only a cover for the real problem. I stared at the gray wall with my eyes wide open. Winston softly stroked my hair just before he drifted off to sleep. Restless as can be, I continued to lay there counting the seconds in between his light snores. Although Winston's arms wrapped around my body to comfort me, thoughts of Dick were the only things that eased my mind. I just wanted to see him and I was not sure what he was going to think if I didn't go over to see him. I really loved that man. How come I didn't love *my* man like that? I didn't know what to do anymore and it just made me upset. I turned my head into the pillow. Even with my heart out of the picture, Dick remained. Closing my eyes, I inaudibly began talking to the Creator.

"Well, I prayed for an effortless party, and I didn't get that. I prayed that I wouldn't hurt anyone and it doesn't look like I'm going to get that either. Now I pray for enough strength to handle this situation the best way possible. I know this seems petty in comparison to world issues like war, floods, and fires. But you are omnipotent and omnipresent and I need a little attention tonight. I'm going to lay real still, listen, and I promise to take whatever advice you have to give."

Amen.

36

What Time Is Checkout Again?

Early the next morning, I awoke alone in Winston's bed. Glancing around the room, I looked for him. Yet I heard him stirring around in the kitchen. After brushing my teeth, I went down the hall to greet him good morning. As soon as I stepped onto the hardwood kitchen floor, hurricanes of negative energy blew me away. Quickly, I grabbed a seat for balance.

"Good morning," I stated.

Winston was quiet.

"Winston, I said good morning."

He looked up from the fridge and asked, "Sleep well?"

"Umm . . . yeah, I did," I said hesitantly.

Winston walked over to the table, sat down with his cup of coffee, and gawked at me as if we were opposing chess players. I stared back, for I was unsure of his next move.

"I want to know right now, right now," he repeated firmly, tapping the table. "Are you sleeping with Dick?"

"No! I haven't slept with him since we started dating," I answered adamantly.

Thankfully, I hadn't slept with Dick and it felt so good to tell that truth.

"Then why are you still seeing him?"

"What? I'm not still seeing him."

"Other than the party, when is the last time you saw him?"

Gasping, I looked down at the table knowing that if I told Winston the truth, in an instant the entire dynamics of our relationship were going to change. I continued glancing at him while biting my bottom lip. He deserved the truth and if I lied, it would just make it easier to lie the next time something else happened. Thus, I swallowed the lie and regurgitated the truth that had been lingering in my mouth for weeks.

"I saw him in Kentucky."

"Goddammit, Lily!" Winston shouted, slamming his fist down on the table.

The pound was so powerful it knocked his cup of coffee into his lap. Winston jumped up, grabbed a towel, and quickly wiped himself off. I rushed to aid him; however, he forcefully pushed me away.

"Get off of me! Just get your stuff and go," he said, walking over to the sink.

"But I didn't sleep with him."

"I don't care. You lied! It's only a matter of time before you do sleep with him. Where is he now?" he shouted.

I was silent.

"Where is he, Lily!" he shouted, louder.

Stuttering, I answered, "I don't know, I guess he's at the hotel."

"Were you going to go see him?" he inquired.

"I don't . . . I didn't . . ." I continually stammered.

Winston turned and moved closer to me. Slow and deliberate, he asked again, *"Were you going to see him today?"*

"Probably," I answered softly.

Winston leaned closer and whispered in my ear, "Then go."

He walked down the hall to the bedroom and slammed the door. I sat down at the kitchen table in shock. Where did this all come from? I had never seen him this angry. As I stared out the window, the minutes passed like seconds. Suddenly I came from my daydream when Winston clapped in front of my face.

"I thought I asked you to leave."

"I don't . . . where . . . why are you saying this?"

"You will not sit here and deny any of this. Last night, I went to sleep holding you in my arms. This could possibly be my wife one day, was my last thought before I drifted off to sleep. Yet I was rudely awakened when the woman in my arms continually called out another man's name. Do you know what that name was, Lily?" he said as his temper rose.

Looking away, I didn't answer. There was no need.

"Dick!"

Quietly, I sat and listened to his anger.

"I will not build a relationship with you only to be made a fool of years later. You may think that I'm ignorant like my father, but I am not. You and I are over! Seriously, get your shit and go!"

I turned and looked Winston in the face. Calming

his temperament, he leaned over with his hands on the table.

"We're over. I can't do this and I don't trust you."

"I'm sorry."

"Me too."

Slowly, I moved my chair away from the table and walked down the hall to retrieve my things. When I returned, Winston was still propped on the kitchen table staring out the window. I walked by him and placed the envelope filled with twenty-five hundred dollars on the table. Although I paused in movement, I kept looking straight ahead.

With a firm murmur I said, "Good-bye."

I walked out the front door, got in my SUV, and drove off. I thought by now that I would be bawling; however, not a single tear rolled down my face. Maybe I was too devastated to cry. Rummaging through my purse, I found my phone and called Tam. As soon as Stan handed her the phone, I spewed out the entire story as she gasped and moaned on the other end. Interrupting, she finally blurted out, "You have to go see Dick. You wanted a way out and this is it. You have to see him, he's waiting on you."

"What am I going to say?"

"You are going to tell him Winston left and that you want to be with him."

Sighing, I hesitated to respond. "I'm not sure if I should."

"What do you have to lose? Your dignity is gone and your man is gone. If you don't go see the guy that caused all of this, you are stupid."

Quietly, I simmered over her words. She was right. I got off the phone, exited the highway, and made my way through town to reach the Residence Inn before checkout. I whizzed into the parking lot and jumped out. Rushing to the counter, I asked the attendant to ring the room of Will Dickson. After punching a few keys, he turned and spoke.

"He's already checked out."

Slamming my head against the desk, I repeated, "No, no, no."

"Ma'am, are you all right?"

"No, no, no," I continued to repeat with my face against the wood. "When did he leave?"

The man punched a few more keys and answered, "This morning."

I placed my chin against his desk and stared at the gentleman. As I blinked, a single tear came down my face. After handing me a tissue, the man took a piece of paper and placed it on the counter.

"Are you Lily McNeil?"

Glancing at him, I replied, "Yes, why?"

He held up his finger and quickly returned with a package wrapped in matte black paper and tied with a big pink bow. "Mr. Dickson left this for you. We were to ship it to this address if you didn't show."

He slid the gift across the counter. Dejected, I took the package and walked away. Sitting in my SUV, I placed the gift on my lap and ran my hands against the smooth paper. In slow motion, another single tear fell and splattered the smooth blackness, leaving a pallid gray inkblot. I tossed it in the bag with the other gifts and drove home.

As soon as I walked in the door, my home phone and my cell phone started ringing. I ambled to the restroom and left them both unanswered. After a relaxing bath I felt a tad better, at least good enough to talk on the phone. I called Tam and Evelyn to finalize our plans for their last night in KC. I could hear the empathy in Tam's voice as I told her that I missed Dick. She couldn't believe that he didn't call, but I wasn't surprised. Dick's big maneuver was crashing the party and if that wasn't enough to make me submit, he wasn't going to call and beg. It was not his style. He passed me the ball and I fumbled. Me not visiting him last night was confirmation that I was exactly where I wanted to be and with whom I wanted to be with. The miscommunication between us was so thick, it seemed as though we spoke two different languages. Ironically, our dialects were one and the same. We both spoke the tongue of fear; fear of loving too hard, fear of getting hurt, fear of the unknown. This idiom, which so carelessly brought us together, had ultimately drawn us apart. Yes, I wanted to call him and I wanted to see him, but I wouldn't be able to answer the first question he was going to ask.

"Why didn't you come see me last night?"

In truth, I didn't want to hurt Winston. However, it was also a fact that I wasn't ready to jeopardize my stable future. But since Winston left on his own accord, Dick would probably perceive his victory as one of default and it would take me a while to convince him otherwise. Personally, I didn't have the energy. Hell, I was even too tired to get dressed. All I wanted to do was sit in the center of my bed, and open my birthday gifts in my birthday suit.

I took the bag of beautifully wrapped presents and scattered them on my bed. First I read all of the cards. I could always tell how a person felt about me by the cards they picked out. I had broken it down into several categories.

1. Generic card, with a broad greeting: meant the distant party felt obligated to buy a card or the card purchaser was an acquaintance who was not quite sure where he or she stood.
2. Specific card, with a humorous greeting: meant the friend was close enough to get my sense of humor or the friend had something more meaningful to say but hid it through witty phrases and funny pictures. In which case, the purchaser always wrote an endearing closing upon signing his or her name.
3. A very specific card with a lengthy greeting: meant the close friend knew exactly what you were going through and they wanted to be there for you or the friend had entirely too much disposable time. Do you know how long it takes to read those lengthy cards in order to find the perfect one?
4. Blank cards with beautiful artwork: meant the friend was excellent at communicating exactly what needed to be said or the friend was a control freak and his or her way was always the best way.

After my cards were read, I tallied the total. I had ten for category 1, seven for category 2, two for category 3, and four for category 4.

Sarah got me a card that folded out with a long scripted message. Sure, she understood what I was going through; however, she had too much time on her hands. From Tam, I received a blank card with a beautiful nurturing statement—control freak. Wealth got a corny card with old ladies doing exercise. He surely didn't get my sense of humor and with his sappy closure, *I truly appreciate our special friendship,* it made me think twice about his intentions. I got the best card from Stix. He created an original card from the new line we had developed at work. The front of the card was a sketch of a naked woman. The sketch started at the neck and ended just above the pubic section. However, there was a pair of lips replacing the belly button. On the inside he sketched a huge B. Beside the B he wrote the phrases *naked, fabulous, misunderstood,* and *you.* So it read like this *B naked, B fabulous, B misunderstood, B you. Happy "B" Day. Stix.*

I loved it. He won, hands down. Now it was time for the gifts. First, I opened Wealth's little aqua box. It was a set of three beautiful bangles with tiny, inset diamonds. They were so sexy and dainty. I immediately put them on. Next, I tore through several other gifts of clothing, books, and gift certificates. Lastly, I came to the matte black gift with the tearstain. Slowly, I removed the pink bow and placed it around my neck. Carefully, I removed the paper and pulled out a black coffee table book with the word *Lily* scripted in light pink trimmed in silver. For seconds I stared, rubbing my hands across the beautiful book that bore my name. Gradually, I turned the first page and it was a letter from the editor, Dick. *Your work should adorn coffee tables across the globe and one day it will.*

Excited, I flipped to the next page, which contained one of my works. More eager, I hastily flipped through the next five pages containing more of my poetry. This was when I realized that this wonderful coffee table book was a book of my poetry. Astounded, I continued to flip through all twenty pages, admiring the sketches, pictures, and poetry. I was in awe. This was why I loved this man. Sure, he was fine and the sex was wonderful, but most of all, he got me. He knew what made me smile, what moved me, and how to touch my soul. Most importantly, he knew how to finesse this knowledge into magnificent acts of thoughtfulness. My eyes quickly began to water. Filled with emotion, I moved the book aside, and this was when I noticed another tiny box within the big black box. I pulled it out, opened it, and saw my old poetry journal and a card. The card was black, just like the book, and inside it had a picture of us. Below the picture was the phrase *I got you, babe.*

That was it, and believe it or not, that was all it took. I quickly rushed to the phone to call Dick. After three rings, his voice mail came on. Nervously, I hung up. His message time was short and I had never been succinct when it came to love, and so I decided to call back later. Rushing back to the bed, I moved the boxes out of the way and saw a tiny piece of paper taped to the outside of Dick's box. Curiously, I read the note aloud. "I hope you're happy. Congrats and good-bye, Dick."

What did this mean? I wondered, staring at his sloppy manuscript.

"Does he think I'm pregnant?"

Suddenly the phone rang. Flopping over my boxes and gifts, I rushed to answer. However, it was only Tam changing our meeting time. Still disconsolate over Dick's message, I mumbled okay and hung up.

"He's gone and he's not coming back. Damn it!" I screamed, jumping down from the bed.

I tried calling him again, but I got no answer. I pushed 1 to leave a message but his mailbox was full. Forcefully, I began stomping around the room. However, I was quickly reminded of my ankle injury when a sharp pain shot up my leg. I stopped and stared at

myself in the mirror. The pink ribbon had fallen from
my neck to across my chest. If I had on a pair of stilettos
to match my delicate diamond bracelets, I would be a
great candidate for Ms. Nude America. Smiling, I posed
for the imaginary judges and the nonexistent cameras.

"Have I lost it or what?"

Did I ever have it? should be the question. I had spent
all last year searching through pieces of a man while
looking for this girl named Lily and now that she'd
been found, I didn't know what to do with her. This year
had definitely been more fulfilling. I was doing things
that meant something to me. I was more disciplined,
more focused, and I had grown. So why was I standing
here naked smiling for invisible paparazzi?

"Have I grown into a nutcase or have I simply shed
the insecurities that kept me from accepting myself?"

Scribbling on the inside of a piece of wrapping
paper, I wrote:

This is who I am:
A thirty-year-old single woman.
I am sensitive and fickle.
I have problems accurately expressing my feelings.
I want to be pursued, 'cause I love adoration.
I am intelligent but I hate to think for other people.
I make others feel secure when I love
But my love is not strong enough to feed my own
*   insecurities.*
I am not needy but I want to be needed.
Passion should be the root of everything I do.
I cry, I'm looked at wrong,
I curse, I'm judged,
I want a lot in a man because I give a lot as a woman.
This is who I am.

I tore the writing from the paper, and placed it inside the coffee table book. Turning, I gave one last smile to the judges and the middle finger to the other contestants. Swaggering back down the runway, I started the first day of the rest of my life.

Although the morning started rocky, the rest of the day was pleasantly smooth. I got tickets for the dinner theater in town, and after Sarah agreed to be my date for the evening, we picked up Tam and the crew from the hotel and had a wonderful night. The play was a murder mystery, and no one at our table guessed the culprit. I thought we were all too engrossed in the flavorful meal. I spoke to Tam briefly about Dick, and yet the night was too cheery to bring up that dismal conversation.

"Que sera, sera." Best summed up that musical. I did, however, bring my wonderful book to show everyone. As the night ended, we sat in the hotel room laughing and talking as my girlfriends looked at my gift with envy.

"I have never received anything so thoughtful," Tam said.

"Me either," agreed Evelyn while eyeing Pierce. "I'm jealous."

Laughing, I thought to myself, *No, I'm jealous.*

A thousand books were nothing in comparison to loving companionship. I loved my gift, but if Dick were lying in my lap instead of this book, I would've loved it even more.

Around one o'clock in the morning, we started our good-byes, since I wouldn't be able to take them to the airport the next day because of work. I squeezed Stan and Pierce while reminding them to take good care of my friends. Evelyn and I cordially hugged and lastly Tam and I embraced. She whispered sweet words of optimism, wished me well with Sam, and finally told me to call Dick again. Everyone said his or her loving farewells and Sarah and I went home. Since Carmen was with Claire, Sarah decided to stay with me that night. I thought we both could use the company. Nothing was discussed. I didn't mention Omar and she didn't mention Dick. We simply walked into the house, said good night, and retired. I walked into my room, cleared my gifts from the bed, and placed them in my closet. I laid my two favorite cards on my dresser, got in my bed, and gazed at them both. Stix's card—I loved for its originality. Dick's card—I loved, well . . . just because. For him, I must create a new card category.

5. Visual cards with meaningful, personalized phrases: meant the friend had an incredible eye and memory for detail or the friend knew just how to touch me in places that other friends never knew existed.

In his case, both definitions applied. I just needed to figure out how to make things nice again. 'Cause life without Dick just wasn't right.

37

You and Me
and EPT

By Monday, my birthday was a blur. I was swamped at work and my mind was still on the weekend's festivities. Constantly throughout the day, coworkers pleasingly commented on the party. Sarah rang my phone all day with nonsense about Omar and I could do nothing but think about Dick. However, when Nehri called at the end of the day and asked me for a tampon, I suddenly remembered.

"My period hasn't come yet."

I rushed down the hall to Sarah. We were supposed to go to dinner that evening and I wanted to stop by the store to get a pregnancy test. We decided on a place for dinner and left work around five thirty to stop by the pharmacy for the pregnancy test, vitamins, floss, and baby wipes. Under my breath I kept praying that the test came out negative. I couldn't bear calling Winston to tell him that I was pregnant. I don't know how he would react, but I knew it wouldn't be pleasant. Sarah and I arrived at dinner close to seven o'clock and were quickly seated by 7:05. Giovanni's was the choice for dinner. Sarah had never been; plus, I thought it would be nice to run into Bruce again.

"I know one of the owners," I mentioned to Sarah.

"Really, is he cute?" she asked.

"Yeah, kind of. His name is Bruce, Bruce Banner."

Sarah concocted a weird face as we giggled like girls. I asked the server about Bruce; however, he was not in tonight. Slightly disappointed, I went ahead and ordered my food and finished my conversation with Sarah. Seconds later, Donnie called inquiring about our whereabouts. Ironically, he was only a few minutes away.

"He wants to join us for dinner," I said.

Sarah shrugged nonchalantly, so I invited him. Before he arrived we discussed Omar. Sarah finally agreed not to see him anymore. I think she was serious this time. The embarrassment was what broke the straw. She knew she deserved better. However, with over fifty people telling her so, she had no choice but to let it go.

"I can't believe Donnie hit him."

"I can. He cares about you. If I were there I would have hit him too."

"But Donnie just came out of nowhere and pounded him," Sarah said with a tiny gleam in her eye.

Pausing, I held my head down and peered into her eyes. She did the same and across the table we connected.

"You like him!" I squealed softly.

"Of course, he's my friend."

"No. I mean you really like him. He's your hero. He rescued you from danger and he wants to whisk you away to a life of happiness."

"He does not," Sarah said, brushing me off.

"Yes, he does."

Sarah looked at me with a peculiar smile.

"He's my friend," she said again with less sureness.

Leaning across the table, I made a funny face while commenting, "But he wants to be your superhero, lover man."

Sarah giggled.

"That's why he wears the patch. It's his secret identity."

"Hush," Sarah said, blushing.

"He wants you," I continued. "And you want him too."

Sarah giggled again, held her head down, and dug into her garlic bread. Moments later, Donnie joined us at our table. He kissed my cheek, handed me a birthday gift, and sat next to Sarah.

"You okay?" he said, softly brushing her face.

Bashfully, she nodded.

"Superhero, lover man," I uttered across the table.

Sarah coughed to cover my murmuring while Donnie obliviously looked at me. As soon as dinner arrived and we began eating, Donnie tactlessly blurted out, "So, Lily, you pregnant or what?"

"Damn, does everyone know?" I said, slamming my fork down.

"Pretty much," he said, stuffing his face with pasta. I didn't bother to respond.

"We'll see tonight," Sarah answered.

The rest of dinner was quiet, just as it needed to be.

All observations on the table were now divulged and digested. Donnie paid for the meal and we all left. Since
Sarah had been with me since yesterday, Donnie offered
to take her home; of course, she eagerly agreed. They
both suggested staying with me while I took the test, but
I wanted to pee in private. Hence, I went home alone to
face my imminent future.

Of course, I stalled as long as possible. Finally before
I went to bed, I pulled out the test and read the directions. Placing it on the counter, I went to the kitchen
and made tea. Just in case the test was positive, I was
going to need something to calm my nerves. At last, I
went back to the restroom and took the test. Now came
the hard part—waiting. To busy myself, I went into the
closet and pulled out my clothing for the next day; then
after three minutes and five deep breaths, I bravely
stepped into the bathroom. Praying to see nothing instead of a vertical pink line, I glanced at the counter. My
eyes widened with glee. My test window was clear and
white.

"I'm not pregnant!"

Jumping and shaking, I began to do the "I'm not
pregnant dance."

"Dick! I gotta call Dick."

Rushing to my phone, I slid into my room and
hopped on the bed. Quickly, I dialed his digits. However, a recording came across the line. Looking at the
phone, I dialed his number again and once more the
lady said the number was no longer in service.

"What is this?" I yelled.

Perplexed, I sat on the bed staring at the phone.
I couldn't get in touch with Dick. Panicking, I began
rocking back and forth. After a few minutes, the swaying diminished and so did my faith that I would ever

talk to him again. Disgusted and exhausted, I finally curled up in a ball and fell asleep on the edge of the bed.

The next day, I informed the cavalry about my test results. I called Winston and left a message on his voice mail, but of course he didn't call back. I apologized to him again for everything that had happened, yet I didn't expect to hear from him.

The rest of the week I impatiently awaited a call from Dick. I even called his home; however, there was no answer and since I didn't know his status with Celeste, I dared not leave a message. I could be catty, but I cared too much about him to be disrespectful and spiteful. Though my week was dreary, I was looking forward to the weekend. Sam was coming to stay with me. It was a pretrial before the trial to become a foster parent. I was excited. There was so much we could do. I had a list to choose from. Knowing Sam, she would want to sit in the house all day and watch television. However, we were going to get out and enjoy this summer weather. I picked her up late Saturday morning, and we went to a park. I had a picnic planned and so we found a perfect spot by a lake and ate the sandwiches I'd made. Sam loved strawberries and I had a basket of them along with whipped cream. We sat on the blanket and talked.

"So, are we going to get to do this every weekend?" she asked quickly after sitting.

"We'll see. It depends. You may not want to hang out with me every weekend."

Sam looked me up and down and then grinned. "You're cool, I guess it won't kill me to be with you."

I playfully mashed her in the face and we continued to eat.

Afterward, we went to American Adventure and spent the day riding go-carts, and playing miniature golf. Of course, Sam challenged me in a few video games, and naturally I lost. I thought this parent thing might work out. Of course, every weekend wouldn't be like this, and I assured her of that, but it was fun. Sam mentioned several times how much she wanted to simply stay. We stayed up late Saturday night, watching television and eating cookies. She asked about Winston and when I told her we were no longer together, she tried to lay my head in her lap and pretend to play therapist. Laughing, I played along and gave her a very dramatic tale of a girl and a boy. Naturally, the tale was fictional, but her advice still served the same.

"Pick yourself up, dust your coat off, hold your head high, and keep walking. Before you know it, you'll bump into Mr. Right."

If it were only that simple; then suddenly I realized, it was. Out of the mouths of babes comes infinite wisdom.

> *The more we learn, the more intellectual we become, and thus the more we discover how to complicate a simple issue. Sometimes, the best guidance requires very little thought and taking that advice requires even less.*

Sam and I eventually retired for the evening and I finally felt a little better about moving on; at least until my phone rang close to six o'clock Sunday morning. Like a private investigator, Evelyn called to update me on Dick and Celeste. While shopping yesterday, she had run into Celeste on the way to the bridal store to pick up her gown. Evelyn, doing what Evelyn did best, pried until she got every detail about the wedding. It seemed Dick told her some line about having cold feet, begged her forgiveness, and she forgave him. They were going to get married on Amelia Island. They wouldn't immediately go on the honeymoon, because Dick was still on tour; however, they were going to Antigua at the end of summer. By the time Evelyn finished giving me the details, I was laughing hysterically. She told me to hold on, and the next thing I knew she and Tam were both on the line. As Tam continually asked the cause of my amusement, I laughed harder.

Finally, my giggling ceased, my breathing subsided, and I calmly asked, "Why are you telling me this?"

Both friends were quiet.

"I can't even get in touch with Dick. He doesn't want to speak with me."

"That's because he thinks you're going to marry Winston," Evelyn said.

"Look, this is my first weekend with Sam and I don't want to ruin it thinking about Dick."

"We understand, we just thought you should know," said Tam.

"Well, now I know. Is that all?"

Again Tam and Evelyn were quiet. At last, Evelyn rolled off her set of words very quickly. "Celeste didn't want to wait and they're getting married this coming weekend."

This time I was silent. After moments, Tam and Evelyn said good-bye and we hung up. Falling back on my bed, I repeatedly said the "F" word under my breath. Sure, Evelyn didn't tell me what to do. However, her call served its purpose. She planted the seed. Bringing Tam on the line was only fertilizer to allow the seed to grow into an elaborate plan. But I refused to let the scheme blossom. I lay there attempting to fill my head with thoughts not concerning this newfound information. Nonetheless, it was useless. I couldn't go back to sleep and I couldn't think of anything but that damn wedding. An hour later, I heard a knock on my door. It was Sam asking me if I liked eggs. She wanted to cook breakfast. However, once she crawled into my bed, she fell back asleep and eventually so did I. When we finally woke up it was time for Sarah's brunch.

We pulled up to the house and Sam went crazy.

"Ms. Sarah lives in a mansion. I didn't know she was rich."

"She isn't. She lives with Claire, Omar's mom."

"That's the baby's daddy, right?"

"That is Carmen's father."

Sam continued to look at the house. "She came up, that's what I'm talking about."

"Exactly what are you talking about?" I asked.

"If you're going to get pregnant by somebody, it'd be great if they have money. You don't want to get pregnant by somebody broke."

"How about you stop thinking about getting pregnant by anyone?"

"Not me. I'm just saying," Sam said.

"Sarah fell in love with Omar. She wasn't trying to trap him. And you make sure you tell all of your little friends that when they think that trapping a man is cute, it's not. You end up biting off much more than you wished you had."

"Okay," Sam griped.

We got out of the car and walked up to the door. Food was ready, and so we ate with Sarah, Donnie, and Carmen. Although Sarah and Donnie were not a couple, I could tell there was something lingering underneath the surface. I didn't believe her at first, but she had ultimately left Omar alone. Claire didn't allow him to come over to the house and unfortunately Carmen didn't know what to think. It was sad that the kids were always the ones who suffered most. Thankfully, she had loving aunts and uncles who made up for the absence of her father.

The day passed quickly and gratefully I made it through the remainder of Sunday afternoon without much deliberation on Dick and Celeste. However, as soon as I dropped off Sam, my mind went into over-drive.

"Who can I call?" I asked myself.

I needed a man's opinion. Sarah was too emotional. Tam and Evelyn were too biased. Donnie was going to have to do. We talked for an hour about the entire situation and he was no help at all. He agreed that I should leave well enough alone. He also agreed that I should get in touch with Dick before the wedding and let him know how I felt. Knowing I could only do one or the other, he said, "Good Luck" and hung up. Totally conflicted, and utterly tired, I felt my mind shutting down around nine o'clock and I watched television until I fell asleep on the futon.

Three days passed and I talked to no one. Other than necessary dialogue at work, I completely shut down. I didn't go by Sarah's desk and I didn't answer my phone. I wanted no outside influences. Part of me wished that I didn't even know about the stupid wedding, and the other part of me wanted to confront Dick and beg for his love. Somehow, Tam must have conferred with the latter part, because when I came home from work Wednesday, I had a parcel package waiting at my door. In the box was a short letter from Tam and a ticket to Jacksonville, Florida, the closest airport to Amelia Island. I picked up the phone and call her. As soon as she answered, I started, "Got your package today."

"Good," she said.

"I cannot go down there and ruin that man's wedding."

Tam didn't say anything, which caused me to continue. "Can I?"

"I did spend my hard-earned money on a ticket," she said.

"And I hate to be wasteful," I added.

"I know."

"What if he curses me out?"

"He may. But at least you tried."

"I don't know, Tam. This could be disastrous."

"That's why Evelyn is driving down to meet you Friday night."

Sighing softly on the phone, I began to rethink the entire idea.

"Once you have said your piece, you will be able to move on. I would join you, but I'm too pregnant to make the drive."

Again I was quiet before responding, "I love you. I hope you know that."

"I do."

We hung up, and I sat on the futon, staring at the ticket that would decide my future. As I started thinking about Dick, there was peaceful contentment. I looked across the room and I saw my heart marching her way toward me. This time completely unarmored, she traipsed across the floor and plunked herself back into my chest. Although she looked like my heart, she felt different. Her beat was much stronger. I didn't know where she had been but it was wonderful to have her back, as I would need her for battle that weekend. Ironically, when she left she was covered from valve to valve in armor; now she was totally naked. Seemed like it should be the opposite, especially knowing that I had a hard fight ahead of me.

But as I thought again, it made sense. It was easier to stab someone covered in armor because metal dehumanized. But to stab a naked heart, that took a low soul, a vile creature.

In a low murmur, I spoke to myself. "I guess hearts are smarter than most minds give them credit for."

Walking into the kitchen, I made a tuna sandwich and grabbed some chips. I tried to call Dick one more time while watching television just to make sure his phone number had changed. I knew he didn't want to hear my voice and I was sure he had changed his number because of me. Surely, the coming weekend was going to be the mother of all weekends. I hoped to make it out alive, 'cause this was going to be one hell of a story to write about.

I went upstairs and prepared for bed. With one foot firmly planted in "rationaleville" and the other planted in "crazytown," sanity was my prayer that night. I needed reason and good sense to be on my side.

"If this is wrong, just keep me from that island," I prayed. "Yet, if this is right, then let me find Dick and say my piece. After that's done, I'll leave the rest up to you."

And, God, if you and me are cool like I think we are, then you will either bring him home to me or let my bare heart walk away unscathed.

Amen.

38

Wedding Party Crasher

The weather in Jacksonville was overcast with cumulus clouds hanging very low. Evelyn was eagerly waiting at the airport to pick me up. This was right up her alley. I, on the other hand, was still very hesitant about the entire thing. The island only had one hotel; the rest of the lodging consisted of condos and town house rentals. Dick and Celeste were having a very intimate wedding. Only Celeste's sister and Coffee, Dick's drummer, were the wedding party members. Once we arrived at the hotel and pulled up to the driveway, Evelyn anxiously started the countdown. With wide eyes and sharp vocals she articulated loudly, "We have exactly nine hours before the wedding."

I glanced at her and placed my finger upon my lips indicating for her to silence. Nodding quickly, she got my point. However, when I stepped from the car, she pushed me onto the pavement and forcefully held up nine fingers. Closing the door, she whizzed around the circular drive to park. I stood in front of the hotel doors staring into the glass windows. Suddenly I saw a group of guys walk by and Coffee was leading the crew. Like a cat burglar, I ducked inside the bushes. When Evelyn came by, I grabbed her arm and pulled her in as well. She screamed and I quickly covered her mouth. The men walked from the building and passed by the bushes. This was when I saw him and all of my nerves sank.

"I can't do this."

"Yes, you can," urged Evelyn.

We watched Dick and his band members walk to the car and pull out of the driveway. Evelyn forced me out of the trees, grabbed my arm, and ran across the parking lot.

"We have to follow them," she said.

The chase began. She followed two cars behind them and when they wove in and out of traffic, we did the same. This was by far one of the craziest things I had ever done. The town was quiet, there was minimal traffic, and I was sure we were going to get caught. Yet Evelyn kept driving. They finally arrived at a bar just on the outside of town. We pulled into the bar a few seconds after and parked on the other side. Spying from the dash, we watched the four jovial men get out and walk into the bar.

"He looks so happy. I really can't do this," I groaned.

Evelyn tugged on my shirt collar while speaking aggressively. "Pull it together. We're here. You will do this."

Closing my eyes, I leaned back in the seat and waited. "So what's the plan?"

"I say we just walk into the bar, you pull Dick aside and talk to him," she said.

Frowning, I disagreed. "His boys may get angry."

"They are a band, not the Mafia. They can't keep you from talking to him."

I sat in the car and fretfully looked out the window. After a few brief sighs, Evelyn stepped out.

"Where are you going?"

"I'm going in to find Dick."

"*No!*" I said, jumping from the car. Pulling on Evelyn's arm, I begged her not to go into the bar. She and I played tug-of-war on the gravel for moments until the bar door swung back open. Panicked, we both ran to hide behind the nearest car. However, when I took off to run, I slid on a rock and fell onto the grated driveway. Although I didn't hurt myself, I tasted a mouthful of dirt and gravel. I remained lying facedown in hopes of not being seen. However, a gentleman came over to assist. He quickly helped me to my feet and saw that I had a scraped elbow. As I kept backing away from the door, he insisted that I should get something to cover my scratch. Finally Evelyn came from behind a pickup truck to help. Eventually, we convinced the guy that I was fine; just then the bar door swung open again and Coffee walked out. Nervously, we grabbed the man's arm and turned away from the door.

"Just keep walking. Say nothing," Evelyn said to the man.

Defensively he tensed up. "Is this a setup? Are you girls trying to rob me?"

Quickly letting go of the gentleman, we fervently discouraged him from his thinking. By now, we had caused a scene in the parking lot and I could see from my peripherals that Coffee was looking at us. The man turned away from us and rushed away to his car, leaving Evelyn and me standing exposed in the parking lot. Arm in arm, we slowly walked backward towards the car. There was no way Coffee could recognize the backs of our heads, and then suddenly we ran into a stalemate. Frozen, Evelyn and I stayed close facing the opposite direction of our impasse. With my right arm, I felt behind me. Our wall was definitely a man, a tall man. He took my arm and spun me around and Evelyn, still hanging on, twirled as well. I looked up and saw Coffee. Our eyes locked and without saying a word, he hoisted me over his shoulder and rushed into the bar. I began yelling and pounding on his back. Evelyn tagged behind joining in on the abuse. Coffee rushed over to the table where the guys were sitting and placed me down in front of it. As though I was back from the dead, the entire section silenced upon my appearance. Evelyn peeped from behind my body and spoke cordially.

"Hi, guys. Having fun?"

No one spoke and no one turned up his beer. Everyone was frozen in midsentence. Abruptly, Dick rose and left the bar. Everyone was still as our eyes followed him out and my heart plunged to the floor. To my dismay, Evelyn poked my back with her skinny fingers. She was coercing me to follow Dick, but my legs were locked. Lastly, she took both hands and shoved me toward the exit.

"Go!" she exclaimed.

Stumbling, I trod to the door and walked outside. I didn't see him; however, I heard a banging noise over by the car they arrived in. Carefully, I tiptoed toward the noise. Once I came closer, I saw Dick kicking the inside rim of the back tire with his boots while cursing. I stood quietly and watched him kick and curse, curse and kick.

Timidly, I eventually cut in. "Um . . . I know you're mad, but please listen."

Dick immediately stopped kicking and walked forcefully up to me. Fearful, I quickly moved back away from him while talking.

"You don't have to come so close. We can talk from here."

Dick kept pressing forward. He clutched my arm and practically dragged me to the front of the bar. Placing me down in the chair directly under the light, he stepped a few feet away and stared into my eyes. Suddenly I was in the spotlight. However, this was not like theater. This was a full-blown interrogation, where I was being charged for unnecessary messiness in the arena of love. Although I was certainly guilty, I had to make him believe that my intentions were true. If that failed, my plea was temporary insanity. I knew he was going to ask me about the night of the party, and so I was going to start off there and pray for the best. Taking several deep breaths, I commenced my appeal.

"I didn't come see you that night because I was with Winston and I didn't know how to leave him. I didn't want to hurt him any more than you wanted to hurt Celeste. I know you can understand that. I came to see you that morning, but you were gone."

Dick stood still with his legs slightly spread and his arms folded. His head was bowed as he peered at me from underneath his eyebrows. He didn't say anything; thus, I continued.

"You threw me off guard by coming to the party. I thought you were still marrying her. When I saw you, I shut down. I couldn't do anything. You had time to plan, I didn't. I love you, Dick, but I just couldn't get up and remove myself from my situation."

Dick unfolded his arms, which was a good sign, and placed them by his side. I couldn't tell from his expression if he was warming up, but he was still listening, so I gave him more.

"I am not with Winston anymore. I want to be with you. I tried to call you but your number has changed and I didn't know what to do so I came here. I know this shit is wrong, but this whole thing has me crazy and I had to see you before you made the same mistake that I was going to make."

And this was when he forcefully spoke.

"The only mistake I made is almost losing a committed woman who truly loves me, for a woman who needs to be committed. You are absolutely insane."

His tone boiled as I lowered my head and nervously began biting my nails.

"You have lost it. You had your chance. I waited for you all night. All night! It was not going to take you twelve hours to say good-bye to him. You didn't even call the next day."

"But—" I began to cry.

"But nothing. You told me that if I came for you, you would follow. You lied to me."

"I needed time to make it right. I'm following you now, please!" I begged as tears began to flow. I reached out for his hand, but he quickly jerked away.

"No! I have made my decision."

"But how could you change your mind so quickly? You were just saying you wanted to be with me. Don't you still want to be with me?" I sobbed. "Please say you want me."

Coldly, Dick leaned over and looked at me. "Hear

this. Celeste is going to be my wife. You fucked up and I'm tired."

"But I love you," I whined, trying to wipe my steady tears.

"Hmm . . . I recall you saying love's not enough. And you were right."

Dick turned and walked away. Devastated, I began rushing behind him. My emotions were completely out of control. He had stabbed my naked heart and it was bleeding all over the place.

"Dick, please!" I called out as I grabbed the bottom of his shirttail. "Don't do this. Please, I'll wait. Just take me back. I don't want to be without you. Please."

Dick, more enraged, whipped around and jerked my feeble body away. Emotionally charged, he threw his hands in the air and yelled, "My fucking wedding is tomorrow! You cannot come down here and make like everything is okay 'cause now you're ready to be with me!"

Weeping, I slid down his pant leg and onto the gravel. Sitting on my knees, I bowed my head and bawled uncontrollably. I had never heard him this angry and it had me broken down.

"I don't want you! Go home!" he shouted, hovering over my shabby remains.

"But she doesn't move you," I said, rocking back and forth. "I move you. I move you," I continued to repeat as he turned and forcefully trudged away.

I never looked up to watch him leave; the next thing I knew Evelyn was picking me up from the gravel and dusting me off.

"I see it didn't go well."

Whimpering, I shook my head very slowly from right to left. Evelyn wrapped her arms around me.

Walking to the car, she commented, "Well, we have at least six more hours before wedding time."

I looked at her, bewildered. There was no way I could approach that man again. Did she not see the bloody trail left by my wounded heart? Did she not see that I could barely walk to the car, forget shielding myself for another battle?

"I'm going home," I said wearily.

"Not yet."

"No. That's it. I'm done."

Evelyn looked at me with disapproving eyes, yet I didn't care. If I could have I would've left that night. However, I was staying in my room until she took me to Jacksonville tomorrow. I was getting on a plane and taking my broken-down, brokenhearted, pitiful, begging ass back to Kansas City. Leaning my head back against the seat, I closed my eyes and tried to stop sobbing. As she drove, I could hear the bits and pieces of my heart juggling around in my chest cavity, for Dick had ripped it to shreds. Clutching my chest, I tried to ease the pain. No, I hadn't thought he would run into my arms, but I certainly didn't believe he would yell and curse at me. My ego had definitely been cut down and I never thought I would act like that. At times when I had seen other women act pitiful and desperate, I would say to myself, "That will never be me."

But tonight, I was that psycho, love-struck woman and then some. I had said my piece and it was time for me to go home.

We arrived at the hotel, parked the car, and I waited by the elevators as Evelyn checked in. The last thing I wanted was to run into any more wedding attendants.

I showered as soon as I hit my room. I stood in the center of the water flow, the hot steamy water splashing my neck and running down my body. Over and over, my mind replayed Dick's malicious remarks.

"I don't want you! Go home!"

Sharp pains stabbed my chest as I balled into the fetal position and crouched at the bottom of the tub. With the water beating me over the head, I wailed, "He doesn't want me."

I repeated this phrase until the hot water cooled and began to wrinkle my skin. Eventually the wails turned to whimpers and the whimpers softened to sighs. I turned off the water, dried off, and looked into the steamy mirror. With my forearm, I wiped away the mist and stared at the disturbing image of myself. My eyes were swollen, my hair was wet and tussled. I simply looked a mess.

"This is who I am?" I asked.

Shaking my head heartily, I remarked, "This is not who I am."

Attempting to hold my head up, I marched into the bedroom, dried my hair, and tried to get some sleep. However, somewhere in the middle of the night, after tossing and turning for hours, I turned on the television while doing some writing.

Tonight, I was not sure if I was completely out of character or evoking a character hidden deep inside. Was that love or desperation? Either way, I never wanted to see her disposition again. Tossing my book aside, I glanced over at the television. An old episode of *X-Files* was on the tube. I thought to myself, *Love has unquestionably got to be the biggest of all* X-Files—*an inexplicable force that causes bizarre behavior, strange occurrences, and baffling outcomes.* Aliens, voodoo, magic, and any other supernatural acts were nothing in comparison to the enigmatic power of love. Falling back onto the bed, I watched television until the sun came up.

Early the next morning, Evelyn came knocking. "Let's go to breakfast."

"I told you, I'm not leaving the room."

"You can't let him win. If you see him, you have to act like you're okay," she called from the other side.

"But I'm not okay," I said while rising to open the door.

"But you have to pretend."

"I don't want to pretend. I want to go home," I said, falling back on the bed as she entered the room. Stomping around in her stilettos, Evelyn placed her hands on her hips and stated arguably, "Damn it, Lily. We are not hiding in this room until tomorrow. You have said your piece so let's go out and do something. If you see Dick, remind him that he's making a big mistake, hold your head up, and keep walking."

"What if I see Celeste?"

"Wish her well and keep walking."

Griping, I placed the pillow over my face.

"The damage has been done. It's over. There is no need to hide now. If you wanted to hide, you should have stayed home. If you're not dressed in five minutes, I'm calling Tam."

Evelyn zipped around me and shut the door.

"I'm grown. I don't care if you call Tam. What's Tam going to do? Punish me?" I yelled through the door.

Frowning, I looked through my suitcase for clothing. Although I wanted to stay in the room, Evelyn did make a point. The damage had been done. I might as well go and enjoy the day.

I met Evelyn in her room fifteen minutes later. She grabbed her purse and we headed down to the lobby for breakfast. Thankfully, there were no signs of the wedding party. We enjoyed our food and began planning our day. Then just when I thought the coast was clear, we ran into the band members minus Coffee spraying the newlywed car. As we approached, they all turned and stared. All of a sudden, one of the guys called out, "You know what you did was fucked up."

Evelyn murmured while grabbing my arm, "Smile and keep walking, smile and keep walking."

I kept walking, but there was no smile. Inside, I was aching. For someone who had said her piece, I sure didn't feel serene. In fact, as the day progressed and the wedding time narrowed to within three hours, I became more unsettled. My chest burned, my stomach ached, and my head was pounding. Although Evelyn had stopped the countdown hours ago, I found myself watching the clock tick and tock.

By the time we got back to the hotel, I was starved and we decided to eat at the bar. The scene was noisy, for there were several men gathered around watching the baseball game. I ordered a chicken sandwich and Evelyn ordered a grilled chicken salad. While we waited, my head pounded heavier. My eyes squinted up as I put my head on the table.

"You don't look so good," she said, rubbing my temples.

"I don't feel so good," I muttered.

While I was waiting for my food, I began scribbling on my napkin. First, I drew a picture of fish. Next, I drew a horn of plenty above the fish. Finally, I drew waves of water. Chuckling, I placed plus signs in between the pictures and slid it over to Evelyn.

"What's this?" she asked, curiously looking at my doodles.

"Figure it out," I responded.

She turned it around and around, but couldn't put it together. Seconds later, the bartender came over to bring our plates. She looked down at my scribble and called out, "Plenty of fish in the sea."

Right, I clapped enthusiastically.

"How did you guess that so quickly?" Evelyn asked.

The lady responded, "I worked the bar late last night and there was a guy here all night getting drunk. Every time I poured him another beer, he would have one of those puzzle doodles on the napkin. I looked at so many last night that I just figured it out."

"Interesting," I responded.

"Do you ladies need anything else?"

Evelyn and I said no, and she walked away.

I glanced up at the clock. It was one hour before the wedding. Miserably, I grabbed a napkin and draw. First, I sketched an eyeball and second, I drew a man in tuxedo tails taking a bow. Last, I penciled an open door with an arrow pointing outward. When I looked up, Coffee, dressed in his tuxedo, was walking across the lobby.

"Oh no," I said as Evelyn turned and looked.

"Just be calm."

I turned my chair to face away from the lobby; however, I kept looking back over my shoulder.

"Here, doodle some more," she said as she took the napkin.

Upon looking at what I had just done, she commented, "I get it."

Evelyn snatched the napkin, hopped up, and walked away from the table. I snapped around to follow her footsteps. But I froze when I saw Dick. The momentum of my breathing swelled. As Evelyn approached him, I snapped back around; however, I was compelled to look again. Holding my napkin, he looked in my direction and with grave disdain he made eye contact. Slowly, he shook his head discouragingly as I mouthed a silent "I'm sorry."

After that, Dick turned and slowly walked through the glass doors to marry Celeste, the one woman he surely could depend on. The way I felt, I couldn't blame him. Within moments, Evelyn came back to the table. Although I was a little upset, I said nothing to her. I simply finished eating my food in silence.

As soon as we were done, my headache eased and I felt a little better. However, Evelyn offered a solution that might enhance my mood even more.

"Let's get drunk."

Smiling like two underage teens, we ordered two drinks. Evelyn got a mojito and I had an apple martini. Now, Evelyn was a social drinker, but I only drank maybe four times a year. Thus, more than two martinis would have me doing the electric slide on top of the bar. We drank, laughed, and drank some more. Three martinis and one Cape Cod later, I was singing my sob story to not only the bartender, but also every bar attendee. The baseball game was no longer the point of interest. The sad, sad tale of a girl named Lily and a boy named Dick had everyone shaking their head in sorrow. The entire scene was quite pathetic. Evelyn sat to my right patting my shoulder while some strange man sitting to my left patted my leg. Even more disturbing, his leg caresses were starting to feel good. As he winked, I blew him a kiss and I winked back. Hunched over the bar, I turned around and finished telling my story.

"He's getting married right now," I said, pointing to the clock.

"That's okay," Evelyn chimed in.

"It has to be," I said, tossing my hands in the air.

"He's settling," said the bartender.

Shaking my head back and forth, I rose from my seat.

"No, no, no! He's not settling. See, Celeste is sweet, beautiful, talented, caring, and loving. She treats him like a king, he said so himself," I slurred while banging the back of her seat. "He's not settling. She's the best thing for him."

"He's still settling," added Evelyn.

"How is he settling?" I yelled, slamming my head onto her shoulder.

Suddenly I heard a familiar, deep voice call out, "'Cause she is not you."

Evelyn spun her chair around so fast that she almost knocked me over. However, when I saw the sight before me, my knees buckled and fell anyway.

"'Cause she is not you," repeated the tall, handsome vision of loveliness.

Repeatedly, I kept blinking as he approached. He looked and sounded like Dick, but I thought the liquor was playing tricks with my mind. Yet when he picked me up from the floor and held me in his arms, I knew this trick was nothing but a treat. I held on tight as he lifted me off my feet.

"Dick. Oh my God, Dick."

Dick embraced tighter and began to twirl me around. However, as he twirled, my head started spinning in the opposite direction.

"Dick. Oh my God, Dick," I said with less excitement and more fret.

This was all I wanted. To be in his arms was why I came and all this time I had been waiting to exhale. Therefore, I took in a deep breath and slowly let it out. Yet my breath exhaled as a pant, and I gagged. The only thing that exited my mouth was everything I had had for lunch hours earlier. I vomited all over Dick's tuxedo. Quickly, he placed me on the floor and rushed to get a towel. The bartender passed the small can from behind the bar and Evelyn jammed it in front of my mouth. I stuck my entire face in the tin can, but nothing else came out. There was nothing left. I looked over at Dick as he disgustingly wiped my digested lunch off his jacket.

"I hope that's not a rental," I said from the floor.

Dick removed his coat and wrapped it inside out. He walked over and lifted me from the floor once more. "We must talk. Where's your room?"

Still high, I took his arm and headed down the hallway. Evelyn handed him my keys and my purse. We got to my room and I rushed to the bathroom to wash my face and brush my teeth. As I looked at Dick standing by the window, I began crying. Dick rushed over to console me.

"What's wrong?"

"I don't know. I don't know," I kept repeating as I snuggled my head into his chest. Dick placed me down on the bed. He slid beside me and caressed my temples.

"I'm happy. I really am. I just can't believe you're here."

"I can't believe it either, but I am."

Smiling, I leaned up and kissed his lips. Holding me close, Dick rocked me in his arms. The entire scene was like a dream. Better yet, something straight from a Julia Roberts romantic comedy. But it couldn't be, because my life didn't consist of great endings. Suddenly I thought, *Could this be the beginning of my great ending?* I closed my eyes and prayed that the answer to that question was yes. Dick softly kissed my forehead and then everything was black.

When I awoke the next morning, I was in my bed alone. I sat straight up and looked around the room.

"I knew it! The shit was a dream."

Falling back onto the bed, I began to scream. "No, no, no! It was a dream."

Suddenly Evelyn came rushing into the room. Forcefully clapping her hands over my body, she called out, "Lily, wake up!"

I opened my eyes and saw her standing over me. With the room slightly spinning, I felt like Dorothy after the tornado.

"Where's Dick?" I asked.

Baffled, Evelyn looked down at me and spoke. "Baby, Dick is gone."

Slamming my head back onto the bed, I yelled, "I knew it was too good to be true. Damn. Damn. Damn!"

Unexpectedly, Dick appeared. Standing over me, he grinned from ear to ear. Slowly, I sat up and realized that this *was* the beginning of my great ending. Smiling, I hugged them both until Evelyn pushed me away commenting on my repulsive breath and body odor. Laughing, I rose from the bed and prepared to shower.

"Hurry, Lily. We need to leave," said Dick as I entered the bathroom.

With a newfound pep, I quickly bathed, got dressed,

and prepared to leave. As we loaded the elevator and headed downstairs, I could feel the nervousness bouncing off Dick's body. I was a little hazy on last night's events. Therefore, I couldn't help but continually think, *What if we run into Celeste?*

The elevator stopped four times on the way down. Each time I visualized Celeste with a machine gun firing into the tiny box killing us all. Now panic was bouncing off my body as well. Once the doors opened to the lobby, I stepped out with trepidation. Evelyn bumped my back and commented, "Go on to the car. I've already checked out."

Hence, like a lightning bolt, I streaked through the lobby, rushed to the car, and hopped in. Evelyn and Dick were not far behind. Once we got to the parking lot, Dick walked to the car, still covered in newlywed foam, and retrieved his bags. Coffee came out of the hotel and briefly spoke to him. They hugged, Dick handed him his keys, and walked toward us. Coffee turned and looked at me. I read his expression as a look of disgust at first, and then out of nowhere came a smile. He threw his hand up to say good-bye. Pleased, I grinned and waved. Dick got into the car and we rode to Jacksonville.

My plane boarded in an hour and I just knew Dick was going to be on that plane with me. However, he explained that he had to go back to Atlanta to resolve some things and get some clothing before meeting me in Kansas City. He had a show Tuesday night, but he agreed to visit in five days. We didn't say much about our future plans. But we decided to discuss them at length that weekend. As they called my flight, I said good-bye to Evelyn and held on tight to Dick. It was always difficult to say good-bye to this man, but this time it was the most challenging. I felt like he was mine now, and if I let go, anything could happen. I almost wished I could ride back to Atlanta with him and Evelyn. Yet I had to work tomorrow and I had to gain control of myself. So I kissed Dick one last time and boarded my plane.

Once I got back to Kansas City, I was deliriously happy. So giddy that I obliviously walked around the parking deck for close to an hour before finding my SUV. I couldn't concentrate. I didn't know how I was going to make it through the week. Of course, I called Tam as soon as I landed, but she already knew the good news. Evelyn had been talking to her the entire time. Quickly, I called Sarah. She didn't answer, so I left her a message to call me as soon as possible. Next, I began calling Donnie, but then a sad love song came on the radio and I couldn't help but think about Celeste. My mood quickly changed from delight to disheartened. I couldn't imagine what she was going through. I knew that I didn't directly break her heart, but I was surely a key player. The song was giving me a guilty conscience.

I flipped through the radio stations, only to hear one sad song after the other. Finally to break the monotony, I plopped in a classic OutKast CD. And as I listened to Dre and Big Boi flow back and forth, I began thinking about balance and how their vocals and lyrical delivery set a nice equilibrium for their songs. Lost in the music, I got home swiftly without much deliberation over Dick and Celeste.

I walked into the house, went into my bedroom, and removed my clothing. I tossed on an oversized shirt and went into the kitchen to eat a snack. The evening hours passed quickly, as I watched a little television and chatted on the phone with Sarah. She was floored as I told her about my weekend. At first she was upset that I didn't tell her ahead of time, but after she heard the outcome all of the disconcertment was erased and she was elated. Around eleven, I made my way to bed. Still keyed up, I found it difficult to go to sleep although my body was very fatigued. As I tried to rest, one word kept drumming over and over in my mind.

Balance.

Everything in the world revolved around balance, the earth's rotation, the solar system, and reproduction. When it's night in one place, it's day in another. Babies are born every day and people die every day. If there were no balance there would be chaos. In love, people get hurt and sometimes their pain is the result of someone else's joy. Not everyone can be happy all of the time. I never set out to hurt Winston and I knew Dick did not set out to hurt Celeste. Yet the outcome was still the same. I prayed that they were able to let go of some of the pain so that they too could one day find happiness. This was my prayer for them and this was my prayer for me. My life had always been a little skewed to the left because I couldn't let go of old things before I grabbed on to new ones. The old boyfriend was still lingering when the new one came along. Old feelings were constantly being meshed with new emotions. There was no balance; thus, there was chaos.

I pulled out my journal, which was nearing its last blank pages and wrote:

If we let go of old baggage, it's amazing how lighter the trip becomes.

I have been given a chance to start anew and I am thankful. I am poised, my scales are calibrated, and I am ready to weigh the ups and downs of love. God, as long as you are there to help keep me balanced, I know I am going to be just fine.

Good night.

39

Beginning at the Happy Ending

I blissfully went through my week, for I was walking on sunshine and it felt good. Friday night, I went by the center and picked up Sam. Over dinner, I told her about Dick and how we were going to get back together and that there might be some major changes in my life. She didn't ask too many details, and I was glad. I didn't really want her to know what I had done, because I knew that would cause even more questions. She was more concerned with the foster care process. She worried about me moving. I assured her that I was going to follow this through. I didn't know all of the stipulations for foster care, but if I had to stay in Kansas City, then that was where I was staying until I could adopt her permanently. I spoke with Dick about it that week and he agreed that it was important for me to focus on fostering Sam. He fully supported the decision, which meant a lot. Sam and I went bowling after dinner and headed back to my home.

When we pull up, I saw a bright yellow package on my door. Immediately, I got nervous. Every time I came home to packages on the doorstep, some major event was about to take place. Sam hopped out and grabbed it. With excitement she opened the package containing a letter and a newspaper. She handed me the letter while flipping through the paper. As I began reading the letter, I bounced with exhilaration. The letter stated that the cartoon strip *Luv & Lil* that was submitted had been accepted in this week's publication. I didn't even know Sarah had submitted the comic. She was so slick, and I couldn't wait until I told her the news.

"Open the paper. Open the paper."

Sam furiously tore through the pages until she got to the comics. "That's my comic!"

Like teenagers in the front row of a concert, Sam and I screamed while jumping up and down. Thrilled, I read the rest of the letter stating that the *Kansas City Journal* would like to pick up *Luv & Lil* as an ongoing comic strip. I immediately called Sarah, and told her the news.

"I can't believe it!" I continued to shout.

Finally, after minutes of veritable enthusiasm, we calmed down and got ready for bed. I nearly tossed and turned out of my skin as I anticipated Dick's visit tomorrow. He was staying for four days; however, that weekend he would be spending his nights at the Holiday Inn close to my home. Yes, I wanted him to stay with me, but if I was planning on becoming a foster parent, I had to set a good example for this curious teenager. She was very intelligent and if she did come live with me, I was not going to have her bringing up any of my old indiscretions as alibis for her possible new ones. For that reason, Dick would stay with me once she went back to the center. I gave up attempting to rest; I sat up in bed and read until my body willingly fell asleep.

Close to eight the next morning, I walked downstairs and cooked breakfast. Dick's plane was supposed to arrive at noon and he was cooking dinner for us tonight. However, while we were eating breakfast the doorbell rang. Sam hastily sprang up.

"Will you sit down?" I said.

"Who is it?" she asked eagerly.

"I don't know."

Sam peered around the corner while I walked to the door; however, before I could get it open I saw Dick's silhouette in the side window. I quickly opened the door and greeted my man.

"I took the first flight," he said, embracing me.

Quickly Sam came to the door.

"Sam, this is Will Dickson, and, Dick, this is Samantha Cordilla."

"So, we finally meet," Sam said very dramatically.

Sam politely extended her hand and Dick graciously shook it. Then he grabbed her up and gave her a tight hug. Sam giggled as he placed her back on the ground. He walked in, handed me flowers, and Sam a gift. Excited, she immediately unwrapped it.

"Every time I come to your house, I get gifts. I love it here," she exclaimed.

Dick pulled me into the dining area as Sam rushed into the living room to finish unwrapping her present.

"I missed you," he whispered before giving me a passionate lip smack.

"I missed you too."

Suddenly Sam squealed. "It's a Wii, with a bunch of games."

She rushed back into the room.

"I hope you like it," Dick stated.

"I do. I do. I'll be the only one at the center with one."

"Maybe we can play later."

"Ms. Lily. I like him. He's a keeper," Sam said.

"Gee, thanks."

As Dick pulled me back into the dining room, I commented, "I want a toy I can play with."

Smirking, Dick responded while brushing his pelvis against my lower body, "I got your toy right here. Play with it as long as you want."

Giggling, I pushed his body away from mine. "Be good."

"Oh, I will." He winked.

Dick joined us for breakfast and afterward we started our weekend. We spent the entire day in the streets. Dick was supposed to cook dinner; however, we got hungry while we were out and decided to eat pizza. Once we returned home, it was past eight and we were bushed.

Dick, Sam, and I sat on the floor while I showed Dick the newspaper. Excited, I told him the entire *Luv & Lil* story. While I was talking, I noticed he was staring at me.

"What?" I asked.

"You are so beautiful," he said with a fulfilled look.

As my heart melted, I responded in my girlish octave, "Thank you, baby."

Lightly kissing his lips, I beamed. Sam quickly made disgusting noises, while sticking her finger in her mouth.

"Get a room," she said sarcastically.

I looked at her and gasped. What did she know about getting a room? That's when I briefly recalled everything that this child had been through. She probably knew more about it than I. I was excited about having her in my life, but I was realizing that she had so many adult tendencies that I had to nip in the bud.

"Don't say that. It's lewd and teens, especially females, shouldn't talk like that."

"What's lewd?" asked Sam.

"Go look it up," said Dick.

"I will." Sam rose to get the dictionary.

Chuckling, Dick and I moved closer to each other. I leaned back in his arms.

"We would be good parents."

"You're getting ahead of yourself, aren't you?"

"Maybe, but we are heading in that direction and if you're seriously considering adoption, then my statement stands."

Looking back at him, I grinned from ear to ear. For the first time a statement like that didn't frighten me.

"Congratulations again on the comic. That's wonderful. I always knew you would be published."

Abruptly, Sam entered the room spouting the definition of lewd. "Rude, obscene, indecent, and lustful."

She looked up at us and asked, "Why is 'get a room' lustful?"

I stared into Sam's inquisitive, innocent eyes. She may have been placed in many adult situations, but she was still a child.

"Because it implies other activities. Just don't say it."

Shrugging carelessly, she responded, "Okay," and took a seat.

"The comic strip is just the beginning." I continued, "I would like to write a novel."

"Then you should," Dick commented.

"I wouldn't know where to start."

"What would it be about?" asked Sam.

"I don't know, maybe my life. Who knows?"

We all sat quiet for seconds; then Sam replied, "I think it should be about you and you should call it Lily."

Thinking over her comment, I stretched out and turned on the television. Dick stayed for about an hour, and then Donnie came over and the two of them went to the studio. Apparently, before the fight broke out at the party they had spoken about collaborating on a few songs. I didn't know how they planned to mix "Bloody Murder" and "Sexy Cotton." The styles were nothing alike. However, like OutKast, it might be the perfect combination of balance that won them both a Grammy. Before they left, I pulled Donnie aside and asked him about Sarah.

Glowing, he stated, "We're just friends."

"You are so full of it."

Laughing, he gave me a hug and whispered, "Things are good and she is happy."

I couldn't explain how much joy that brought to my heart. Patch was a wonderful friend, Donnie was a wonderful man, and that was just the combination Sarah needed to let go of the old and start anew. Once the guys left, I walked back into the living room and lightly shook the sleeping teen. She went upstairs and prepared for bed. After my shower, I lay down and looked through my journal.

"It's almost full," I whispered as I flipped through the pages.

Landing on the page of likes and dislikes, I pressed the book open, and counted the number of dislikes and the number of likes. They both had eight on each side. As I slowly worked toward removing some of the dislikes, I realized that there would be another to quickly replace it. If I liked everything about me and had nothing to dislike, how could I continue to grow?

I guess it's important that we recognize our negative characteristics and work toward turning them into positives. Yet not obsess over eradicating them entirely, 'cause all pluses and no negatives equals an unbalanced equation.

Eight and eight on each side was a great base to work with. I liked who I was; in fact, I love her and I was thrilled to be in her company. If I claimed her happiness, she would ultimately be happy.

Staring into the mirror, I looked at my reflection.

"I have full lips. I could be Julia Roberts." I laughed quietly and wrote on the last page of my journal.

I could have that great Hollywood ending. Better yet, I didn't want a "Happy Ending." I wanted a "Happy Beginning."

I will embrace it like a new thought
I will adore it like a new lover
I will protect it like a newborn
I will inhale it like new rain

And
I will watch it blossom like a new lily

Because this is my life and no one can live it better than me.

Good night.

Love,

Lily